By Force or Fear

Meredith Ryan Mystery
Book 1

Thonie Hevron

ROUGH
EDGES
PRESS

By Force or Fear

Epigraph

Theodore Roosevelt said:

"It is not the critic who counts; not the man who points out how the strong man stumbles or where the doer of deeds could have done them better. The credit belongs to the man who is actually in the arena, whose face is marred by dust and sweat and blood; who strives valiantly; who errs, who comes short again and again, because there is no effort without error and shortcoming; but who does actually strive to do the deeds; who knows great enthusiasms, the great devotions; who spends himself in a worthy cause; who at best, knows, in the end, the triumph of high achievement, and who at the worst, if he fails, at least fails while daring greatly, so that his place shall never be with those cold and timid souls who neither knows victory nor defeat."

He also said, "Speak softly and carry a big stick…you'll go far."

California Penal Code Section 646.9 Stalking

(a) Any person who willfully, maliciously, and repeatedly follows or willfully and maliciously harasses another person and who makes a credible threat with the intent to place that person in reasonable fear for his or her safety, or the safety of his or her immediate family, is guilty of the crime of stalking, punishable by imprisonment in a county jail for not more than one year, or by a fine of not more than one thousand dollars ($1,000), or by both that fine and imprisonment, or by imprisonment in the state prison.

California Penal Code Section 211 Robbery

Felonious taking of another's property, from his or her person or immediate presence and against his or her will, by means of force or fear.

Chapter One

Winter 2014

"You've got to be kidding." Meredith Ryan groaned as she looked at the clock on the wall of the Russian River substation. "I never got a subpoena."

"Yeah. The judge is going out of town. He wanted to get this motion heard so he could rule on it." The deputy district attorney's voice oozed over the phone, conciliatory but insincere. Meredith recognized the woman's name as a new DDA. She sighed as the woman justified the summons. It was a simple burglary case, the suspect was arrested at the scene with the goods.

Why is nothing ever simple once the lawyers get hold of it?

The Russian River Substation was a satellite post thirty miles from the Sonoma County Sheriff's Main Office in Santa Rosa, California. A handful of deputies rolled from here every shift to cover the predominantly resort area filled with a meandering river and Redwood trees that led to the stunning Pacific coast. Most of the population was year-around with a significant summer uptick. However, the affordability of the area also attracted runaways, homeless, and vagrants, commonly known as River Rats.

Meredith wouldn't need her Taser at the DA's office. With her phone propped on her shoulder, she waited behind another deputy at the equipment closet. At her turn, she shoved the Taser battery into the charger and scratched her initials under the "in" column on the log.

"We need to talk to you in person before court at ten o'clock," the DDA continued. "Whether you have to appear will depend on what you say when you get here."

"I'm just now getting off work. I work graveyard. You only reached me because I had a late arrest." Meredith could see the probability of crawling into bed evaporate. "I'm already an hour into overtime."

"Good, then you'll be in uniform, right?" The DDA's tone took on a distant quality, as if she was now looking around for another person's day to ruin.

Meredith realized she wasn't going to get out of this. "Yes, I'll be in uniform." Even the prospect of overtime didn't cheer her up. She didn't need the money like when she first started out.

"Good. Be here as close to nine as you can."

Meredith hung up. She rubbed her eyes and reached for the coffee mug she'd put away hours ago. Dayshift's pot sat on the burner. The need for more caffeine was now a priority to make it through the morning. No time for a coffee shop, even a drive-through. She poured a half cup into her mug, then glanced at the clock—again. Her husband, Richard, would be on his way to work.

Time to call him.

Slipping behind the wheel of her patrol car, she pulled out her cell. Her finger hovered over the screen. For the second time this week, she would be home late. Richard hated that. He said it threw off his whole evening schedule.

Chapter Two

After meeting with the DDA, Meredith walked across the Quad toward the courtroom, her report in her hands. She skimmed through the pages, trying to remember the details of the year-old case. She must look professional, something she always strived for, but particularly now, since she put in for the detective unit.

The second person who bumped into her made Meredith stop. People swept past her, not pausing to excuse themselves, rushing toward an exit. In the middle of the courtyard, a small crowd pulsed with excitement. A few more women and a pair of men scurried away.

What's going on? Meredith slipped into her street patrol mindset. She wedged her way through dozens of observers. It grew easier once they noticed her uniform. Breaking through a knot of young women, she made it to the center.

An old man wobbled in an untidy circle spitting words she couldn't quite make out. His grizzled face screwed up in what? Confusion? Anger? Both? Which emotion didn't matter. His skin flushed. A vein throbbed in his temple.

Meredith recognized him, Rusty Webber, a regular River Rat. She remembered him as a harmless drunk who ended up in the tank after getting hammered and thrown out of a bar on the first of every month. But it wasn't like him to call attention to himself like this. *Something's wrong here.*

She grasped the arm of a heavy-set young woman. Meredith's voice snapped with authority. "Call 911. Tell them an officer needs assistance in the Courthouse Quad." The woman's wide eyes inspired little assurance that she would make the call. "Do it," Meredith ordered, moving toward the old man.

She was ten feet from Rusty when he pulled the buck knife. His rant escalated into a hoarse yell. Spit flew from his lips. One spindly arm waved the blade over his head. She noted his eyes were glassy, his words still unintelligible. Meredith wasn't convinced he knew what he was doing. This looked like a mental-health breakdown. His history indicated alcohol probably had something to do with his state of mind, but she'd never seen him this wild.

"Rusty, put the knife down." Meredith's command resonated throughout the Quad. The normal Wednesday morning noise halted. The courtyard occupants held their collective breath.

He shook the knife at the sky. The blade sliced side to side through the air. Meredith moved around, keeping her focus on him but still alert to anyone intruding in the circle of danger. Now the foggy morning glare was in his eyes.

Should she back off and wait for help? Did she have enough time before he went off completely? No radio, she'd checked that in. The closeness of the crowd watching Rusty's escalating rage told her she couldn't wait for backup. "Get back, everyone. Move." One or two left.

She felt a flash of irritation at the minimal response to her direction. There was danger here with all these civilians around a weapon in the hands of an irrational drunk. This had to end as quickly and peacefully as possible.

This was what she did for a living. She'd wrestled drunks with weapons often enough in seven years as a deputy to respect the fear that rose in her chest. This is who she was. A niggling worry found its way into her mind. *Whatever happens here will be a big deal.*

Jesus, don't let this mess up my chances for detective. Too much is riding on it.

Meredith moved in.

Rusty turned toward her, six feet away, unsteady and squinting. He stumbled over a frayed trouser cuff and fell, landing on a bony hip. In a spike of fury, he yelled at the gaping crowd as if they were to blame. He struggled to his feet, twisting away from Meredith. One gnarled hand grabbed the worn denim, hitching up his pants. The other jabbed wildly with the buck knife.

Meredith shouted again. "Everyone get back." Her gaze swept the Quad. Had the crowd moved? Were they far away enough? "Someone call 911," she yelled. Better to have multiple callers than none at all. She didn't want any casualties. The crowd moved, like an amoeba spilling against obstacles. People retreated until trapped against the concrete walls. Some hid behind cement planters, peeking around the corners to see, morbid curiosity outweighing their own safety.

Help was close by, with the entrance of the Sheriff's Office a mere twenty feet behind Rusty. But Meredith was still alone.

She reached for her Taser. Damn, it wasn't there. Momentary confusion erupted—then she remembered putting it in the charger an hour earlier. At least she still had her gun and vest on. She stepped toward Rusty.

Her mouth was parched; she had to swallow to get the words out. "Rusty, put the knife down. Nobody wants to get hurt." She could rely on some things without thinking. Training and experience kept her prepared for facing armed suspects. Keeping an eye on his hands, she unsnapped the safety strap on her holster. Her fingers spread around the grip as she shifted her body to position her gun side away from him. While she focused on his actions, her eyes softened to observe movement outside the target area.

"Rusty, it's Deputy Ryan from the River. You remember me? Tell me why you're upset. Maybe I can help." If she could get his attention, she might be able to talk him down. She didn't want to pull the gun and shoot here where so many bystanders could get hurt.

The old man's head snapped towards her. "Ryan," he grunted.

For the first time, she saw a glimmer of awareness in his eyes. Another grunt. "Rosemary. Rosemary's gone. They won't give me my money."

Then, it dawned on her. Rosemary, Rusty's sister, who acted as his caregiver, was found dead of natural causes last week. "Rusty, I'm sorry about Rosemary. She took good care of you, didn't she?" The County Social Services Offices were several blocks away. Rusty must've come here in error—the courthouse would be his logical reference point looking for his allowance. He would've had to appear in court many times for petty crimes, maybe even for his conservatorship under Rosemary.

His watery gaze moved from Meredith to the stream of olive, drab, and tan uniforms pouring out of the office to her right. He stood, scowling as the commotion registered. In her peripheral view, a trio of deputies hustled onlookers to sheltered offices. Other uniforms slid into tactical positions.

A bulky, green and tan-clad figure moved in an awkward tiptoe toward the old man. Dismayed to see it was Cooper, the traffic court bailiff, she watched both men. On a good day, Cooper would be considered clumsy. This was not a good day. He hid a canister of pepper spray behind his chubby hip and lumbered closer.

Meredith shifted her attention back to Rusty. As poor as the bailiff's plan was, she didn't want to expose him to danger. "I thought you were in a program, Rusty. Last time I saw you, you told me how much better you were feeling. Isn't there someone who can help you?"

Rusty sputtered the beginning of an answer, but the words drifted away. He cocked his head. He must have heard Cooper's shoe scrape on the loose gravel. Then the bailiff stumbled and lost his grip on the small black canister. Grasping while trying not to fall, the can bobbled in his hands. As he reached for a better hold, his index finger jammed the trigger downward. The pepper stream squirted seconds too early, arcing away from his target.

Cooper's momentum plunged him into the toxic vapor, grunting as the can fell. Lurching away from Rusty, his eyes welled with tears. A coughing fit seized the bailiff. He stumbled toward a garbage can, choked, and lost his balance. He dropped to his knees while trying to rub the toxin from his eyes. Deputies behind Cooper yelled.

The old man turned and pitched toward the bailiff, knife weaving from side to side, lower now. His face twisted in anguish, tears coursing down his cheeks.

"Rusty, stop. Drop the knife. I can't let you hurt anybody. Drop it!"

He ignored her.

Meredith pulled out her Beretta, making sure no one was behind Rusty in the line of fire. The old man stumbled toward the coughing bailiff—eight feet away now. She sighted in on Rusty as his outstretched knife came closer. He advanced toward Cooper. Six feet away.

Meredith pulled the trigger.

Her body absorbed the percussion, just like at the range. What she hadn't been prepared for was the shock, the image of the old man's body jerking as her bullet slammed into his chest. The small spurt of blood was a surprise, too.

Suddenly the 9mm felt like an anvil in her hand. Her arms wobbled with spent tension. She summoned the control to lower the gun to her side and, without thinking, pressed her index finger flat across the trigger guard. She caught the bitter smell of spent gunpowder as she sucked in a breath. A gray cloud of smoke hovered, then evaporated in the deafening silence.

Meredith began to shake, damp with sweat under her vest, despite the morning chill. Her heart hammering, she felt each thrust of blood pulsing through her veins. The muscles in her arm quivered as her muscles strained to keep hold of the gun.

A sense of detachment took over. It was like an impenetrable fog had rolled into her brain and she was staring down a telescope, watching the scene unfold from outside herself. A profound numbness seeped into her, but she felt totally rational. What did the academy teach about officer-involved shootings? Tension, anxiety, and grief. *All that and so much more.*

Slowly, the haze cleared. She became aware of the events around her: a woman sobbing, men shouting, the clang of aluminum doors slamming, the distant wail of a siren. Her shock wore off as the reality of what she'd done settled in. She braced herself against a concrete planter to keep steady. A deputy sprinted to Rusty, kicking the knife away before he leaned over the body. As if the first one opened a gate, a horde of paramedics, firefighters, and deputies flooded in. Then, uniforms swarmed and obscured her view.

If only there had been another way to end this. She couldn't take those moments back. She hadn't wanted to hurt him. Her heart stung as she saw paramedics loading him on a gurney. She'd seen enough to know he wasn't going to make it.

Through the jumble in her mind, Meredith heard a lieutenant barking orders. Then he was beside her, whispering in her ear. She answered, then immediately forgot what either of them said. He leaned across her, his hands gently taking the pistol from her grip.

Meredith couldn't take her eyes off the throng of emergency workers. Her mind split into two worlds as she took in the para-medics' practiced choreography while listening to the lieutenant. Policy, department policy. That's why he took her gun. More proce-dures would follow. She couldn't remember exactly what and, at the moment, didn't much care.

Meredith watched while they carried Rusty to an exit.

In slow motion, she replayed the bullet blasting into Rusty's chest. He had been standing sideways, so she aimed at his right shoulder. Still moving, he turned just enough for the round to hit his chest. A slash of crimson oozed across his shirt. He fell, something she would see forever in her dreams.

What could she have done differently? Wait for another deputy to take the shot? She couldn't depend on that. A second later would've been too late for Cooper. Rusty removed her choices by going after the bailiff. She had done the only thing she could. At least, by God, she hoped so.

A mandatory Internal Affairs Investigation would follow, as well as an investigative team from the DA's office and Santa Rosa PD detectives.

Just yesterday, she received an email informing her she'd passed the promotional detective test. A resignation settled in. This would ruin her chances to make detective. And she'd missed court.

But she was too drained to give it any more thought. She allowed herself to be led away to an office. She wanted a cup of coffee and a long sleep, in that order.

She was so very tired.

Chapter Three

ON THE SECOND FLOOR OF THE COURTHOUSE, THE HALLWAY OUTSIDE the courtrooms was lined with floor-to-ceiling glass that overlooked the Quad. Inside, a tall, striking blond man with a commanding posture slipped through the cluster of onlookers at the window. He found an alcove next to a stucco pillar and pushed aside a clerk to capture the best vantage point. From his second-story position, he watched the crowd below. All eyes were riveted on the Quad's center —an open courtyard nestled in the heart of the Sonoma County Hall of Justice. The man had a full view of the spectacle playing out.

An old man gripped a knife. A raised fist waved the weapon toward a female deputy. She remained at a safe distance, waiting, moving side to side; evaluating, talking to the old man.

As he watched, the blond man's interest in the deputy grew. He hardly noticed that several other uniformed law enforcement officers poured out of the Sheriff's office. They eased the crowd back from the center and herded them through breezeways to parking lots and safety.

Even though he couldn't hear her words, he could tell the female deputy was trying to placate the old man, who continued waving the knife. The blond man noted that, even though she was tense, she stood tall and confident. Through her bulletproof vest and dress wool uniform jacket, she was trim and athletic. He judged her as strong and capable. Here was a woman certain of her role in life.

Spellbound, he couldn't take his eyes off her.

The sun burned off the last of the morning fog, bringing out glints of gold in a simple auburn ponytail. Large, dusky eyes caught his interest first, then the well-defined nose, perched above lips set in a faint grimace. A handsome woman, yet her face was a mask of professional concern as she'd tried to calm the old man. Her periodic glance around the Quad seemed to take the measure of her surroundings.

From his experience in criminal trials, the man knew the deputy would attempt to draw out the old man and keep his attention. As long as he was talking or yelling, he wasn't hurting anyone. She kept well out of range of the knife.

After a minute of watching, a bailiff appeared at the blond man's elbow and tried to move him away from the window. If there was gunfire, bystanders could be in jeopardy. Irritated, he waved the uniform aside. The bailiff's eyes sparked in recognition. He nodded respectfully and moved on.

The scene below was like a night at the opera, in a box seat. This stalwart woman handled an impossible situation with resolute grace, alone. When a bumbling effort came and fell into jeopardy, it was the point of no return. She took decisive, irreversible action, a gunshot, with no hesitation or break in resolve.

Afterward, when paramedics rolled away the loaded gurney, the blond man sighed. He felt his shoulders droop. Only then did he realize he had been holding his breath. The scene below him grew busier as more deputies arrived, tacking up crime scene tape and taking information from onlookers. He couldn't take his eyes off the remarkable woman deputy. She acted with such courage that a bud of fascination took hold in his heart.

This was truly an exceptional woman.

Chapter Four

THREE DAYS LATER, SHERIFF WILLIAM "BUCK" FLANNERY SETTLED his bullish frame onto a delicate chair at a trendy Indian café. The oppressive aroma of curry wafted inside the batik-fabric-covered walls. He hated curry.

Flannery looked across the table at his companion. Judge Stephen Giroud was about the same age, early forties, but carried himself like a man a decade younger. Short, blondish hair flecked at the temples with gray and styled, yes, it looked like a stylist cut his hair, not a barber. Buck kept his disgust to himself as he wondered why the Judge insisted on meeting here. Buck was a big man, a barrel-chested cowboy from a local pioneer ranching family. He took pride in his significant role in county politics. The Judge, however, was a new Sonoma County resident due to an appointment by the governor. The man had political ambition written all over his Brooks Brothers suit.

Buck disliked him and certainly didn't trust him. But when it came to doing his job, the Sheriff was an expert at parking his feelings.

This was a working lunch. Both men occupied seats on a county youth crime task force. A committee of two, Buck thought this was an odd place to take care of the few pressing problems. This could've been done by email. Did the Judge have something else on his mind? That was fine with Buck. He was sure he wasn't in trouble. If he'd stepped in crap, the Judge would have already told him, in no uncertain terms. Lunch must mean that he wanted something. *Alright. I'll play along. Let's just see what's on his mind.*

A salad arrived, four sorry leaves of romaine, one faded radicchio leaf, and some wilted endive. Buck sighed. Chic or not, this restaurant never served enough food. Flannery scooted his flimsy chair closer to the tiled table. The two men discussed school crime over their salads, School Resource Officers over lentil soup, and juvenile sentencing issues over portobello mushroom lasagna.

Then, with business done, the Judge leaned back in his chair. The check remained unopened in a black folder on the table between them. Buck figured the Judge was working up to asking for a favor. What was he up to? He hated to admit it, but the Judge intimidated him a little. His chest puffed with importance at having something this guy wanted. He had a feeling it wasn't about the task force.

"You must be gratified to have such a capable staff, William."

The Judge's insistence on not calling him Buck was annoying. Not the right foot to get this conversation started on. Buck answered, "You referring to someone in particular?" He shoved away his dessert plate with more force than he intended. He'd heard about the Judge witnessing the shooting in the Quad last week. He'd always made it his business to know things like that, incidents that could bite him in the ass later.

"Yes, as a matter of fact." The judge toyed with the last piece of coffee-colored cheesecake. He sat upright. "At last week's shooting at the courthouse, your deputy, the female one, handled it quite well."

The judge tried to look casual, but the intensity of his eyes gave him away. "I heard you were there," Buck said. *What was he getting at?*

The Judge studied his plate, using his fork to push crumbs into a mound with an obsessive-compulsive deliberation. "Lucky for you, that bailiff wasn't the only deputy present. He's fortunate that she was there to rescue him. She did a fine job."

The Sheriff nodded. *Where the hell is he going with this?* He sipped his diet soda.

The judge placed the fork precisely in the middle of the plate, sat back, and asked, "Who is she?"

Buck had the feeling that the Judge knew her name and was just being coy. *What was his game?*

Buck answered, "Meredith Ryan. Been with the department for seven or eight years now. Married to an architect; he's got a different last name—Taylor, I think. Lives in a big, new house that I couldn't afford, on a cliff overlooking the Russian River outside of Forestville." The Sheriff paused. Ryan had made him look good in the media. "I remember when she was hired. I knew she'd be a real go-getter. She's a trouper with good judgment, and she can scrap with the best of 'em. None of the guys complain about her backing them up." He basked in the reflected light of his deputy's success.

"I am not surprised, William."

Why did the judge's tone make Buck feel like he was an idiot?

"I noticed that in her conduct the other day." Giroud paused. Buck knew the judge was going in for the kill. This is what this whole lunch-deal was about. An obvious motive sprang into his mind; his gut clenched in disgust.

"Yeah, she's a good cop, that one," Flannery agreed.

"It seems a waste to have her in patrol, don't you think? She should be somewhere where her skills and talents are fully utilized. I mean, I would have her in some specialty position..."

The Sheriff's neck hair prickled. *Who the hell do you think you are, telling me how to run my department?*

"...just based on the soundness of her judgment under pressure. I would wager she didn't fall apart after the shooting, either, did she?"

'I'll bet...I'll bet...you pretentious bastard,' Buck thought. *Why couldn't he say, 'I'll bet' like a normal guy, instead of 'wager'?*

"If she did, no one saw it." The Sheriff sniffed and continued, although it wasn't the Judge's business. "But psych counseling is mandatory in officer-involved shootings, so she may have let her hair down behind closed doors."

Then, another thought struck him; he sat back in his chair. "You know, I seem to remember that she put in for detective last month." He met the Judge's gaze. "You may have something there. It's not the way specialty assignments are normally picked, but she'd be a real asset in Violent Crimes Investigations." He twisted the napkin for a moment. "Technically, I can pick whoever I want for the job. There may be an opening soon, anyway." He nodded. "I'm gonna look into it."

As soon as the words were out of his mouth, he realized this was the judge's objective all along. At least he had the sense not to be obvious about trying to run Buck's department.

———

A WEEK LATER, as the Sheriff's pen was poised over Meredith Ryan's promotion paperwork, it occurred to him that was exactly what the other man had done.

Chapter Five

"I want to ask him straight out, 'Richard, are you having an affair?' No, how about, 'Richard, are you seeing someone else?'" Meredith kept her eyes on the leaf-strewn asphalt ahead of them. "Damn, they sound so Dr. Phil."

She huffed in frustration, wondering if Christy would think her a fool.

It wouldn't be the first time.

They were on one of their favorite runs, a trail along the redwood-studded creek below her house. Rainwater from last night's showers cascaded down the hillside, filling a creek that joined the swollen Russian River a quarter mile away. Running under the giant trees was like being in a cathedral. Redwood spires pierced the dull morning sky. Up top, boughs knit together to form a ceiling more spectacular than any church she'd ever seen. In the stillness, the water played a prayerful chant. She preferred to run alone, but when Christy had invited herself, she was happy to have her company. Christy was an emergency room nurse. They'd met the first week Meredith worked patrol seven years ago. She'd been in three times with arrestees needing medical clearance and quickly established a friendship. Christy understood Meredith's weird hours and met the same kind of clientele.

"What if he says, 'yes'?" Christy countered.

"Richard? Admit he colored outside the lines?" Choking back a laugh, she said, "I've thought he might admit it. I'm ready for it. The uncertainty is what's driving me crazy." She brushed away a fern drooping over the trail.

"Are you going to throw him out on his ass?" Christy was on the brink of divorce. She didn't have a high opinion of men in general and Richard in particular.

"I don't know," she said, sensing Christy's disapproval. She knew the real answer. Christy was her best friend, and she deserved the truth. "No. I can't give up on our marriage. This is a lifetime gig for me. But Richard may have other ideas."

"Do you still love him?"

Meredith felt Christy's eyes on her. "Yes," she answered too quickly. She'd been brooding over the same question for weeks. She wasn't as confident as she sounded.

"I think you'd be better off without him." Christy didn't bother to hide her exasperation as she glanced at her friend. "I think you're scared. I think you'll stay with Ricky-baby because you're afraid to be alone. Maybe you're afraid of history repeating itself, I mean, with your parents and all." Christy was working herself into a frenzy.

Meredith clenched her jaw, biting off her sour response. With a flat tone, she said, "You're wrong."

"You'll get the detective promotion. You're at the top of the list, so it's just a matter of time." Christy's voice took on a convincing urgency. "Richard's never liked that you're a cop. He's always made it so difficult for you to do the one thing you ever wanted." They'd been over this ground before.

"It could be months. There has to be an opening, and just because I interviewed for the job doesn't mean I'll get it." She didn't dare to hope for the position on her first try. Some deputies tested for years to get into the Investigations unit. Meredith planned to make her Irish stubbornness work for her—she could wait. She propped up her disappointment with the idea that she'd get it when she earned it.

"Anyway, until January, I would have said we were building a good life together," Meredith snapped.

Richard had been the opposite of her father: responsible, sober, and ambitious. They'd met at a mutual friend's college graduation party. She'd been instantly attracted to his intelligence and drive.

As for him, he'd been attracted to her from the beginning. There had been no game-playing, no doubts about his love for her. In retrospect, Meredith thought he was exhibiting controlling behaviors. He seemed impressed by Meredith, an athlete with plans to teach Physical Education in high school. He laughed at her jokes, listened to her stories, and empathized when she bared her soul to him. Now she knew part of her appeal was that he felt he could groom her into an excellent wife for an upwardly mobile architect.

As a junior partner in a top-notch San Francisco architectural firm, he specialized in residential design. Hoping to break into the Marin/Sonoma Counties area, he'd used his expertise to design and build a modern, glass-walled home, a showcase, for the newly married couple. The home reflected his character. Meredith never felt the home was half hers. He'd set it in Forestville above the Russian River resort area, close to River Road for commuting yet surrounded by heavy forest that provided privacy.

Meredith had denied the pull of law enforcement for years. But when she reached the crossroads to make a career choice, she knew in her soul she was meant to be a cop.

Meredith remembered how he'd raged when she told him of her career change to deputy sheriff. There had been an ugly scene where Richard threatened to call off their wedding. In the end, he gave in, and they were married. Meredith sometimes wondered if it wouldn't have been better if she'd been single.

"Things changed, sometime last winter." Meredith's manner softened as she continued. "He seemed different, moodier, gone a lot, and not truly 'here' when we were together. I was dealing with it, but since the shooting, he's shut down all the time."

Christy usually discounted Richard's feelings. She knew how miserable he'd made Meredith. All she wanted was happiness for her friend. "And you've been off the past three weeks, so you're home to notice his bad attitude."

"My friend, Nick, remember him? He was my FTO—Field Training Officer. He used to tell me to trust my gut. I should have done that more at home, too."

They fell silent. Meredith's breaths came rhythmically, little puffs of exertion.

A mile later, Christy slowed to a walk, then halted. Her chest heaving, she bent a leg to stretch a hamstring. "Refresh my memory. Why are you off work?"

Meredith stopped beside her friend and pulled her foot up in a quad stretch. "It's department policy: I'm on paid administrative leave pending the conclusion of the investigation. Then I'll have to finish mandatory counseling sessions to check and double-check my mental health and fitness for duty."

"Ahh, that makes sense," Christy said. "I wouldn't want someone who couldn't pull the trigger in a tight spot."

"Or pulled the trigger when she shouldn't," Meredith added.

They set out again, picking up a slow pace. On one side of the trail, the creek splashed and burbled, carrying February's rainwater.

Meredith's mind drifted, recalling a conversation with her husband four days after the shooting. In the quiet gloom of the foggy morning, she replayed the confrontation. She couldn't quell the churning in her empty stomach.

Richard had been angry when she asked him to accompany her to the psychologist. "So just because you shoot some asshole, I have to lie on some couch and bare my soul to a complete stranger—a shrink contracted by the department, I assume. Give the department access to my private thoughts? Not a chance."

"Come on, Richard. It's not like that, and you know it." She wrapped her worn chenille robe around her. Meredith had gotten up early to see her husband before he left for work. "You're making it a bigger deal than it needs to be. The counselor just likes to have the spouse present so she can explain the process."

"What d'you mean? Flashbacks or post-traumatic syndrome or

some other horseshit like that?" He stuffed his briefcase with papers, avoiding eye contact.

Meredith was done arguing. She dropped onto the sofa. "Actually, yes." She wouldn't beg for his help. It looked like she would be on her own.

Finally, he turned to her, his spine straight. "Do you realize what this job has cost you?" He swung his arm around the room. "WE live in paradise in a showplace for a home, and all you want to do is wrestle with drunks and arrest tweakers. We have things that most people would kill for, and you don't seem to give a damn about any of it. You sleep all day and work all night, and I'm alone."

She sighed, irritated for feeling a twinge of guilt. She had done nothing wrong. "We've covered this ground before, Richard. You knew my career choice when you married me. All I want to do is be a cop, a detective if I can. The promotion list will be out next week. I know I did well on the test, and if I get the job, it'll be an 8 to 5, Monday through Friday gig. Isn't that what you want?"

He hesitated but didn't say anything. He snapped his briefcase closed and marched to the front door. "I won't be home tonight. I have a late meeting, so I'll just stay in the city."

"Sure," Meredith said as the door slammed shut.

BACK ON THE TRAIL, Meredith said, "He isn't home much anyway." Her voice trailed away. She sounded pathetic.

Christy stayed silent, huffing alongside Meredith as they came out of the trees into a grassy meadow.

"Richard's been coming home late. He started sleeping in the guest bedroom three weeks ago, and he leaves without saying anything but the bare minimum to me." Her frustration grew like a black hole in her stomach. She saw it coming—the failure, the loss, the anger. Just as she had with her father, she'd messed up her relationship with Richard. Her father had called her single-mindedly selfish. In a man, the preoccupation is called focus. Why was it such a bad thing in a woman?

Aw, hell, she was tough, wasn't she? She could make it through anything, and she wasn't alone. Christy was about the best friend a girl could have. And there was her friend Nick, though she hadn't seen him much since she married Richard. She even had a shrink if she needed one.

"The thing is, when I'm alone, I feel miserable. I start to feel sorry for myself. Even though it's been three weeks, the shooting still disturbs me. That won't go away any time soon, I guess. But I'm so frustrated with Richard's lack of interest. I need his support more than ever." She thought for a second, then continued. "Intellectually, I suppose I could second-guess the shooting, but that won't change the outcome. It was the only action I could take. Richard's distance, lack of interest, and moodiness make all of it worse."

Christy's trot slowed again. "You've got a lot going on now. I could stay with you for the next few weeks if you want. It's not like I have anything to keep me at home." She sighed and sucked in another giant breath.

Meredith was breathing hard too. "Have you heard anything from my wayward brother?"

"Just what I told you a month ago—he called to tell me he got some sweet gig in Ontario. I don't even know if he's in Canada or Southern California. Haven't heard anything since."

"I'm sorry…"

Christy seemed to expect this. She interrupted Meredith's apology. "There's no reason for you to apologize for David. He must've been on a coffee break when they passed out the common sense. Besides, he's a grown man. He made his choices."

"Did you file for divorce yet?"

Meredith felt the intensity of her friend's gaze. "That was the reason I invited myself over this morning. I wanted you to hear it from me." With the back of her arm, Christy wiped droplets of sweat from her forehead. "Yes, yesterday."

The women stopped. Meredith put her hand on Christy's shoulder. "I'm so sorry…"

"Sorry for what? That I fell for my best friend's brother, knowing that he was an irresponsible musician? And I went ahead and married him anyway? What do you have to be sorry about? I've still got my best friend. That means a lot to me."

"Right," Meredith sighed. Tears threatened Christy's eyes. Meredith hated to see her friend upset, so she nodded toward the path. They picked up their run again, dodging damp fern fronds and puddles.

"Hey, you have a trip planned to visit your aunt in Illinois, don't you? Next week, right?"

"I have plane tickets for Thursday. If you want me to stay with you, I can change them. I'd like to help."

This time, Meredith stopped first. She looked into Christy's eyes. "You're going to help your aunt after her surgery. She needs you. No, Christy. You go. I'll be fine. Besides, you need to get away, too."

"You're sure?" Christy's eyebrows lifted.

"Yeah, I'm sure." Meredith set out with Christy falling in beside her.

Chapter Six

STEPHEN GIROUD STARED AT THE REFLECTION IN THE REAR-VIEW mirror. He signaled Esparza to duck out of sight in the leather seat of the Mercedes. Giroud did the same. He glanced at the luminous dial on the dash, noting the time. Nine P.M. Meredith would call it twenty-one hundred. The mirror reflected his target: the 1940s stucco façade at the River Substation of the Sonoma Sheriff's Office. Esparza made a soft groan of protest, but Giroud ignored it.

Soon, when Briefing was over, the aluminum-frame door would swing open. Then he could watch her stride out to the parking lot with the other deputies.

Giroud now knew her routine. He had watched her every workday for the last two weeks while discreetly parked in an adjacent lot. He even followed her home one morning—almost all the way to her house. He had driven past when she turned onto a steep driveway, but it hadn't been a wasted trip: he had seen where she lived. William Flannery was right. It was a large house set on an expensive knob of real estate that overlooked the Russian River. The house struck him as an austere modern structure, which conflicted with the landscape. It surprised him a little, too, that she lived in such a house. This angular, modern style seemed to contradict what he knew of her down-to-earth, unfussy personality. So far.

His sources told him she was well-liked and respected, with a reserved but easy nature. She kept her composure in tough situations, a trait of much value to deputies.

The substation door flew open. Meredith Ryan and another deputy trotted toward their patrol cars, both carrying large black fiberglass "pursuit baskets" that contained forms, reference books, and some supplies required during a patrol shift. Bundled against the nighttime cold in her bulky "Tuffy" jacket, she looked rougher than normal. Her face, though, held the same expression as that day in the courtyard: purposeful and professional—her lips set in a determined scowl. He decided he rather liked that look.

While speaking to his driver, Giroud kept his attention on Ryan. "She's like an Amazon, isn't she?" It was rhetorical. He didn't give a damn if the man answered.

The deputies started their cars, then flipped on spotlights and overhead rotators. Sirens chirped as they finished their equipment check. Meredith hit the accelerator, zooming out of the lot with the second patrol unit on her bumper.

"They're going on a call." The driver's voice was raspy.

An intense light strobed through the interior. Giroud's breath caught. A spotlight. He slumped deeper into his seat. Adrenaline throbbed through his system. Tires screeched as more cars left the lot. He dared not look for several minutes more.

The driver spoke so quietly that it was almost a whisper. "This is too risky sitting in the parking lot like this. It's a cop's job to look for things out of place. That's *us*. We don't belong here."

Giroud sighed. Esparza was right. This surveillance needed to end tonight. They had almost been discovered. Still, he had learned much. It almost felt like her schedule was something he had arranged for her.

Giroud scooted upright in the seat; his head swung side to side, looking around. Finally, his lips spread into a grin. "Wasn't I right? Isn't she unbelievable? Beautiful and capable. Just perfect for what I have in mind." He didn't wait for an answer. He didn't care what

Esparza thought. He just wanted to show how spectacular this woman was. It was satisfying to tell someone else about Meredith Ryan. It might make his task that much easier.

Esparza started the car, then pulled onto Sebastopol Road. Traffic was light at this time of the evening. Giroud laid his head on the headrest. Things were working out just how he planned. Just today, the calendar judge moved him out of his courtroom for a change of venue from Tehama County. His offer was accepted to work mornings for incidental things like looking over search warrants. He was essentially free except a few hours each weekday morning.

In a month, Meredith's promotion would come through. He could wait. He was a patient man. Soon she would be close enough for Giroud to see her regularly. After all, he'd waited his entire life for this. In four weeks, six at the most, she would be at the Main Office every day—just across the courtyard from Giroud's office.

Then, he could see her any time he pleased.

Chapter Seven

Rap. Rap. There was a knocking at her door.

Meredith dragged her fuzzy mind into consciousness. Gus, her white, longhaired cat was curled on her chest. She had fallen asleep on the couch, waiting for Richard. Richard? She glanced at her watch. It was after nine p.m., the day after her run with Christy.

Did Richard forget his keys? As the thought faded, she realized he would have used his remote door opener and pulled into the garage.

She set the protesting cat on the floor. *Who's banging on the front door?*

Meredith rubbed the sleep from her eyes and forced herself fully awake. She was in her bedroom, pulling out her Beretta, when she heard, "Mere, it's Nick. Open up!"

Nick Reyes stood on her doorstep, the evening breeze enough to ruffle the collar of his jacket. His face was drawn, and his eyelids sagged with either lack of sleep or sadness—she couldn't tell. He was still dressed in his office clothes: a wool sport coat and khaki chinos.

"What the hell?" Her auburn hair blew into her face. "Come in before we both blow away." She hugged her sweatshirt around her as another gust swirled through the doorway.

He plodded in to stand, shivering away the cold as she closed the door. His gaze took in the living area. "Nice place."

"Thanks." She studied his bloodshot eyes. "You didn't drop by to see the house. What's up?"

From the set of his shoulders, Nick was not merely stressed. He was uncomfortable. A gnawing dread formed in her chest. *So why is he here?*

"Can we sit down?" He pointed to the couch in the living room.

"Not a good idea, Nick. You know how Richard feels about you and me together. I can't wait to see his face when I tell him about the promotion."

Nick stood in the living room. "Mere, sit down and shut up."

She stared at him. Usually, it made her smile when he called her "Mere." He was the only one who used the nickname. Now, she was a little indignant he would take that tone. Then she noticed the quivering muscle in his jaw. This was Nick Reyes *stressed*.

"Nick…" Meredith already didn't like this. She didn't sit. She needed to stand, to be ready. *Ready for what?*

He waved a hand to dismiss her objection. "Meredith, please." He ran his fingers through his wavy hair. Then, facing her, he clasped her shoulders. "Meredith, there's been an accident. It's Richard— he's dead, Mere."

Shock wracked through her. She pulled away and doubled over. It was like a huge hand grabbed her innards and squeezed. *Breathe,* she thought, although it seemed impossible to take a breath. "Richard?" Did she say it or think it?

Nick steered her to the couch. Struggling to put her words together, she asked, "What happened?"

"Sit down. I'll tell you what we know so far. There was a traffic collision—a hit-and-run. Since you have the confidential law enforcement vehicle registration, CHP called our watch commander. He said a car registered to you was involved in a hit-and-run at an offramp in South San Francisco. It was Richard's Beemer—an unknown suspect hit it. Impact must've been at a high rate of speed because the car was pushed up against an overpass abutment, totaled. He was pronounced DOA at the scene."

Meredith held her breath, trying to keep her mind on the facts and her emotions under control. *Tears, where are my tears? DOA at the scene? That meant a catastrophic injury when first responders would pronounce him dead.* "When?"

"At five-fifteen this afternoon. Looks like he just left work. No one at his office knows why he was going southbound instead of northbound." Nick bent his head toward her and asked, just above a whisper, "You have any ideas?"

Meredith felt like she was in the crosshairs of a terrible weapon. There was no way out of this. She had to be honest, yet she didn't want to admit the state of her marriage. She hated being vulnerable, especially to Nick.

She looked away from his gaze and focused on the sleeve of her sweatshirt. She had dealt with victims many times before, but this—this was *her* life. The change in perspective forced a terrifying reality on her. "No. No idea, but things haven't been so good with us for a while." She paused, and the seconds ticked away. *Did Ferrua send Nick to question her on purpose? Is she a suspect? Does she need a lawyer? Still no tears.*

"Go on," he urged.

"I can't prove it, but I think he was seeing someone." She exhaled. This was the first time she'd admitted it to anyone except Christy. "He's been coming home late for the past several months. I was waiting up tonight to talk to him about it. I…this morning, I got a call from Lieutenant Ferrua. He told me I got the detective position. Did you hear?" She went on without waiting for his answer. "I was going to tell Richard about the promotion. It means I'll be home more on evenings and weekends."

The doleful tone of her last sentence echoed in her mind. She covered her face with her hands. Tears threatened, halting her words.

Nick leaned over—his arms encircled her shoulders. The gesture broke through her wall; tears gushed out. She had never felt more alone. She was always picking up the broken pieces when she lost someone she loved. Abandoned by her father, her mother's death eight years ago, her AWOL brother, David—now, Richard. And there was so much left unsettled between them.

Why did she wonder about crying before? Now, she couldn't stop.

It was some time before Meredith could talk. She tried to move her mouth to form the words. It felt like she had no control over her muscles. Her mind was a hurricane. She couldn't process the information.

The room pressed in on her. "I've got to get out of here," she moaned.

She shot to her feet and rushed to the sliding glass door. Unlatching it, she flung it open and took three long steps onto a small patio. In the late winter, dormant wood rose vines bordered, giving it the feel of a secluded haven. Redwoods towered over the outdoor room, while a vine, maple and laurel trees formed a sub-canopy. Wood and bracken ferns lined the patio pavers. Lichen spread across the stepping stones while moss grew between them. There was life everywhere here. This was always a place of renewal for her. But not today. She gulped in the moisture-laden air and tried to steady her breathing.

When her head cleared, she found she was leaning against Nick. After a few minutes, she pulled away, sniffing into the soggy pile of tissues in her hand. "How did you find out about this?"

Nick shivered. "Let's go back in."

INSIDE, Meredith perched on the edge of the couch, clasping a cup of coffee with Nick beside her. "The watch commander phoned Lieutenant Ferrua to see if he wanted to handle the notification. Ferrua knew we'd worked together and asked me to notify you."

Poor Nick. Every cop hated death notifications. It would be worse if you knew the parties involved. *Ferrua was a jerk.* What seemed like sensitivity was more about passing on an awful job. "What about the other driver? Did they catch the guy?"

"No. No solid leads so far." He hesitated.

"No witnesses at that time of day?" That didn't sound right.

"I know. It's weird, right?" He looked at her.

"Almost like it was planned. At first, it sounded like a road rage situation." She shook her head.

Nick kept his eyes on her, searching her face, like he could see if she lied, this woman he knew so well. "Meredith, you realize that this is a homicide investigation?"

Hearing the compassion in his voice, she squeezed her eyes to shut out the tears. Damn, she hated crying in front of people. Nick wasn't just anyone, but she didn't want him to see her like this. *Really, it's okay. You've just lost your husband. You're entitled to a few tears.*

She whispered her answer. "Yeah. I got that."

"You know I have to ask you." His tone was low and slow; the way it was when he was doing something he didn't want to do. "Where were you at 5:15 this afternoon?"

A spurt of anger shot through her, and just as quickly, it was gone. This was Nick—doing his job.

She replayed her afternoon activity. "I was at my bank in Santa Rosa at five-fifteen. It'll be on their cameras."

She smiled when she heard him exhale in relief. "Good. The CHP investigating officers are on their way here. You want anyone with you when they interview you?"

"Like an attorney?"

"No, I mean like Christy. Or me, maybe. I could hang around." He stared at the sullen cat curled in a chair.

She thought this over. Christy would provide moral support but not much else during an interview. Besides, she was still in Illinois. *An attorney?* No, she had done nothing wrong. *Nick?* Yeah. She wanted him here.

"Will you stay?"

Chapter Eight

Raul Esparza pulled a metal currycomb from the wooden tack box. He grimaced as he pulled a handful of brown horsehair from the tines and hurried to clean it up before the boss saw the mess.

Esparza had just combed a chunk of dried mud from the flank of the boss' favorite stallion, Patrick. The thoroughbred threw his head, gnawing at his cross ties and stretching his lips toward the nearest patch of Esparza's skin while stomping side to side.

Esparza's elbow jabbed into the soft side of Patrick's muzzle. The horse pulled his head back and stiffened, wide-eyed at the correction. It was more severe discipline than he'd needed, but Esparza didn't like animals that misbehaved. Patrick needed to be taught better ground manners.

Esparza straightened when Giroud entered the barn a moment later. He felt the judge's gaze as he finished brushing the horse's hide. Esparza bent, his wiry fingers, squeezing the horse's leg above the fetlock to make Patrick raise his hoof for cleaning. Above, Giroud threw a navy saddle pad on the horse's back. A lightweight English saddle and cinch strap followed.

Esparza straightened. "Hey, slow down. I'm not finished cleaning his feet."

Giroud seemed to welcome the challenge. "Then get your ass in gear. I can replace you in a second with any number of wetbacks. Grooms are a dime a dozen."

The muscles in Esparza's lower back tightened. "Maybe. But what I do is more *specialized*." He dropped the hoof and stood tall, a dare to the pompous creep. "You need me to do your dirty work." Esparza's jaw set like concrete.

Giroud's head dipped as he considered Esparza's words. "Right now, you need me more than I need you. Look at you: a disgraced cop, one with a record of violence. No law enforcement agency would touch you, let alone private industry. You are a walking liability." Giroud finished up like he was on the bench. "You need a salary to keep your gambling buddies off your back. You're at a dead end, and I am your last option."

Esparza squeezed the hoof pick until the iron dug into his hand. Staring at his fingers, he released them slowly, one by one. "I'm the only one who can do your wet work and keep the cops off your trail, and you know it."

Giroud's piercing blue eyes penetrated Esparza's damaged soul. It was a gaze the groom would never get used to. It was like Giroud saw into his conscience, like he knew what he was thinking.

Esparza had to look away. He didn't intimidate easily, but this guy was just far enough off-center to worry him. And Giroud was right. He was boxed in. Working for the judge helped to keep the enforcers away. He paid them when he could, but his position with a Superior Court Judge was threatening enough to keep him safe —for now.

Giroud was right. He did need him.

"The deal in South San Francisco went okay." Esparza decided to change the subject.

Giroud looked askance at him. "I assumed it had, or you would have said something."

Esparza picked up the face brush, fingering the soft bristles. "You're going to have to come up with another method if you have any more of these 'accidents' planned. Too many hit-and-run homicides can look suspicious."

"I know that. I'm no fool. Don't you worry."

Esparza ran the brush over Patrick's wary eyes. *You don't know how lucky you are, dude. Still, the same guy is riding us both.*

Chapter Nine

"THANKS FOR COMING BACK." MEREDITH PUT A HAND ON CHRISTY'S arm. They stood in Meredith's stainless-steel kitchen, caterers bustling around them. Trays of savory canapés, citrus juice drinks, and wine rushed out as fast as the lively wait staff could move. Christy posted herself next to Meredith. Christy standing guard for her? That was a switch. Meredith cast an ironic smile.

"Of course I'd be here. I wouldn't let you go through this alone." Christy's eyes were dark with sadness. Her friend's dislike for Richard made Meredith suspect Christy held no real grief for him— only for her. They'd weathered many storms together in the seven years of their friendship. They'd first met when Christy was the ER nurse who attended to a lacerated knee on one of Meredith's arrestees. Forged by suffering other people didn't want to see, they worked similar shifts and dealt with a clientele on the margins. Christy and Meredith understood each other. They'd seen a lot, but this was the worst.

Christy slipped a hand under Meredith's arm. In a careful tone, she asked, "Any word from the bank about the house?"

"It was as bad as we thought." Meredith grimaced. "The house has two mortgages against it. I'll have to sell to pay all the debts."

Christy shook her head, her eyes wide with amazement. "What a shitty deal he left you with, huh?"

Meredith shrugged, numb from the loss of her husband and yesterday's illusion of security.

Christy caught a server's attention and pointed to a knot of guests with empty glasses. "Where's Nick? He came, right?" She craned her neck to see into the living room.

"He's here." Meredith managed a thin smile. "He's like you, a friend I couldn't keep away." She glanced at the front door. "Last I saw, he was outside."

"What's he doing, walking security?" Christy's eyes swept around the room.

"I don't know. He's checking out all the cars if I know him."

Christy eyed Meredith. "He's a car geek, right?"

Meredith nodded.

A server approached Christy. "Where's a soup ladle?"

Christy pointed to a drawer next to the oven. "Over there."

Meredith sighed. "You know my kitchen better than I do. Thank God you're here." They embraced for the umpteenth time since Nick brought the terrible news.

Over her friend's shoulder, Christy made a low snort of surprise. "Who's that?"

Meredith turned to look in that direction. "Shopping for your next husband already, Christy?" Meredith frowned as she heard the unintentional snark in her voice. Catching Christy waving the remark aside, Meredith focused on the new arrival.

The warm fall breeze stirred up orange and yellow leaves that danced across the threshold. Posted inside as a greeter, a uniformed patrol sergeant, Tim Leonard, welcomed the new guest—a tall attractive man.

Sergeant Leonard extended a respectful hand to the man on the threshold. The new arrival's gaze scoured the room. Then he entered, nodding absently to the sergeant. A moment later, his attention settled on Meredith. She wondered at his interest.

A server whispered something in Christy's ear, and the pair were off to the kitchen. Meredith stood alone. As she observed the guest, an unsettling shiver ran down her back. She shook it off and studied him. He was in his early forties. Tall and blond, he looked like a gracefully aging preppie. Broad shoulders capped a well-built physique that was apparent even through his tailored black suit. When he entered, almost everyone turned to look at him. She shivered again. Her mother would have told her someone walked over her grave. She dismissed the old wives' tale, and as the newcomer approached her, she glanced away, hoping to break his notice.

A half dozen guests grasped the man's hand and begged his attention as he walked through the room. He shook hands, brushing them off politely as he made his way to Meredith.

Then he was in front of her. "My sympathies for your loss, Mrs. Ryan." Bowing slightly toward her, he extended a hand. "I am Stephen Giroud."

Meredith murmured something she hoped was appropriate, then took his hand. It enveloped hers. "I recognize you. You're the new Superior Court Judge." Managing her surprise, she dropped her hand from his.

With a furtive glance, he nodded. "Don't tell anybody." A wry grin crept to his lips.

She smiled at the humor, searching for what to say next. "Did you know Richard?"

"We met at the County Bar Association Golf Tournament last spring. I didn't know him well, but I took an immediate liking to him. We ran into each other this summer and had lunch a few times. He spoke of you with great respect." The judge's blue eyes bored into hers. They were so blue. Almost ice blue.

She couldn't say why she was so taken aback. "I didn't realize you knew him." Richard had never told her. She didn't even know he'd attended the golf tournament. Or was she surprised because Richard had spoken highly of her? They must've been getting along better then.

"We weren't close by any means. But I liked him. When I heard about this tragedy, I felt compelled to pay my respects." He took her hand again and squeezed it. "I hope you don't mind that I came."

"Of course not." Meredith forced herself to focus on his words.

"I'm sorry." She shook off the vague discomfort as she freed her hand. People wanted to touch her for consolation. She never liked being pawed, even during this period of grief. She was okay with a hug from Christy and maybe Nick, but they were exceptions.

Wait. Lunch? Richard told her he usually worked through lunch so he could leave early to get ahead of the ugly commute. Why wouldn't he have told her about meeting the judge? *Why, why, why— a lot of whys.* "I'm honored. Can I get you some wine, coffee, or something to eat? The dining room is around the corner. There's plenty of food."

Trying to be a gracious hostess, she steered him to the table. He waved away the food, so she introduced him to a pair of her lieutenants standing over the crudité platter. The Judge was courteous, but when the conversation lulled, the burden of entertaining him drained her. A little irritated at this pressure, she guided him toward the Sheriff.

At Meredith's voice, Buck Flannery turned to her, then the Judge. Flannery's brow wrinkled. It was almost imperceptible, but she noticed. He recaptured his composure, then stretched his hand out in a formal greeting. She thought it peculiar that the Sheriff looked so startled.

To Meredith, Flannery said, "We know each other."

The Judge nodded. Meredith felt the chill in their greeting.

The next moment, another new arrival got her attention, and their meeting was pushed out of her mind.

Chapter Ten

STEPHEN GIROUD MARVELED AT WHAT A GREAT LITTLE ACTRESS SHE was. She appeared stunned when he showed up, but he knew it was an act. No one else saw the way she looked at him. Her message was for him alone. He read it in her eyes. She wanted him the same way he wanted her. The feeling went beyond mere physical attraction. It was something deeper. She saw the two of them fulfilling their potential together.

Chapter Eleven

"REYES. MY OFFICE, NOW." DONALD LEAHY'S STRIDENT COMMAND boomed over the normal workday bustle. The gangly detective sergeant pivoted smartly on the heel of his gray cowboy boots and disappeared into his office without waiting for a reply.

Nick Reyes' fingers paused over his keyboard. He was glad he wasn't on the phone with his sergeant bellowing like a weaning calf in the background. Nick frowned, saving and closing a document. A summons to the sergeant's office was never good news.

Leahy was pacing behind his desk when Nick walked in.

The detective said, "Yes, sir?" Nick waited. Leahy took his time, clearly building himself into a frenzy. His head was shaped like a long cube, except for the underbite that gave his jaw a bulldog look. One of his least offensive nicknames used by deputies was 'block-head.' As usual, he wore a Western-style polyester shirt with mother-of-pearl buttons down the front and on the pockets. A silver belt buckle the size of a garbage can lid glinted in the fluorescent lights. He raked his fingers through his wiry salt and pepper hair. "Shut the damn door."

Nick raised an eyebrow and did as he was told. It was rare that

Leahy didn't want spectators when one of his tirades simmered. Nick wondered why he was needed to be an audience.

As lead detective, Nick got along with the sergeant out of necessity. Nick had worked for worse, although no names sprang to mind. He navigated his way around office politics with solid ethics and considerable silence. By the mere fact that Leahy had never yelled at him, Nick knew the sergeant trusted his ability as a detective and a leader. Leahy's temper was legendary, so Nick often had to "translate" his rants into orders for the squad of detectives. It was tough to respect a boss like that. While Nick wasn't afraid of Leahy, he took pains to avoid him when he could. Yet, under Don Leahy's insistent control, Nick found himself in his boss's presence too often.

"Sit down!" Leahy fired the command like Nick was an enemy prisoner.

Nick didn't need to be told to sit. He leaned against the doorframe, keeping his silence.

The sergeant would need no prompting to continue. "Fucking brass. I can't believe they did this to me." Leahy stomped around his desk. "You know what they did? You wanna know?" Leahy squinted at the detective.

Nick didn't need to answer.

"Lieutenant Ferrua fucking ordered me to take a bitch into my unit. My unit." The sergeant stabbed a proprietary finger at his own chest. "I'm supposed to call the shots here. We've got a good thing going. The guys in this unit get along just fine. Now, putting a split-tail into the room is a bad move. And I don't have any choice."

Nick remained calm despite Leahy's disparaging language. The detective didn't like bias, race or gender. He'd experienced racism first-hand and spent enough time in a patrol car with Meredith Ryan to know she'd lived through similar gender prejudices. This woman had proven her worth on the street. Too bad she landed Leahy as her sergeant in her first investigations assignment.

His sergeant had begun to pace and was spitting mad, and Nick didn't give a crap. He figured he must have endured enough of Leahy's tirades that they had lost their impact.

Maybe, though, he should try to calm Leahy down. "Sarge, it's overdue. Given how few women are in the department, it was bound to happen."

Leahy stopped pacing and leaned his long arms on his desk. His face twisted in an ugly sneer. "I don't give a rat's ass how many women there are. I don't want one in my unit. I don't even want to see her." He made a fist as if the woman had challenged him personally. "She'll be yours to break in. You give her the welcome pep talk." He picked up his pacing again, building up a head of steam like a train engine chugging over a mountain. Stopping suddenly, he pointed an index finger in Nick's direction to punctuate this atrocity. "When I took this position ten years ago, the Sheriff promised me I could hand-pick my people. This is bullshit." He wrapped his arms around his chest, a high priest unable to ward off the evil headed this way.

Nick scratched his chin. "Get real, Don. That was two sheriffs ago. Your buddy is long gone. Flanagan isn't going to honor some back-room deal made in ancient history. Besides, it's illegal."

Leahy swiveled toward Nick, his face registering something between fury and resentment. "Don't tell me the law. Bullshit is bullshit."

Nick fought back a smile. It was about time Leahy got treated like a regular guy—fairly. Nick chewed his lower lip, considering how past administrations had tiptoed around Leahy. Nick always thought Leahy had something on a ranking officer. His ass should've been fired but wasn't. Oddly enough, they'd shown him favoritism as if to make up for his earlier time on the beach. The lawsuit was for sexual harassment, and the county had paid out big bucks to settle before it went to court. No law enforcement agency likes to be on trial—especially for something that was blatantly illegal.

"Looks like you don't have a choice." Nick shifted, dropping his hands into his pockets. He had to ask. He wasn't supposed to know before his sergeant. "Who is it, anyway?"

Leahy shut his eyes tight, as if to will the name away. Finally, he blew out a breath of exasperation. "Meredith Ryan—the one who shot the old River Rat in the Quad." The sergeant's indignation crested as his gaze landed on Nick's face. "Now, what the hell am I supposed to do with this one? Watch every word I say? Ride ramrod over you guys? She needs a babysitter, not a sergeant. She can't even show up until next week. She's on some personal leave or something —probably having her head examined." Leahy's head shook in disbelief. "What the hell am I going to do now?"

Irritated, Nick turned to leave but paused at the door, looking back at his red-faced sergeant. A blast of excitement blew over him. It took an effort not to smile. "I guess you have to follow orders, just like the rest of us."

Chapter Twelve

THE DISPATCHER'S BROADCAST DRONED ON LONG ENOUGH FOR NICK to lose attention. He didn't care. He was off duty and on his way home. He reached over and snapped off the radio.

Home. It was too quiet these days, without Angela. It didn't feel like home, even with his mother there. Sometimes, he even put off going home to avoid all the silence. At first, it had been the loss of his daughter. Then, a year later, his wife. Now, after eight months, the shock still surprised him. The loss he'd felt over her departure, the hole in his heart that she had left behind—he wasn't sure he would ever get over it.

Losing the baby was a different matter. He felt like he'd fallen down a hole with no bottom. He'd heard once that one never gets over the loss of their child. He was sure of that. She'd died in her sleep almost two years ago—SIDS, they'd told him. Neither parent could have done anything, but just the same, the guilt and anger moved in to stay. The feelings were as fresh as if it had just happened. Angela told him she couldn't live with it—or him. In those last few days, she couldn't even make eye contact. Being a good Mexican Catholic, Nick accepted the blame, even though there was none to assign. He thought it better that he shouldered it rather than Angela. He loved his wife enough to take that burden from her.

It cost him their marriage. At first, she'd assured him she wouldn't file for divorce, but when she fled to her brother's house in Bucerias, Mexico, he didn't feel quite as certain. He didn't hear from her for months, seven, to be exact. Family members filled him in on what little news they heard: she'd worked as a receptionist at her brother's law office, she still lived with her brother and parents, and yes, she was healthy, although still melancholy.

The Spanish word *melancholia* is a much prettier word than the miasma it represents. The English word *depression* always sounded too clinical. *Melancholia* conjured up images of Angela's bloodshot eyes, red from endless weeping. His beautiful, dark-haired, energetic wife had lost her drive. She'd become listless, refusing to bathe, dress, or leave the house for days. Although she had never exhibited symptoms like this before, he was sure some of it was due to genetics. He recalled the whispers at family dinners about Angela's mother, uncle, and two brothers also suffering from *melancholia*. He hoped that she eventually could understand her grief, manage her sadness, and return to him —with or without medication.

Until then, he sent her money so she could live comfortably and he kept her health insurance premiums paid. He prayed to God that she would come to her senses—soon. He considered going to Mexico to bring her back, but at the urging of her family, grudgingly agreed to be patient.

Nick's mother had moved in with him just days after Angela's escape. What began as her intention to care for her son reversed itself within a few months. Exhaustion dogged her, and Nick noticed that she often braced herself on furniture. She denied being dizzy, but he was sure something serious was going on. Even so, Mama still cooked. He overruled her protests and hired a house cleaner. With Nick's help, Mama still managed the laundry, but otherwise spent her time either cooking (often sitting at the kitchen table) or resting on the couch. She refused to see a doctor. The more he pushed her, the firmer she dug in her heels. Nick couldn't figure out how to force her to go. When Mama tended toward stubbornness, her daughter Sofia was her only match. Maybe Sofia would convince Mama to go to the doctor.

Ah, women, he sighed. Why were they so obstinate? And now, he'll have a woman partner—Meredith.

He smiled.

Chapter Thirteen

MEREDITH PULLED OPEN THE HEAVY GLASS DOOR OF THE SHERIFF'S
Main Office. The pride of the county in 1966, the building was now
a dated, overweight diva. Built in an era where the word "technol-
ogy" had one dimension, plans were already underway to replace it.
For now, it would be Meredith's new home.

Dressed in a blue sweater, black slacks, and a tan blazer, she
showed her ID to the desk officer and the door buzzed open to the
inner sanctum.

The Violent Crimes Investigations office was at the far end of the
building. Gathering her nerve, she walked a long narrow hallway that
bisected the open Administration and Records offices. Nodding at a
few familiar faces, she saw a few looks of sympathy. She smiled but
continued walking. Meredith wasn't sure she could manage small
talk yet. She didn't want to cry, particularly on her first day in Detectives. It had just been a month since the funeral, and she was still
feeling raw and vulnerable. This was the job she always wanted, but
now it felt bittersweet. Richard wanted her on a normal schedule so
badly, and Meredith believed this would've ended his discontent.

Nick stood as she entered the office. His broad grin welcomed
her.

The knot in her stomach loosened at the sight of him. She hadn't realized how much tension she felt at this new beginning.

"Since we've worked together before, I've been assigned as your orientation adviser. Jacket, umbrella, and personal stuff over there." Nick pointed to an alcove with coat hooks and wall shelves.

The office was a huge, high-ceilinged rectangle framed by pale, colorless walls. Worn, dingy brown linoleum ran underfoot. The space was broken into ten three-quarter-height office dividers. Each cubicle held two desks, a pair of computers, monitors, and phones. On the floors, equipment cables were tacked under vinyl runners.

Nick explained the Monday morning caseload. "The sergeant assigns new cases that come in from the weekend. We're down two positions now because of the budget, so we have a total of twelve in the unit, plus the sergeant. Our immediate supervisor is Lieutenant Gil Ferrua."

Meredith followed Nick as he moved through the room. He seemed so comfortable in his surroundings.

Emil Anderson and Jerry Peters occupied the cubicle nearest Nick's. Anderson—a tall, square-jawed blond man of obvious Nordic heritage—stood and extended his hand. "Pleased to meet you. We hear good things about you."

Pleased with the cordial welcome, she returned his smile. "Don't believe everything you hear."

Peters, a dark-eyed man in his mid-thirties, pumped her hand. "We never believe anything we're told until we see it for ourselves." His thin lips curled in a half-smile that included her as an ally in a world worthy of their skepticism. Peters looked more like an accountant than a cop.

Nick greeted each detective in his low-key manner, introducing her along the way. He mentioned their assignments, specialties, and something personal about each detective, which made it easier for her to remember all the new faces. Overall, she was more welcomed than she'd expected. She wondered how much it had to do with being Nick's former partner.

She had watched each man's response as he'd shown her around. They'd know her, of course. She hadn't worked with any of them before, but Sonoma County Sheriff's Office was a small enough agency that every deputy carried a reputation with him or her, deserved or not. At the very least, she'd be on their radar from the courthouse shooting. Without exception, they'd offered respect. In the younger men, it was elevated to deference. She smiled to herself at the wave of pride that her friend was so well regarded. As Nick's partner, she held a special place. She hoped she wouldn't blow it.

"Did you bring lunch?"

"Nope."

"Good, we'll go out. You're buying."

Nick pointed to the cubicle containing his desk. The adjacent vacant one would be hers. It was standard issue drab county furniture, undetermined vintage, by the look of it. "This was Newell's desk. He's gone back to patrol since he made sergeant."

"Yeah, I heard that. You going to give me the low-down on this job?"

"Don't rush me." His eyes narrowed, and his lips curled. "When I'm ready."

Like he is awaiting inspiration. She folded her arms across her chest, casting a warning. "You ready?"

He took the challenge with a smile. "Yeah." With a glint in his eye, he launched into his spiel. "VCI, Violent Crimes Investigations, consists of a lieutenant, sergeant, eight detectives, and half of the steno pool. Like I said, the unit sergeant, Don Leahy, assigns our cases." Nick motioned to an empty office at the other end of the long room. "You know Leahy?" His deep brown eyes peered at her.

"I've heard about him." Yeah, she'd heard about him, all right. Leahy's name made her hesitate when the lieutenant offered her the job. The sergeant had a reputation as a humorless, uninspired deputy, promoted mainly for his relationship to a county supervisor—his twin. He was also known for his resistance to women in law enforcement.

Nick continued, "Rumor has it that he had a personality once, but his ex got custody of it after their divorce."

Meredith smiled. When Nick stepped out the back door into the cool, damp morning, she followed.

He asked, "Do you know about his lawsuit?"

She wrapped her arms around herself for warmth. "Just from the rumor mill. I was on graves out at the River, so I didn't hear much of anything."

Nick leaned against the stucco wall, watching some Canada geese honk their way into formation across the leaden sky. They sounded like an airborne riot. "Leahy doesn't like women in law enforcement. In 2014, he was one of several sergeants involved in a high-profile discrimination lawsuit. The county supposedly paid out millions of dollars in damages to the three women who filed the suit. Leahy took his time on the beach without pay and returned with an even bigger chip on his shoulder."

"Nice. How's that going to work? He's meeting with me today to give me a pep talk?" Supervisors regularly met with new unit members to discuss the unwritten rules. The thought made Meredith's stomach turn.

"I'm going to give you the talk."

Her relief was short-lived. "Wait, he won't even meet with me?"

"You're the first woman to come into the unit." He shrugged. "We'll see how it works out."

"Maybe this wasn't such a good idea." Too soon after Richard's death? And now all the financial hassle. Too much stress?

Nick looked down his aquiline nose at her. "You wussing out? You wanna go back to patrol with your tail between your legs before you've even given your dream job a shot? Let the job politics sort itself without you. Trust yourself on this decision."

She sighed. "No, I'll deal with him." She thought a moment and then straightened. "No, I'll be fine. I am not a victim."

Nick said, "That's what I wanted to hear. I've got three open cases—all assaults. Two have follow-ups that are time sensitive. Let's get to work."

Chapter Fourteen

"JUST PUT THE FUCKING THING ON." STEPHEN GIROUD SOUNDED irritable, even to his own ears. He didn't care. He wanted to get on with it. He grabbed the thick leather bridle out of Esparza's hands and pushed him aside. The animal dipped his head and opened his mouth to accept the bit. Giroud adjusted the throatlatch and noseband and then fastened them securely. He was pleased with the horse's good ground manners.

Esparza dropped the halter onto a hook next to the stall. He stepped away, and Giroud was alone with Alegre.

"Let's see what kind of polo horse a hundred and twenty thousand dollars buys." Giroud slipped his boot into the stirrup and, in an agile leap, sprang into the saddle. He leaned from side to side, adjusting the stirrup leathers. "Did you check this saddle to be sure it fits him?"

Esparza nodded with a sullen set to his jaw. Giroud watched his groom's face, and for a second, he thought the man was going to say something. But he remained silent. Good, the judge thought. He didn't need attitude from a fucking wetback today.

From his vantage point, Giroud could see rain blowing through the breezeway that led to the covered riding arena. He was glad he'd invested the fifty thousand dollars in the roof. The past month's rains would've never permitted working the horses out in the open. Now he would be ahead of everyone else when the season arrived in May.

Giroud tickled the reins, tightened his seat and calf muscles, and settled in as the horse trotted out.

In the arena, Giroud set about moving the animal into specific patterns, cantering, halts, slowing, half and quarter turns, neck reining, and then a full gallop. He sank his seat into the saddle, tugging on the reins, settling the horse into a smooth, firm stop. He was satisfied with the horse's responsiveness. Good enough for practice. How would he do with a mallet?

"Esparza." He yelled across the breezeway. "Get a horse and come on out here. I want to take him through some moves with another horse."

A few minutes later, the groom joined Giroud on a dark bay mare named Roxanne. She was an experienced Argentine horse that the judge had used for the past four seasons. She wasn't his favorite, but she was solid enough to match the new horse as he was put through the paces.

Esparza handed a mallet to Giroud, positioned his own, then tossed the ball.

Roxanne burst into a thunderous gallop. Giroud nudged Alegre's flanks, and the animal exploded after the ball. Alegre caught up. Giroud steered him into Roxanne's shoulder. The horses thumped into each other, narrowly avoiding smashing their tack. After a snort of frustration from Roxanne, both horses took the bump in stride. They trotted apart and lunged after the ball. Esparza came to it first, leaning into the ball with his mallet. He struck it downfield with an energetic swipe. Alegre's ears pointed toward the ball, and Giroud let him have his head.

Their horses' hooves pounded after the ball on the packed sand. Giroud was out of the saddle, leaning over Alegre's mane, spurring the animal forward. Soon, he was two lengths in front. Giroud shifted, pushed his leg into the horse's side, and yanked the reins into a sharp turn. A fierce swing and Giroud's mallet smashed the ball off to the side. Roxanne twisted her nose away but had too much momentum to stop. The mare slammed into the back of Alegre's saddle, her chest pushing Alegre's haunches sideways. Anticipating the collision, Giroud remained firmly in the saddle.

Startled, Roxanne reared, trying to free herself. Esparza tumbled to the ground. He landed on his back, then shook his head to clear it. His brown face darkened. "You fuckin' t-boned me."

In a move Esparza hadn't seen coming, Giroud slipped from the saddle in one fluid movement. A puff of dust rose as he dropped to the sandy surface inches away from Esparza's face. The groom leaned on one elbow, the other hand covering his brow. With a firm grip on the handle, Giroud shoved the mallet head under Esparza's chin. He pushed on the handle.

Esparza fell back, coughing. "Hey."

Giroud pushed the mallet head harder against the groom's throat.

Esparza coughed again, grunting out something like, "What the fuck" but Giroud wasn't sure and didn't care. The groom's muscular arm shot out from below and knocked the mallet away.

Giroud smirked as Esparza scrambled to his feet. A few steps away, the judge bent to retrieve his mallet.

Esparza shouted. "What the fuck was that about?"

As Giroud pulled himself back into the saddle, the past minute evaporated from his mind. He left Esparza standing.

Giroud settled into the smoothly worn leather and wrapped his long legs around his new horse. Alegre handled the collision better than Esparza. Giroud chuckled, slamming his ankles into the horse's flanks.

His mallet cracked the ball downfield, and the horse chased after it.

Chapter Fifteen

ESPARZA HELD THE REINS, GIVING ROXANNE A CURSORY CHECK FOR injuries. Still furious, he mounted and trotted after Giroud, thinking that Giroud didn't give a shit about how he won. Horses are disposable as long as he maintains his five-ball status, as long as he's the local big shot.

Giroud hit the ball toward the imaginary goal line as Esparza caught up. Roxanne spun to put Esparza into position to block the ball. He missed, and the ball rolled to the goal. The two men straightened in their saddles. Giroud's voice was calm. "Toughen up. The horse did fine back there, but I had to test him. I cannot have him shying in the middle of a match."

"That's crap, and you know it." Impulse control had always been a weak point with Esparza. He'd blown his law enforcement career because he didn't know how to keep his mouth shut. He'd pay for the smart remark.

Esparza didn't mind doing Giroud's dirty work but hated being made a fool of. Seeking a remnant of justification, he spat. "I bet this kind of bullshit didn't go over any better in the Santa Barbara Club."

"You don't know what you're talking about." The judge's eyes narrowed. "You are too soft."

Esparza nudged Roxanne into Giroud's line of sight. "I'm tough enough to do your wet work." The horse snorted with confusion, unable to anticipate his next move. The ball lay still.

Giroud's eyes shone like flint. "And smart enough to keep quiet? For your sake, I hope so."

Esparza returned the threat. "I got plenty on you, Judge." He stopped short of saying that he'd kept enough information to turn over to the police should he ever be arrested. He'd keep that ace in the hole tucked away. An ex-cop, he'd saved evidence that showed that Giroud generated and planned all the crimes. If he was ever sent to prison, he'd make sure that Giroud went with him. The idea of Giroud sharing a cell with an armed robber satisfied Esparza's thirst for vengeance.

The judge raised his chin. "Don't convince yourself that any cop would listen. A low-life like you could never challenge my impeccable record."

"I still have friends."

"You have no friends." Giroud's lips turned downward in an ugly sneer. "In the law enforcement world, you're a leper. You beat a prisoner and lied about it. No cop can tolerate a liar, especially one who got caught."

"Man, what you don't know."

Giroud crossed his arms over the pommel, the mallet dangling from a strap on his wrist. "I know what I need to know about you, Esparza. For instance, you cannot find a job anywhere in the state. Probably on the entire west coast."

"I have—" Esparza started again.

"You have nothing." Giroud straightened, his voice deepening. "Nothing."

Esparza's lips pressed together as Giroud's words found their target. For sure, he was a pariah in the cop world. No one would touch him. The judge was also right about finding a job.

"You are mine. I own you. You are little more than a slave."

Esparza studied his worn gloves, at a loss for words.

"Now get to work." Giroud stuck his spurs into Alegre's sides, and the horse jumped onto a gallop.

Chapter Sixteen

"Are you sure there's not some mistake?" The crack in Christy's voice shattered Meredith's façade of calm.

Meredith cleared her throat and took a deep breath. Her fingers tightened around the phone. "I'm looking at it right now. The credit card balance is five digits." The computer screen glowed against the dark room. She scrolled to a different page. "From the statement, it looks like Richard spent money like water." Meredith gasped. "This card was for a cash advance, $20,000. I didn't even know we qualified for that much."

Christy sighed into the phone. "Mere, what did he use the money for?"

Dread gripped Meredith's chest. "Let me see." Going into his file, she found his password list.

"This can't be right." All she did since Richard's death was learn how little she knew about her own life—especially her husband. "Four different credit cards are listed here. I only recognize one of these." She fumbled through the log-on for the Visa card. Nothing unusual there—a small balance outstanding for the newspaper subscription.

She clicked back to Richard's password list. "I'm still here. Checking for passwords."

Christy said nothing. Even over the long distance to Illinois, Meredith considered her friend's silence alarming. "I'm going to look at the mystery cards. Just a minute." She was scared. She couldn't think of a reason for her husband to have secret credit cards. She'd always been careful with money. She'd been raised without much and tended to put money away for a rainy day. She'd felt it was a good balance to Richard's tendency to spend what they made.

"Meredith, there's only one reason for a husband to have secret credit cards."

Scrolling down the list, she found an American Express account. She re-checked the password he'd chosen—Jennifer. "Who's Jennifer?"

"I'd say she was your husband's floozy." Christy's clipped tones conveyed her disgust.

Meredith logged into the account. The numbers flashed before her eyes: Twelve hundred dollars for a hotel charge in Utah, another eleven hundred for lift tickets and restaurants. "How am I going to pay for this? This is unreal." She read the items to Christy. "That was three months ago, when he was supposed to be in San Jose for a conference."

"At these numbers, the lift tickets must be for two." She paused. This would wipe out her rainy-day fund and then some. Scanning through other charges, she saw that Richard had made minimum payments on the card. The balance was eleven thousand dollars —maxed out.

This went against her natural frugality. She'd always paid the balance in full when she got a credit card bill. She didn't even know he had these cards.

"Time to go. I'll call you back later." She couldn't stand dumping all this dirty laundry on anyone, even Christy. She pulled up their credit report. Her stomach was in knots when she looked at the balances of open accounts—forty thousand dollars in credit card debt. But her stomach flipped when she saw the second mortgage on their home. The balance was over two hundred thousand dollars.

Chapter Seventeen

"THORNTON WOULD HAVE A FIT AT THIS EXTRAVAGANCE." THE OLD lady spoke to her steering wheel. She waved the thought away with a wrinkled, age-spotted hand. *Not to worry. He isn't here to nag me about the cost.*

Contentment seeped through Violet McMurray's wizened body as she pressed the remote button. Her new, custom-painted aluminum garage door opened before her eyes. Her home in the senior community of Rolling Hills was nestled in the far eastern part of Sonoma County. The winter rains watered the lush vineyards stitched across the hills down to the Valley of the Moon. The weather was Mediterranean, dry summers with mild, wet winters, but this year's heavy rains made the automatic garage door a very handy expenditure, indeed.

A twinge of guilt struck her. She thought of her husband's death last fall. She did miss him. Their forty-eight years together had been more habit than happy. George annoyed her with his quirky practice of hiding cash in odd places: the sofa cushions, the backside of paintings, even coffee cans in the freezer. She found money in the oddest places. But Violet didn't miss him harping about her spending too much. She didn't miss that one bit.

"Yes, this little extravagance is just what I needed," she said out loud. She loved the convenience of getting the car into the garage without getting drenched. It's about time she enjoyed the fruits of their labors.

Another jab of remorse. Thornton would never know the comforts of their retirement nest egg. Nevertheless, she hooked her thin arms around two bags full of groceries, closed the trunk of her new Cadillac, and shuffled to the garage door.

The kitchen smelled of furniture polish and Pine Sol. "Good," she thought. "Theda's been here." She savored the sheer delight of a clean house and the joy that she was not the person who cleaned it.

The heel of her black leather pumps crunched on something against the tile. She peered under her grocery bags. What did she step in?

Raw eggs splattered across the floor, along with lettuce, celery, and some frosted packages of frozen ground beef. Confusion muddled her vision. *Did Theda do this?*

She slid the grocery bags onto the counter and picked her way through the kitchen, taking care not to get egg yolk on her shoes.

"Oh no," escaped her lips. In the living room, paintings had been pulled from the walls; the canvas sliced off their frames. The plates from her china cabinet were smashed, and vases and boxed silver service had been dumped from her sideboard. In the living room, couch cushions were slashed open, the contents thrown on the carpet. These were places where George had hidden cash.

She'd been robbed! How did the burglar get in? How did the burglar know where to look?

She reached for the china cabinet door, then stopped. A man's face reflected in the glass. Fear shot through her body. *He's still here.*

Suddenly, rough hands gripped her throat and pressed from behind. She tried to twist toward the source of her pain. What was happening?

Violet caught a brief glimpse of pale, moody eyes. The young man tightened his hold on her neck. Panic gripped her as her vision blurred. She saw a mural of fireworks just before she lost consciousness.

Sometime later, she came around. There was no way to tell how long she'd been out. *Why can't I move my hands? Or legs? Oh, my shoulder hurts so much.* Dried tears almost sealed her eyes closed. She fought to open them, to see what was happening. The man had tied her to a chair. Something like a cord pressed into her skin.

The man's face dropped to hers—right in front of her nose. He spat on her when he yelled. "Where are they? Where's the rest of the money? And I want your jewelry, too. The good stuff."

She tried to tell him, but the words came out as sobs. She didn't care about the money or the jewelry for once in her life. He was welcome to all of it if he would only leave her alone. She wanted to live to see her grandchildren again.

She tried to picture the moment when she saw them last. She loved the way little Logan's nose scrunched up when he smiled. *Oh, please stop.*

But he didn't stop. He hit her, his rough palm across her face, screaming at her, spittle dripping from the corner of his lips. Then, his fist to her jaw, the side of her head, and her shoulder. The more he hit her, the more she cried. Tears of desperation, the anticipation of loss, and a touch of anger, too. She kept trying to picture Logan's darling face to take her mind off the physical beating. *Oh, no!* The man knocked her over, chair and all. She saw the knife snap open and her naïve mind leaped to what she had hoped for. *Maybe he's going to free me.*

Leaning over her body, he cut the cord that tied her feet. It was a ragged, awkward movement. When she struggled, he sat on her hips. He leaned over to her face again, and the knifepoint pricked under her chin.

The warmth of the blood trickling down her neck shocked her out of her tears. "The jewelry is in a safe in the bedroom closet. The safe is behind the shoe rack. It's not locked."

Grunting, he shifted the knife to his other hand. "Where's the rest of the cash?"

She sighed, knowing he wasn't going to like her answer. "I don't know—all over. My husband hid money everywhere." Her chin trembled.

"That's not good enough." He stabbed his knife into an end table. He straightened and got to his knees, unzipping his jeans.

Violet couldn't believe what she was seeing, so she slammed her eyes shut. She nudged her face into a sofa cushion lying beside her. Logan's playful expression filled her mind and took her away from this terrible place.

After some fearful grunting, scratching, and horrible pain between her legs, the man shuddered. The pumping stopped. Her lovely house smelled like sweat, blood, and now this. He rolled off her.

When Violet opened her eyes, anger finally took hold. Even if she got out of this alive, she would never be the same. She studied the man's face so she could identify him to the police. The beady gray eyes, hawk-like nose, and dingy blond hair. Before he looked away, it dawned on her. He looked like Theda, her housekeeper.

"I know you." An ugly cloud of betrayal grew in her chest. This was someone her housekeeper brought into her home to do odd jobs. "You're Theda's grandson." The words were out of her mouth before she realized what danger they'd put her in.

He snorted, then faced her. In a second, he was on her again, this time with his hands wrapped around her soft neck.

Chapter Eighteen

THE SHRILL RINGTONE OF HER CELL PHONE SHATTERED THE SCANT sleep Meredith had managed. She groaned and rolled over, keeping her head on her warm, down-filled pillow. Her arm swung out from the sheets to drop on the ringing device. She punched "accept."

Meredith grumbled into the phone, then heard Nick barking out orders. He concluded with, "I'll pick you up in ten minutes." Nick's words fought a battle with her body's need for sleep.

He waited on the other end of the phone.

She asked, "Okay, did you call out CSI?"

"Yes." He hissed his answer, then hung up.

The question was ridiculous, of course. He'd been doing this a long time and didn't need any reminders. She'd better get moving. When Nick said ten minutes, he meant ten minutes.

An assault or potential homicide. Her first call-out as a VCI detective.

The phone clattered to the bedside table. Meredith rolled over and reached out to touch her husband. Her hand dropped to the mattress, and a moment of horrifying disorientation spun through her mind.

"Richard," she whispered in a panic. Then she realized that she had called out to the emptiness next to her.

Chapter Nineteen

EDGY AND EXCITED, EARL SUTTON GRIPPED THE STEERING WHEEL SO hard his knuckles went white. His Grandma's old Toyota pick-up sputtered through the wet Sonoma night. He made himself relax his fingers, then gripped the wheel again as a flush of excitement shot through his body.

He remembered the moment he'd found the first of the hidden cash. The rush threatened to make him black out. Finally. Finally, some goddamn good luck. He'd found some easy money. For once, Grandma had been right: there was money stuffed everywhere. He'd searched the house, from kitchen to bedroom to living room, not caring if the old lady knew he'd been there. He ripped open seat cushions, tossed open books, and busted flower vases on the floor. He'd yanked pictures and paintings off the walls, pulled the food from the fridge and freezer, and, in place after place, found still more cash. Plenty of it. A fifty here and a hundred-dollar bill there. All there for the taking. A quick tally totaled almost three thousand bucks, cool, untraceable cash.

The windshield wipers smacked against the truck frame, he recalled how fast it went south when the old biddy came home. He'd heard she would be gone all day. Now, he was glad he'd given some advance thought to her returning.

He heard the garage door open from a back bedroom. Damn, he was almost done. Now, he'd have to tie her up. He picked his way through the debris on the floor and hid behind the dining room door. She waddled into the kitchen while he watched her through the gap in the doorframe. The woman stopped and looked down at the linoleum. She huffed at the mess, dropped the groceries on the counter, and tiptoed between the mess on her way to the dining room. She flipped on the light in the dining room. At the china cabinet, she gasped as the full scope of the damage was revealed.

Sutton hoped the old woman would run from the house. But no, she was as stupid as she looked. As she stood in front of the cabinet, her sobs grew over all her precious broken shit. With each new discovery, the wailing increased.

Then, twisting around in her old lady drama, she met his eyes in the reflection of the cabinet glass. She stood very still as if he was a snake, maybe he'd slither away.

An electric ribbon of excitement unrolled down Sutton's spine. He'd been getting a kick out of watching her reactions, but now she'd seen him. The point of no return? Maybe she didn't recognize him. If she left the room, he could get out through the kitchen. He needed to be outta here. He'd been inside the house too long already.

But he really dug this shit. The old bitch freaked out when she saw her precious crap smashed. All his handiwork.

Before she moved, he slipped in behind her and closed his fingers around her soft neck. He held on tight during her feeble struggle until she went limp. Then, he propped her in a chair, tied her hands, and smacked her face when she finally came around. Just like in the movies.

A few more smacks, and she finally told him where to find the jewelry. The old girl wouldn't give up any cash, so he made her pay for it. By then, she had eyeballed him real good. She saw his face; she knew who he was. After all, wasn't the resemblance to his grandmother, Theda, noticeable? The tiny eyes and big hawk nose.

So, his little game had backfired. Now he had to shut the old bat up. He couldn't have her ratting him out to the cops. That would screw up his plans royally. He got her by the throat again, and this time he didn't fool around. A fine gold chain cut into his hand as he pressed his fingers on her throat. A necklace.

He held her airway closed for a long time. When he was sure she was dead, he released his fingers and stretched them until the cramping was over. He studied the chain and whistled a long, low note. A fine gold chain and pendant, some religious stuff on it. He yanked it from her bruised neck and stuffed it in his pocket alongside the cash.

An hour later, the old Toyota putted down Highway 12 toward Santa Rosa. Sutton was hot, like he had a fever. His breath still came in short bursts. He had to lay low for a while. He pulled out his cell phone, scrolled through the numbers, and punched the "send" button.

Fredo Pilchard, H-block, three cell doors down. Released six months ago. "Fredo, buddy." Sutton smiled into the phone.

"Dude, what's up?" Fredo answered.

"You got a trip planned anytime soon?"

"Yep, day after tomorrow. Why?"

"Need to get out of town for a while. I think I need some sea air." Sutton believed in being blunt. That way, no one misunderstood.

"Um, I got a full crew going out now. Hey, ain't you on parole?"

"Yeah, so?" Like that had anything to do with his plans. Parole didn't mean shit, and he'd be off it tomorrow.

"So, nothing." Fredo spat out a shallow laugh. "I thought you had a slick hide-out in your granny's trailer."

Sutton ground his teeth. "It's a tunnel. Good for getting away but not for hanging out."

"Don't be testy. Getting tired of living with your granny?"

"Yeah, she's been making my life hell, telling me what to do and when to do it. Man, my Parole Officer made me live with her. Any place would be better. Living with her is worse than life in Pelican Bay."

"I hear ya, man." Earl could picture Fredo, working his mouth with a toothpick, drooling on his undershirt. "Wait, can you cook?"

"Yeah, I can cook." Which was a stretch, but Fredo couldn't expect him to tell the complete truth.

"All right, show up at Spud Point Marina day after tomorrow at 3 am. That's 3. Not 3:30. We'll be leaving on the early tide."

"Day after tomorrow? That'll work. It'll give me time to get some stuff done before I go."

Fredo grunted. "You gotta take care of your granny?"

"That bitch?" The words were out of Earl's mouth before he could think. He took a moment to consider Fredo's question. In a way, he was going to take care of his granny. He chuckled at the thought. "Yeah, I'll be setting up the old witch."

Fredo sympathized with a, "yeah, yeah," then said, "Later," and ended the call.

Sutton's mind whirled like a blender, chopping up ideas and spinning them around. Theda was a problem. Theda would snitch him off in a heartbeat if the cops put any pressure on her. She was the old bitch's cleaning lady. They'd for sure talk to her.

When the cops talk to her, she'll know it was him. Earl knew he'd been clever, getting information from her about the old biddies she worked for. Theda never seemed to catch on.

But she would if the cops hauled her ass in. He still needed to return to the trailer to pick up his baby, his pride and joy, a midnight blue 1973 Pontiac GTO. "Goat" to those in the know. He would dump this heap of crap he was driving. It had served its purpose. No one would think twice about seeing the Toyota in the neighborhood as it was there every week. He might catch a catnap, too. It was too early for anyone to discover the old lady's body. Earl figured he had a little time.

His hand pawed at the cash In his pocket. Better find a safe place for this, he thought.

He'd take care of Theda, too.

Chapter Twenty

FORTY MINUTES AFTER HIS PHONE CALL, NICK STOOD NEXT TO Meredith outside the open front gate of Violet McMurray's precisely landscaped retirement home. Mist dampened the night, a light fog draping a row of juniper topiaries. "You ever see trees cut like that? Perfect and straight, like everything's right with the world." But it wasn't. The junipers were an illusion. The elderly lady who lived here had suffered grievous injury tonight. There was doubt whether she'd survive. He shook his head. A shitty thing, to work all your life, retire to a quiet life in the Wine Country, and get beaten to death.

He scanned the home, yard, and neighborhood, taking it all in. "Get your notebook out and start writing. Anything I say, write down."

Meredith pulled out her spiral notebook.

When Nick spoke, he talked in cop shorthand. "Upper middle-class neighborhood in the unincorporated area of Santa Rosa." He glanced at his watch, "It's three-oh-five, Tuesday, January 19, 2014. Units who arrived first, directed by Sergeant Robbie Jacks of the Valley Substation, have secured the scene. Presently, I am the lead investigator and accompanied by my partner, Meredith Ryan."

He watched the redheaded Sergeant Jacks follow the path from the backyard. Jacks nodded to Meredith in a professional acknowl-edgment and extended his hand to Nick. The detective introduced her as his partner, then shifted his focus to the case.

"What have you got so far, Robbie?" Nick asked.

"Aggravated assault, potential homicide. The medics got a weak pulse on the victim, but it doesn't look good. The suspect left her for dead." The sergeant's thick fingers dipped into his breast pocket for his own notebook. He flipped the dog-eared pages. "The call was received in dispatch via 911 at zero-two-oh-five. The reporting party was a neighbor returning from a trip." He nodded toward the street where a tall, gray-haired man slumped in the back seat of a patrol car. "He saw the lights on in Mrs. McMurray's house at midnight and recognized it as unusual. He thought she'd fallen or something. When he went to check on her, the front door was ajar, so he walked in. He found her lying on the carpet in the dining room. She was unconscious, bleeding, and her breathing was shallow. The medics said the clotting on her lacerations indicated she had been there for several hours."

"Yeah," Nick calculated the time with his fingers. "If the lights were on when she was found, it looks like a six, maybe seven-hour window when this could've taken place." He looked at Meredith. "Sunset is about five pm, right?"

She nodded, and he turned his attention back to Sergeant Jacks. "Rob, what have you and your guys done so far?"

Jacks thumbed to another page and began, "We secured the perimeter. Didn't use crime scene tape because of the location and time of day, but a deputy is logging movements of all personnel involved since we arrived. EMS showed up within four minutes, and we have all their horsepower. Since the victim was still alive, I sent a deputy along in the ambulance. He's collecting her clothing and standing by. They're going to Community Hospital."

Nick was pleased with the sergeant's foresight.

Jacks continued, "I had dispatch call out you guys, and the Crime Scene Investigators to process the crime site. I knew you'd call them out anyway, so I thought I'd give them a jump on the response time." He broke off his narrative, and for a moment, you could see on the sergeant's face how bad this was. "The medics said she's pretty busted up. I figured I'd better treat this like a homicide."

Nick said, "Good call."

"I pulled in everybody available to help with the neighborhood canvass." Jacks went on. "No witnesses, so far. All we have is background info which I'll give you when you need it. According to the neighbors, her housekeeper was here yesterday during the day, then again before suppertime. Her white Toyota pick-up was spotted in the guest parking area. We just have a first name on her: Theda."

"Wait." Nick held off the impulse to grip Jack's forearm. Most cops didn't like to be touched. "The Toyota showed up twice on the same day?" Nick's eyebrows drew into a V.

"Yeah." Sergeant Jacks frowned. "We have to check if that's normal or not. One of the neighbors said the woman cleans at another house around the corner on Wednesday mornings, so as soon as we can get hold of the resident, we should have the housekeeper's last name."

"Good. We'll get someone to sit on that house and wait for her to show up." Nick glanced at Meredith to be sure she wrote that down, then back to Jacks. "Is there family around who can help with a property list of stuff that was taken?"

"I have the names of the son and daughter-in-law. They live in San Francisco. I didn't notify them; I figured you'd want to do that yourself." Jacks tore off a sheet from his notebook and handed it over. Nick slipped it into his jacket pocket.

"Yeah, Robbie. Thanks."

"That's about it. So far, no one saw anything unusual last night. Jacks fastened the button on his breast pocket. "We're available for anything else you need." With two fingers, he massaged his temple. He didn't move, although his briefing was over.

Nick waited.

"Nick, I hope you catch this guy. He strangled, beat, and raped her, an eighty-three-year-old woman. This was as brutal as I have seen." Jacks' eyes were bloodshot and weary, glassy from too many graveyard shifts and too many crime scenes. Nick knew the look. The sergeant's lips thinned into a humorless smile. "We take that stuff personally out here in the Valley. These old folks have done their time. They deserve a safe place to live, and we try to provide it for them. When something like this happens, well, it impacts the whole community. Even us." With slumped shoulders, he turned and walked away.

He understood Jacks' dejection. More than being territorial, the sergeant was charged to keep safe a vulnerable segment of Sonoma's population. In his eyes, he'd failed, and an old woman who should've been bouncing grandbabies on her knee was in the hospital with grievous injuries.

Nick pulled a pair of latex gloves from his jacket pocket, snapped them on, and turned to Meredith. On her cell phone, she told dispatch to look up the history on the house and the victim. Holding McMurray's driver's license, she gave the information for a computer check. Meredith told dispatch to get everything they could on "Theda." It was such a unique first name; they might get a match on the computer. It was a long shot, but one that any good detective would take.

Nick caught Meredith's attention and jutted his chin in the direction of the house. He was going in. A slow walk past the lush foliage in the entry atrium and he stopped at the two doors. One was the front door to the house the other led to the garage. The front door was open. He'd have to confirm that the neighbor found it that way and the light on inside. Down three steps into the garage, he noted the neatly stacked shelves to his right, boxes labeled in a tidy script identifying the contents. To his left, a shallow pantry stocked with canned and boxed foods, paper towels, and such. The wall directly in front of him held a newer stainless-steel washer and dryer and a door that opened to the kitchen. His hand hovered over the engine compartment of the light blue Cadillac STS. It was cold.

At the door, he waited for Meredith to finish her call. When she joined him, he spoke just above a whisper. "You only get one shot at this scene. Look at everything, no matter how small it seems."

Her head dipped in a silent acknowledgment.

"It took me a year in VCI to learn how to *see*." It was a rare disclosure but one he hoped she'd learn from.

Nick took two steps inside the kitchen and scanned the house. He cemented his first impressions in his mind, then fired his observations at Meredith. She scribbled notes and, in moments of silence, also scanned the messy scene. "Record date, time of dispatch and arrival, and address. Upon our arrival, it was dark outside. The house was lighted inside in at least one room. Victim's car parked inside garage, engine cold to the touch."

Through the kitchen, Nick and Meredith picked their way through to the dining and living rooms. Furnished with sapphire and rust-colored brocade drapes, a matching upholstered couch, and color-coordinated recliners worn but maintained over two previous decades. Dark cherry wood tables dotted the room in strategic positions. An aged and well-polished dining table and chairs with a matching china cabinet occupied the dining room. It had been a comfortable space.

But there was nothing comfortable about it now: the intruder had left his mark. Cushions were pulled from the sofa and ripped open; pictures and family photos were ripped from their frames. Vases and lamp bases were shattered methodically. Canvas paintings were slashed and pulled apart, books were ripped from the shelves, opened, and scattered.

Nick scanned the dining room again. He judged by the dust-free tables that the house had been cleaned recently. He could still smell furniture polish. While the house was clean, almost everything in the front three rooms was upended. Someone had made a huge effort to search the house and didn't care who knew about it. The mess didn't strike Nick as particularly organized, but there was a single-mindedness about it that caught his attention. There was a specific search pattern. This wasn't an impulse crime. The suspect knew what he was looking for and had lots of time to find it. Or beat it out of the victim.

From the full grocery bag on the kitchen counter, it appeared the victim had interrupted a burglary. Then it had turned bad.

The electrical cord lay on the carpet where it fell after deputies cut it from her wrists. The kitchen light shined into the dining area.

Nick began a mental inventory of items to be covered for the investigation.

Meredith was quiet. He looked sideways, keeping his silence while she scanned the area as he had. He liked her, trusted her in the field seven years ago. But he wondered how much of it she was getting. Standing in the middle of the havoc, Nick thought of the irony of his cautious, meticulous steps like a strange, uneven dance with the criminal. He remembered how hard he had to concentrate on his first assault or homicide cases. He was pleased to see Meredith's gaze lingering at different points inside the rooms. She's a quick study.

He noted the tiniest shadow of sadness in her eyes. He turned to face her. "Not like the movies, huh? You gotta figure a way to not let this bother you if you're going to do this job." He thought about his own situation. When was he able to get the job done without letting emotions get in the way? He couldn't say. Every case was different. This one had trouble written all over it.

Meredith said nothing.

Nick's phone rang. He answered, listening intently to the caller. A few quick questions later, he snapped the cell shut. "Now it's official. It's a homicide. McMurray died four minutes ago."

His gaze took in a small series of blood splatter soaking into the carpet. All that's left of the violent taking of a life.

Chapter Twenty-One

EARL SUTTON YANKED OPEN THE TRAILER'S FLIMSY DOOR. HE charged up the steps, calling for his grandmother. One glance told him the messy trailer was empty. He considered his next move, then dodged his way to the bench that folded into a bed. He closed it up in a hurry, and the edge of a gray blanket dangled from the plywood storage box underneath.

In a cupboard, Sutton found a metal bandage can, its hinges lightly rusted. He dumped the bandages on the bed, then pushed the roll of cash into the can. After sliding it into the plywood box, he covered it with a blanket.

Mission accomplished, he stretched, releasing the tension from his shoulders, and glanced out the dirty window to the morning mist.

Where the hell is she? He needed to find Theda before she said something stupid to a cop. She always was a dumb bitch. He couldn't trust her to keep her mouth shut.

With that thought, he sat down. He lit a smoke, and his mind drifted back to the first time he gave her a little payback. They were in a trailer a little larger than the one he was in now. The place even had a bedroom with a door that closed.

GRANDMA SLAMMED the front door after her and growled at twelve-year-old Earl, stretched out on the carpet before the TV. "I told you to take out the garbage and clean this place up." A cigarette dangled from her lined lips as she used her hip to hoist a grocery bag on the kitchen counter.

Earl pushed himself up to his knees and reached for the remote sitting on the coffee table. Eyeing her with a 'fuck you' expression, he held up the controller so she could see and pushed the volume up. A Knight Rider rerun blared from the TV. He loved that car.

She stood motionless in the kitchen while the challenge sank in. Her shoulders curved as she launched herself toward her grandson. Earl got to his feet. They were eye to eye when she got to him, her hand arcing toward his cheek.

This time, he was ready. He grabbed her scrawny wrist and held it. Her momentum blocked, Theda stumbled and shot him a look of disbelief. She caught her balance while Earl still had her trapped, and her rage rekindled. "What're you doing? When did your pants get big enough that you think you can challenge me?"

"I'm tired of your shit. Time for you to get a little payback." He slapped her across the face. Then he hit her again.

She cried out, pleading for him to stop. She looked so pathetic and old, blabbing her useless whining. It grated on his nerves. Her tone was so unnatural, a pitch that busted his eardrums. It made him angrier. The more she begged him to stop, the more he hit her. On her face, her head, and shoulders. Her wispy, bottle-blond hair shook with every blow. His chest heaved with the exertion. He sighed with satisfaction when he finally released her wrist.

He noticed her reddened face, a trickle of blood from a cut on her cheekbone. "Touch me again, bitch, and you'll get more."

Chapter Twenty-Two

NICK SLOUCHED BEHIND THE WHEEL OF THE WORN-OUT COUNTY FORD Taurus, steering them back to the Main. The sun had burned off the morning fog and with it went Meredith's somber mood. She was pleased with the progress of the investigation. The crime scene techs found several usable prints, blood samples, and the electrical cord used to tie the victim to a dining room chair. The autopsy would yield even more. The victim was raped, so the exam might yield the suspect's body fluids. There were plenty of potential leads here; Meredith was anxious to get to the office to work them out.

Meredith had sensed Nick's approval of her, the rookie detective at the crime scene. Back in patrol, her job would have ended when the detectives showed up. Now, the work was just starting. She watched Nick and the techs and made notes as needed. It had been seven years since her basic investigations class in the police academy. She'd long forgotten the specifics. Although the fundamentals remained the same, the science changed—almost daily—and she would need Nick to point her in the right direction. In the upcoming weeks, she was scheduled to go to forty or eighty-hour technical schools. But she was here now. She pulled out her notebook and glanced over the pages.

Nick cleared his throat. "Pretend I'm Leahy. Tell me what you got so far."

Meredith considered where to start. At the beginning, of course. She recalled that from her training days. The same, only different—seven years later. "A neighbor called dispatch to report a suspicious circumstance at zero-two-oh-five. Lights on and front door open at this address. Sergeant Jacks and Deputy…" she turned a page in her notebook. "Deputy Rico Gomez arrived on scene at zero-two-thirty-six. They found the victim, Violet McMurray, an eighty-three-year-old white female, unconscious. She was tied to a chair with an electrical cord. The ambulance transported her to Community Hospital, where she was pronounced DOA at zero-three-thirty."

"Okay, so far. What time did we arrive?"

She flipped another page. "At three-oh-five. Sergeant Jacks briefed us. We did the initial crime scene overview, then the crime techs arrived. We observed and directed them for a half-hour, then turned our attention to the field interviews done by Sergeant Jacks' guys. Nothing workable there." She looked over at her partner. "We'll have to go back today during the daylight hours. Guess most of the old folks had their hearing aids out."

"No reason to wear them to bed, is there? No one would expect trouble in this neighborhood."

Meredith continued. "We have the name of the victim's son in San Francisco, so we'll call him after SFPD does the death notification. Maybe we can get them to do a walk-through today or tomorrow to see what's been taken. I'd like to get a list of stolen property ASAP." Her glance took in his nod of approval. She tucked her notebook under her arm and finished up. "That's about it so far. Oh, and we checked for any license plates run in the area last night that were out of place, but none came up."

"Leahy will want to know about the usable prints, electrical cord, hair and fibers, and blood."

"I wasn't sure how much detail he needs."

He tipped his head in a gesture that indicated the importance of his statement. "Leahy has to know what we know. It doesn't always work out well for us, but those are the rules."

Meredith smiled, not feeling it. "And we always must abide by the rules."

"Yep, it's the way I work. If working by the rules is a problem for you, you better find another job."

"Ouch. Feeling a little defensive?" She turned in the passenger seat so she could study his face. "You know me better than that. You know what my standards are and how I work. I take umbrage at your comment."

"What the hell is 'umbrage'?" His jaw set as he turned the ignition. The engine sputtered to life.

"Never mind. I don't take umbrage, so it's not important." She sighed.

"Another stupid white man word." He switched gears. "Back to the investigation. What evidence do we have so far?"

"We have a half dozen different fingerprints. The lab will process them. Blood found on the carpet near the chair the victim was tied to would be hers. Hair and fiber samples taken are waiting to be matched up with a suspect. The autopsy is scheduled for tomorrow morning, so we'll see if any body fluids turn up there."

His head bobbed with approval. "Good. You can brief Leahy when we get back. In the meanwhile, call the victim's son and see if we can meet with him today or tomorrow afternoon." He pulled onto the road, driving slowly, inspecting the neighborhood. After a few minutes, he made his way to the highway.

Nick steered the Taurus northwest on Highway 12 toward Santa Rosa under picturesque oaks that formed a canopy over the roadway. To the west, upscale retirement homes dotted the rolling hills. Vineyards sprawled over the opposite hill, stunning even now, in the dormant stage. It was scenery that tourists spent millions of dollars a year to see. As Meredith glanced out the window, she thought it atrocious that Violet McMurry had to suffer such a horrible death in this beautiful setting. "You probably know this, but I'm going to give you my take on dealing with the victim's family."

"Okay." She wondered if his philosophy had changed since her training days.

"We treat the family with the utmost respect. This isn't a

vandalism report. It's a murder. Someone the McMurray family loves has been taken from them, violently. But it's crucial to get any information they may have immediately." He glanced at her. "And we do it with care."

She thought about the conversation in her living room two months ago. He'd demonstrated his philosophy then.

A half-hour later, Meredith finished briefing Sergeant Leahy in his office. Nick looked on while she added, "The son is going to the house this afternoon to check for anything missing. We'll meet with him afterwards; should be about midafternoon."

"Are you thinking robbery's the motive?" The tall, thin sergeant looked past Meredith and focused on Nick. The detective shrugged, then jutted his chin toward his partner. "Ask her, she's doing the briefing."

Meredith grew warm under Leahy's glare. "Yes, sir. That's a guess from the condition of the home, upholstery and paintings cut up, drawers, boxes, and vases opened and smashed. She interrupted him, and he raped, then strangled her."

"The autopsy's tomorrow? Reyes, be sure you're there so this rookie doesn't foul anything up."

Meredith blushed at the slight but stood, happy the briefing was over.

As they walked the hall from Leahy's office, Nick said, "Why don't we go to Crime Analysis to see if there are any similars. They only keep stats on stuff in Sonoma County, but they get crime bulletins from all over Northern California. Maybe there's something."

Nick's cell phone rang. He listened a bit, mumbled something into it, then grabbed Meredith's elbow. "C'mon. We're going to Crime Scene Investigations. They got a hit on the prints."

Chapter Twenty-Three

HARVEY CLAYTON'S LIPS MOVED AS HE READ TO HIMSELF FROM THE top page of Sutton's file. He pulled his glasses off, looking at Meredith across mounds of documents with the perpetually tired expression of a career state employee. His wiry gray hair, clip-on tie, and rumpled off-white shirt matched his job enthusiasm. Clayton cleared his throat for his summary, then snorted to clear his sinuses.

The heavy-set parole agent's chair squeaked in protest as he leaned back. His eyes studied the ceiling as if that would help him remember. "Earl Redmond Sutton. Oh, yeah. I recall this guy," he commented in the flat tones of a Midwestern accent. Clayton seemed pleased with himself that he could place Sutton, even though the booking photo was old.

Meredith and Nick had folded themselves into parole agent Harvey Clayton's dusty, cramped cubicle. Frameless bifocals crept down the man's bulbous nose as Clayton scanned one of a score of papers in his meaty paw. The detectives hoped the parole agent would fill in the background that a rap sheet couldn't provide.

"Yeah, he's off parole as of midnight yesterday." This was not new information. The parole termination date was on the criminal history record and had been noted. The detectives had reviewed Sutto''s rap sheet: three armed robberies, several assaults of varying degree, and physical violence against his domestic partner that included a weapon. This demonstrated an inclination to physical violence. There was enough to tie his past behavior to this type of violent crime.

"Sutton reported to this office as required on…" Clayton glanced at his report. "…March third of last year: He was released from Pelican Bay twelve months ago. Been living with his grandmother in Sebastopol. Job as a dishwasher at a restaurant on the River. Usual terms: a urine analysis test every month. He did that and didn't do anything to cause any concern on our end."

"Then none of his UA's turned up dirty?" It sounded like Nick was searching for motive. Money to buy drugs is often a reason.

"No. I would have violated him if he had." A vein throbbed in his temple.

Meredith leaned toward him and motioned for the report. Clayton handed it over. She looked at it while Nick asked, "Off the record, what are your impressions of Sutton?"

"What are you looking at him for?" Clayton chewed the earpiece on his glasses. Nick had told Meredith about this tactic. He called it the "I'll show you mine if you show me yours" game. It was common in law enforcement when dealing with different jurisdictions. There was no reason for Nick to be coy, so he answered the question.

"Homicide. His prints showed up at a murder scene."

Clayton's eyebrows shot up. "Hm. That SOB has graduated to the big leagues, huh?"

Nick gave a cursory outline of the investigation. When he finished, Clayton frowned, settling back into the worn Naugahyde chair. It hissed with the weight. The parole officer released a lengthy breath as he collected his thoughts.

"I'm not surprised," Clayton sighed. "The psych report said he showed no remorse for his victims. I can't say for certain, but I remember getting the impression his grandmother was afraid of him. She never said so, but I was sure."

Clayton nodded at the memory. "Yeah, his grandmother raised him after his mom went to prison for fraud."

His eyes searched the ceiling. "Dad was absent. There was a girl-friend he got knocked up, too. She's the one he went to prison over. He beat her up when she was pregnant and killed the fetus."

Nick's voice was lower when he asked, "Did she testify against him?" This guy was scum. Beating a woman was something Nick couldn't tolerate, much less understand. But killing your own child?

Clayton's vacant expression told them he didn't remember. Meredith scanned through the court report. "Here," she said, pointing to a paragraph on the page. "Yes, she did."

"Uh—yes, she did," he repeated, giving a nervous laugh. "Now I remember: She was so afraid of him, she left the area afterwards." Clayton rested his elbows on the desk. "He threatened her and her family. In fact, they filed terrorist threats charges on him while he was in jail. Yeah, he did a number on her, all right. He carved his initials on her stomach." His chubby face screwed up with disgust.

"We still need a motive to kill a defenseless old lady." Nick rubbed his temples.

"Talk to his Grandma. She knows him best. Her name's Theda something."

"Theda?" She heard Nick's impatience. He was excited. Maybe he's on to something. "That's an unusual first name. It's the same as Violet McMurray's housekeeper. What's her last name?"

"Simms, Theda Simms. You may be right about that." Meredith stared at the report. "She lives in a trailer park in Sebastopol on Highway 12 with Sutton."

Nick rose and stretched his back. He glanced over Meredith's shoulder at the documents in her hand. "That's the same address we have for him. Let's go see her. Maybe he'll be home, too."

Meredith stood. "We have to meet with the victim's son at the victim's house in twenty minutes."

"Oh yeah," Nick said, like he hadn't remembered at all.

As she rounded the corner, leaving the cubicle, Meredith stopped. She turned to ask Clayton one more question. "What's Sutton's weapon of choice?"

"Knives mostly, but he's been known to pack a gun. Basically, anything he can get his hands on."

"Great," Nick said.

Chapter Twenty-Four

"QUIT YOUR WHINING, COUNSELOR." JUDGE STEPHEN GIROUD sighed. "I've ruled against your motion for the reasons I have articulated. It's not my fault you are not prepared." Giroud pursed his lips to show his disgust. Truthfully, he didn't care.

The defense attorney's ferret-like face colored as he dropped into a chair. The client grabbed his lawyer's arm and whispered urgently into his ear.

Giroud didn't try to hide his smirk. There was no challenge with this worthless excuse for an officer of the court. Ill-prepared, shy with no discernable personality, Giroud would have to force himself to concentrate.

Ferret-face sulked while the prosecutor took the jury on a tour of the defendant's crime. The deputy district attorney matched the other attorne"'s dismal skills. It was going to be a long morning. Giroud sighed again and his mind drifted to Meredith Ryan.

He'd not seen her today. She was mired in a homicide case, her first. His administrative assistant told him that she'd been assigned to partner with Nick Reyes.

Giroud sat back, making a poor attempt to look interested in the proceedings.

He wasn't worried about Reyes getting romantically involved with Meredith. He'd done some checking around and found out that the detective was married and a committed Catholic. The Reyes family suffered the death of their infant child. The wife, Angela, went to Mexico to be with her family to recover. While religion was as good a reason as any to stay on the straight and narrow, Giroud quashed his natural jealousy. He was quite sure Reyes would honor the partnership with Meredith.

Giroud wouldn't tolerate anyone else imposing on Meredith's attention. He wanted all of hers. In time, He would get it.

No need to worry about Reyes.

Chapter Twenty-Five

IT WAS LATE IN THE AFTERNOON WHEN THEY FINISHED TALKING TO Violet McMurray's son and daughter-in-law. They had walked the family through Violet's home for details that would help form a picture of her life and to determine the loss of property.

Nick got the feeling the son hadn't spent much time in Violet's home. Jared McMurray had been stunned by the chaos in the house. He seemed at a loss to name any valuables taken from the emptied jewelry box. But Nick understood that shock did surprising things to people. Anger, denial, tears, but McMurray just seemed in shock. No matter what their relationship had been, this woman was his mother. The horror she'd endured tainted the air with an undefinable foulness. It wasn't until they got outside that Jared shook himself sensible. They stood on the sidewalk when he remembered his mother had recently done a valuation of her jewelry. The jeweler's appraisal was attached to Violet's will. Jared had a copy at home and promised to fax photos as soon as possible. "One more thing, detective. There was cash hidden in the house, too." Jared's face reddened. "My dad was old school. Didn't trust banks much, so he tucked cash, usually larger bills, 50's and 100's, around the house."

"That could account for the scale of damage inside," Nick said. "Any idea how much?" Nick knew no one could answer this question. At Jared's shrug, Nick asked, "Who knew about this?"

Jared looked at his wife. "I don't know. I'm the only child, and Dad wouldn't have advertised it."

"How about someone who comes into the home, like a caregiver?" Jared shook his head.

She offered another idea. "A house cleaner?"

Jared perked up. "Could be. I know she had a lady come in every week. I can't remember her name, though."

The wife pulled a check register out of her purse. "I have your mom's checkbook. Let me see if I can find who she made the check out to." A minute later, "Here it is, Theda Simms, housecleaning. There's a check written every week."

BACK AT THE MAIN, Nick led Meredith to VCI offices to brief Leahy. The sergeant was on the phone, so Nick propped himself against the doorjamb to wait while Meredith took a seat. It was late afternoon, and the long day was catching up with him. When he yawned, Meredith found she didn't have the energy to do anything but yawn back.

Leahy hung up. He turned to Nick. "What did the family say?"

Nick stood. "No surprises. We'll check out their alibis, but they both were at a political fundraiser in the city. They claim all the jewelry, and some cash was taken. No idea on the amount of cash—all large bills hidden throughout the house. The good news is that her jewelry was appraised last year, so there are photos, descriptions, and valuations available. The victim's son is going to email the files to us. Then we'll fax them to all the local pawnshops. I'll show Meredith how to do a Trak flier to pass this on statewide."

"All right."

Meredith spoke up. "We're going out to the River now to talk to Theda Simms. We'll ask if we can search the place. She's on probation. Unfortunately, the search terms don't include her home, just her person. We might get lucky and find Sutton home."

"Nah, that would be too easy." The cliché slipped from Leahy's lips. He cleared his throat, aiming his attention at Nick. "What time did you get the call this morning?"

Meredith answered, "Two-oh-five."

"And it's..." Leahy twisted his wrist to check his watch. "It's almost five now. Why don't you call it a day and get some sack time? Simms'll be there tomorrow." He pulled a file toward him and flipped open the cover, appearing to dismiss them.

"We're fine." She'd never heard Nick speak to a supervisor with such firmness. "We need to get to those two as soon as we can."

Leahy closed the file and sighed. "All right, I can't go with you, but I'm sure the Lieutenant will. Take whoever's on duty from SWAT in case he is there. Don't want to pay overtime if we don't need to."

Meredith read the frustration in Nick's squint. "We got it handled."

IT WAS dark ninety minutes later, and Nick had Theda Simms stashed in the back seat of the Taurus. The sodium vapor lights from the twenty-foot pole at the entrance to the trailer park cast a ghoulish pallor on the old woman's face.

Nick leaned onto the car, eyeing Theda. "Where's Earl Sutton? He's living with you, right?"

Theda's whole body shook. Meredith couldn't tell whether she was nodding or plain scared. "Haven't seen him in a couple of days."

"Does he still live here with you?"

Theda met Nick's eyes. Hers were awash with unshed tears, her chin quivering. "He does whatever he wants."

"We're going to search you. In accordance with your probation terms, you must submit. For our safety, we're going to check the trailer."

Theda rubbed her eyes. "Go on then, I can't stop you." Dark splotches of mascara dirtied up the bags beneath her eyes.

She waited in the car with a deputy while four SWAT personnel, Lieutenant Gil Ferrua, Nick, and Meredith cleared the trailer. Sutton was not there.

Chapter Twenty-Six

T̲H̲E̲ ̲L̲A̲S̲T̲ ̲P̲A̲T̲R̲O̲L̲ ̲C̲A̲R̲ ̲K̲I̲C̲K̲E̲D̲ ̲U̲P̲ ̲G̲R̲A̲V̲E̲L̲ ̲A̲S̲ ̲I̲T̲ ̲L̲E̲F̲T̲ ̲T̲H̲E̲ ̲P̲A̲R̲K̲. Theda led the detectives inside the trailer and snapped on the light over the sink. Blond ash plywood, old and cracked, paneled the walls. A dinette with bench seating sat close to the door. The kitchenette's dingy avocado-green sink and stove bisected the trailer. An unmade double bed was opposite the bathroom, a wadded-up pile of jeans and sweatshirts in the corner, men's clothing. The color and pattern of the upholstery on the benches were unrecognizable. Thin cotton curtains shrouded the interior windows, giving the trailer a dreary feel. Empty beer bottles, crushed soda cans, and filled ashtrays were used as accents to the décor. The smell of rancid grease from meals past mingled with stale cigarette smoke.

Theda motioned toward the table, grabbing an open can of Diet Pepsi from the small counter. Meredith studied her as she fussed with the soda can.

Theda Simms was a stooped, worn-down woman with sagging skin and a thick paunch. A hawk-like nose punctuated the frizzy, bottle-blond hair that framed her wrinkled face. Her stained gray sweatshirt and skinny jeans were too big for her scrawny frame. She settled into a seat at the table, facing the detectives with a trembling chin and an air of resentment. The set of her thin lips said that she'd faced cops before and wasn't happy about this interview. Her posture told them she had been beaten by life.

Whatever work she'd done in Violet McMurray's home yesterday was not repeated in her own. The dinette table had smears of grease and pale crumbs of something unidentifiable between condensation ring stains from drink containers.

Meredith was reluctant to put her notepad on the filthy table. Feeling a little prissy, she decided to hold it in her hand. Nick would record this interview, but she wanted to back it up with notes. Earlier, he told her to pay attention to Theda's body language. He wanted her take on Theda's truthfulness. She winced at her own foolishness, flipped her notebook closed, and stuffed it in her pocket. She couldn't take notes and watch at the same time.

Nick positioned the small recorder. He pressed the "record" button, giving the date, time, and name of the person to be interviewed. "Theda Simms, you are being interviewed in the matter of Violet McMurray's homicide. Are you her cleaning lady?"

Theda's head bobbled up and down.

Nick said, "Mrs. Simms, please use words and not gestures for the tape."

"Okay." Theda cleared her throat and leaned into the recorder. "Yes, I am Mrs. McMurray's cleaning lady."

"When was the last time you saw Mrs. McMurray?"

"A few days ago."

"That would be…" Nick prompted her. "What day?"

Theda shrugged impatiently at the triviality of his question. "It must've been a week ago."

"According to Mrs. McMurray's kitchen calendar, you were scheduled to clean yesterday. Did you?"

She nodded, then remembered the tape machine and leaned toward the mic. "Yes."

"Did you see Mrs. McMurray then?" Nick's jaw muscle started to flex. Theda wasn't uncooperative, but she wasn't giving up anything without an effort. Meredith could almost see the gears shifting.

Theda's head went from side to side. She paused, then said, "No."

Nick slouched back in the seat. "It must be a pain to have to clean houses for those rich, old people." His tone was conversational; his face seemed relaxed. Meredith knew better.

Theda leaned toward Nick. "Uh-huh."

"Working all day in other people's houses, taking orders, cleaning up after them. Then, working at night at the restaurant, serving people. I bet you get tired of it."

"Yeah," Theda answered. Her mouth opened to say something more, but then shut it with resolution.

Nick prodded. "How was Mrs. McMurray to work for? A little demanding?"

Theda's focus dimmed, as if replaying some scene in her mind. She snapped toward him, spewing the words. "Yeah, she was demanding. Ya know, last week, she had me wash the windows in the living room twice. They weren't crystal clear enough for her. The old biddy."

"I thought she might be like that." Nick said, "Go on."

"Once a week, she wanted me. There was never anything to do. She kept the place pretty neat, but she had me doing the stupidest things, like..."

Nick's voice was deep when he cut across her tirade. "Did you ever get so mad that you wanted to wring her neck?"

"No." Theda sat back like she'd been struck. Her eyes flashed at Nick for a second, then swept away to the floor. "No, never."

"So," Nick asked in the same conversational tone as before. "Do you know of anyone else who did things for her? Did she have a gardener, a handyman? Anyone like that?"

"No, the grounds are done by the homeowners' association. I don't know about anyone else."

"She never mentioned needing anyone to help hang pictures, change the furnace filter, or batteries in the smoke detectors?"

Theda shook her head. When Nick pointed to the tape recorder, she said, "Not that I know of." She stared at her soda can.

Nick sat back with a sigh. "Theda, do you live here alone?"

"No." She eyed him with a sour look that told him he already knew the answer.

"Who lives here with you?" Nick pressed.

She took another drink from her can. "I run a halfway house for parolees."

"Is one of those parolees Earl Redmond Sutton?"

"Earl," she whispered.

"I asked you about Earl because we found his fingerprints in Violet McMurray's living room." Nic"'s voice was soft, but Theda reacted like he'd shouted at her.

With wide eyes, her spine straightened. "No. No..." She sucked a breath into her lungs and reached toward a shelf for a Marlboro.

Nick blocked her arm and shook his head. "Not now. Wait. Earl is your grandson, right? And he lives here with you. Yes or no."

Theda's thin arm dropped. She looked at the detectives, then stared at her soda can. "Oh yeah. Now I remember. Violet asked me to have Earl do some work for her. She needed furniture moved." She sighed as if she was pleased with her lie.

"When was that?" Nick's jaw flexed. He didn't believe Theda any more than Meredith did.

"Last week sometime, maybe early this week. I don't remember."

"So you don't remember the date? What day of the week was it?" Nick shifted in his seat. Meredith noticed the intensity in his eyes. "Theda, when was the last time Earl hit you?"

Theda's emaciated arm waved the question aside. "It's been months since he laid a hand on me. What does this have to do with Violet?"

Nick smiled. Lines crinkled around his dark eyes, and his lips spread in an engaging grin. Meredith had seen him smile many times. It was his nature to always stay professional, and smiles didn't often factor into police work. However, it did today. Meredith knew the effect it had on women. She almost fell for it herself.

Meredith's gaze flew to Theda. The woman was softening when Nick said, "Humor me, Theda." The smile evaporated, but the effect remained.

He let the mood settle on the older woman, then said, "I'm

concerned that Earl might have hurt you more recently. If he's done it once, he'll do it again. It's a proven fact."

She shook her frizzy, blond head and dropped her gaze to her lap. "No..."

His tone carried the softness of concern. "Theda, look at me." He waited for her to focus. "Did he hurt you to get information about Violet? Did he tell you not to talk about him?"

"No," she said, a little too loud.

"I thought so." Nick sat back, his suspicions confirmed.

"No," Theda said again.

"You can't make me believe that, Theda. I think he's hurt you to get information. I believe he's threatened more harm if you say anything about him to the police."

"No, I said, no." Theda straightened, her small gray eyes darting from one detective to the other. Meredith read fear, desperation, and something else. Nick had zeroed in on it. She was scared of her grandson.

Before Theda could bolster her defenses, Meredith rushed in with a question. "What kind of wheels is Earl driving these days, Mrs. Simms? Nice muscle car?" Nick knew Meredith took a chance on the prompt. There were no vehicles registered to him in the DMV database. He was pleased that she'd kept up with the rhythm of the questions.

"Yeah, a Goat." Theda bit her lip; she winced as it dawned on her that she'd given up info that Earl might not want the police to have.

Meredith tipped her head to appear impressed by the model. "Is it the black one I see on River Road sometimes?"

"I got nothing more to say. Earl did odd jobs for Violet. That's it."

Meredith tried another tack. "Theda, if we could look around..."

"You want to search this place, you're gonna have to get a goddam warrant. The old woman cut across Meredith's words and glared. "As a matter of fact, I think I need an attorney. I got nothing more to say."

Chapter Twenty-Seven

THEDA SLUMPED INTO THE SHAPELESS CUSHION WHEN SHE HEARD THE detectives slam the door behind them. They were gone. With them went the risk for her to say something that would get her into trouble. Earl always accused her of talking too much.

She rubbed her knuckles trying to ease the arthritis pain, then stood and reached into a shelf. Setting the liter of drugstore vodka on the table, she twisted the cap off and lifted the bottle to her lips. No time for a glass. She was in a hurry. She needed another place to crash until things cooled off or the cops caught Earl. It was just a matter of time. He's so sure of himself. He thinks he knows it all. He's not as smart as he thinks. But she was still afraid of him. She'd been a fool to come back here for her clothes. She hadn't planned on getting caught by the cops.

Sooner or later, Earl would figure out she had taken his cash. Cash that belonged to Violet McMurray. Three thousand dollars was nothing to sneeze at—and, by God, she deserved some of it. Hadn't she slaved for that old battle-axe for the past four years? If she hadn't told Earl about the money, he wouldn't have known about it, much less where to look. Violet and her old man stashed it all over the house.

Earl owed her, but he'd never share it. So, while searching his things this morning, she found an old bandage can. Because it was so out of place, she opened it and found a bundle of bills. She simply took it. She hadn't even been looking for it specifically. Weeks ago, she had found his hiding place, the plywood box tucked under his bed. She'd made a project out of checking it regularly. She wasn't completely surprised to find the cash but didn't expect the large amount.

Too bad, most of it was gone already. So fast, it was like she'd never had it. She paid her sister back the grand she owed her, then put almost all the rest on a pony with a lucky name. Only it wasn't. She patted the roll of fifties in her bra. $350.00 was all that was left, and she'd buy some really good vodka with some of it.

Her eyes lost focus as her mind drifted to the years when Earl was a baby. When she was excited to see him—when she wasn't afraid of him.

SHE BLINKED, and it was 1984. Jerrold, her son, was still in prison. She remembered because Nellie, the bimbo he'd shacked up with, showed up to ask her to babysit little Earl. Theda was living in a room at the Motel 6 until she could move into the trailer she'd rented out at the River, so everything was a mess. She didn't have that much, but her clothing, two boxes of dishes, assorted pots, and dry goods were scattered across the stained carpet.

Theda opened the door coming face to face with her worthless son's woman. While Theda stood deciding whether to let her in, Nellie elbowed her way into the room. The girl was a tiny woman, more a girl, really. Theda was annoyed when she remembered the baby fat she'd gained from Jerrold. She still had that damned spare tire around her waist. Not like Nellie. Skinny with stick-straight blond hair, she had deep blue eyes perched above an upturned nose. She was pretty and knew it. Too pretty to sit home with a baby while her man was in prison, Theda thought.

The baby's head bobbed over Nellie's shoulder as she dumped a grocery bag on the rumpled bedspread. The bag toppled over, and Theda saw diapers, faded onesies, and assorted baby supplies fall out. Mixed emotions flooded her. She loved seeing her grandson, but she had all this packing to do. And Nellie never appreciated what she did for her, anyway. No way in hell she'd help her.

"I need a favor." Nellie laid the baby on the bed and ducked into the bathroom. Before the mirror, she pouted, smoothing her blond bangs across her forehead. "Can you watch the baby? I have a job interview in a half hour." Without waiting for Theda's answer, she tugged her black leggings to her ankles, dropped her butt to the toilet seat, and peed.

Theda made herself look away. "I'd love to but..." *She's not going for a job interview. No way.*

Nellie cut her off fast. "Thanks, Theda. I knew I could count on you. You're not like the bum you raised. That piece of shit just got another seventeen years tacked onto his sentence. On top of the twelve he already has. Did he tell you?"

Theda's stomach roiled. What now? She heard the snap of elastic as Nellie pulled up her leggings. Theda glanced back toward the bathroom. Nellie was arranging her powder-pink oversized turtle-neck sweater, smoothing it against her large, pert breasts. Then, she shook her hair in a nervous gesture, and she padded across the room. She faced Theda and her mouth twisted with contempt. "I didn't think so."

Nellie leaned over the bed to her purse, pulled out a smoke, and made a production of lighting it. Theda kept quiet. Afraid to ask, she was sure Nellie wouldn't keep the bad news to herself. It wouldn't have killed her to offer her mother-in-law a smoke, either. Gawd, she hated bad news.

"He got caught planning to do a hit. Can you believe that? I mean, how friggin' stupid can he be? He's already in prison. He'll never get out at this rate. What does he expect me to do? Sit here and wait for him?" Her pale face flushed with exasperation.

"Well, I can't take care of the baby today, Nellie..." Theda began.

Nellie crossed her arms, then raised a lazy hand to her mouth.

She sucked on the cigarette and blew out the smoke, looking thoughtful while her little finger tapped her lower lip.

"You're my last chance." Nellie's eyes glimmered with quickly summoned misery. "Theda, I have to have a job to support myself. And little Earl. I gotta make some money."

"I can't. I have to finish packing and move by tomorrow. I don't have time to take care of Earl." Theda felt her determination wobbling. She loved the little boy. He represented all that was good in her life. The only scrap of innocence left in the family. She loved the smell of him, the silkiness of his infant skin, his feathery blond hair. She loved holding him. It was almost like having another chance to make it right.

Nellie must have sensed Theda's weakening. She went in for the kill. "You know, if I don't get this job, I'll lose the apartment. That means I'll have to move in with you. *We* will have to move in with you."

Theda put a hand up to halt the onslaught that was coming. "All right, all right." Resigned to her fate, she bent over Earl and checked his diaper. He needed a change.

Nellie was just warming up. "Imagine dirty diapers in that dinky-ass trailer. Hoo, in the summertime." She fanned her nose at the possibility of the smell. "It'd get downright nasty. And the fucking formula. That stuff gets rank, too—when I forget it and leave it out." She stabbed her cigarette out on a paper plate that held the scraps of a pineapple and ham pizza.

Theda straightened as the baby began to whimper. She glanced at Nellie. "I said I'd do it. Now go, so I can get my crap done." Theda grew louder as she said each word. The baby began to howl in earnest. "Get going before I change my mind," she shouted over the screaming.

Some minutes after the door closed, after she'd cleaned Earl up and he was freshly diapered, Theda remembered she hadn't asked when Nellie would be back. She tucked the baby's head under her chin, thinking that she didn't care when she got back. She'd have her little man all to herself for a little while.

THEDA SMILED AT THE MEMORY. She did have him—forever. The next time she saw Nellie was at her arraignment on forgery charges. Neither woman could come up with bail money. The pimp Nellie had been working for never even showed up.

Nellie was found guilty and sentenced to seven years in prison. Theda never saw her again.

Theda heard a car stop at the entrance to the trailer park. She took another swig of the vodka and looked out the window. A gray Honda Civic was pulled over beside the Shady Acres sign. Earl got out of the passenger seat. He must have hitched a ride.

Crap. She had to get out of here. She grabbed her parka and opened the front door. Her heart dropped as she stared into her grandson's face.

Earl's lips curled in a snarl. "Going somewhere, Granny?" His grimy hand went to her chest and pushed her back inside. "You're not going anywhere, not before we have a little talk. Get inside."

Earl's clothing was wrinkled and dirty. His blue flannel jacket looked like he'd slept in it. His face was dark with fury as he pushed her down on the bench seat. Glancing around the trailer, his gaze homed in on the area by his bed. Three steps, and he was bending over it, pulling bedding away into a pile. He yanked the thin mattress as his fingers scrambled for the plywood box. He opened the door and shouted, "I knew it. You fuckin' took my money." He squinted, and his gaze caught his grandmother's. "I heard that you've been flashing cash around, buying drinks for your friends, spending like you won the Lotto. I want my money back."

Theda backed up on the seat until she touched the wall. "I didn't know about any money. One of your lousy friends must've took it."

The flat of his hand met the flaccid skin of her jaw in a loud smack. She grabbed her face with both hands and whined. "I didn't take your stinking money. Honest."

"You wouldn't know honesty if it bit you on the ass." He bent over and hit her again on the other side.

"Earl, you might've dropped it down the back of the bed or something. Look before you do something bad!"

Grumbling, he stepped away. "You don't know how important that money is for my future."

Theda felt a laugh escape her lips. "What future? You don't have a future any more than I do." She should've kept her mouth shut and not antagonized him. Damn, she had a big mouth.

He whirled and faced her, a fierce finger pointing at his granny. "Yes, I do. You're going to sit around here and drink yourself to death, but not me." The finger re-directed to his own chest. "Not me. I'm gonna find my girl Faye, make her believe we can have a life together, a family, build something. Not like you, but a real family with Christmas and birthdays and...."

"Faye?" Theda scooted to the end of the seat and pushed herself to her feet. "She's so scared of you that she's in the wind, you asshole." Theda stood closer to Earl. This was her chance. "Look, Earl. There's your money, over there." She pointed to the farthest corner of the trailer. As soon as he turned to look, she whirled and was out the door.

Cold rain splattered her face, but it soothed her swelling cheeks. She ran hard, making for the stand of laurel trees, pine, and black-berry brambles that bordered the creek. She stumbled but made it before Earl saw where she'd gone. Theda climbed into the crook of a laurel, squatting to watch for Earl.

She was safe. He'd run out of the trailer, but the rain had already filled in the imprints of her shoes. He searched for a few minutes. Then, she watched him slam the trailer door, get in his car, and leave.

Chapter Twenty-Eight

NICK SAT BEHIND THE WHEEL OF THE TAURUS IN THE SHERIFF'S Office parking lot. He'd been silent the whole way back, but now he turned to her and asked, "What just happened back in that trailer?"

"You mean aside from the justification that Theda gave for Earl's prints to be in Violet's house?"

Nick flashed her a look that told her she was a smart ass. What he said was, "Explain it to me." Sometimes the best part of having a decent partner was bouncing ideas off her.

"Theda's statement that Earl did odd jobs for Violet McMurray made it reasonable for his fingerprints to be in her living room. Do I believe her? Not for a minute. I think she's scared to death of him."

"Good observations. Yeah, you're right. But you realize that this puts a kink in our case. An hour ago, fingerprints alone were good enough to prove that Earl Sutton killed Violet McMurray. But now, we've got *nada*." He slammed the heel of his hand on the steering wheel. "We have to find more. Something: hairs, fibers, DNA."

"Something might turn up at the autopsy. But that's not until tomorrow." She had some thoughts of her own.

"Tell me what you would do."

Meredith took a deep breath. "First, I'd go back to the office and see if the victim's son has faxed us the descriptions and pictures of the jewelry. If he has, I'd fax them to all the local pawnshops, like we told Leahy. Then I'd follow up with a personal visit to as many as we can."

Nick agreed. "Good start. We need to get some more guys on this case. I'll clear it with Leahy: Put someone on Theda's place and the restaurant where Sutton's supposed to work. But we need to be careful, or we'll spook him."

She smiled at him. "Good thinking."

WHEN THEY GOT INSIDE, Nick showed Meredith how to send a "be-on-the-lookout" or "BOL" fax. The bulletin would go to a network of pawnshops, gold brokers, and second-hand dealers. Then he coordinated the stakeout assignments on Theda's home and the roadhouse where Sutton worked. His clothes were still in the trailer, and a paycheck was waiting for him at work. It was unlikely he would try to return to either spot, but they couldn't afford to rule it out. Nick wanted all the bases covered. The partners wouldn't pull a shift until the next afternoon unless Sutton showed.

They'd done as much as they could today. Nick yawned. "Let's quit for the day."

"Good idea."

The evening was damp with drizzle. In her car, on the way home, Meredith's mind drifted. Home. She thought about her marriage and what a sham it had been. She was glad she and Richard had not had kids.

Fatigue washed over her. She rolled her window down an inch to get some fresh air, drizzle be damned. What had Nick told her on their first night together in training?

HER MIND WANDERED BACK to a time when she was just out of the academy. She was a rookie, her first night on patrol. The Field Training Officer to who she'd been assigned was Nick Reyes.

She could still hear Nick's words pinning her down. "What do you want out of this job?"

"I want to help people…"

"Bullshit," he cut across her trite answer. "What's the real dope?" His dark eyes penetrated hers in the shadows of the patrol car. She felt like he was seeing things inside her. She exhaled while she formulated the words to sound sincere.

"My father was a cop. I wanted to keep the family tradition." There, that should be enough of an explanation. It's worked for everyone else.

"Really?" His eyes tracked a motorcycle accelerating onto a nearby highway onramp. Staring out the windshield, he continued with renewed energy. "You picked this job for tradition? What does your father think? I bet he told you it's not the job for you." His forearm flopped over the steering wheel. The fingers of his other hand tapped a metal box on the console between them. "No father wants this for his daughter." His square jaw jutted toward the dashboard. Every square inch was filled with computer screens, radios, a shotgun mounted vertically between them, and such. These were the physical tools of his trade, the means to get the information he needed to do his job—to serve and protect the people of Sonoma County. "This isn't a dance floor where you show him that you measure up. You make a mistake, and you could die. Worse yet, you could get someone else hurt or killed."

She chose her words with care. She didn't want to lie… "He doesn't know," she whispered. She left it at that, hoping there was enough finality in her tone to stop this line of questions. She wasn't sure about Reyes. She'd heard good things about him at the academy, but recruits who'd been through his FTO told her he was one of the toughest trainers.

She heard his breath hitch like he was starting to say something then stopped. Then, "Okay, the original question was: what do you want from this job?"

She studied his face, dark in the shadows but strong enough to hold her attention. "The truth?"

He nodded once.

"I want to solve crimes." Her voice rose as she saw the beginnings of disgust twisting his lips. She needed to explain. "No, don't jump to conclusions. It's not from watching too much CSI."

He waited.

"Investigating has always been fascinating to me. I love putting the puzzle pieces together to form the whole picture. I have a logical mind and an aptitude for that kind of reasoning. It will be satisfying to be able to tell a victim that I figured out who did the crime."

He chewed the inside of his lower lip as he considered her words. After a moment, he said, "Just because you know who did the crime doesn't mean you can prove it in the courtroom."

"I know."

"You realize that we don't get to do much crime-solving on patrol. And you will spend years on the street. You have to earn getting into the dick bureau. If you're in a hurry, you might look elsewhere for a job, say, the State Department of Justice or the feds."

Her head bobbed. "I know I'll have to wait till I get some tenure." She met his gaze. "I checked all that out before I applied here."

"What about your husband? You're married, no?" His words came faster after her nod. "Kids? No kids?" He fired questions at her like a machine gun, not waiting for an answer. "These are the questions the courts have prohibited us from asking in interviews before you get hired. It's time someone says something so you think about all this. What are you gonna do when you get knocked up? Because kids are a game-changer." He stopped, pressing his lips together like he was considering saying more. But he didn't.

He was pushing limits. He was an authority figure asking questions that put her on the spot. She'd take care of this. "You leave my family to me. I know what I have to do." She heard the strength in her own voice and hoped her trainer heard it.

A MOMENT TICKED BY. The radio crackled with static. Nick Reyes cleared his throat and straightened behind the wheel. "All right." His head bobbed with enthusiasm that surprised her. "Let's rock 'n roll then."

Chapter Twenty-Nine

NICK AND MEREDITH ARRIVED AT THE MORGUE EARLY. THE NIGHT attendant recognized the detective and buzzed them into the work area. Meredith had attended an autopsy while at the academy seven years ago. The smell hadn't changed, disinfectant losing the battle against the odor of decay. Her stomach took a tumble of revulsion as she walked through the doors.

They were early enough to catch Ross Proust, the medical examiner, in the break room dumping sweetener into his coffee. Proust was a forty-something male who cultivated a preppie image with Brooks Brother's suits, oxford shirts, and Wingtips.

"Hey, Nick, who's your new partner?" His smile showed even, white teeth.

Nick introduced Meredith. Ross nodded. "Ah, yes. I heard about the thing in the Quad." At Meredith's silence, he seemed to think better of saying anything more.

Meredith gave him a polite smile. She glanced through the double doors. "I haven't been here since the academy. Is that the autopsy room?"

Proust nodded. "I just finished with her. Sorry about the timing, but I had an opening in my otherwise tight schedule, so I went ahead.

Give me a minute to collect my file, and I'll go over the results." He blew on the coffee. "Where are my manners? Java, anyone?"

"No, thanks," Nick answered for both. They waited while Proust donned white scrubs, slipped a fine net over his helmet-like hair, and capped off the outfit with a splatter mask and gloves.

In the autopsy room, Proust's assistant rolled in a gurney carrying a sheet-covered body with a file folder lying across it. Meredith glanced away while the two men positioned the body. The assistant moved away to finish putting the room in order. The large room was immaculately clean. White tiles covered the walls and floor. A large red Craftsman toolbox stood to one side of a Formica counter that held a large stainless-steel sink. On the shelf above were a scale, a row of six X-ray illuminators, and a shelf with boxes for paperwork. Meredith stifled a shiver when she saw the sign above a 50-gallon garbage can: *No trash, organs only.* The assistant rolled the garbage can through a door.

Proust adjusted the huge swing-arm lamp over the corpse. He took the clipboard off the body and pulled off the sheet. "V. McMurray?" He checked the paperwork, then the toe tag, and nodded to himself. He began reading, "Today is February 20th, 2014, seven am. Attending is myself, Ross Proust, and assistant Gary Tucker. The subject is Violet McMurray, a Caucasian female, eighty-three years of age. Death occurred on February 18th. Body appears intact with multiple bruises and contusions on her upper body as well as bruising about the neck. The victim was sexually assaulted, but we were not able to collect any semen." Proust glanced at Nick. "He must have used a condom. Clothing has been removed by hospital staff and will presumably be examined elsewhere. Both hands have been bagged."

His clinical tone chilled Meredith. That could be my grandmother, she thought. Then she corrected herself. Proust had to be unemotional, the same way she had to be during an investigation. Emotions were messy things that got in the way of doing the job. For cops and coroners, feelings had to be kept out of the equation.

Meredith squared her shoulders, re-adjusted her focus, and listened to Proust's external exam notes.

"Bruising on her throat indicates she was choked." He pulled a large magnifying glass from his tool chest and showed them the bruising. "The imprint of a fine chain—like a necklace—is imbedded in her skin."

Proust straightened, eying Nick. "I took the liberty of gassing the body when it arrived from the hospital. I was able to lift several partial prints mostly from her neck area. The victim's own perspiration washed away the best impressions, but I got fifteen points— enough to match your suspect Sutton."

Nick frowned, then told Meredith, "Fifteen is enough to use in court, but not enough to stand on its own."

She nodded. "Still, it adds another nail to his coffin, doesn't it?"

His lips splayed in a humorless smile. "Yeah." Then to Proust, "Can you make a copy of the chain impression?"

Proust waved to Tucker as he entered the room. The assistant pulled a narrow strip of photo paper from a shelf. "Already done. And Tucker here has photos of the neck injuries and the chain impression for you. I collected hair and some fibers, too."

Chapter Thirty

THAT AFTERNOON THEIR FOOTWORK PAID OFF. MEREDITH PLAYED A voicemail from a pawnbroker on the south end of Santa Rosa Avenue, then grabbed Nick and headed to their car. In his briefcase, Nick carried a file folder of the photos of Violet McMurray's jewelry that her son had provided. Nick drove while Meredith briefed him on the contents of the message left late last night.

"The caller said he was the owner of South Side Pawn. His nephew took in some of the jewelry described in the faxed BOL. He had several of the pieces still there, and he took them off the floor so they wouldn't be sold."

Nick frowned as he dodged a pothole. "Don't expect too much help from this guy. He's doing what he's required to do and nothing more. If we take the jewelry for evidence, he's out the pawn money with no way to recoup it."

"Do you know him—Hasan Hasani?"

"No, but pawnbrokers are all the same." Nick rolled to a stop at a red light, pushing the lever to clear the mist from the windshield. "Out for a buck no matter who gets stuck."

"That may be, but he did call us."

THE PAWNSHOP'S metal accordion gate rattled open as they pulled into the parking lot. They approached, and a tall, Middle Eastern man of indeterminate age stood inside at the front window, pulling up the shades. The shop window displays overflowed with watches, clocks, jewelry, musical instruments, and other such valuables. Then, he disappeared into the back room.

Nick pushed open the door and shouted, "Hasan Hasani? Sheriff's Office here to talk to you about your phone call last night."

An old-fashioned saloon-half door pushed open. The man sauntered into the room. With eyes half-closed, he blinked gravely and stood behind the largest counter. Nick wasn't sure whether he was tired, suspicious or his eyes were just like that.

The man said, "Here so early, Detectives?"

"Are you Hasan Hasani?" Nick had to be sure he was the right person. He flipped open his flat badge, sliding it under the clerk's prominent nose.

Hasani ignored the badge. "Yes, I called you, Detective."

"We'd like to look at the jewelry you put aside." Nick wouldn't tell him any more than he had to. Even though he had cooperated by calling the sheriff's office, Nick kept the details from the pawnbroker. There was no way of knowing what kind of involvement he might have. Sometimes, the tiniest detail will give a suspect away.

"Sure, sure." Hasani reached down without taking his eyes off Nick. He grabbed a box covered in dusty, faded brown velvet from a drawer beneath the display shelf, and shoved it toward the detectives.

Nick took it with both hands. This was Violet's jewelry. He knew, even before he opened it.

Meredith had spread out the faxed pictures of the jewelry on the scratched glass countertop. The two detectives went through the list and accounted for almost a third of the jewelry. Hasani kept an eagle eye on them.

"You going to take them with you?" Hasani asked, but the misery in his eyes told them that he already had the answer.

Nick shrugged. "We have to take them for evidence, but I'll give you a receipt." He reached into his jacket pocket for the receipt book.

"And the chances that I'll get them back?" There wasn't a glimmer of hope on the man's face.

Nick's pen hesitated over the form. "To be honest, unless we find, prosecute, and get a conviction, they won't be released to anyone. Because this is the proceeds of a theft and capital crime, the court won't find you rightful owner."

Hasani was silent as he pushed his finger into an unfortunate gnat on the glass case.

Meredith shuffled the papers back into a folder. "Were you here when they were brought in?"

Hasani looked toward the front window. He shook his head, "My good-for-nothing nephew was here last night. He's the reason you're here now." He squinted at Nick. "Me? I would've seen trouble coming with this stuff. Too expensive." He flicked his fingers at the jewelry, shaking his head.

Nick asked, "When will your nephew be in? We need to talk to him."

"He's done working this week. He won't be back until Monday."

"We'll need his name, address, and phone number."

Hasani's resigned eyes focused on Nick. "The kid's not answering his cell, and I don't know where he's sleeping these days. I called my sister—his mother. She doesn't know where he is either."

Nick waved the man's irritation aside. "Write down his name and cell and your sister's. We'll find him."

Meredith spoke up. "I notice you have closed circuit cameras. Are they working?"

Hasani shook his head. "No, the system is fouled up, and it's too expensive to fix. There is more overhead to this business than it looks, and the economy..." He shrugged, finished scribbling his nephew's phone number, pushed the paper towards them, and turned away.

Chapter Thirty-One

THEY SPENT THE REMAINDER OF THE MORNING TRYING TO LOCATE Hasani's nephew, Robert Kareem. Kareem's mother offered up some names and a hang-out or two but was no help.

Meredith put together a photo line-up that included Earl Sutton's driver's license photo, along with five other similar-looking white males. She put it in her briefcase, ready for Hasani's nephew to view.

They ate lunch on the run while they checked out three more places Kareem hung out but turned up nothing. After stopping at a market for snacks, bottled water, and coffee, they relieved the stakeout team at the Guerneville restaurant an hour early, hoping for Sutton's return.

Meredith pulled the car next to Anderson's faded blue county Impala. He and Peters pulled the first shift. Yawning, Anderson handed over an activity log sheet and said, "Nothing going for the past seven hours, except my partner had gas. Hope you have better luck on your shift." He winked, threw his Chevy into gear, and sped away down the potholed drive to River Road, clearly happy to be out of there early.

Meredith nosed the Taurus under a Laurel tree at the far corner of the parking lot, facing the restaurant's back door. An afternoon mist graduated to light rain as the detectives settled in. The car radio blared over the quiet sheriff's radio channel. An anxious-sounding newsman barked cautions about the incoming storm. Flooding in low-lying areas was predicted. It was winter in Sonoma County.

Nick pulled the plastic lid off his cup and blew on his coffee. "So, tell me why we're here?" He kept his eyes on the roadhouse.

She sighed. "Sutton works here—or he did. According to his boss, he hasn't been here in four days. But," Meredith wiggled an index finger in front of her nose, "he has a paycheck waiting for him. He might be by to pick it up sometime." Her lips thinned in an expression that told him this was kindergarten stuff.

Nick nodded.

Meredith smiled; she'd passed the test.

"Quit with the attitude," Nick said, still with eyes forward.

"What do you mean, 'attitude'?"

"The sigh, the snotty answers, you know." He glanced at her, then to the roadhouse.

"Well, Nick, since you brought it up: let's talk about this. You know that I know the answers to your little quizzes. I've been in patrol for seven years, so I recognize what's going on. I can conduct an investigation." She pressed her lips together so she wouldn't say anything she might regret.

He was silent for a few moments. "I can't assume anything." His jaw muscle flexed. "What if I was wrong—it could cost us the case, or someone could get hurt. Either is unacceptable."

She saw his jaw clenching and releasing. *Uh, oh. He's pissed.*

Nick swung his head toward the roadhouse, inhaled, then exhaled. "I am your Orientation Officer. What I teach you now will set the tone for your whole career. This is a responsibility that I take seriously." The lines on his face softened, and he continued, "I know you want to do this the right way. I am making sure you know how to do it."

"As opposed to doing it wrong? I thought you knew me better than that." She hadn't intended to snap.

"I know you better than anyone, Mere. You know that," he said quietly.

She pushed at her cuticles, waiting.

"We've been through a lot together, Mere. More troubles than most friendships ever have to go through." He cleared his throat and, after a heartbeat, resumed. "I'm doing this because I want you to be the best. You could do the job on your own, but with my help, you can go to the top of the class—fast." He paused; she thought he was trying to measure her reaction. "Don't get me wrong: this isn't a competition. It's about doing the job the right way and the safe way. You need to trust yourself more. You have solid education, experience, and training. You need to trust your intuition, respect your training, and listen to your common sense."

"I know you're doing this for me. It's just your method: I resent being treated like a fourth grader." She started to cross her arms over her chest but stopped. She stared at her hands in her lap.

Before she could say anything more, he laughed. "You never did stand for any of my shit, did you?" He stretched up in the seat and draped his long arm on the threadbare upholstery where it met the window.

Feeling an absurd pride, she answered, "Nope."

"All right. I get it. I'll back off." He smiled the same way he had at Theda. Her pulse jumped.

"Speaking of trials, have you heard anything from Angela?" Meredith looked away when she asked him about his estranged wife. He was still raw over their breakup.

"No, her uncle told me she went to visit her brother in Mexico about a month ago. She's still there, as far as I know." Nick's face was blank. Meredith was almost certain that he practiced being expressionless in the mirror at home.

"Is she still talking about you both going to counseling? I mean, it's been three years since the baby died. You can't pretend it didn't happen."

He spat out the words. "She's not talking about anything. She's not here for me to talk to." He paused, then said, "I don't want to talk about this anymore."

The silence stretched out between them, his terse words evaporating. Meredith thought about these quiet moments. They were usually amiable. Without having to discuss it, they each appreciated the silence.

"It's weird, isn't it?" Nick turned to her. "I mean, we've both had unexpected deaths in our immediate family." Nick paused, staring out the windshield.

Meredith followed his gaze, then, with a jerk of her head, said, "Hey, there's Sutton!"

Chapter Thirty-Two

MEREDITH FIXED HER ATTENTION ON THE MIDNIGHT BLUE PONTIAC GTO creeping into the parking lot, engine throbbing. The driver moved slowly, avoiding attention, yet the car shook the entire lot. Only one person in the car. With any luck, Sutton would be at the wheel. Against the steely gray sky, she couldn't tell for sure.

Nick struggled to balance his coffee. The cup teetered on his knee, and after a moment, he rolled down the window and tossed it. He snapped his seat belt into place.

He whispered, as if Sutton could hear him. "Doesn't look like he's spotted us. Let's wait…"

The GTO slowed at a plywood lean-to sheltering garbage cans. Next to it sat the back door of what appeared to be the kitchen. Meredith saw the driver's head swivel in the opposite direction, towards her.

Sutton. It was him. She recognized him from booking photos, even from this distance. "What if he bails on us?"

Before Nick could answer, the GTO's tires burned out a damp cloud of rubber. The car headed for River Road, eastbound toward Santa Rosa.

"Follow him," Nick shouted.

Meredith ground the Taurus' ignition to life, threw it into gear, and thanked God it wasn't raining. The road was damp but not wet. She took a deep breath, collecting her thoughts. It had been a long time since she was in a car chase with a partner. For the past seven years, she'd been in a patrol unit, mostly alone. Still, each officer has a role in incidents like this. Now, she checked with Nick to be sure of their responsibilities.

"You got the radio?"

"Yes, and cross traffic, too. Keep your mind on your driving. I'm calling for marked units now."

"'kay." It had long been department policy for unmarked units pursuing a motorist to call for patrol cars to take up the primary position and make the traffic stop. The courts had been reluctant to recognize the "failure to yield" section of the California Vehicle Code if the pursuing vehicle was an unmarked car. Defense attorneys found it too easy to dispute whether a fleeing driver knew police were behind him.

After calling for back up, Nick yanked the glove box open, pulled out the red plastic mini lightbar, and mounted it on the dashboard. He plugged the cord into the power receptacle and flipped on the siren.

Weekend tourist traffic crawled along meandering River Road. The scenic two-lane rural highway ran east from the bohemian town of Guerneville to the small community of Fulton at Highway 101. The GTO wove in and out of traffic, driving on the right shoulder or plowing towards the opposite lane of traffic. Some motorists scattered in panic, driving off the road. Others froze in place. Sutton dodged them all.

Meredith stuck with the GTO, working at the fine balance between keeping the public safe and letting a possible suspect in a homicide escape to kill again. She held her breath as he slid around a Volkswagen Bug, narrowly missing the bumper. "Another half mile, and we'll be on Highway 101. Damn, where's a marked unit?"

Nick dropped the mic into his lap, his voice controlled and calm. "Santa Rosa has a couple of patrol cars on their way to set up at Mendocino Avenue off-ramp."

"Why not Steele Lane? Or Bicentennial?"

"They're working on those two exits."

"What about CHP?"

Sutton pulled onto the southbound onramp to Highway 101, accelerating as he hit a straightaway. Meredith followed, then braked for a merging red Nissan.

"No help there. They're all working a triple fatal in south county."

Dang it. Southbound traffic was thick, lanes packed with travelers returning from wine country. Sutton pulled onto the soggy, weed-covered median. He slowed but bypassed the gridlock.

Meredith stayed with the GTO, slowing on the wet, mossy median for safety.

Sutton went straight through a knot of traffic at 40 miles per hour, flipping a sharp turn to the offramp onto Steele Lane, eastbound.

A light mist covered the windshield. Meredith waited until the last possible moment to use the wipers, then agonized through the few seconds of obscured vision before the windshield cleared. She heard bits and pieces of Nick's radio conversation as she watched the GTO's brake lights. Traffic was heavier here, slowed by signals.

Two car lengths behind, Meredith followed the GTO north on Mendocino Avenue. Sutton honked his horn and rode the bumper of a Honda Civic until it pulled into a parking lot. He forced his way past four more vehicles. One long city block later, Sutton peeled off to the right onto Chanate Way.

"Mere, ped on the right," Nick said.

"Got her." Meredith's pulse thumped in her ears as she noted the pedestrian catching herself before stepping into the crosswalk.

Sutton took another turn. This led them up a hill and into a tidy post-World War II neighborhood. The next block, a quick left toward the hospital, this time without brake lights. He pulled away from the Taurus, behind by half a block. A signal light dumped traffic onto a busy parkway leading to a large hospital complex, slowing their pursuit. Sutton's GTO plowed toward protesting drivers headed in the opposite direction.

For Meredith, the siren had little effect. With nowhere to pull over, most vehicles hugged the right side past the white fog line. She fought her frustration, willing herself to take deep breaths.

The shoulder was just enough for Meredith to squeeze her way around, trying to remember the routes of the connector streets ahead on the other side of the medical buildings. Her knuckles whitened on the steering wheel.

Nick spoke calmly on the radio, giving dispatch the cross streets, estimations of vehicle speeds, and weather conditions. He released the transmit button and updated Meredith. "Santa Rosa PD has four units on the way. They're positioning two on the backside of the hospital—on Chandler Street. The other two should be behind us soon."

"Okay." She played out the possible moves in her mind like a chess game. "If he heads up there, I'll pull over and let the marked unit take the lead on the parkway."

The GTO hesitated a half second at the red light in the intersection, then its wheels spun, plunging through oncoming traffic north toward the hospital. Nick flipped on the siren to an alternate tone to alert motorists as Meredith aimed the Taurus toward the intersection. Most of the cars had already peeled off to the shoulder after the GTO flew past them. Meredith's foot hovered over the brake pedal until the last vehicle was out of her way. She stomped on the accelerator. Still, the Taurus was no match for the muscle car. The county car slogged up the hill, barely able to keep the GTO in view.

"Keep an eye on the taillights," Meredith said to Nick.

"I will. You just get us closer."

When the GTO crested the hill, it dropped from sight. Meredith stepped on the gas again, but it was no use. She had wrung all the power she could from the car. "Damn, I hate to lose him."

The Taurus chugged up the road. Meredith's stomach twisted into a knot. Would they have to abandon the pursuit?

Then Nick yelled, "Taillights. He turned off to the right."

That would be the hospital overflow parking. Meredith tried to recall if there was an exit.

Nick answered her unspoken question. "He may have boxed himself in. There's no way out from that lot."

"Good, but we need to get ready for a foot-bail." She glanced in her rear-view mirror. "A PD unit just pulled in behind us."

Meredith weighed pulling over and letting the marked unit assume the primary position but hesitated as the Taurus met the rise where they had lost the GTO. "There's the car, under the trees at the far end of the lot." Nick's words cracked like a machine gun as he pointed.

The GTO sat under a scrub oak tree, parked with the door open. Sutton was nowhere in sight. He'd taken off on foot.

The Taurus skidded to a halt at an angle behind the GTO. The inside of the car had to be checked to see if Sutton had hidden. She pulled out her Beretta and nodded toward Nick, signaling that she would watch the driver's side while he kept an eye on the passenger side. The Santa Rosa PD unit screeched to a stop behind their car. In seconds, a young patrolman hunkered down behind the Taurus.

Nick made the announcement. "You in the car: this is the Sonoma County Sheriff's Office. Follow my directions carefully." Meredith kept her eyes on the GTO. With the patrolman's help, they cleared the car, finding it empty. The partners holstered their weapons and did a closer search of the interior.

More patrol units arrived. Nick walked to the back of the Taurus, taking the lead and positioning the uniforms strategically. The hillsides bracketing the lot needed to be cleared.

Meredith studied the grounds beyond the lot. She was sure he'd gone into the woods. Several acres of flat, oak-studded land with what looked like a cliff on the far side. *He could be anywhere in those trees.*

Something moved in the oaks to her left. It looked like a red shirtsleeve behind a tree trunk in the middle of the grounds. *Sutton.*

"Got him," she yelled and started after him.

Third tree behind the big one in front? Or was it farther back?

Her feet pounded the asphalt to the end of the parking lot, then she headed to where she'd last seen the flash of red fabric.

There. Sutton broke away from the trees and bolted to the back of the property—toward the cliff. He fit his grandmother's description: medium height, shaved head, and scrawny. His red KISS tee-shirt flapped in the breeze.

"Earl Sutton... Sheriff's Office. We want to talk," she yelled. She didn't sound convincing, even to herself.

Sutton never even slowed.

Still at a run, she picked her way through a scramble of dead limbs underfoot. Raindrops grown fat from the oak leaves above splashed on Meredith's head. But she was gaining. He had a muscle car that could out-run her Taurus, but on foot, she was faster. Nick's heavy footfalls followed her.

When Sutton's head twisted back to see where she was, Meredith knew he'd made a big mistake. Curiosity slowed him. In the mucky, uncertain terrain, he tripped, kept his forward momentum, and went to his knees.

Meredith slammed him with her shoulder in a solid tackle, the force spinning them both around. Sutton fell on top of her, his elbow jamming into Meredith's chest. The weight of his body knocked the breath out of her. She rolled to her side while he lurched in the opposite direction. She lay breathless in the mud, struggling for air.

Sutton was on his feet in an instant. He took a precious moment to glare at her, then, suddenly, he kicked Meredith in the jaw. Without waiting to see the result, he took off toward the cliff. Gripping her cheek, Meredith saw a blur running past her. Nick.

She heard Nick yelling as she struggled to her feet, but she couldn't make out the words. Her jaw throbbed. A spike of anger shot through her as she took off after Sutton. He was close to the edge of the tree-covered acreage. He'd be at the cliff in a second.

As Sutton reached the precipice, he paused. Without looking back, he took one step forward and disappeared.

Nick halted at the rim, his chest heaving, then took one big step back. Was he going after Sutton? *What was he waiting for?*

Meredith reached the clearing. The turf was loose here, hardly any vegetation to hold the dirt together. She stopped, an arm's length from the edge, as she tried to catch her breath. Nick stood away from her, oddly distant.

Oaks continued up the undeveloped hill to the right, but below the terrain gave way to a sheer drop. Erosion had carved an S under the bluff. The cliff fell about twenty feet to what looked like an abandoned quarry site, now a small pond, dotted with debris from rotting trees. The mist had turned into a steady rain. Bold, round drops soaked the entire hillside.

Meredith took another step backwards. She couldn't see Sutton. From the soggy tracks, Sutton had plunged down the cliff. She hadn't moved fast enough. He was gone.

She didn't follow. Better to stay safe and catch him another day. Nick's voice penetrated her thoughts. "Don't move, Meredith. Stay there…"

The ground thrummed. A heavy sloshing sound gave warning too late. The soil beneath her feet liquefied. She lost balance and pitched down the muddy slope, along with mud, tree branches, and rocks. Plummeting with the muck, something rough struck the side of her head. Pain shot through her skull. She saw flashes of brilliant white light, then nothing.

Chapter Thirty-Three

"MERE, MERE. WAKE UP." NICK'S TONE POSSESSED A QUIET urgency that surprised her. *What's going on?*

"Come on, wake up." His insistence penetrated the fog that enclosed her mind.

Was she dreaming? She must wake up to see why he was so demanding. She tried to open an eye, then quickly shut it. Pain shot through her skull. She moaned.

"She's coming to," said a voice from outside her head.

A muscular arm cradled her. *Nick?*

Fingers pulled debris away from her face. Then a gentle tugging at her hair as someone pulled something out. Again, she tried to open an eye, only to find mud clogging her vision. Then, something wiped her eyelids. She pushed her eyes open. It was a moment before she recognized the hazy outline of her partner leaning over her.

"Nick?"

"Meredith, take a deep breath. Are you hurt?"

She wished he would stop yammering. Her head was spinning. She put a hand out to steady herself, but there was nothing solid to grasp. Where was she?

The confusion began to clear. She lifted her head, blinked, then choked. She was in Nick's arms.

"Mere, where do you hurt?" Nick, even more insistent.

She groaned, dropped her head back, and asked, "Did I fall?"

A PD uniform hovered over Nick's shoulder. "Dropped like a rock."

Someone told the uniform to shut the fuck up. Nick said, "You got tangled up in a mudslide. Looked like you got hit in the head by a tree branch or a rock."

She eyed a blurry Nick. "Sutton?"

"He's in the wind," he shook his head. "We've been searching for the past ten minutes but can't find him."

"Aw, crap. I let him go, dang it." She pushed against his chest in a feeble try to get up.

"Not so fast, kid." Nick grasped her upper arm. "Are you hurt anywhere?"

She did a quick inventory. "My head feels like someone dropped an anvil on it, and my jaw hurts, but everything else seems okay."

"Okay, we'll have EMS check you out. They're up in the parking lot, waiting."

Meredith shot him a look to convey her unwillingness. "Not hardly. We gotta get that son of a bitch. I'm fine, really." She looked away. She wasn't very good at lying. "Just a little headache."

Nick frowned. "First, we have to get out of this mess." He glanced at the activity at the top of the hill. Someone yelled, "We're going to send down some more help and a rescue basket."

Meredith was more than a little annoyed at this production going on for her. Really, she felt fine. But the three firefighters who accompanied the basket were so patient and kind, she found her resistance waning. Even in their rain gear, they all were dripping wet.

Resigned, she whispered, "Okay."

With practiced movements, they eased her into the basket and strapped her in.

Nick followed them up the slope. At the top, she was handed off to another pair of firefighters. Someone threw a thermal blanket over her. A gurney clattered over the asphalt toward her. She eyed it with caution. *This is a waste of time for a simple headache.*

Nick picked up the subject of her getting checked out. "Mere, you have to be seen by a doctor. You don't have a choice. You were knocked out. Even if it wasn't just plain sensible, I'd make you go."

She noticed the worry crease on his forehead.

"Oh yeah?" Someone draped another blanket around her shoulders. She lifted her arm to shift it, sending a sharp stab of pain across her shoulder blades. Sitting on the gurney, she re-considered seeing a doctor. *Blacking out is always cause to be checked. Nick would bulldoze her into going. There's probably some departmental regulation, anyway.*

She sighed. "If it'll get you off my case, I'll go."

AN HOUR LATER, Meredith tried to get warm on a hospital bed in a draped-off ER cubicle. Left to wait for the wrap-up paperwork and a ride home, she studied her toes. She shivered despite two thermal blankets and the dry scrubs an attendant had scrounged for her. X-rays and a cat scan were completed; a neurologist had determined she'd suffered a mild concussion. She'd been given acetaminophen, but her head still throbbed. She felt the goose egg on her scalp and decided she'd been lucky.

Even with her mind still spinning, a part of her was grateful for the controlled atmosphere of the hospital. At least she couldn't get hurt here. She was glad the past hour was over. All she wanted was to go home and sleep, but that was still hours away.

Where was Nick?

He rode in the ambulance with her and stayed with her most of the time. They'd sat together in the ER, wordless. Finally, a while ago, he had grumbled, "Be right back," then walked out to the hallway. She couldn't remember how much time had passed.

Her shivering had stopped. She adjusted the blankets, trying to cover herself better. Her toes were purple and aching from the cold.

One of the blankets fell from her shoulder, slid down her leg, and dropped to the floor. Now she had to retrieve the blanket. She sighed, wondering how to summon the energy.

Where is Nick? She glanced around. *No one here. No one. Not Richard, not Christy, not my mother, or my father. I'm alone.*

No Richard. No Richard, ever again.

Her breath caught in her throat. The reality of her husband's death settled upon her.

Gone. He was dead, and their last words had been in anger. Had he loved her when he died? The question sent a slice of pain through her soul.

She moaned, slumping back onto the hospital bed. Her emotions had been boxed up and shelved for too long. Tears erupted, a dam finally burst. She covered her face with the bed covers and struggled to be quiet so no one would notice.

Then, she felt a hand on her shoulder, a firm but gentle pressure. She looked up and saw her partner. He leaned onto the bed, wrapping his arms around her, then pulled her to him.

She tried to say, "Oh, Nick," but it didn't come out like that at all. With her sinuses puffy, her throat thick with emotion, and her mind like mush, her words made no sense. Her own ears heard more of a growl than his name. She let it go, giving in to the tears and long-overdue grief. Occasionally offering her a tissue, Nick held her with a firm grip.

Finally, she didn't know how long, her tears ran out, and her sobs waned. She had no strength left.

Nick laid her back on the bed, telling her to wait. She smiled at the irony. Like she could move.

He told her that he would expedite the release paperwork.

She sighed. Thank God for Nick.

Chapter Thirty-Four

"I LET SUTTON GET AWAY." SHE BIT OFF THE WORDS AS SHE GOT into the passenger seat of the Taurus. The neighborhood search had turned up nothing. Nick would've waited to tell her at this point, but she'd insisted on knowing.

Nick leaned in to snap the seatbelt in her lap. "Yeah, but you're okay, and that's more important. You'll live to catch him another day." He didn't try to baby her. She was so dang independent, snapping at him anytime he did things like open the door. Sometimes, he had trouble reconciling his Latin upbringing with her self-reliance. Now, he thought she would cooperate, as rummy as she was from medication. She needed him, or someone, especially today. He suspected she'd held in her grief too long. She had to get this out of her system. He understood all too well.

"Yeah." She seemed about to say something but didn't. Her head lolled to one side of the headrest, tired and beat up. She sported a golf ball-sized bruise on her jaw. He was amazed at her strength, even after having seen her break down.

"Let's get you home and to bed." He debated touching her again to reassure her but decided against it. He wasn't sure why.

He felt her eyes on him, but she was silent. Then, her eyes were closed. Her face was drawn and pale, even in sleep.

As they approached Mirabel Road, she stirred. He noted the firmness in her voice when she asked, "What next, Nick?" Fatigue still flagged her eyes, but she sounded more alert than she had been in hours. He decided not to go into all their options. That would get her all stirred up again. She needed to get some rest.

"Probably a search warrant. But we'll talk about that tomorrow." He tried to sound casual, like he wasn't giving her an order. "You know, the lieutenant said you can take time off if you need it."

"The lieutenant? How did he know?"

Nick frowned. "I had to call him, Mere. Leahy was out of town. Lieutenant Ferrua had to be notified. He has to write a report for your injury on duty. Actually, I'll write it, and he'll sign his name."

"Crap," she whispered, looking out the window at the swaying redwood boughs.

"Don't worry about it, Mere. IOD reports are part of a supervisor's job."

"I'm more concerned about letting Sutton get away."

He tried to change the subject. "Almost home, Mere."

The storm that had been circling all day finally ramped up. As they turned onto her street, Nick flipped on the windshield wipers. Their frantic beat couldn't keep up with the pelting rain. They both struggled to see.

Meredith straightened. "Someone's walking down my driveway."

Nick couldn't see anything but deepening shadows in a storm-darkened late afternoon. The steep canyon walls surrounding her house obscured his vision even more.

"I can't see anything in this rain, Mere."

"Ah," she pronounced, slumping back into the seat. "I'm probably hallucinating. I don't see anything now, either."

Nick kept his tone even. "Probably an animal or something. Living out here in the wilderness, you must have all kinds of wild things."

She didn't answer.

He had to get her into bed.

Chapter Thirty-Five

"How do you feel, Meredith?" The next morning, Lieutenant Gilbert Ferrua's broad brow furrowed as he leaned both elbows on the paper-covered desk.

"I'm fine, Lieutenant. Ready to get this guy." The throbbing behind her eyes contradicted her words, but she'd never tell. She sat in the lieutenant's office with Nick. The morning had started early, when Anderson and Peters called Nick. They'd caught up with the pawnshop owner's nephew. "Now that the Kareem kid ID'ed Sutton from the photo array, we can bring him in."

The fourth person in the room was pale and fleshy with salon-dyed hair and a gray Brioni suit. He stood near the Lieutenant, eyeing the detectives. Deputy DA Edwin Traber finally spoke up. "Glad you're feeling up to par, Detective Ryan. Changing personnel on the case at this point would waste precious time."

Meredith smiled at the lack of compassion.

Ferrua picked up Traber's line of thought. "The Press Democrat had this story on the front page, headlining 'no arrest.' They're turning up the heat on this case." He shook his head in a 'what is this world coming to' manner. "An eighty-three-year-old woman is burglarized, raped, and murdered in one of the safest neighborhoods in the county. People are scared."

"There's an area meeting tonight at the community center," Traber continued. "The Sheriff and the DA will both be there to reassure the public. We'd like to be able to tell them an arrest has been made or is imminent."

Silence hung in the room.

Nick cleared his throat. "We can't compromise this case to make the press and the public happy. I won't make shortcuts and lose a conviction so you can win in the newspapers."

Traber's eyes widened. "No, I didn't mean..."

Ferrua cut him off. "Ed, I just okayed a search warrant written for Sutton's trailer. Feel free to review the report and their paperwork, but my detectives have an appointment with a Superior Court Judge to have it signed." He checked his watch. "In ten minutes. We'll execute it tomorrow, when we have enough members of the Special Operations Unit for an entry team."

Traber grabbed the report from the desk and glanced at it, then the warrant request.

Five minutes later, Ferrua took them from Traber and handed them to Meredith. "Here are your papers. You better get a move on."

Chapter Thirty-Six

THE JUDGES' CHAMBERS OF THE SUPERIOR COURT OF SONOMA County were impressive. Rich walnut paneling lined the front room. A judicial assistant sat sentinel at a desk in the center of the office, blocking the entrance to the Judge's inner sanctum. She made them wait, even though they had an appointment.

Every time up here, Meredith had to fight the intimidation factor. She flipped through the report. Like all Cops, she wanted to be prepared and hated to look like a fool.

Nick looked her over with sleepy eyes. "Don't worry so much about this. You've written a search warrant before."

"I know." She dropped the pages onto her lap. "I can't help it. It's been a while since I did one."

"Ferrua and I both went over it. Traber, too. Nothing to worry about."

"I'm not worried..."

"Yes, you are. Quit it, or you'll jinx the whole thing." He sat back in the uncomfortable chair. Nick was self-conscious about his superstitions. Cops were a hard-assed bunch. Admitting you believed in a rabbit's foot showed a measure of vulnerability. Weakness wasn't tolerated in this world. Therefore, one who showed it was subject to ridicule to toughen him up or send him running for the exit. Yet, everyone had their secret superstitions.

Meredith opened her mouth to say something, but the judge's assistant interrupted. Her perfectly coiffed gray head bobbed, "You can go in now."

Nick pushed open the heavy wooden door.

Judge Stephen Giroud rose from behind his massive mahogany desk, extending his hand to Meredith. She took in the man's magnetism during the handshake. His charisma was tangible. She had met him, but not on his own turf. He didn't merely belong here, he owned the room. The very air seemed to pay obeisance to him. A tall man, he gave the impression of youth tempered with experience. His posture was remarkably correct, as if he carried his pride on his shoulders.

"Good to see you again, Meredith."

"Sir, do you know Detective Nick Reyes? He's the lead on this case."

The two men faced each other and shook hands. "Nick, I've heard good things about your skill as an investigator."

Nick's head dipped, but he remained silent.

She handed the judge the search warrant. Giroud motioned for them to be seated before settling into his plush leather chair. He studied the document for several minutes, then read the accompanying police report. It was normal for a jurist to have questions before he signed a warrant authorizing the search of a person's property.

The detectives waited. Meredith's eyes wandered as she reviewed the case and evidence. They needed one more solid piece of proof to tie Sutton to Violet McMurray's assault and murder. Cash usually wasn't traceable, and she doubted any would be found. Nick told her he expected Sutton would hold back some of the victim's jewelry to be pawned later. That would be best-case scenario. She was certain that if they could get into the trailer, something would turn up that would convince a jury.

"You have all the elements that satisfy my need for a search of

Earl Sutton's trailer." He focused on Meredith. "This is a good report, good solid police work."

"Thanks. Nick did most of it." She smiled. She'd slept through the report writing. Nick had stayed the night at her house, sleeping on the couch after he finished working on his laptop.

"I heard you made a trip to the ER." Giroud's eyes bored into her. "You must be feeling better?"

"Good enough to catch Sutton."

He nodded, an approval of her determination. Giroud shifted his attention to her partner. "Nick, is there another warrant in the works for Sutton for the assault on Detective Ryan?"

"Yes, sir, the DA has the complaint now. I expect a warrant to be issued in the next few days. The charges are 148PC: resisting; 243(B) PC: assault on a peace officer; and 2800.1 VC: evading a peace officer."

While they talked, Meredith's eyes wandered over the dark paneled walls. Elegantly framed pictures of the judge were everywhere: shaking hands with the governor, with a casual arm over the shoulders of a senator, a group photo of celebrities during a fundraiser, a team shot of him and three other polo players.

She craned her neck to see the photo better. *Polo on horseback.* Her heart quickened as she took in the picture of a sleek, athletic Thoroughbred.

Giroud noticed her attention. He stood to point out the photo. "That was taken right after our win at the Wine Country Polo Classic last summer. That's me. My groom, Esparza, is standing behind the horse. There's the trophy on my credenza." He pointed to an engraved silver cup, one of a dozen trophies.

Meredith rose, hoping she made appropriate noises of appreciation, but her mind wasn't on the trophy. She was back in her childhood, in San Francisco, with her father in the police stables. Terence Ryan was a sergeant in the SFPD Mounted Unit. They had never been close, and Meredith had hoped her love for horses could break through their barriers. In her early teens, she'd taken riding lessons, paying for them by ironing, cleaning neighbor's houses, and babysitting. Under her father's tutelage, she won or placed in dozens of equitation and jumping shows. This was the only place she felt successful at bolstering the failing relationship with her father. It became a cornerstone of their relationship, the only positive in the fourteen years he parented. Once off the trail, they stumbled.

She cleared her throat while studying a well-muscled bay in the next photo. "He's a beauty. Thoroughbred?"

The Judge's eyes opened in surprise. "You know horses? That guy is my oldest stallion. He's seventeen and never seen a lame day."

"I rode a bit as a kid. Every girl goes through the phase." She waved the topic aside, uncomfortable with the memories. One good overruled the bad, though, as she acknowledged a soft spot in her heart for horses. "Still, I really loved riding."

"Great." Giroud leaned toward her. His excitement made his blue eyes shine. "I'm riding in a match this weekend. Would you like to come?"

The words stunned her. She should have seen it coming, but she hadn't. She looked away, trying to organize a refusal.

Giroud's words rushed in to fill the awkward silence. "I'm sorry, Meredith. That sounded like a date. It was inappropriate. I know you are a recent widow. I let my enthusiasm get the better of me." He took her hand and placed it between both of his. "Will you forgive me?"

Without thinking, Meredith yanked her hand away. Then, mentally, she shook off the shock and softened. "Yes, of course. Maybe some other time."

Giroud collected himself and bent over the papers to scratch his name on the specified lines.

Nick's spine was straight as he stood. "Thanks for your signature, Your Honor."

Meredith noticed that Nick didn't offer a handshake to the Judge. She followed her partner to the door.

The Judge called after them. "When do you plan to execute this warrant?"

Nick paused at the door. "In the morning, early." An oddly vague answer from Nick.

A heartbeat passed. Then, "Good hunting, detectives."

Chapter Thirty-Seven

TWO MINUTES LATER, THE STAIRWELL DOOR SLAMMED. NEITHER detective said anything after leaving the Judge's chambers. The late afternoon sunlight, filtering through a window at the top of the fourth floor, threw slanted shadows across the walls. Nick pulled at her elbow.

She stopped to face him, a question in her deep brown eyes.

Nick's control slipped away. "He frickin' hit on you."

"Yeah, I know. I was there, remember?"

"He knows you just buried your husband. I know, because I saw him at the reception after the service."

"Yes, that's right. He was there." Those beautiful, intelligent eyes were staring at him, waiting.

Nick felt his face flush. He was having trouble saying what he wanted her to understand. "It's just not done."

"Who are you, Emily Post? Of course, it's done." She hesitated. "That doesn't make it right. I think he understood a line was crossed. He did apologize."

Nick replayed the scene in his mind. "I don't think he was sincere with the apology. He was testing you, seeing if you'd go for it."

"Why on earth would he test me?"

The improbability sunk in. "I don't know. Maybe he's one of those guys who likes to mess with people."

"Well, I didn't go for it."

"Yeah, but," he paused. "You liked it."

Was she *smiling*? "I guess it was flattering."

"Flattering?"

"Yes, I was flattered. Why the hell are you yelling at me?"

His voice thundered, "I'm not yelling."

She turned away and continued down the stairs.

Chapter Thirty-Eight

STEPHEN GIROUD SMILED AT THE MEMORY OF MEREDITH IN HIS office. The chair was still warm when he put a hand on it. He took a deep breath, savoring the moments they faced each other. He sank into his leather armchair as his mind drifted into his secret place. His fingers met and flexed into the shape of a temple.

She'd gone right to the polo photo. He wasn't surprised, given the information Esparza had supplied him. Daughter of the SFPD's Mounted Patrol Unit, her history in hunter/jumper shows in her teens. This was the right hook to pique her interest. Giroud had seen her reaction when he asked her to the match. She had been so busy trying to mask her excitement that she didn't know what to say. He wondered at the lift of her eyebrow, the press of her lips.

She was sending him another message. *Subtle, wasn't she? What was she trying to say?*

Giroud played the moment over in his mind's eye, listened to her breathing, watched her head turn toward her partner.

There was the problem. She was saying she'd have accepted my invitation, but with her partner by her side, it would have been awkward. Esparza assured me that there was nothing between the two detectives.

But with Reyes as her partner, his invitation fell on unwelcome territory. It was of questionable taste to make a date while she was still mourning. Not to mention do it in front of her partner. She had shown admirable self-possession. Surely, she would have joined him otherwise.

He chuckled at the thought. Things were moving along nicely. He wanted her *now* but realized that a woman as sensitive as Meredith Ryan would observe the proprieties. Her husband was barely cold.

Giroud's smile grew wider.

And getting colder by the minute.

Chapter Thirty-Nine

WITH NICK'S HELP, MEREDITH SPENT THE AFTERNOON ARRANGING for the SWAT team. There was a lot to do to put together a search warrant. With the Special Operation Unit Sergeant Carl Wells, Nick oversaw the tactical aspect involving personnel transport, weapons, and other special equipment. Meredith wrote the operations order, lined up Peters, Anderson, and Leahy in addition to the SWAT unit, and notified DA Traber.

Late that afternoon, Nick dropped Meredith off at home. Everyone else was to be at the office the next morning at five am. Meredith would drive her own Subaru to work.

Home felt still, vacant. Even her fussy and demanding cat, Gus, was not around. Meredith's head still ached, but it was a manageable dull throb. Her stomach growled as she rummaged through the kitchen, looking for something edible. She settled on a can of Campbell's tomato soup and some saltines. After eating, she left Gus half a can of cat food in the laundry room and fell into bed.

JUST BEFORE FIVE the next morning, Meredith shrugged off her damp raincoat in the women's locker room. Thankfully, she'd awakened headache-free. She checked her hair in the mirror, smoothing wisps into her ponytail. Lipstick at this hour was out of the question. She was dressed in jeans, a navy-blue sweater, and lightweight hiking boots to ensure comfort for the long hours ahead of her. The walk down the hallway into the VCI office gave her time to review the plan. She'd been taught in the academy, and Nick often emphasized, that a winning mindset won battles. She had to prepare and pre-plan before they got on site, to wrap her mind around what she was about to do. The incident in the county courtyard with Rusty Webber illustrated how nothing should be considered routine, not even a court appearance. She hoped not to kill anyone today. But if she had to, she would.

With this on her mind, she turned the corner into VCI.

At his desk, Nick straightened abruptly, a look of surprise plastered across his broad, tan face.

"What?"

"This was sitting on your desk." He nodded to her desk. The shock had exhausted Nick's meager catalog of expressions. "It was here when I got in."

Her desk almost groaned under the burden of two dozen crimson roses in a crystal vase. A small, white card stood sentry over the bouquet. Meredith exhaled her own astonishment.

"Open the card." Nick shifted from foot to foot, waiting.

Mildly irritated at his pushy manner, Meredith opened the envelope, read silently, then closed it. "It's from the Judge."

Nick had to lean toward her to hear her words.

He waited another moment. "What does it say?"

"It's none of your business." She'd tell him eventually.

He squinted, then shrugged. "Okay." Leaning onto his desk, his jaw set as he stuffed his ballistic vest into a go bag.

"'To Meredith, with sincere respect for your courage. Yours, Stephen Giroud.'"

She looked at her partner's eyes but thought of another man. *What was this about?* To Meredith's mind, the judge had crossed some indefinable line. Judges and cops didn't mix any more than engineers and ditch diggers. It wasn't something taught in any classroom, it was just understood. Besides, how the hell did he get someone to deliver these so early in the morning?

Peters, Anderson, and Bingham, another detective on the team, strolled into the room. She tucked the card into her pocket.

"Nice flowers. Somebody get lucky?" Peters hooted at his own joke as the three detectives ambled to their desks.

Ignoring them, Meredith whispered, "This is unreal."

"Hey, you guys, get over to the squad room for briefing," Nick said. "I'll be there in a minute."

When just the two of them were left in the room, Meredith's head shook in amazement. "I can't believe this."

"Really? A guy sees a girl he likes, and he sends her flowers. It's simple, isn't it?" Nick leaned against the cubicle frame, his face a study in stoicism.

She glared at him. "Quit your fishing expedition. I'm not going out with the judge. I'm not going out with anybody. I've been a widow for three months. I can't even consider it."

He nodded, staring at her for a long moment. A smile crept onto his lips; he jutted his chin toward the squad room. "Let's get this briefing done."

Chapter Forty

HEAVY MORNING FOG SWEPT OVER THE COASTAL HILLS, BARELY visible in the emerging daylight. Nick and Meredith pulled the Taurus into the pre-arranged location, a lot one block away from Shady Acres Trailer Park. An aged blue Buick sedan with Anderson, Bingham, Peters, and Sergeant Leahy followed. Both cars tucked into the edge of the asphalt under a thick stand of laurel and scrub oak. The grove formed a crescent around three-quarters of a derelict Chevrolet dealership outside the small town of Sebastopol. The car lot entrance was off Highway 12. The far end tipped into a blackberry-snagged creek path that wound to the end of the trailer park. Theda and Earl Sutton's trailer sat at the far edge, overlooking a lagoon filled with reclaimed sewer water. Abundant rainfall had created a surge of vegetation that threatened to overrun the lot. Nick thought that might not be a bad thing. Good concealment.

On his previous visit, Nick had seen the detritus of unsettled, transient lives, abandoned appliances, household garbage, car parts, and other throwaways littering the space between the trailers and the brambles. Most of the trailer park residents were one rent payment away from homelessness. In planning the raid, Nick took the debris into account. Anderson had taken some good photos of the grounds.

Warnings had been issued to deputies about obstacles and the potential for cover or concealment when needed.

The trailer itself was an early sixties' vintage canned ham-style, resting on a ragged foundation of broken cinderblocks, which were visible through gaps in the battered aluminum skirting. Most of the other trailers had open areas under them, but Theda had upgraded.

Nick didn't want to think about the crawlspace underneath. A faded turquoise slash across the trailer's midsection divided the rusty, dented white skin. Nick guessed the length at about sixteen feet. Sealed windows front and back offered a view of neighboring trailers. The far side looked out on the junkyard and brambles beyond, with the nearby pane facing the park entrance. Two louvered windows on each side offered scant ventilation.

The SWAT van took up a position at the park entrance. The occupants swarmed the perimeter, assuming their assigned posts. Nick had requested nearby residents be evacuated, but Leahy preempted this as unnecessary. No one truly believed Sutton would be stupid enough to return to the trailer, but Nick was irritated that Leahy denied a reasonable precaution.

He was surprised when Leahy included Meredith on the entry team. When he allowed women deputies on his operations, Leahy didn't usually put them at that position, but Nick had said he wanted her at his back.

The mist shrouded the conifer-covered hills. It dampened sound to create an eerie silence. Everyone held position: the breach officer at the point, Nick behind him to announce the warrant, Meredith, Bingham, and Peters to the sides. Everyone outfitted with standard vests, radio headsets dialed to a secure channel, and duty weapons. Bingham and Anderson had chosen to add AR-15s, as did the Special Weapons crew.

The SWAT officer banged a huge fist on the trailer door, standing off to the side.

Nick shouted, "Sonoma Sheriff's Office, search warrant."

They held for five long seconds waiting for a response. Then, after checking to see if it was open, the breach officer used a specially designed pike to punch the door handle.

The pike did the trick. The door flailed open. Two deputies swept through the opening. Nick heard a thundering explosion from inside. A gunshot.

Both deputies backed out and scattered for cover. Nick ducked behind an upturned picnic table to the west of the trailer. East of him, Meredith bounced to one knee behind a broad redwood stump. Bingham and Peters took cover to the south. Meredith, Beretta in hand, waited for the next move.

Another round blasted from the trailer through the entry door. It sounded like a large-caliber handgun. It was unlikely that Theda had enough body weight to hold a gun like that, much less use it. It had to be Sutton.

"Sutton, Earl Sutton. This is Detective Reyes of Sonoma County Sheriff's Office. We have a search warrant." An arrest warrant had not been issued yet for Meredith's assault the day before. But by shooting at the deputies now, Sutton had provided the cause to arrest for attempted homicide of a police officer. They didn't need an arrest warrant.

Nick watched the windows. At the one closest to him, the plane of the glass louvers shifted slightly. He saw the muzzle of a gun.

"Gun, front window!" He ducked for cover at the sound of a half dozen rounds. Nick felt the impact of a slug that hit the picnic bench mere inches away from him. The sound of glass breaking meant return fire must have knocked out the window.

The SWAT officer in charge, Sergeant Carl Wells, halted fire. He called Nick on his headset. "Reyes, how do you want to play this?"

"Give me three minutes. If I can't get him out, then we'll go in. You guys at point can do your stuff."

The sergeant grunted his response.

Nick announced himself once more. No response. A full minute elapsed. Silence. Nothing moved inside the trailer. The curtains were still.

Nick spoke into the mic, Leahy replied, then the SWAT sergeant. Low voices hissed in his earpiece as units reported in. He glanced at Meredith and motioned her to get ready.

A canister flew over Nick's head and through the broken window.

Good throw. Gray smoke billowed through the shattered glass and the open door. With masks on, the SWAT entry team rushed the door. Four times, Nick heard strong masculine shouts, "Clear."

That fucking Sutton had escaped again!

The bulk of the teargas dissipated; three of the four officers came out, one of them, Sergeant Wells. With the easy rolling gait of an athlete, he strolled over to Nick. "No one inside, but you're gonna want to see this." Leaving the safety off, he settled the AR-15 into the crook of his arm and led Nick and Meredith inside.

They followed. The acrid gas smell lingered. Meredith coughed.

Wells walked three paces to the middle of the messy trailer, stopped, and faced them. "He got away through here." He pointed to a squared panel in the floor. "I forgot about these. The manufacturer had to build escape hatches in these things because they caught fire so often."

Nick knelt to study the hatch, a 16-inch by 16-inch square with a swing latch recessed into the lip of the frame. The latch was open, and the door was ajar. "Is this cleared?"

"Yeah, I sent Lopez down there. He's our littlest guy. It leads under the trailer, to a tunnel made of garbage, and out to the lagoon." Sergeant Wells shook his head. "I've called for a K-9 unit, but the ETA is extended, about 45 minutes."

Nick nodded, containing his dismay.

The sergeant added, "Sutton's in the wind. We'll search the entire place, but he could be anywhere."

"Yeah, yeah," Nick muttered to no one in particular. Glancing back to the hatch, his eye caught a sparkle on the damp ground below the hatch. He reached for it and pulled out a pair of diamond earrings, a brooch, and several rings, all familiar from the photos of Violet McMurray's stolen jewelry.

Chapter Forty-One

"Fuck, fuck, fuck," Earl Sutton mouthed into his tee-shirt. He had to keep quiet. No telling if the cops were still waiting for him out there. God, that was close. He shoved the gun, a Raven .25 caliber semi-automatic, into the back waistband of his jeans.

Sutton shimmied along the tunnel that he had assembled a week ago. He crawled under a greasy oven door propped up by mildewed plywood, then under a stack of carefully balanced truck tires. Taking a moment to smile in self-congratulation, he was glad he'd put together this quick escape from the trailer. He just didn't think he'd need it so soon.

He'd come back to catch Theda. He wanted his money. When it was dark, and she hadn't shown, he'd shoved what was left of Violet McMurray's jewelry in his pocket and turned in for a few hours of rest. He didn't plan on staying so long, but exhaustion overtook him, and he fell asleep.

He couldn't trust Theda to keep the cops away from him. The old bitch would do anything to keep herself out of trouble, and that included giving him up. He shook his head in disbelief as he considered her lack of reliability. He should have beat some loyalty into the old hag long ago.

He inched forward inside the tunnel, dodging sharp edges of rusted aluminum siding and weathered wood scraps. When he reached the end, he waited for what seemed an eternity. He wanted to be sure the cops were gone before he came out.

The escape tunnel would take him east from the trailer park and onto a walking path surrounding the marshland. At this exit point, his view was east beside Highway 12. He saw nothing; no cops, no patrol cars, nothing. He stretched out on his stomach, listening for sounds from the entrance to the park or any of the trailers.

He chanced a quick look when the noise of the raid was over. Damn, another cop car driving up. A K-9! Sure as shit, the dog will find me. Time to change plans. He mulled over some possibilities. Patting his pockets, he realized his cell phone was still inside the trailer. Fuck!

No money, no phone, and no haul. Fuck!

Ten seconds later, he settled on another simple idea: get the hell out of here, make it to the gas station two blocks away, and call Fredo from the pay phone. Have him pick him up. Maybe he could hole up in Fredo's commercial fishing boat.

Scooting from the exit hole, Sutton crawled to the walking path. Once there, he pulled off his flannel shirt and tossed it into the brush. With the K-9 on his tail, this might buy him a few minutes. A sprint along the path for a quarter mile left him winded, standing at an abandoned barn behind the gas station.

He leaned against the rough wood, alternately shivering and sweating in his tee-shirt. When his breathing returned to normal, he walked as calmly as he could to the pay phone, fingering the change in his pocket.

Sutton dropped the coins in the slot, quarters, all he had. He ground his teeth as he waited for his friend to answer, thinking about where his money was. He bet Theda had already blown it all. Damn. He fingered the sharp points of several pairs of earrings, a necklace, and three rings. They were too hot to unload around here.

Answer, buddy, answer your phone. You're the last chance I got. He felt his waistband, checking for his pistol. It was still there.

Finally, his friend picked up. "Fredo, buddy."

"Sutton, my man. Whassup?"

"Hey, I need a ride and quick."

"Ride? What happened to your GTO?"

"The fucking cops impounded it."

"Dude, bummer. Sure, I'll give you a ride. Where are you?"

"The gas station on Highway 12 by the Sebastopol Grange, the Chevron Station. I'll watch for you from inside the bathroom, around the backside of the building."

Fredo's voice lowered. "You on the run, dude?"

"Yeah, I'm kinda hot right now." He grimaced at his choice of words. He was freezing; the morning mist had intensified to rain, and now he was soaked.

"Hey, this may work out for both of us. I'm short one guy for our trip tomorrow. If I bail you out, you'll work for me, for pay."

"Yeah, yeah, man. That's great." He shivered. He needed cash and a safe place to lay low.

"But you gotta think about what you're gonna do when you get back. I can't let you live on my boat forever, dude. This is the second time in a week you needed help. What's your plan?"

"Yeah, Fredo. That's what I need. A plan."

"I'll be there in about twenty minutes in the pick-up."

By the time Fredo's step-side truck pulled up beside the station, Earl Sutton had the basics of a plan.

First on the list was to find a blanket. Second, he needed to get his GTO back.

Chapter Forty-Two

THE OPERATION ENDED JUST AS THE RAIN STARTED. IT WAS AS IF THE heavens wept for the failure of their mission. When the evidence tech van left, the two detectives sat in the Taurus. They were silent as they mulled over the past few hours. Judging by the set of Nick's mouth, their failure today had strengthened his resolve. Nick hated losing.

On the drive to the Main, Meredith spent the trip mapping out their next steps to catch Sutton. Their plans included updating the BOL to include 24I) PC: "assault on a peace officer," and sending it for statewide broadcast. Meredith would supplement the original report with the morning's events, and they'd re-check the places Sutton frequently visited. The stakeout at the restaurant had been terminated. No one believed Sutton would return for a measly paycheck. Besides, they'd needed the manpower at the trailer park this morning.

The wipers slapped a monotonous rhythm at the rain pelting the windshield. Nick watched them for a moment. "I'm tired of rain."

The cell phone in his pocket vibrated. He answered it, listened, then said, "I guess this shouldn't be a surprise." He glanced at his watch. "We're on our way back to the Main now."

She could hear Lieutenant Ferrua's raspy voice.

"Okay." Nick looked to Meredith as he corrected his direction. "We're on our way to the sub."

Meredith glanced at him. The sub was behind them, several miles from the trailer park. She pulled over on the shoulder and waited for a break in traffic.

"That was Ferrua. He just got word to mobilize for evacuations from the River area. He wants us at the River substation."

"All righty." She whipped a U-turn and started toward the sub.

"The river reached flood stage an hour ago, and the tide is coming in. The campground at Monte Rio is already underwater. It's getting into houses along the highway. High tide is in another hour."

"This sounds the same as five years ago. I hope the sub has extra raingear. Mine's at the Main."

"Uh, yeah. Mine too. I guess we should put it in the car with our other gear for next time."

"Right. At least for the rest of the winter."

They pulled up in front of a colorless one-story building trimmed with glass blocks along the top of the cinderblock wall. It looked like a neglected dentist's office. A painted wood sign in front had large block letters, 'Sonoma County Sheriff's Office River Substation'.

Inside, the River sergeant Marco Donato smiled at Meredith. "Everything went to hell in a handbasket after you left. Ready to come back?"

"Nope, I've got a good gig in VCI." She grinned. "This is my partner, Nick Reyes."

"We met at the last qualification shoot," Nick said, shaking hands with Donato. "What do you need us for?"

"I have one problem area at the moment." The burly sergeant tapped a knuckle on a wall-mounted map. "Up in Laurel Tree Canyon, a cabin that slid down the hill belongs to an elderly couple. The bridge washed out, so the only way to get to them is by boat. I have a County Park Service guy coming in with a 17-foot aluminum fishing boat. You'll be on your own getting them out. Can't spare any bodies. Take them to the parking lot at Monte Rio Beach. Shuttle buses go to the Red Cross Center in town."

Meredith studied the map. "I know where that is. We've had domestic beefs up there."

Donato's voice boomed. "Any questions? No? Then go suit up."

When both were outfitted in scrounged-up raingear and boots, they waited in the small briefing room for the boat.

After twenty minutes of *hurry up and wait*, Meredith stood and stretched. Nick studied the map but glanced up when she drifted toward the door.

"Where're you going?"

"Out in the hallway to make a call. That okay with you, boss man?"

"You can't have your conversation in front of me?"

"I can, but I don't want to. I want some privacy."

Nick shook his head like she was a child caught stealing candy. "You're going to call Judge Giroud."

"What if I am?"

He shrugged. "I suppose you're going to tell me you want to fill him in on the search warrant fiasco. That's why you're calling him."

"It's none of your business, Nick." A flutter of anger stirred in her.

"Yeah. Don't forget to tell him thanks for the roses."

Her anger melted away as she realized what was behind his intrusion. "You're jealous."

"Don't be stupid." He turned away.

"You are." She bit her lip to contain a laugh. "You don't like him because you're jealous. You don't like that a man has shown interest in me."

Nick ignored the comment, scrutinizing the map.

She pushed the tease. "A superior court judge, no less. I hear he's got lots of money, too."

His complexion darkened. "Don't be crude."

"Then stay out of my business. If I choose to call him, it's none of your concern. If I wasn't going to do it before, I certainly will now." She mentally dug her heels in. Who was he to tell her what to do? Not in her personal life, for sure. The judge was interesting. She was curious about him, not romantically, but she wanted to know more about him.

Still, there was a nagging feeling the judge was playing her. He seemed to be after something, but she couldn't imagine what. She had no money. Richard had seen to that. Sex? He could get that anywhere. And Meredith possessed no influence socially or politically. She was just a cop, nothing more.

She shook off the thought and stomped out to a deserted hallway. Boxes filled with reports were stacked along the wall. She found a solid looking one and perched on it. Reaching through the layers of her clothing, she pulled out her cell and a card.

She punched the numbers into the phone.

"Giroud."

"Your honor, this is Meredith Ryan."

"Meredith, I am glad to hear from you. Please, call me Stephen." Even when he was happy, his voice sounded like he was giving orders.

"Yes, sir. I thought you might want to know about the search warrant we served today."

Giroud's voice shifted reluctantly to business. "All right, how did the search warrant go?"

"Not so good. Sutton was there but got away after taking a few shots at us."

"That's disappointing. No one hurt, I hope."

"No, just some damaged pride. We didn't expect him to be there. We found some of the victim's jewelry under the trailer at his escape route, though. That's more evidence to go to trial with."

"It always helps to have an abundance."

"It helps even more to have the suspect in custody."

He laughed. It was a pleasant sound. It had been a long time since she'd heard a man laugh like that. Richard seemed to have forgotten how the last year they were together.

"Thank you for the flowers. They are lovely."

"You are welcome. The red stands for respect, I hope you know."

She exhaled. "I didn't." Again, she had the feeling he wanted something from her. Maybe he was just smooth.

"A small symbol of my esteem."

Sergeant Donato's order boomed over an intercom. "Reyes, get your partner. Your boat's here."

"Time for me to go. Thanks again for the roses." Ready to disconnect, she popped her head into the briefing room and nodded to Nick.

"I hope to see you soon, Meredith." The judge's voice deepened, like his words had heavy importance.

She made her response light-hearted. "You bet, Your Honor. Hopefully with Earl Sutton in handcuffs." She ended the call before he could say anything more.

SHE SPENT the next two hours bobbing around with Nick in an aluminum fishing boat. It was cold, the scant afternoon light faded fast as another wave of showers descended. The rescue went smoothly despite the steady downpour. Most River residents were veterans of rain and mudslide evacuations, but the anxiety was always there. Even in rain slickers, the couple shivered and stomped with worry at the wait.

Nick steered the boat to a footpath not yet covered in water. Meredith tied the line to a stout Bay tree and waved them over. The residents were ready.

The boat was at capacity with Nick and Meredith, the couple and their six cats in carriers, two leashed dogs, and a parrot in a cage. The wife fidgeted and fussed over an iguana left behind, agitating the dogs. The cats howled, the dogs whined, and the husband groused about the boat taking on water. Meredith stroked the dogs to reassure them and keep them still. The husband's complaints almost became real as they slogged up to the boat ramp at Monte Rio Beach.

The family off-loaded while Nick got their next assignment. Another rescue completed, the rest of the evening was filled with hurry up and wait, hurry up and wait, until, finally, Donato called Meredith's cell. "Go home. Water's going down, rain's stopped, got everyone moved out that needed to."

They were released at eleven p.m. Rather than going back to the Main to pick up her car, Meredith told Nick to drop her off at home. He'd have to pick her up in the morning, but they were both wet and exhausted. Better to get some sack time now.

Nick waited in the Taurus while Meredith unlocked the front door. She smiled as she heard him shove the car in gear and hit the gas pedal. It was almost like an old-fashioned date. But no, she corrected herself. It was one partner respecting the other. She was pleased to admit she would do the same.

A wet, furry, feline bowling ball rushed past her into the house. "Gus, what were you doing outside?" This happened yesterday, too. What's going on?

She called a few more times but realized the cat was in a snit over getting wet and he would be no one's friend now. Inside, Meredith leaned her hip against the kitchen counter, watching her sweet kitty turned Franken-feline. He perched on the dining room windowsill, furiously licking his coat. She found a can of his food in the fridge and served it up. In due time, he meandered over to the plate and nibbled at it.

Pleased he was settling down, she spent the next ten minutes going through the house. How had Gus gotten out? She checked windows and doors but found them all secure.

Then, as she walked into her bedroom, a scent reached her nose. It took her back in time to a better place. Her stomach flipped with excitement. Then she realized it was Richard's cologne.

Startled, she caught her breath. Richard. *Richard?* What the hell?

She moved to the dresser still filled with his clothes, things she wasn't ready to part with. Silly, she thought. His cologne was sitting on the dresser as he'd left it months ago. She touched the bottle, feeling the same glass he had touched almost daily, then stopped. She jerked her fingers away as if the bottle was on fire.

Stop it, she thought. *Stop.*

Chapter Forty-Three

THE NEXT MORNING, MEREDITH STIRRED THE SUGAR INTO HER coffee and watched people coming and going in the Hall of Justice cafeteria. The cavernous room was yellowed institutional white, with a buffet line on one side and accidentally vintage tables and chairs on the other. Large wall-mounted placards displayed the menu behind the buffet line, as most diners had trouble distinguishing Itree from another.

Lawyers, secretaries, cops, clerks, Joe Citizen on jury duty, defendants waiting for their court appearance all mingled together in the unspoken truce over the partaking of a meal. People rubbed shoulders with those who would be prosecuting, testifying, or documenting their proceedings.

Nick slipped into the chair next to Meredith. She shuddered at the cinnamon roll on his plate. "That stuff is going to kill you. Why do you bother working out?"

"Quit being my mother." He shoveled a piece of roll into his mouth.

"Speaking of your mother, how's she doing?"

"She's fine." He chewed.

"That didn't sound convincing."

Nick avoided her gaze.

Meredith liked Nick's mother. She was the traditional Mexican mom who reared her children with an iron glove. "She's still living with you, isn't she?"

He swallowed. "Yeah, for another month. Then she's going to my sister's in Modesto, but my sister is an RN. She'll get her to the doctor and find out why she's so tired all the time."

"She still nagging you about Angela?"

He put down the cinnamon roll. "She doesn't get the split up at all. She thinks Angela is coming back from Mexico and we'll pick up where we left off."

"Which is not going to happen, right?"

"She's a good Mexican Catholic mother. She thinks that when your son gets married, it's forever."

"Well, it should be." Meredith looked away.

"Yeah, it should, huh?"

Nick was having his own trouble understanding Angela's escape, just as he would always suffer the loss of their little girl. He'd told Meredith the baby had no choice, but Angela did. He also once believed that marriage was forever.

Meredith sipped her coffee, wondering how the county could charge for this swill. "So, about Sutton: what do we do now?"

Nick sighed. When he spoke, his tone was quiet. "Bottom floor…"

"Ground floor…"

"Oh, yeah, ground floor." He waved the correction away. "Start over. Look at everything again from a different angle. See if we can come up with something new." He rubbed his eyes with his fingers.

"We can do that." Meredith paused. "What about setting a trap?"

"Set bait to catch him?" Nick's eyes widened.

She cocked her head. "We could talk to Theda. See if she knows of anything he would risk his freedom for. We might have to get tough with her, though. She's scared enough of him, she might not want to talk."

"Pam in dispatch called this morning." Nick brushed crumbs off his fingers. "She'd just entered a warrant for Theda. It's a little one, a grand for bad checks, but it'll give us some leverage."

"What are we waiting for?" Meredith was already on her feet.

Chapter Forty-Four

RAIN PELTED THE ALUMINUM TRAILER AS THE PARTNERS GOT OUT OF their car at Shady Acres. The trailer's door was still trashed. A tangle of bungee cords was strung through the hole where the doorknob had been and looped around to the doorframe.

Theda's Toyota pick-up pulled into the oil-drenched parking space next to the Taurus. She glared at Nick and Meredith through the windshield wipers, then pulled a cigarette from her purse, stuck it in her lips, and lighted it. A cloud of smoke filled the cab.

Meredith was damp and getting wetter by the moment. Enough, she thought. With Nick following, she dodged oily puddles, uneven gravel, and mashed food wrappers to stand next to Theda's truck. Nick pulled open the driver's door as Meredith returned Theda's glare. "You want to go inside and talk about the warrant we have for your arrest?"

Raindrops splattered Theda's faded pink sweatshirt. "What warrant?"

Meredith slipped a hand under the woman's upper arm and firmly pulled her out. "Let's go inside and talk it over."

The not-so-subtle aroma of Old Crow drifted from Theda's wrinkled lips. Meredith wrinkled her nose at the stench. "Theda, you haven't been drinking and driving, have you?"

The old woman ignored the question. "What warrant?" She stood next to the truck, pulling away from Meredith. "What bullshit are you handing me now?"

Nick asked, "Remember the bad checks you wrote on a closed account last December?" He had researched the report that generated the warrant.

"That was Christmas presents for my daughter-in-law. The bank made a mistake."

"Daughter-in-law?" Nick cocked his head to the side as he looked at Meredith. He looked back at Theda. "I thought his wife was common law."

"She is. She dumped him before the trial. But we stay in touch. I call her my daughter-in-law for convenience." Theda started toward the trailer, holding the damp cigarette between her lips. From the bottom step, she untangled the bungee cords and backed up to let the door swing open. Nick and Meredith guided her up the wobbly steps. The trailer hadn't been cleaned since their last visit. Dishes were piled in the sink, clothes strewn about, and ashtrays overflowed with cigarette butts. It smelled like no one had cleaned for the last decade. Theda flicked her half-finished smoke into a water-filled bowl stacked in the sink.

They settled at the table. Nick looked around. "Dang, Theda. It's hard to believe you clean other people's houses for a living."

The older woman's lip curled like she wanted to spit at him, but she thought better of it. "I get tired of cleaning. By the time I get home, it's the last thing I want to do."

She reached for a cigarette pack on the table. Meredith pushed it out of her reach. "Not now, Theda. Let's talk about that warrant." Neither detective had any idea whether Theda would help them find the bait they needed, but it was worth a try.

"What about the warrant?" Theda pulled a matchbook from her jeans pocket and twisted the cover back and forth. "I don't want to go to jail." She shifted in her seat. Meredith caught sight of what looked like cash peeking out of her jeans pocket. From the bulge, it was substantial. Meredith filed that info away. Cleaning houses didn't pay like that. She could have taken the money from Sutton. No chance he'd given it to her, judging from the rancor they seemed to feel toward each other.

Meredith considered how she could lawfully get to look at the cash. Violet's son couldn't produce serial numbers, or a final amount of the cash taken from McMurray's house. She believed the money stashes were random, with no final tally. Probably a dead-end anyway. There was a slim chance of getting usable prints from currency, especially after it had been handled by others.

If they could gain Theda's cooperation, they'd need to put her in protective custody in the jail.

Nick answered. "Maybe we can work with this, Theda. You help us out with information, and we look into it, as long as you appear in court when we tell you."

Theda creased the matchbook cover and bent it opposite, then back again. "Will I have to pay anything?"

"You help us with good information, then maybe we'll talk to a judge for you. In fact, my partner has a friend who's a judge. We might get him to help."

The matchbook cover shredded in her fingers. "What do you need to know?"

"What happened between Earl and your daughter-in-law?" Meredith asked.

Meredith watched Theda's mouth as she began to tell her story. A small tremor worked the corner of her lower lip. "Her name's Faye, Faye Zelman. He knocked her up about four years ago when they were living in another trailer with me. I told them they had to get out. I had no room for a baby and no patience for a squalling kid. So Faye found some Section 8 housing in Santa Rosa, and they moved out. Then things got a little rocky. Faye dumped him and moved to Southern California with an uncle or something."

"They split up over the baby?" Meredith asked.

Theda grabbed a room-temperature Pepsi from the counter. Popping the top, she eyed the foam. "Earl beat her up real bad. She was pregnant at the time, and she lost the baby. She was in the hospital for a month."

"What happened to Earl?" Meredith asked.

Theda sighed. "He got arrested and sent to prison for three years. He got out about eight months ago."

"I saw the Domestic Violence arrest on his rap sheet." Nick nodded. "I didn't know there was such serious injury."

Theda laughed. "Yeah, he pled to a lesser charge, and now the damn fool wants to find her to get back together. He wants to be a family. Can you imagine? After doing that?"

Meredith smiled and asked her, "Earl said he wanted to find Faye? Is that right?"

Theda's lined lips twisted in irony. "I never said brains ran in our family." She took a swig of the Pepsi. A thought struck her, and she met Meredith's gaze, her forehead wrinkled. "I didn't tell him where she is. I'd never do that. He might kill her."

Nick leaned in close. "Do you think Faye would come back?"

Theda slammed the can on the table, splashing soda as a sarcastic cackle escaped. "No way." She straightened up and leaned toward Nick. Their noses were about four inches apart. "He damn near killed her. She's scared to death of him."

"What would it take to convince her?" Nick sat back.

Theda pulled her head back until her chin disappeared. "I don't know—a million bucks? No, I don't think she'd do it for nothin'."

"Theda," Meredith pulled the old woman's attention to her. "Let us talk to her. Will you give us her address?"

She hesitated. "Why? Won't do you no good."

"What if we could put him in prison until he rots?" Meredith offered.

Theda glanced from Nick to Meredith. "You could do that?"

"We're working on it." Nick's eyes met hers. He seemed to sense her fear. "What are you afraid of?"

"Nothin'," she began, but the shallowness of her protest stopped her. She was so scared she couldn't even lie about it. Meredith marveled at the level of fear that Earl inspired in Theda. She lied like she breathed yet couldn't formulate anything believable to the detectives.

"You see," she traced the trim on the table with a broken thumbnail. "Yesterday, I borrowed some money he hid. I know he'll be pissed. I'm afraid he'll hurt me. I only came back today to get some clothes." Her wizened gray eyes held the faintest flicker of hope.

"We can get you into protective custody. Maybe book you on that warrant, then put you into a secure part of the jail where no one can touch you." Nick spoke with lazy authority. Meredith wondered how he could offer this.

"You're sure? No one can get to me?" Her chin quivered.

Nick rested a palm on her bony shoulder. "I'll make the arrangements airtight."

Theda mewled with resignation. "Hand me my purse," she nodded to Meredith. "I'll copy off her address for you."

Chapter Forty-Five

"JUST LOOK AT THAT FRIGGIN' HEADLINE." LIEUTENANT FERRUA tossed the offending front page of the Sonoma County Press Democrat toward Meredith, Nick, and Sergeant Leahy.

"These reporters are killing me." Ferrua ran his stubby fingers along his bald head. He slouched back in his swivel chair and blew out a sigh that came from his toes. To Meredith, Ferrua always seemed at the end of his rope. As prone as he was to drama and lacking in leadership skills, she wondered how he made his rank. At least he had the good sense to listen to Nick. Professionally, her partner had it all over her boss.

"The brass is on my butt to find this clown. The DA's parents live out there in Rolling Hills, and everybody's got their knickers in a twist."

Leahy slithered to the lieutenant's side and poked his jaw toward Nick and Meredith. "Where are you in the investigation?"

Nick brought them up to speed, ending with Theda's contribution of Faye Zelman's address in San Luis Obispo.

Leahy curled his lip. "What good is her address going to do you?"

Meredith started to answer, but Nick cut across her words. "We want to use her as bait."

Leahy's eyes bugged out. "Bait?"

"We're at a dead end." Nick was calm in the face of his sergeant's reaction. "If we catch Sutton, the evidence will convict him. That's according to DA Traber. The trick is to find him. We've looked everywhere. Granted, this should be a last resort kind of thing, but it looks like maybe we're there. We don't even know if the ex will go for it."

Meredith put in. "We think it's time to do this, sir."

Leahy's attention rested on Meredith. "What makes *you* qualified to decide this?"

Ferrua's hand clamped onto Leahy's forearm. "Don't be so hasty, Don." The lieutenant turned to the detectives, his face barely concealed shards of hope. "Do you think he'd try to make contact with the ex?"

Nick repeated Theda's information about Faye, adding his own conclusion. "She says he wants to re-unite, to be a family. We have no more active leads. So yes, it's worth a gamble."

Ferrua glanced at the headlines, silent for a moment. "All right. But the ex has to be a willing participant. We don't want to be accused of strong-arming her if this goes south."

Meredith spoke up. "We know we can't coerce her. I've thought of several approaches…"

Leahy cut across her comment, his face reddening. "Who's going to pay the OT for these two? Tomorrow's Saturday. And their airfare to LA?"

"San Luis isn't that far from LA. We're going to drive," Meredith said.

"There's still your mileage," Leahy insisted. "And a hotel. What if you have to stay the night? That would be two rooms and meals."

Ferrua jerked his head at the sergeant. The squint of the lieutenant's eye made Meredith think he was going to tell him to shut up. She was disappointed when he didn't. "Don't worry. If this works and we get Sutton off the street, we're golden."

"And if it doesn't work?" Leahy sneered at his lieutenant.

Ferrua stood, puffing his chest up. "Then it's my ass, not yours." He looked pleased with his decision. "Any more questions?"

Leahy's lip stiffened into a pout. Nick shook his head, and Meredith continued to bite her tongue.

Ferrua nodded. "Then take off tomorrow morning, early. Let's get this guy off the street."

Chapter Forty-Six

MEREDITH MET NICK AT HIS HOUSE AT 4 A.M. RATHER THAN MAKE him drive all the way out to Forestville. They were heading south, and passing that detour saved an hour's travel time. Nick convinced Leahy to let him take his personal truck and pay mileage rather than use the department Taurus. He reminded Leahy how expensive it would be to have the Taurus towed if it broke down. Nick's new Chevrolet half-ton was comfortable and dependable. Meredith's car wasn't an option, even if it was a station wagon. Her four-year-old Subaru Forester embarrassed Nick. He wouldn't be caught dead in the styleless, gutless vehicle.

They made good time. Because it was Saturday, there was little traffic on Highway 101. Darkness still shrouded the Golden Gate Bridge, broken by the amber roadway lights and occasional head-lights. They drove down 19th Avenue, the Chevy's suspension evening out the terrace-like street as Nick surfed the green lights. They drove through Daly City as the sun rose, then ducked behind a low cloud mass to the east. They turned off at the Highway 280 exit, Nick's truck ticking off the miles on the wide, smoothly paved high-way. At Tully Road in San Jose, he pulled off and found a gas station for fuel and a greasy breakfast biscuit. Meredith scrounged a greenish banana and a granola bar.

They returned quickly to the freeway and headed south along the Bayshore Freeway. Any other time, Meredith would have enjoyed the ride, but today she was preoccupied with the elements of this case.

Down the road, the terrain south of Atascadero impressed her as being similar to Sonoma County, without the redwoods. Laurel, valley oak, and digger pines dotted the gently rolling hillsides. Intermittent patchworks of vineyards, vegetable crops she couldn't identify, and gentleman horse ranches spread beneath the trees.

They reached San Luis around lunchtime. Meredith suggested meeting with the local police department before they tried to find Zelman. They eased off the two-lane highway at Exit 203A, circled the block, and crossed over Highway 101. On the corner of Walnut and, ironically named, Santa Rosa streets, they parallel parked into a space in front of the police station. SLOPD was a pale stucco single-story building at street level, a structure probably built in the 60's. Behind it, a lower-level lot was reserved for police parking. The mission-style font used on the sign was also used on the street signs, a quaint hometown touch.

The business office was closed for the weekend. Nick picked up the handset in the red telephone box next to the locked front door. He introduced himself to the dispatcher and asked to see a watch commander. A second later, the entrance door buzzed. Inside, the pair waited. Nick raised his arms in a stretch, groaning as he worked out kinked muscles. A minute later, an interior door clicked open, and they faced a uniformed officer, a lieutenant. They both had their ID's out as Nick introduced himself once again. "We need to talk to you about finding a person of interest in a homicide case."

The lieutenant stretched a hand to Nick and Meredith. "Lewis Brody. Be glad to help." Lieutenant Brody, a spindly, short man with a tight mass of curly gray hair, wore chevrons on his sleeve representing twenty-five years of service. "Let's go to my office so we can get to a computer." As they followed him down a tiled hall, he said over his shoulder. "I take it this person is local?"

"Yes," Nick answered as they settled into a tiny cubicle.

The lieutenant sat at a dark wood-finish aluminum desk facing the two detectives. "We don't have any detectives on duty on weekends. I should be able to help you, but if need be, I can call someone out." He folded his hands on his desk, a look of polite curiosity spread over his face.

Nick repeated the essentials of their case, finishing his narrative with a request. "We're here to find Sutton's ex-girlfriend, Faye Zelman. We'd like a local record check to see if she's had contact with you guys, if she's changed her address, and anything else you might know about her."

He nodded emphatically as Nick told his story. He couldn't wait to answer.

"The Zelmans are a piece of work, for sure. We have a whole family here. Faye was a decent kid in high school. I remember her from DARE—I was the school resource officer. The odds of her turning bad were high, given her family life. They are shitbirds from the git-go. I was convinced at least her father, maybe her brothers, physically abused her, too. Anyway, she stuck it out to graduate from high school then she moved away. Three years ago, she showed up on her mother's doorstep. She moved in and has been here since. She got a job at the Circle K over on Higuera. I see her when I get coffee sometimes."

"Has she been staying out of trouble?" Meredith asked.

Brody's gaze searched the ceiling, came up with nothing, then spoke, "Can't remember anything off hand. Let's check our computer." He swiveled his chair to a monitor, shook the mouse, waited, then tapped the keyboard. Tiny lines around his eyes creased as he read the results. "Yeah, nothing for your purposes. She's called in shoplifters, reported vandalism to the store...that kind of thing." A wiry eyebrow raised as he considered something on the screen. "Parking tickets, too."

Meredith leaned over her notepad, her pen poised. "We show an address of 227 King Street. Is that still good?"

"Yep, that's the last one we have from a month ago."

Brody gave them directions to both the Circle K and Zelman's home, then suggested a local deli for lunch. They shook hands, said their thanks, and got back on the road.

The partners stopped off at the deli for a couple of sandwiches to go. Zelman's apartment house was easy enough to find. They ate in the truck so they had a chance to study the neighborhood. The building was a two-story square box, matching a half-dozen others on the block. It had been sage green at one time, but the first-floor exterior was mottled from spot painting over gang tags. The lower floors had wrought iron grills bolted to door and window frames. Cockeyed, bent, or absent shades gaped in the windows. Weeds grew from the roof gutters. Children's scooters and other toys were scattered on the dried-up patches of Bermuda Grass.

After they ate, Meredith rang the doorbell, but it went unanswered. She knocked, then Nick tried. Still no answer.

"Maybe she's at work." He nodded in the direction of the Circle K.

NICK PULLED the truck into the store lot less than ten minutes later. A tall, skinny redhead clerked at the counter. From Theda's description, it had to be Zelman.

They waited until the store emptied. They hadn't quite made it to the counter before she volunteered, "What can I do for you, officers?" Her thin lips clamped shut without any hint of friendliness. Meredith was never surprised when people recognized them as cops. Not that they all looked the same, but they carry themselves with authority, have an observant eye, a no-nonsense set to their jaws.

They showed their IDs and introduced themselves. Zelman's eyes widened. "Sonoma County? Wow, you guys are a long way from home."

Meredith began, "Faye, we came down here to talk to you..."

"No shit. Let me guess. Earl Sutton, right?"

Meredith answered. "Yes, we'd..."

"You wasted your time. I don't have anything to say to you." Zelman looked over her shoulder as a customer came in.

"Faye, this is really important. He's killed someone…"

"I'm lucky it wasn't me." She hissed, leaning over the counter. "See this, and this and this?" She raised the sleeve on her light blue smock and pointed to several heavy scars. "I've had a dose of Earl's temper one time too many. I'm not smart, but I learned that lesson good."

A truck driver came to the counter. She rang up his RockStar and candy bars, giving him the obligatory smile as he left.

"Is there anywhere we can go talk that's more private?" Nick asked.

"Detective, there's nothing you can say that will make me talk to you."

"Okay, we'll talk here." Nick leaned toward her. "Sutton killed someone. Not just anyone, an 83-year-old lady. She could've been your grandmother. She had no defenses to fight back. We think he's getting desperate and might hurt someone else."

Zelman rested her hip on the counter, arms folded across her chest.

Nick bit the inside of his lower lip. It was a sure sign of his sincerity. Meredith hoped Zelman picked up on it, too. He continued, "We need help finding him. We need someone who knows him, knows how he thinks, where he goes."

Meredith studied the interaction. Nick didn't dump the bait idea on her right away. Zelman was so resistant to anything having to do with Sutton that it would take time to convince her. It was encouraging that she was listening now.

"What about Theda?" Zelman asked.

Nick shrugged. "Theda knows what Sutton tells her. And she's not dependable."

"You mean you don't trust her." Her lips twisted into a crease of irony. "That means you *do* trust me?" She sputtered a nervous laugh.

"Good question, Faye. You're pretty smart." Meredith said in her best no BS voice. "You've been on the straight and narrow since you moved down here. Starting over takes a lot of guts."

Faye's forehead wrinkled. Her thumb rubbed a spot off the worn Formica.

"Have you figured out what you're gonna to do if Sutton comes after you?" Nick scratched his chin. "Run again?"

Faye's curly red hair shook frantically. "He doesn't know where I am."

Nick shrugged. "We found you."

"Get out."

Chapter Forty-Seven

IT WAS RAINING AGAIN, NEARLY MIDNIGHT WHEN NICK DROPPED Meredith off at her house. She slid out of the truck, stepping into a puddle. "Crap."

Nick's eyelids drooped with fatigue. His face reminded her of a basset hound's as he said, "Not a good omen for the rest of your night."

"There's only sack-time in my immediate future."

"Yeah. It's hard work, sitting there snoring."

"I didn't snore."

He smiled at her indignation. "See you on Monday. I'll pick you up."

Too tired to speak, she turned away as Nick drove off.

"Damn it," she fumbled with her house key, wishing she'd turned on the front porch light. Beyond the driveway, the front door was bordered on each side by rain forest. In the three years she and Richard had been in the house, the vegetation had thrived in the damp Russian River atmosphere. The lush plant life always calmed her; cool, welcoming, and peaceful.

The leaves of the giant dieffenbachia at the front door swayed, betraying a slight breeze. But the movement was more than the wind would make.

Startled, she dropped her keys and bent to retrieve them. In a fluid motion, she straightened, Beretta in hand. For a half second, she felt a little silly. A lot of wildlife thrived in this neighborhood. She'd feel foolish if she drew down on a skunk.

She gripped the pistol with both hands. "Sheriff's Office! Come out where I can see you." Adrenaline fueled a stampede of a thousand thoughts through her head. The last time she aimed her gun at someone Rusty Webber died. No, that wasn't right. She'd got off a few rounds at Theda's trailer yesterday.

"Mere?" The last voice she expected to hear.

"*David.*" Keeping her stance and aim, she realized she was yelling.

"Mere, it's me." The huge leaves separated, and a shadow stepped out.

"David." She reached around and holstered her gun.

When he heard the holster snap, his arms wrapped around her. She returned the hug, and a part of her wanted to keep holding him, never let go. Her little brother was back. She held him tightly, afraid he'd take off again.

"Sorry I dropped out of sight like that." He broke the embrace and leaned his forehead against hers.

She was silent as memories flooded her mind. Unable to decide whether to be relieved or angry, she turned away, groping for the door lock. "Let's go inside."

David followed Meredith and stood in the middle of the living room, with a glance from one side of the room to the other. A low whistle escaped him. "What a showplace. How can you live here? It's like a page from a magazine."

Meredith shrugged off her jacket and tossed it on the sofa. "It's home. You want something warm? Coffee, tea?"

"Bourbon?" He flashed a hopeful smile.

Pulling a wine glass from a kitchen cabinet, she nodded towards a bar in the dining room. "Lift the top. The bourbon is in there somewhere. Pull out the open bottle of red wine for me."

David poured himself a tall one.

She swirled the pinot noir. "Where's your stuff? Do you need some dry clothes?" Curly blond hair plastered in a dark mass around his head, the denim jacket hanging around his hips was heavy with rainwater, and his aged Birkenstocks were drenched.

"My things are in a car that's about halfway through Central California by now."

At her questioning look, he explained, "I hitchhiked to Santa Rosa. The asshole I got a ride with took off with my stuff when we stopped to take a leak." He smacked his lips after taking a sip. "Tastes good. Where's the old man?"

"Sit down."

"I'm still wet." He took another sip.

She got up and walked to her bedroom. When she returned, she tossed a pair of sweatpants and a Tee-shirt at him. "Go change."

He squinted at her but didn't argue.

Ten minutes later, David settled into the sofa, balancing his drink and a pillow. He asked, "So, what's up? Where's Big Dick?" He laughed at his wit. His sister's frown silenced him.

She dropped into a chair across from him. "Richard died three months ago. Three months, two weeks, and two days ago, to be exact."

David pitched forward, splashing his bourbon. "What? What happened? Aw, Mere. I'm sorry I wasn't here for you." He put his drink down and crossed to her chair. He knelt and swung an arm around her shoulders.

She focused on a spot on the carpet. "He was killed in a hit-and-run accident in South San Francisco. They didn't find the guy who rammed his car."

"I'm so sorry. You were alone for all this. No one to help."

Her eyes filled with unshed tears. She glared at him. "Christy was here. She and Nick were here."

David pulled back as if he'd been stung. "No one in the family, I mean."

"Christy is more family than you are, David Ryan. She's always here for me. It's more than I can say for you or our father, wherever he is. Richard didn't have a choice about this. It's not like a divorce or anything."

"Divorce? That came from left field." David dropped to the sofa. "Divorce?"

Meredith considered what to tell her brother. In the end, she told him all of it. There was no reason not to. He was, after all, her brother.

His drying curls shook when he finally spoke. "I'm so sorry, Mere. I didn't know."

"Of course, you didn't know. You were playing at breaking into the big time. Christy doesn't even know where you are."

"I kinda want to keep it that way." He picked at the sweatshirt. "And I wasn't playing. I was working."

"Why keep it from your wife?" Meredith felt her temper rising. Same old David.

"It's one of those things better left to the privacy of the people involved." His voice wavered as if he was unconvinced of the truth of his statement.

"Bull." Her glass clattered against the coffee table when she put it down. "Christy is my best friend. We don't keep secrets from each other. She told me you left her for a life on the road. With bills and an overdrawn checking account."

"Mere, it's not that simple."

She held up her hand. "Okay, okay. I see that I need to stay out of this for my own sanity."

He took another long swig of his bourbon.

"I suppose you need somewhere to stay," Meredith exhaled her pent-up frustration.

A wry smile was his reply.

"Don't scare me like that again. I could've shot you." Meredith was too tired to sustain the irritation. She stood. "I'm done in. I'll get you something to sleep in." She motioned to the back of the house. "Pick either of the spare rooms. Both beds are made up. I'll find some of Richard's clothes for you to wear tomorrow."

He cocked his head sideways. "Thanks, sis."

"We'll talk more later. I've had a bitch of a day. Time to turn in. You look tired, too. Let's go to bed."

"Hey, since when is Gus an outside cat?" David's glass motioned to the redwood deck.

"Never." Meredith jumped up and ran to the French doors, eyeing her wet cat. She flung one side open, cooing at Gus to come in.

He didn't, of course. He hunkered down and backed away when he saw David striding toward the door. The cat hunched in a corner, watching. The deck wrapped around the back and side of the house, covered by the roof at the living room doors. The wind blew rain sideways and dampened the railing.

"He's not usually so aloof." Meredith sighed. "He'll come in. He hates the rain. When he figures out who you are, he'll come back. I guess I have to check out the house again tomorrow and find where he's getting out. This is the third time this week."

Rain splattered on David's damp hair as he stepped onto the deck. "Wow, that's quite a drop." He looked over the balustrade at the blackness below him and shivered. "I can't see the bottom."

"It drops down fifty feet. There's a seasonal creek down there and a walking path that leads to the River. I like to run there sometimes."

He whistled a low note of amazement.

She sipped her wine. "We can go out to dinner tomorrow night at Cabañas if you want." She referred to his favorite restaurant. "Christy is in Illinois with a sick aunt, so she won't see you. Maybe Nick'll want to come, too."

Relieved, he nodded. "Anything to avoid your cooking."

She smiled and punched his shoulder.

Gus' need for dry turf outlasted his unusual wariness. Meredith closed the door as they watched him saunter inside. He made for the laundry room, where dinner awaited him.

"You're off graveyards, then?"

"Yep, working in VCI, Violent Crimes Investigation."

"A promotion? Wow, you deserve it, Mere."

"Quit sucking up, David. I've already said you can stay. Let's get some sleep."

Glass in hand, he turned toward the door behind the sofa. "Okay, show me where to go."

"That's my bedroom. You go the other way." She put her wine-glass on an end table. In spite of the hurt he pressed on those who loved him, she couldn't keep from hugging him again. "God help me, I love you." She grinned into his shoulder. "You're as dependable as an earthquake, but you have a big heart."

He hugged her back fiercely, glass bobbling in his hand. "Love you, too, Mere."

"I need to see that you have towels." With an arm around his waist, she steered him through the door and down the hall towards the spare bedrooms.

Chapter Forty-Eight

STEPHEN GIROUD WAS HOT, ANGRY ENOUGH TO BREAK SOMETHING. Ignoring the pain, he pressed his fingers into the angular edges of the Swarovski binoculars, snapping them in half. He'd listened to the conversation on the deck from his hidden position. He was able to see them through a potted tree set at the corner of the house. When he watched them embrace, the judge's temper spiked. He almost lost control at Meredith's words, "I love you." He had wrapped his fingers around the binocs, wrenching until they gave way. He dropped the two halves into a dirt-filled flowerpot.

Watching Meredith walk down the hall with her arm around the blond man's waist infuriated Giroud. He didn't know who the man was, nor did he care. The stranger was another impediment to catching and keeping Meredith's attention. The guy would have to be dealt with, and soon. Giroud didn't want anything taking hold in the vacuum following the collapse of her marriage.

Giroud watched as Meredith and the man went to the back of the house—the spare rooms. He stood back to re-group his thoughts. Can't leave the binoculars behind. After tossing them over the balustrade, he glanced at the dark chasm below.

He found the solution to his problem.

Chapter Forty-Nine

THE NEXT NIGHT, THE DIM ATMOSPHERE OF THE UPSCALE MEXICAN restaurant provided a level of discretion for Meredith. Santa Rosa was a small town. She hoped to avoid running into someone she knew. She was worried Christy might find out that she was harboring her brother. The odds were slim, but the Irish Catholic upbringing dictated she was guilty, whether she was or not.

While Meredith looked around at the other tables, Nick tossed back a Corona. David knocked over the saltcellar reaching for chips and salsa. Nick slammed his beer on the table, stretched toward David, and righted the shaker. He pinched some salt between his fingers and tossed it over his shoulder. David's mouth hung open in surprise.

"Holy crap," Meredith whispered. Looking past David, the judge sat in a dark corner, enjoying the company of another woman.

Nick followed her gaze, then snorted into his beer.

"What?" David eyed one then the other, twisting in his chair to follow his sister's gaze. Then facing Meredith. "What?"

Nick's lips curled into an unpleasant smile. "That guy in the corner with the fat girl is a Superior Court Judge who's been after your sister."

"Double dipping, huh?"

Peeling her eyes off the judge, Meredith reached for her wine. "Shut up, both of you."

Nick's smile was small, almost artificial. "Well, you didn't expect him to live a celibate life waiting for you, right?"

"Mind your own business."

David forked a *relleno* with enthusiasm. "Man, I love this restaurant. This's gotta be genuine Mexican food, isn't it, Nick?" He shoved a mass of oozing cheese into his mouth.

Nick shrugged a 'no' and took another swig of his beer.

Meredith pushed her chair back from the table. "I'll be right back."

"You're not leaving, are you?" Nick asked.

"I'm going to the restroom." She shoved her chair to the table with too much force, tipping it sideways. It clattered on the uneven tile, making other diners look up at the commotion. Meredith strolled to the bathroom, fighting the inclination to run. Inside, she needed a moment away from nosey friends and family. She slumped against the bright blue tile. Why did she care? It pissed her off, seeing the Judge with another woman, but she couldn't figure out why. It wasn't like she had something going on with the judge. She didn't even *want* that. Still, the attention of a powerful, attractive man doesn't happen every day.

Grow up, she thought. Flattery is no basis for a relationship. She summoned more rational, adult feelings. Maybe not, Judge Giroud could mean financial security. Embarrassed at her mercenary heart, she pushed the idea away.

A toilet flushed while Meredith hunted in her pocket for a lipstick. A waitress with a blond ponytail came out. She stood at the sink, washing her hands.

The bathroom door swung open. The Judge's lady friend glided into the small room. She was a voluptuous redhead with an excess of make-up and flirting manner. On a closer look, the woman looked familiar.

After a smile to both women, the waitress left.

The redhead looked intently at Meredith. "You're a deputy, aren't you?"

Meredith nodded.

A satisfied smile spread across her lips. "I thought so. I'm Astrid Vachon. I work in the Court Clerk's office."

Meredith flashed a polite smile.

"Meredith Ryan, right? I thought so. I saw you in the Quad when you had to shoot that old guy who went postal."

Meredith remained silent.

"That was so gross, the blood and all the screaming."

Meredith thought about her reply, as she had every time someone mentioned the incident. "I wish it had never happened. Rusty wasn't a bad guy. He just flipped out under pressure. He didn't deserve to die." She needed to make people understand. She didn't need a locker-room pat on the back and a 'good job.'

Astrid stared for a moment, then bent over the sink, pumping soap into her hand. She smoothed the liquid over her hands, massaging it, luxuriating in the moment. "Are you and your boyfriend enjoying the food here?"

Alarms went off in Meredith's head, confusing her. Why did a conversation with this stranger signal high alert? "Cabañas is an old favorite," she managed to say.

"I'm here with Stephen Giroud. You must know of him. He's a Superior Court Judge." She rinsed her hands, a vague, expectant stare hinting that her next words were important. "He's totally taken with me, I can tell."

Whoa, too much information. Meredith said, "How lucky for you."

Astrid dried her hands. "Yes, isn't it?" She smirked, applying lip-gloss with a deft motion. Her gaze slid over the detective, head to toe. She seemed to find Meredith wanting.

At the door, Astrid turned to Meredith one last time. "I always like to look my best when I go out with my man. You should think about a makeover. Put a little spice in your life." She shrugged one shoulder like a seductive gypsy. She pulled the door open and left.

Meredith felt like she'd been slapped in the face. What just happened here? Who the hell is this woman? What right did she have to...

When she returned to the table, Nick had started on another beer. David was on his third tequila shooter.

"I just got a call from dispatch," Nick said. "Someone busted Sutton's car out of the impound yard."

"We can look for it Monday. Let's get outta here."

David's face screwed up in confusion. "We haven't eaten yet. And I've got a righteous tequila high started."

Nick studied Meredith. "That's a new one. I thought you liked this place."

"I do, but the mood's gone sour. Let's tell the waiter our order is to go and take it home." It took an effort not to look at the pair in the corner, but she managed.

Chapter Fifty

A BEAD OF PERSPIRATION TRAILED BETWEEN ASTRID VACHON'S ample breasts. Her hairline was damp, too. *Afterglow.* So, what if she had to do it herself to come? Stephen wasn't an attentive lover, but did that really matter? This was how she was gonna get him. She was tired but excited at the same time. This was how she was gonna make him hers.

Alone in the room, she snuggled under the silk sheets, savoring the smell of her man. Maybe calling him 'her man' was a bit premature, but not by much. He'd belong to her, soon. Those skinny, athletic types like that damned Ryan bitch weren't the only ones who could catch a man. Full-figured women know what a man likes, even if she didn't learn it in college.

She heard the shower start. Stephen would be busy for a while. She had a fleeting thought about joining him but decided to use the time to get to know her man. She eased out of bed, glancing around the room. It was formidably masculine. Dark coffee-colored walls, plantation shutters, crimson leather armchairs, a huge, matching mahogany armoire, and a four-poster bed. Right now, the room was in disarray from their hastily dropped clothing.

Astrid felt a little overwhelmed by this room that permeated his presence. She looked inside the walk-in closet, pausing to caress his suits. Beyond the closet, the armoire across the room piqued her interest. Looks like an old-school TV cabinet, she thought, grabbing the brass knobs. They were stuck; she pulled even harder. Finally, they swung open. Surprised at the weight of the doors, she stepped back.

There, occupying the entire space, was a shrine-like display of Meredith Ryan. Pictures, newspaper articles tacked on the cabinet's back and sides, a wilted red rose lying on the shelf.

She fingered a newspaper article with a trembling hand, scanning words that didn't register. It was old news, the local story of the Quad shooting.

That bastard, she thought. He was using her to get to the twit. Her face flushed. Running into Meredith Ryan tonight wasn't a coincidence. The judge had played her. He'd made a fool of her so he could…what? Make the Ryan woman jealous?

But Astrid was nobody's fool. She'd see Stephen Giroud pay for using her.

"You stupid bitch." She jumped as his silky voice sent a shiver up her spine. Did she hear menace in his tone? Astrid spun around, pausing when she saw his face twisted with rage. The judge stood at the bathroom doorway, still wet, with a towel tied around his waist. Three steps across the carpet, and he was inches from her nose.

"What are you doing?" Giroud's face was nearly purple.

Astrid threw the clipping at his chest. "I should ask *you* that question." She glanced back at the shrine. "What the hell is this?"

"It is none of your business." He reached past her to slam the armoire closed. His masculine scent made her falter. Once again, she was sure she could make him forget about the deputy, come to love her. A few more romps in bed like tonight would do the trick. Then he'd fall for her, hard.

"Get dressed and get out." Stephen's complexion had faded, and the set of his jaw was like granite.

"I will, in my own time." Astrid settled her fists on her hips. Her back was against the open armoire door. She wished she had some clothes on, but she continued anyway. "I want you to know that I don't appreciate being used. It's obvious you have a fixation for this girl, though God knows why. I sure don't. You set me up to make her jealous at the restaurant."

Stephen squinted as her words hit their mark. "Whether I did or not is irrelevant. Get out. Get out now."

Astrid stooped to grasp the clipping from the carpet. She waved it in Giroud's face. A giddy desperation rose in her chest. "You're a pervert, a freak. What would she say if she saw this stuff? What would the Judicial Council say? This is sick."

His tanned arm reached out, grabbing her white neck. She saw it coming but was too stunned to move. How could she have been so wrong about this guy?

With one powerful thrust, he pushed the web of his hand across her throat. Thumb and index finger curved enough to mash into her carotid vein and jugular artery.

She saw a checkerboard spread across her eyes, turning all black, then nothing.

Chapter Fifty-One

THE CIGARETTE SMOKE WAS THICK ENOUGH TO SLOW A PERSON down. A "closed" sign hung outside The Blue Flamingo Bar. Closed to the public. Six men sat around a table littered with chips, cards, drinks, and ashtrays. A crowd of a half dozen watched without any visible enthusiasm.

A short muscle-bound biker type, the sergeant at arms for the proceedings, opened the door for Earl Sutton. After Sutton said Fred's name, the biker nodded and went back to his post.

Sutton's boat had docked two hours earlier. He still wobbled on sea legs, so he eased between the tables and chairs, careful to avoid the poker game. He wasn't here to gamble; he was here to meet someone who could help with a problem. He'd been told to look for a Rasta guy with two filled teardrop tattoos under his eye.

Sutton sauntered to the bar, scanning faces. There, in the corner. All by himself. A light-skinned black man with dreadlocks and a black leather jacket slouched in a cushioned booth. He toyed with a non-filtered cigarette as Sutton approached the booth.

"You Jamaal?"

The man nodded as if to the beat of a song no one else could hear.

Sutton remained standing. "I hear you do favors for people."

Jamaal's glance swept over Sutton, then dismissed him. He'd been found wanting in the black man's estimation. Jamaal stuck the stub of the cigarette into his mouth. Smoke curled upward, disappearing into the cloud hovering above the coils of his hair. "Sometimes, if the circumstances are right."

Sutton expected him to have a Jamaican accent, but he sounded like a New Yorker.

Jamaal nodded to the seat across from him. Sutton slid onto the torn vinyl bench. "I need this woman to be out of my life." He shoved a yellowed snapshot of Theda across the table. "Her address is on the back."

Jamaal took the photo without looking at it. "How far out?"

"Permanently out."

The dreadlocks bobbled. "You know the deal?"

Sutton reached into his jeans pocket, pulling out a roll of cash, everything he'd earned on Fredo's boat. He pushed the money over to the ashtray, where Jamaal cupped a hand over it. It was gone in seconds.

"Will I know when it's done?" Sutton propped his elbows on the table. "How can I be sure it's taken care of?"

Jamaal's eyes darkened. He studied Sutton a moment. He spoke so softly that Sutton wasn't sure he heard right. "You'll hear about it."

"Yeah, but…"

"We're done." Jamaal caught the eye of the biker at the door.

Sutton jumped up. "All right, all right, all right." He felt blood rushing to his cheeks. He murmured, "I got it. I'm leaving."

Sutton scooted out the back door of the bar like a scalded puppy. He hated dealing with punk asses like Jamaal, but he had to get rid of Theda before she spilled her guts to the cops. She knew everything. Besides, she'd taken his money, and he fucking hated her.

The bar where he'd met Jamaal was off main roads. At this time of the morning, he figured it was unlikely a cop would see him. He raised the collar of his borrowed Pendleton jacket against the morning breeze. Glancing around the parking lot, he headed for his GTO. As he was slipping behind the wheel, he noticed a familiar white Taurus passing the Blue Flamingo.

Shit.

Chapter Fifty-Two

"HERE, YOU DRIVE. I'M BEAT." ON MONDAY MORNING, NICK STOOD at Meredith's front door and tossed her the car keys. "I was up all night with my mother."

"Sure." Meredith squinted through the drizzle as she dashed to the driver's side. Behind the steering wheel, she asked, "Was she sick or something?"

"Yeah, something." Nick slipped into the passenger seat, balancing a takeout coffee cup he'd bought at a drive-through coffee kiosk.

Meredith waited while he pulled the lid off the cup and blew on the coffee. "Don't know what. Last night, she was throwing up, won't drink any water to stay hydrated. Doesn't go to the doctor and won't tell me the truth about her symptoms." He looked out the window. "Stubborn old bat."

Meredith started the car, flipping on the windshield wipers. It rained hard enough to be annoying. "Now I know where you get it."

Pulling out onto Mirabel Road, she peered through the streaky windshield. "How about we drive past the restaurant where Sutton worked? Maybe we could stop in and see if anyone there has seen him or his car."

Nick rubbed his eyes, agreeing. "We've got to start at the ground floor elevator…"

"Just 'ground floor.'"

"Whatever." He waved aside such trivialities. "As long as we're going to do that, let's take another look at the crime scene. It's already been released to the son, but we should be able to get permission. Turn left there."

"Quit being a back-seat driver. I know where I'm going."

They took a left at the next intersection. "Now, turn right at the Blue Flamingo. It's the kind of dump where Sutton would hang. Probably wouldn't hurt to drive slowly past there…"

"Sutton," Meredith pointed. "Look, the GTO."

"He's going to run, Mere."

Meredith stomped on the accelerator, steering the car into the parking lot. The heavy morning mist had dampened the asphalt. She braked the Taurus into a 180-degree slide. They came to a stop facing the opposite direction. Surprised that the car had done exactly what she wanted, she hesitated to make sure of the man in the other car.

Nick tightened his seatbelt, pulled out a blue bubble light from the glove box, and pressed it onto the roof. "Hit it!" He flipped the siren on, bringing on a full wail.

Sutton's GTO pulled from the driveway onto the two-lane road, turning west. The back end dragged a moment in a fishtail. Smoke and steam billowed from the coupe. The tires found purchase, and he was off.

Meredith stepped on the gas pedal again, this time with gradual pressure.

Nick reached for the radio. He spoke calmly into the mic. "David one, we're in pursuit of a 187 suspect, Martinelli at River Road."

"Code 33 for David One in pursuit of a 187 suspect, Martinelli at River Road. Routine traffic to tac 3. David One, go ahead." The dispatcher prompted him to continue, the channel was now cleared for pursuit-related transmissions.

"He's turning westbound at River Road." He gave the vehicle description and license plate. Meredith concentrated on driving while

Nick gave the GTO's estimated speed, traffic conditions, and cross streets.

"David One, that vehicle is reported stolen from our agency's impound yard."

"David One, copy."

Westbound traffic on River Road was comprised of one plodding Citroen, blocking Sutton, slowing him down. However, the eastbound lane was solid with cars, all moving at the speed limit. Meredith fought tunnel vision, making herself watch oncoming traffic.

Nick shouted over the siren, "Ready to listen?"

Her partner needed to update her, and this seemed as good a time as any. The mist had lifted enough to turn off the wipers. Sutton set a steady pace, neither pulling away nor slowing. He was solo in the car, and he hadn't displayed a weapon. "Yeah, go ahead."

"Pretty much, we're on our own. None of our units are even close. The coast deputy is in court, and Santa Rosa is too far away. CHP will get back to us with an ETA, but they're down on the southern end of the county. They're sending their chopper, too, but it's responding from Napa."

"No State Parks Police, nothing?"

"Dispatch is trying to contact State Parks, but so far, no luck." Nick glanced each way, gauging oncoming traffic. "He's headed toward the coast."

"This way T's out at Highway 1 in Jenner." They both knew that, but she said it anyway.

Parallel to the Russian River, they followed for twenty minutes, meeting little traffic on the winding road. She knew this stretch of road well. It had been part of her beat in her River patrol days. She smiled to herself at the advantage. She'd be damned if she'd let him get away again.

Sutton opened up the GTO and moved a quarter mile ahead. Meredith couldn't get any more out of the Taurus. She was grateful it stayed steady at the top speed of seventy.

"He's turning." Nick pointed.

Meredith did mental calculations of how fast she could take the same turn. She eased on the brakes, leaning with the car, then, as the road straightened, she stomped on the gas pedal.

The GTO turned south, toward Bodega Bay. As they crossed the Russian River, the Taurus made unexpected gains on the GTO.

A spurt of adrenaline jolted through Meredith as the GTO flipped a left turn at the Russian restaurant onto Willow Creek Road. Clear of oncoming traffic, she followed, wondering what the hell he was up to. On the riverside, less than a dozen vacation cabins perched above the water, then—just road. All she remembered out here was cattle pasture. The roadway was mostly gravel, lined with residents' cars. Scrubby manzanita and coyote brush covered the hillside.

The Taurus almost bottomed out at the drop in the road. Then over a small rise and the pavement narrowed even more into a damp, pot-holed country lane. Barely enough room for two cars to pass. Meredith dropped her speed. She lost sight of the GTO but didn't feel safe going any faster.

He's still up there, using his stick shift to ease into the turns so he can blast out the other side. She gave a silent nod to his driving ability. She'd learned much the same in defensive driving classes.

Sutton pushed ahead, making a little progress. She focused her attention on the GTO's taillights. The road began to dip, twisting into gullies and small timber stands.

"He's going to have to slow soon." Nick said, "The road gets real curvy." The rain was a consistent mist that made for sloppy driving, but no flooding, so far.

"Willow Creek dumps out on Freezout Road in Occidental," Nick dropped the mic into his lap. "We lost the radio for the moment, so don't crash."

The road dipped and snaked around hills and into gullies. They had lost sight of the GTO behind a rise when her eye caught movement behind the juniper hedge to her left.

Oh crap, it's a driveway.

A battered green GMC flatbed backed slowly onto the asphalt. Meredith took in the truck and the roadway. *There's no way through.*

She stood on the brakes. The wheels skidded off the asphalt onto the loose gravel shoulder. The tires were unable to grip. Her correction was wasted. The Taurus plummeted into a four-foot-deep drainage culvert next to the roadbed. Meredith's head whipped around by the sudden stop and slammed into the doorpost.

A blinding barrier flared into Meredith's face, she yelled, "No, no, no!" Then there was nothing.

Chapter Fifty-Three

IT WAS FOGGY, WHEREVER SHE WAS. SHE COULDN'T SEE ANYTHING but felt Richard's presence. Men's voices spoke in urgent tones, like orders.

Where am I? I can't see anything. She smelled anise and hay. So, someplace familiar. Men's voices, again. What're they saying? Listen, Meredith. Maybe you'll get a clue. No, I'm too tired to listen anymore.

Later, the "whop, whop, whop" of helicopter rotors. Voices, talking but not making sense.

Voices kept prodding her. *All I want to do is sleep. Quit talking. Be quiet, please.*

Then: the kind of jarring, upsetting noise where people don't even try to be quiet, the acrid smell of antiseptic. Ouch, a jab in her left arm. Her eyes fluttered open only to squeeze shut against the bright lights. She had a headache. After a while, she managed an inventory. A headache to end all headaches, mouth dry, arms and legs stiff, right knee throbbing. Felt like she was swimming in taffy. Sleep, all she wanted to do was sleep.

A female spoke. "She's coming around."

The fog again.

"Meredith, dear."

Her mother. Dead, felled by breast cancer the year Meredith graduated from college. Yet this was her mother's voice as sweet and thick as honey, with hints of the Irish. "He's been bewitched by that hussy. It's not his fault; it's herself that made all this trouble."

"All this trouble" was a simplified summation of the destruction of a family. Her father had found someone new, someone who wasn't her mother. So, he left the family, abandoning his wife and children, forcing them to survive on a prayer and a pittance. Meredith was fourteen, David barely ten.

Even now, she could hear her mother weeping behind a closed door.

The doctor was in a hurry but stopped by her room to tell Nick that the CT scan showed no sign of a fracture. She suffered some bumps and bruises and a twisted knee. Nick had been cautioned about the symptoms of concussion, black-out and headache afterward. Nick worried that two head injuries in three days could be more serious than the doctor believed. They had assured him more than once that she would be fine, but he didn't trust them.

Meredith groaned, turned her head, then settled down again. Nick sat in a vinyl-padded chair next to her bed. Watching her chest rise and fall with the peace of chemical creation. Her chestnut hair tousled over the pillow. Her tranquil face looked more vulnerable than she would have liked. Once she woke up, she'd be in a frenzy to pick up the search for Sutton. He'd have his hands full trying to make her rest for the next day.

If not him, who would keep her quiet? David? Not hardly. He'd have to speak to with her brother.

Meredith groaned, turning her head his way.

"Nick? Did he get away?"

If her head didn't ache so much, she would've been irritated at him when Nick rolled his eyes. But her head *did* ache, and her knee, too. She shifted to get comfortable, but the movement twisted her leg further. "Ahhh," she groaned.

Nick rose and leaned over her. "You need to rest, Mere. The doctor said so."

The ice pack on Meredith's knee made it awkward to get comfortable. She changed her position again, finally finding a place without pain. She retreated into the covers, trying to keep inside the cocoon of her body heat.

"Doctors. You can't listen to them. They just want to make money." Her thoughts drifted off. She couldn't remember what she was telling him, but it wasn't important anyway.

Then, her mind cleared. "Tell me what happened."

He ran through the pursuit from the crash to now.

She felt as if a hand grabbed her gut. "You're okay? You didn't get hurt?"

"Nah, I'm okay. I got a bruise on my elbow, but that's all. No one else got hurt, either."

"Thank God," she whispered. "And Sutton? What happened to him?"

She took in all the details as Nick caught her up. "So he got away again."

"An effing Houdini."

Meredith sighed and closed her eyes.

A zillion ideas fought for her attention. What if...

But Nick's voice interrupted. "Good afternoon, your Honor."

Meredith's eyes flew open and searched the room for the doorway.

"Detective. Good to see you again."

"Your Honor..." Meredith began but didn't quite know what else to say.

Giroud's long stride crossed the shiny hospital tiles to her bed. Again, she inched around on the uncomfortable mattress, this time trying to sit up so she could greet him appropriately. His long fingers grasped her forearm. In his other hand, he carried a bouquet of spring flowers.

"Meredith, I heard about the accident. Thank God you are all right." His eyes were bright with concern.

She struggled to one elbow.

Nick cleared his throat. "I'm going back to the office. CHP will be coming to take your statement. I'll see you later, Meredith." His lips clamped shut as he glanced at the Judge, then left. Her attention trailed after him, wishing he'd stayed.

What to do with her new visitor? Some common ground, something to talk with him…Oh, flowers.

"They're beautiful," she said as he handed them to her.

"Yes, they are. But, even lying banged up in a hospital bed, you outshine them."

She didn't answer. Nothing in her upbringing had prepared her for flattery like this. Her father barely spoke to her. David would never think of praising her appearance. Richard had used teases for left-handed compliments. As for Nick, his approval came from a more professional perspective. He didn't talk like this at all.

Giroud saved her. "I heard Sutton got away again, but the most important thing is that you are okay." He put the vase of flowers on a shelf across from her bed, then pulled up the chair that Nick had occupied. He sat near her.

"We'll get him. It's a matter of time." Meredith hoped to distract the judge from wherever he was going. This weird attention was more than she could handle right now.

"Still, the accident is a reminder to me of the fragility of your life. I want—"

The hair on the back of her neck stood up. "Your honor, how did you find out about this?"

"Call me Stephen, please." He smiled, proud of his cleverness. "I have a secretary who keeps me informed about people of interest."

People of interest? Yikes! She didn't want to be of interest to him. He was giving her the creeps.

Another change of subject was in order. "I've been here since nine a.m." She glanced at the plastic clock on the wall above the TV. "It's now three, and I won't be here much longer."

"You're being released?" Giroud's eyes grew wide. "So soon? Did they do a CT scan?"

Meredith raised a hand to brush away his concern. "I'm fine. The doctor said I need rest." She shook her head. "Which is tough as I can't get any sleep here. As soon as I get a ride, I'm going home."

Even though he's kind of a pest, it was nice getting this attention from a gentleman.

"Are you sure it is not too soon?" His brows set in concern.

She started to shake her head, but the pain stopped her. "I'm fine."

His lips drew into a cautious smile. "My car is in the parking lot. I would be happy to take you home, if you would like."

His offer wasn't totally unexpected, but her voice caught anyway. "Thank you, but I have already made arrangements." Did Giroud think he was a knight in shining armor? She could use a good solid rescue right now. Someone who could offer a stable financial life. She pulled her covers to her chest and sat back into the mountain of pillows, wishing Nick had shown enough sense to stick around. "How did you say your secretary heard about this?" She wanted to know.

He looked toward the door. "She has a scanner."

Meredith doubted an administrative assistant to a superior court judge would have a scanner in her office, much less listen to it. She also noted his averted eyes. *He's lying.* But then again, so had she. She hadn't made any arrangements to get home. She didn't want to be around someone who was virtually a stranger when she felt so crappy.

Guess it's not much of a lie. Lighten up, Mere. Still, something held her back.

His smile came too easy. "It's a big deal when a deputy gets hurt. Word travels fast around the Hall of Justice."

He's too smooth, she thought. What's he hiding? She was just too suspicious. *Let it go.*

"It was a stupid mistake. Thank God no one was injured." Tired from the effort of dodging his obvious interest, she dropped her head back onto the pillow. Her fingers rubbed her temples, thinking about the truck pulling out in front of her. Unavoidable. "It just dawned on me what Nick said about the CHP. There's going to be an IA on this. There always is after a wreck. I hate going through IA again."

Giroud scooted his chair even closer, taking her hand. "Meredith, you should not worry. You have done nothing wrong."

"That's irrelevant. There's always an IA after every incident. You know, 'how could this accident have been prevented?' kind of thing."

"I did some checking. From Nick's statements, you are not culpable." He squeezed her hand.

She pulled it away and rubbed her eyes. "I know that." Her words sounded sharper than she'd intended. "It's the investigation, the interviews, trying to recall the moment and all the details. I don't have the energy for it now." She turned her head away.

"Meredith. Look at me." He spoke in a whisper, but with such command that she couldn't resist.

"Do you want this to go away? The IA, I mean?" His eyes drilled hers. "I can help with that." His lips set in a firm line.

In spite of her exhaustion, she sat up, her eyes level with his. "Help?" Her heart thundered. How could he offer this? Restraining her temper, she continued. "No, *your honor*. I don't need your help. I'll be exonerated in good time. Besides, you can't control the California Highway Patrol. They still have their own accident report." She hesitated, about to thank him. Realizing she had no business thanking him for interfering in her life, she remained silent.

As if on cue, a fresh-faced CHP patrolman strolled in, then pulled up short. "Sorry to intrude." He shoved a rain-soaked cap under one arm and held out a clipboard.

"Speaking of the CHP..." Meredith said, nodding to the patrolman. She faced Giroud, extending her hand. "Thank you for stopping by. The flowers are beautiful." She hoped he caught her dismissive tone.

Giroud rose and grasped her hand, still holding her attention. "I will be going now."

Meredith smiled with relief as he walked out the door.

Chapter Fifty-Four

MEREDITH'S CELL PHONE BEAT A MUFFLED RINGTONE. BONNIE RAITT warbled while Meredith stumbled out of her hospital bed, running toward the sound. She found it after the ringing stopped and checked for a missed call. Nick. She pressed the keys to call him back.

"Hey," he answered.

"Sorry, the phone was buried in the closet."

"Yeah, I didn't get a chance to tell you, but that's where I put your stuff."

"Thanks."

Nick whispered into the phone. "Are you alone?"

"Yeah, the Chippie just left. Told me we both said the same thing."

"The truth is usually easier for that reason."

"Yep."

"I don't think there'll be any department repercussions." He paused. "You did everything right. The other driver didn't look before he backed out. If anything, he might get cited."

"That's reassuring." Although she didn't see the point in this becoming an even worse day for the driver.

"The IA should be cut and dried. They rely on the accident report for their facts."

"So, when are you going to spring me from this dump?"

"I'll come get you now." She pictured his smile. "The doctor wanted to release you tomorrow morning to keep you under observation. But I convinced him to let you go. I told him you'd walk out AMA if he didn't."

"AMA?"

"Against medical advice. That's what the hospitals and medics use when patients don't do what the doctor tells them. He compromised and will release you tonight before dinner. Having David home to keep you in bed was key."

"What are you waiting for?"

"Actually, I'm on the way to your house to pick up David. He wanted to be there for you."

She smiled wryly into the phone. "How thoughtful of him, making you drive thirty miles out of your way."

"Aw, it's okay. I think he needs you as much as you need him right now."

"Who needs who?" She felt a tickle of indignation.

"Hey, I gotta go. These roads are a mess. See you in an hour."

Chapter Fifty-Five

"Sir, you have a call on line two. I told him you were done for the day, but he was very insistent."

Buck Flannery sighed. He was tired; it had been a long day, and he had one more stop before he could go home and put his feet up. His secretary was usually good at screening his calls, which meant this guy must be a pain. He dropped his briefcase and raincoat on the corner of his desk. *All right.* This was one of those moments when he hated being a public servant.

"Okay, Peggy. Put him through."

Flannery settled into his chair. After a series of clicks, the voice came through.

"Sir, what can I do for you?" Not a public servant, a private servant.

Flannery listened a moment. "Yes, but she's alright. Still in the hospital. I was on my way to go see her."

The orders boomed in the sheriff's ear. "Yes, sir. It's our policy to do an Internal Affairs Investigation after a critical incident. Anytime a deputy is injured, it becomes a critical incident to me." Flannery leaned into the phone as if the caller could see him emphasizing his sincerity. "No, sir. This is not discretionary. Precedent has been set. We do this with all deputies."

The Sheriff pulled the receiver away from his ear to keep the volume manageable.

"No, sir. This rule isn't written down. I can appreciate how you feel about this..."

Flannery listened, and then answered, "Sure, the CHP will complete a report, and we'll get a copy. We base most of our investigation on it."

The voice kept the Sheriff quiet for a few moments. "Sir. This conversation is inappropriate, at the least. You're asking me to..." Flannery hoped Peggy couldn't hear through the closed door. Then, Flannery spoke into the mouthpiece. "Is there something I should know about you and Ryan? I mean, are you seeing each other?"

The short answer did not appease Flannery. "This doesn't change anything, sir."

The pause on the other end emphasized the weight of the coming words. The caller spoke. Then it was Buck's turn to listen. He recalled the photo the scumbag PI had shown him leaving Peggy's house late one night. His wife thought he was at a meeting. It wouldn't do for her to see the picture.

After a short while, Buck cleared his throat. "All right, sir. If those are the terms, you've made the decision for me. I'll call my IA Bureau now and stop the investigation."

Flannery didn't wait for any further comment from the other man. He slammed the phone down.

Chapter Fifty-Six

DRIZZLE CONTINUED INTO THE LATE AFTERNOON AND DID LITTLE TO improve Stephen Giroud's mood. His conversation with the fool, Flannery, had not gone easy. Giroud got what he wanted, but he had to spell it out for the idiot. The Sheriff had no concept of subtlety.

Giroud sat in his plush Mercedes, hitting the wipers intermittently to watch the entrance of the hospital. Who would pick up Meredith? He expected it was the partner or the tall blond guy who spent nights with her. His mind replayed the images of last evening. He watched her laughing with this who-ever-he-is—Blondie, for lack of a name—then strolling down the hall together, arm in arm. If she hadn't been there, he would have broken into the house and beat the guy to a pulp.

The dark green Chevy pick-up pulled under the hospital portico. The driver looked like Reyes. Someone rode in the passenger seat, getting out. It was Blondie.

Giroud's head dropped onto the headrest. He watched the front door. After a few minutes, Nick and Blondie loaded Meredith in the front seat of the truck. Blondie folded into the back. As they pulled away, Giroud stayed where he was. He knew where they were going.

His chest roiled with fury, disappointment, and passion. He needed a better hold on his emotions before he left.

He closed his eyes, and his mind drifted back to another adulterous woman from many years ago.

STEPHEN'S MOTHER'S musky scent drifted to his eleven-year-olds nose when he opened the back door. He hesitated; the teacher's note burning in his pocket, then hollered his usual after-school greeting. No answer.

Stephen Giroud dumped his books on the breakfast table and yanked out the paper from a back pocket. Angry fingers wadded it into a tight ball, then stuffed it in the trash bin under the sink. His parents wouldn't see the stupid note.

Pleased that he wouldn't have to face his mother's hysterics over Mrs. Wagner's tattle of a missed English assignment, he grabbed an apple from a Limoges bowl on the kitchen counter.

He checked the kitchen for the maid du jour. No one here. It was no real surprise. The Giroud family could never keep help because Mom was so "high-strung." That's what his father always said. Between her drinking and her temper, his mother scolded the staff frequently. She said they needed guidance, but Stephen knew, even at his age, that she loved the drama that went along with a problem maid.

A whiff of a stranger's aftershave told him that his mother's guest was a man.

A thought struck him: *If I'm very quiet, maybe I can listen to Mom and her visitor. Maybe they're talking about something interesting.* Stephen had long ago perfected his stealthy stride. He loved to spy on people: his parents, neighbors, even Mrs. Wagner.

His Keds were silent on the hardwood floor. Holding the apple, he halted at the corner separating the kitchen pantry and the hallway.

Glasses clinking together in what sounded like a toast. *Cocktails this early?* Goosebumps rose on his neck. This wasn't normal. His mother's laugh sounded deep and teasing. *She is flirting. I wonder with whom?* A man's reply, in tones so low that Stephen could not make out the words. She laughed again.

Weird.

Stephen dropped the apple as he rounded the corner into the parlor.

His mother sat draped over the sitting figure of their neighbor, Abraham Rosen. The pair sat on the white velvet davenport that Dad complained cost too much. Mr. Rosen leaned toward her on one elbow, balancing a martini while Mom giggled. His comb-over was askew, his suit wrinkled, and shoes unlaced. The cocktail table held a half-filled ashtray and Dad's silver-plated martini shaker.

They were so enthralled with each other that the eleven-year-old had to clear his throat to make himself known.

"Stephen." His mother slid off Mr. Rosen's lap. She stood, shaking her blond curls, trying to straighten her lilac silk skirt. High heels made her a little wobbly. "Stephen, you're home early." Her voice wavered.

Stephen was silent. His father taught him to keep his mouth closed if he couldn't think of anything to say. It was unwise to agitate his mother. Dad taught him that, too.

And yet this was so wrong.

Mr. Rosen was on his feet, smoothing his jacket and making for the front door. *He wouldn't even stay and face me like a man?* Stephen shouted after him. "Chicken!"

"Stephen," his mother whispered, dropping to the sofa. Her tone was almost a scold, but she knew better than to do that. "Don't jump to conclusions, honey."

The front door slammed. Stephen stared at his mother. "What kind of conclusions should I jump to, Mommy? What were you two doing? What's Dad going to say?"

"Stephen..." His mother looked away, looking for words to explain.

He knew what to say. He didn't care if he upset her. So what if his psychiatrist said he needed to control his anger? So what if he told his mother she was a whore and this fact hurt her feelings? The whole neighborhood saw this shameful behavior when Mr. Rosen came and went. *The whole world knew Elizabeth Giroud cheated on Father. Dad will be crushed. Everyone at school will know...that bitch.*

"This is what the pastor says is despicable behavior. I know because I looked it up in the dictionary. This is the kind of thing that sends you right to hell, Mother." His anger swelled in his chest, growing like a new life. His mind churned with emotion. He tried to sort this out, but an odd fog drifted in and out of his brain, preventing a complete thought. He stopped, then set himself straight. He was not going to let her win. Willing himself to slow his breathing, he concentrated on her face.

Elizabeth Giroud's face twisted in a cruel smirk. "I'm not going to let an eleven-year-old kid ruin my life." She searched his face.

Stephen caught a glimmer of another way to go with this. "What? You want this to be our little secret?" No, that would not work. She had been indiscreet. His father would find out from someone else. "That ship has sailed, Mother. I will tell Father."

"You manipulating twit," she began in disgust, then stopped. Her whole demeanor changed. Her face softened, and she chewed her lower lip in a child-like pose. Then she stood and lunged toward him. "Don't tell your father, please, Stephen." Her plea was a whine. Scarlet fingernails reached for his arm, but as he pulled away, they raked his skin.

Stephen cradled his arm, squeezing the three stripe-like wounds to make them look worse than they were. He wanted Mother to think she had hurt him. She tried to play the 'I love you' and 'I'm your mother' and 'You don't understand' scenes again. But now, they would not work. His love and sympathy for her evaporated. The emptiness inside him filled with disgust.

"Oh no. Oh, honey. I'm so sorry. I didn't mean to hurt you..." She stepped closer, still unsteady on her heels. He saw the pain in her mascaraed eyes. Was she acting? It didn't matter. She would pay for this.

Covering his arm, he turned away, moaning.

She took another step toward him, hand outstretched. From the corner of his eye, he saw she was in range. He whirled with his unin-jured arm to block her.

She tried to stop her momentum, but the heels undermined her balance. She reached out to him to steady herself. Stephen ducked, then reached out, his palm pushing her shoulder. His mother grabbed nothing but air. She wobbled for a half-second, still trying to right herself. Her face was set in sheer panic as she fell backwards into the cocktail table.

He heard an indelicate grunt as she landed hard. Tufts of curly blond hair clotted with skin and blood adhered to the corner of the heavy glass table. He peeked at her, prepared for another whiney plea. He was tired of her stupid justifications, tired of her lame excuses. He didn't care. He didn't want to listen to her ever again. No.

He took a quick inventory. He knew his psychiatrist would ask. What was he feeling? Guilt? Shock? Remorse?

More like relief, but he realized he couldn't tell the shrink that.

He squatted over his mother. She lay stretched out before him, her eyes sightless while her chest gave one great surge, then ceased moving. Blood oozed in a puddle on the white carpet under her head. Soon, it stopped as her heart quit pumping.

She would never embarrass him again.

Chapter Fifty-Seven

"WHAT THE HELL?" MEREDITH STIFFENED AS SHE GLARED AT HIM. "Why? That doesn't make sense. Did he say there won't be an investigation?"

Nick poured cold coffee into a cup and then looked at it with a disappointed squint. "Don't get your panties in a bunch." He walked across her living room, smiling at his mastery of yet another silly white man cliché.

"C'mon, Nick." She blew out an exasperated sigh.

He dropped into the white leather chair next to her, putting the coffee on the side table, untouched. He caught her gaze and held it. "Okay, okay. Here's the deal: Leahy had already contacted IA when Ferrua told him to call it off. Leahy said the Ell-tee wasn't happy, but this came from the top."

"The top? You mean the Sheriff?"

"Sounds like the top to me." He sipped the coffee.

"What the hell?"

Nick put his mug back on the side table and leaned toward Meredith. "Not normal protocol, is it? Sounds sketchy."

Meredith covered her face with her hands. "More than sketchy. I don't get it." Her hands dropped to her lap.

Nick was reluctant to bring the subject up. But if his hunch was right, it would explain a lot. "Leahy said from the top. Sheriff Flannery doesn't have any reason to drop this, right? Maybe someone else got to him."

Meredith's eyes widened. "Judge Giroud?"

Nick cocked his head sideways. "That's what I was thinking."

She groaned and sank back into the sofa. "In the hospital, he asked if I wanted his help to make this go away. I thought he was trying to make like a big man."

Nick waited.

"I told him no, anyway." She sat up, frowning. "You really think it was him?

"I never liked that guy." Nick shook his head.

"I can't believe he did this. It's wrong, against protocol. An investigation will protect me if the other driver changes his story. I certainly didn't want to have to endure an IA, but it's a necessary evil."

"Not to mention putting you on Flanagan's shit list." Nick chewed the inside of his lower lip.

"Aww." She sank back into the couch again, and he suspected she began calculating the damage.

Nick was satisfied that she had no hand in this. "Not much you can do. You can't go in and demand an investigation."

She sighed. "I guess not."

"Next time, tell the Judge to keep his hands in his pockets." Nick's jaw flexed.

Chapter Fifty-Eight

IT WAS TOO SOON TO GO BACK TO WORK, BUT SHE DID IT ANYWAY. She couldn't stand the idea of lounging around the house. She got bored just thinking about it.

Meredith had expected the headache, but the pain in her knee was a surprise. She plodded to the cafeteria for coffee, irritated that the coffee station in her office was out. She needed a cup and maybe a bagel. And some aspirin.

A few minutes later, she settled into a corner table. Her coffee sat on the chipped gray Formica, next to a glass of water and three Excedrin.

She could almost tell he was there. The way the air in the room changed. Her arm was stretched out for the mug when she heard Giroud.

"Meredith, I can't believe you came to work today. You should be at home, resting."

She managed a smile. "I'd go stir crazy. Besides, there's too much to do."

He slid into the seat across from her. "But Detective Reyes is more than capable."

She swallowed the aspirin, then sat back. Headache, knee...and now the aspirin would bring on heartburn. "No question about it. But I can't sit at home while he does everything."

"You should take better care of yourself." His face was solemn.

"What are you doing in here?" She made small talk while she searched his face for tells. Was he sincere or playing at some weird game? "I've never seen a judge in the cafeteria before. Don't you guys have a secret place with special judicial coffee?"

He smiled. The change of topic seemed to suit him. "I, too, needed a cup of coffee." He looked at the line-up at the cash register. "I will be right back."

When Giroud returned, he sat across from Meredith. He swirled in the cream with a plastic stirring stick. "The timing of your accident is unfortunate," he said. "I wanted to ask for your help at a polo match this weekend. Esparza, my groom, injured his arm. I can do all the grooming and loading, but I need a handler during the match so I can change horses." His eyes came up with an invitation.

Meredith's heart jumped at the idea of being near horses again. "I'd love to help. I'm sure I can do something."

"Maybe you can. The match is still two days away. You won't have to ride, just be sure the horses are ready—bridles fastened, cinch straps tight, drop the stirrups, that kind of thing."

"Just thinking about it makes my headache go away. I used to love being around horses."

He nodded. "I remember you said you had horses when you were a child."

She sat up. "I didn't own them. I rode other people's horses to exercise them. It helped pay tuition."

He leaned forward, making the conversation more private. "How old were you?" His face was close to hers.

She straightened, surprised at her need to put space between them. "I started riding when I was eight."

He waited.

"My father was in the SFPD Mounted Unit."

"Did he teach you to ride?"

Meredith nodded, as much an acknowledgment as she could muster.

Giroud stirred his coffee. "Were you close to him?"

She shrugged.

"Was he difficult?"

"You could say that." She paused. It wasn't an easy thing to say. There was a time when all this rolled around in her head, but that was long ago. "My father was pretty much absent during those years. He worked a lot. When he wasn't riding on duty, he was training officers and horses, making sure the stalls were clean, taking animals to the vet and farrier. He did it all."

"Sounds like quite a guy."

It was a matter of perspective, wasn't it? "He was my dad." Her gaze dipped to the coffee mug. "Aren't all dads like that? Spectacular in their own way." Dang, why was she telling him this? It wasn't normal for her. Why couldn't she keep her mouth shut? Reluctant to encourage him but, honestly, it felt so good to talk about it. "I mean, he had his faults. Everyone does. We never got along except around a horse. I learned early that was the way to establish a relationship with him." That was the only time he ever talked to her like she was a human being. There was the hope of a bond with him while horse-hair wafted in the air. The hope that he'd see how badly she wanted him to view her with respect. And the hope that maybe it would spill over into their lives at home.

The Judge took a sip of coffee.

"Like I said, he was always working." Her mind played through several scenes from her youth: him forgetting her 14th birthday party, mom struggling to change a flat tire alone, nights when he didn't come home from work at all. Hearing her mother crying, alone, in her bedroom.

"Does he live around here?" Giroud asked like he already knew the answer.

She sighed. "I don't have a clue. We don't talk anymore."

Giroud sat up straight. "I am sorry. I didn't mean to bring up an uncomfortable subject."

She scratched at the mug handle with her fingernail. "It's all right. I'm a big girl. I dealt with this years ago." It was a lie. She hadn't come to terms with their estrangement. She never would.

Mere resignation would have to do. But she wouldn't say any more about her father to Giroud. She already told him too much. At least she hadn't gotten into the sordid reason for the ending of her parents' marriage, that Dad left his family for some young piece who dumped him in the end, probably. For all she knew, Terence Ryan was alone, and she didn't care.

Giroud cleared his throat. "We don't always make the right decisions, especially when they involve people we love."

She bobbed her head in agreement, as she thought about her father and Richard. "You've got to wonder how much of these 'decisions' are based on lust versus love. For some people, those two emotions are the same."

"True. But the bottom line is to never hurt the one you love."

He was steering the conversation, but she couldn't make out the direction. "No one should hurt those they love. It happens when people put themselves first."

"Maybe loved ones don't recognize what is being done is motivated by love." He drained his mug.

"I don't get your point. It should be what's best for both." The judge's attempt at intimacy made her impatient. Where was this going?

His sigh was almost patronizing. He spoke so softly she had to lean toward him to hear. "I know what is best for you."

Her heart hammering, she said, "You presume too much." So, he knew what was best for her? He had some *cojones* if he believed that. What was he doing butting his nose into her life? He seemed to care about her, but…he…this crossed the line between deputies and jurists. This was about him messing with her professional life. What the hell? She reined in her anger and tried to answer calmly. She still had to show him some respect, right? *Some.* "You don't even know me."

"But I do know you." He smiled, staring into her eyes.

For the first time, a small tingle of fear inched into Meredith's head, a hunch that something was wrong. Then, a sudden spike of anger pushed the feeling away. She wouldn't participate in his fantasy. "I know you interfered with the accident IA."

When the judge tried to protest, she held up a hand to shush him. She worked hard to control her temper. "I didn't need your help. I would've come out fine. Don't assume that you can meddle in my life. I'd appreciate you not doing it again."

"All right, Meredith. All right. I stand corrected. I am sorry for any problem I created." His downcast eyes should have made her think he was sorry.

She didn't believe him for a minute. She stood and limped away before Giroud could say anything more.

Chapter Fifty-Nine

TUESDAY WAS A RARE MORNING WITHOUT RAIN. GIROUD WAS grateful he didn't have to bundle up in a raincoat. From his usual spot, sheltered among the redwood trees on the southern edge of Meredith's property, he could see most of the house's living area. There were no window coverings. Why should there be? The house was isolated and surrounded by dense forest. *All the better to see you, my dear.*

Except he was not watching Meredith. She'd gone to work at her usual time this morning. He was observing Blondie rummaging through cabinets, looking for food, and drinking the beautiful deputy's scotch. Then the man stretched out on the sofa to watch television.

It disgusted Giroud that Meredith would allow such a lay-about in her home, much less in her life. What did she see in this moron? She did seem attached to him. Why was he living in her house?

Giroud shook his head. There were always obstacles to things of great value. Tricky situations required a delicate touch. It was time for action. He could not allow someone else to dwell in his special place, Meredith Ryan's heart.

Giroud crept through the brush and mounted the back stairs to the deck. The muscles in his back twitched in anticipation. He flexed his biceps while grabbing a piece of ornamental driftwood, then hid it behind his body. He'd found the wood in the sideyard earlier. He liked the heft of it.

Giroud glanced over the railing at the fifty-foot drop. Below was a rocky cliff with ferns and brambles bottoming out to a hard-packed running path. It was as steep as he remembered. No way anyone could survive the fall.

The French door was unlocked. Giroud opened it and took a bold step inside.

Blondie jumped off the couch, puffing up his chest. "What the fuck? Who are you?"

"The next person to move into her heart." Giroud didn't expect this fool to understand his answer. "There won't be room for two."

A quizzical look flashed across Blondie's face as he stepped closer. Giroud backed out to the deck, baiting the other man to follow.

Blondie rushed Giroud. When he got within two feet, Giroud sidestepped. Blondie had too much momentum to stop. The Judge swung the driftwood like a bat. It connected with a solid thump at the base of his victim's neck. Rolling awkwardly onto the rail, Blondie put up a weak struggle trying to stay upright. Giroud grabbed the man by his wobbling knees, tipping him up and over the railing. A beat-up sandal caught on the deck rail as Blondie's shrieking echoed downward. He thumped into the underbrush, rolled down the slope, and was lost to Giroud's view. A slight scuff mark on the redwood was the only sign Blondie had ever been there.

For a moment, Giroud was alarmed that someone might have heard the scream. No, he thought, looking around. No one heard anything.

He wiped his fingerprints off the door, picked up the sandal, then tossed it over the rail. This kind of thing was getting easier...and oddly satisfying, too.

Smiling to himself, he fished a piece of paper from his pocket. The paper drifted to the deck as he left.

Chapter Sixty

MEREDITH STIRRED HER TEA UNTIL THE TEA BAG BROKE OPEN. "AW, darn it. What a mess." She should've stuck with coffee. She pushed the white ceramic mug aside. Checking the almost empty room, she noted a knot of clerks sipping coffee in the corner.

"You weren't listening to me." Nick sounded like a neglected housewife.

"Yes, I was. You said we should make another try at Faye. The Ell-tee is threatening to turn this over to the DA's office." She pulled the mug back, inspected the mess, and pushed it away again.

Nick sat back. "Okay. What's going on?"

"What do you mean?"

"You have great short-term memory, but you're not listening. We have a real problem here. If we're going to be partners, we have to work this together. I won't be giving you orders or telling you what to do."

Her shoulders relaxed. He was right. But this thing with Giroud was seriously bugging her. "Okay. I've let the Judge distract me from the case."

"I told you." His mouth drew back into a grim smile. "He wants to get into your *pantalettas*."

"I guess so. I should be straighter with him."

"He's manipulative as hell. He used his horses like a pedophile uses puppies."

She nodded, closing her eyes to change her train of thought. "Enough of him. Do you want me to contact Faye again? She didn't seem to like you very much."

"Yeah, I can't see any other place to go with this investigation. We know Sutton did the homicide. He could be anywhere now. We need help finding him. But I don't want the DA's office taking this over. Don't like to leave a case unfinished."

"I'll call her now." Meredith gathered their trash.

Across the room, a group of clerks wound their way through the maze of tables toward the door. One, a tall, slender black woman, nodded to the detectives. Meredith recognized her as a particularly friendly civil division supervisor.

Meredith smiled. "Trisha, what's up?"

Trisha stopped, pulling out a chair. "Did you hear?" She sat down as if she couldn't bear her own weight.

"Hear what?" Both detectives asked simultaneously.

Trisha's somber voice lowered. "Astrid Vachon's been murdered. Do you remember her, from my office?" The woman's gaze searched Meredith's face like the detective might have answers to her questions.

Meredith was stunned to silence.

"What happened?" Nick recovered faster. "Do you know any details?"

Trisha's head moved from side to side, still unable to conceal her shock. "Not much. A friend from Santa Rosa PD called. They found her body in a dumpster behind a gas station in the north end of town." The woman's face contorted into a terrified mask. "She was strangled."

Nick and Meredith were silent as they digested the news. Trisha blinked back tears. "I've got to get to my office. This is so horrible. I'm considering bringing in a counselor for my staff."

With Trisha out of earshot, Meredith eyed Nick. "I don't know about you, but I'm going to find out who's the lead in that homicide and have a chat."

Nick spoke more deliberately. "No, I'll do that. We'll talk to him together if you want. For now, let's get hold of Faye and get her up here."

Meredith was about to agree but stopped when she noticed Ferrua coming their way. The lieutenant met them near the cash register. His face was serious. "Ryan, I need to see you in my office."

"Lieutenant, can it wait? We just heard one of the court clerks was murdered. We saw her just a few nights ago. We need to talk to—"

Ferrua put a hand on Meredith's shoulder. "No, it can't wait. C'mon." He steered her toward the door.

She turned back to Nick for any hint of what this might be about. Nick shrugged, following them to VCI. Her stomach clenched as Ferrua closed the door, leaving Nick outside.

Meredith stood by the closed door, quelling the urge to run through it. Ferrua's face twisted in a knot of suffering.

Judging by the look on the Ell-tee's face, this couldn't be good.

The lieutenant stood stiffly next to his desk. He motioned for her to sit in the chair, then propped a substantial hip on his desk. "Meredith, do you have a brother? David Ryan?"

She clamped her teeth shut on her apprehension. "Yes."

"Is he staying with you? Living with you?" Ferrua opened his hands in a rolling gesture meant to encourage her to talk.

What now? What did he do? "Yes, he's staying with me, temporarily. Is he in some kind of trouble?"

The lieutenant's head bobbed. "But not the kind of trouble you might think." He rose and put a hand on her shoulder.

She looked at his hand, then his face. This had to be serious. Ferrua was prone to touching. She'd heard he'd been warned about it.

"Lieutenant, you're scaring me. What's going on?"

He yanked his hand away, as if he suddenly remembered not to be so familiar. "Meredith, your brother has been found near the Russian River. It appears he fell off your deck. He's badly injured."

Ferrua clasped his arms across his chest. "In fact, he's in a coma." His eyes found hers. "It's not looking good, Meredith."

She struggled to catch her breath. She heard her own voice but couldn't make out the words. Were there words? No, it sounded more like a quiet wail.

Then she found them. "Where is he now?"

"Community Hospital. Nick'll drive you." Ferrua leaned back to his phone, punched in an extension, and told Nick to get his ass into the office.

Chapter Sixty-One

MEREDITH'S BODY ACHED WITH WEARINESS. SHE'D SPENT TOO MUCH time in hospitals recently. Still, this time, it was worse. It was her brother. Her little brother. Studying his rigid face, she re-played the tapes of the conversation with the neurologist. *Diffuse brain injury... a 40 percent chance of recovery... brain stem damage... decerebrate response.* David's seizure-like posturing affected all four limbs. The reaction to the injury made him stiff. A pair of IV needles poked from his veins. Both arms were secured to the bed frame so he couldn't hurt himself. Monitors, IV stands, clear plastic lines, wires, remote control devices, oxygen tubes, and a hundred things she could not name surrounded his bed. His left side was affected: his arm and leg were extended stiffly, fingers flexed. He looked like an angelic pincushion. But, Meredith reflected, David was no angel. Even as a child, he'd been full of mischief.

The memory of her father's deep, rumbling voice sounded like a dog's growl. "Where is that brat?"

"He's at the school skateboarding with Jeremy."

"You go get that little fucker so I can beat the crap out of him."

Meredith's mind spun through the memory of the beating David got after she summoned him. He'd stolen a five-dollar bill from

Dad's wallet. David admitted it, then Dad took his leather belt off and strapped him good.

After Dad left for the bar, Meredith and her mother tended to David's injuries. She recalled pushing her mother away from David, so her mother's tears wouldn't sting his lacerated back.

A year later, when Meredith was fourteen and David ten, the pair was trying to ignore an argument in the next room. Daddy was laying down the law. Mother was pleading with him and crying again. Sister held on to brother tight.

She couldn't protect him, not now. They were both grown-ups, capable of taking care of themselves. Obviously, he'd done a poor job. *And me? I can't sustain a relationship. Everyone I've ever loved has either left or died. All I have is my career. All of it, all the stuff with my father while growing up made me different. I was destined to be alone.*

Nick interrupted her reverie. She was relieved to see him, the one person able to lighten her burden. Even so, his eyes held sadness.

"Hey. How is he?"

"As bad as he looks."

"I went to your house. Peters caught this case, so I walked through with him."

"Did you find anything? Was he drinking?"

"We found this." Nick pushed his cell phone at her. The screen contained a photo of a piece of white paper with the word 'sorry' on it. It looked like it had been printed from a computer printer.

"Sorry?" She looked at her partner in disbelief. *Sorry?*

Meredith pushed the phone away. "I don't believe this."

"What? You think I made this up?"

"No, I didn't mean that. I'm sorry it came out that way. I mean, I don't believe he tried to commit suicide."

"It looks like he tried." He spoke softly as if it could lessen the weight of his words.

His arm draped around her shoulders. She twisted her wedding ring, considering Nick's words.

Chapter Sixty-Two

THE STREETS WERE DRY WHEN NICK DROVE MEREDITH HOME IN HIS truck. The sun hadn't come out, but at least it wasn't raining. The partners were silent. Nick knew to keep quiet as Meredith sorted through the debris that made up her life.

She spoke up abruptly. "I've got Faye's phone number in my briefcase. I'll call her when I get home."

Nick nodded. "Okay, good." He was hoping she'd change her focus. It would be tough enough when she got home. He'd cleaned up after the deputies. Fingerprint powder all over the house was a crappy welcome home.

"In a way, it's a blessing the nurses won't let me stay there." She fingered her seat belt.

"Yeah, we've got work to do. Tomorrow, I'll take another shot at Theda. Maybe she knows something that she doesn't realize is important."

"Does being in protective custody help her recollection?"

"Funny, but yes. I think she feels safe in jail where Sutton can't get to her."

On Guerneville Road, the canopy of trees blocked the opaque

light. The world got colder. Meredith turned sideways to watch Nick's face. "I'm concerned about Giroud, too. He's pushing, trying to get too close too fast. I don't know what he wants from me."

"Well, then stop encouraging him." Nick mentally kicked himself. He knew that sounded patronizing. Relationships were never simple. He wasn't sure what she wanted.

"I'm not encouraging him. I don't want his attention. I'm having a hard time drawing the line in the sand with him. He keeps pressing. Because he's a judge, I don't want to piss him off."

"And he's using his position as leverage?" This wasn't a surprise. He'd suspected it. He'd seen this kind of behavior before, but so close to home made it especially abhorrent.

"No, not overtly. But he won't accept my 'no.'" Her sigh came from her depths. "Maybe confusion creeps into our conversations. Maybe I sound ambivalent enough that he can grab my attention. You see, I feel like I need to be polite and respectful due to his position."

"I get that. It'd be professional suicide to estrange him. Not only could he prejudice your cases, but he could influence other judges." But he felt she had more to say.

"Right, my thinking exactly." She looked out the window. Vineyards with low spots flooded, wild grape vines tangling in redwoods, and soggy wetlands, but she didn't see any of it. "I get so confused sometimes. I mean, it's only been a few months since Richard died. I feel alone, but I don't want another man in my life to fill the hole. Especially a high roller like Giroud. I'm definitely not in his league."

"Fuck that idea, Meredith." He didn't like to hear her talk like that. "You've got more class in your little finger..."

She held her hand up, stopping his protest. "You're taking that the wrong way. I mean, I can't be a socialite like him. Cocktail parties, opera, and polo. I don't have the energy that it requires, and my BS meter won't shut down."

Nick smiled at the image of Meredith holding a martini and listening to a windbag politician, trying to be tactful.

"Then there's the creep factor."

"Huh?" Creep factor?

Meredith tipped her head in a way he thought was particularly endearing. "Yeah. There's something creepy about him. He won't accept a 'no'. Today, in 2014, there are rules against pressuring women for sexual favors. He hasn't gone there yet, but I see it coming."

"Have you gone to Leahy to complain?"

"No." Her face twisted in disgust. "Of all staff officers, he wouldn't take it seriously. Even if I had evidence, which I don't."

Relief filled his chest as he considered her words. He was pleased that Meredith didn't have feelings for Giroud. He'd been unsure what she thought about the slimeball in light of her confusion. Now he was clear.

"Well, okay." He set his shoulders back, taking the lead. "Whatever comes, I'll be on your side. You know that." He tipped his head, searching her face.

A weak smile emerged. "I know, Nick. You're always there."

"I have an idea. Let's concentrate on catching Sutton and doing what we can for your brother. Those should be priorities."

Back in more familiar turf, her voice was strong. "What about your mother?"

"I'm working on that. I figured out a way to get her to the doctor's office tomorrow. So, I'll be gone for a couple of hours."

The Chevy truck pulled into her driveway. "And expect SRPD to be contacting you about the Vachon homicide. Brad Kingston is in charge. I talked to him today while you were at the hospital. I gave him your cell number."

Meredith nodded, but she wasn't looking forward to the interview. She slid out of the seat and walked to her front door.

Nick opened the passenger window to yell, "Call me after you talk to Faye."

She held up a hand in acknowledgment while she fished for her keys. The front door was swinging open as his truck pulled down the driveway.

The timing of David's accident seemed too close to be a coincidence. In three months, Meredith had lost her husband to a hit-and-run accident, survived an officer-involved shooting, and now this. It was more bad luck than anyone deserved.

Just one thing. Nick didn't believe in luck.

He couldn't say why, but when he turned out of Meredith's driveway, he turned left on Mirabel Road instead of right. This would take him the long way around.

Irritated, he searched for a turnout or driveway. A half block away, he found what he was looking for, a gate with a short apron that led to an abandoned pasture. He drove into the apron and slammed on the brakes. Tires skidded on loose gravel as he came to a stop inches away from the bumper of a black Mercedes SLS550.

He knew this car.

Nick flipped out his cell and punched in the code for dispatch. He recognized the voice who answered. "Hi, Maria. It's Reyes from VCI. I don't have access to a computer. Can you run a plate for me?"

Three minutes later, he thanked the dispatcher and closed the phone. He sat in the car, thinking. He could find no reason why this car should be there. No logical reason at all.

He called Meredith's cell. When she answered, he plunged right in. "Hey, Giroud's car is parked about a half a block from your house in a pasture driveway. Lock your doors."

She was quiet for a moment, then had a question. "It's the pasture on the north side of my house?"

"Yeah. He's got no business there." He snapped, irritated she didn't see the trouble after their conversation minutes ago. "What if he's watching you right now?"

She spoke slowly. "Nick, that's an old pasture. It's almost flat terrain. He might keep horses there."

"That's a long shot, and you know it. This is too close to be a coincidence."

"Yeah, but there is reasonable doubt in your mind now, isn't there?"

"Lock your damn doors."

"I did."

"I'm coming back to your house."

"Okay. This creeps me out, but he's a judge, you know. Judges don't do this stalking thing. Do they?"

Just the same, Nick was at her front door two minutes later to check inside the house. Outside, he didn't find anyone. No footprints, but the undergrowth was more leaves than mud. He didn't find anything to tell him why Giroud's car was parked so close by.

Chapter Sixty-Three

MEREDITH ANSWERED THE DOOR TO FACE DETECTIVE BRAD Kingston. With an apology, the lanky detective wiped his shoes on the mat. In a blue sport coat and khakis, he looked like the classic police investigator. The short brown hair and mustache clinched it. "I'm sorry for coming so late, but I needed to talk to you as soon as I could."

She waved him in, reluctant but still wanting to get this over with. "Not a problem. I know you want to get everyone interviewed as soon as possible. Coffee?"

"No, I'd rather get right down to it." These things were touchy. Jurisdiction issues were a big deal. For cops from one agency to interfere in another's investigation was like a poodle pissing on a terrier's fire hydrant. It wasn't illegal, but it wasn't welcome. Giroud's ties to the victim were entirely too close. Even though Meredith couldn't prove it, the judge was somehow involved in Vachon's homicide.

Meredith pointed to a chair and sat opposite on the edge of the sofa. When his notebook was open, pen poised, he asked, "Are you aware that Astrid Vachon was found murdered this morning?"

She nodded. "That kind of news gets around fast at the courthouse."

"I understand you saw Astrid two nights ago."

"Yes, at Cabanas."

"Was she alone?"

"No, she wasn't."

He sighed. "Ms. Ryan…"

"It's Meredith."

"Okay, Meredith. This isn't court. You can help me out here."

"This is kind of awkward for me." She rubbed her eyes. "I'm not sure how much you want to know."

"Meredith, I'm a violent crimes investigator. Just because a Superior Court Judge is involved doesn't mean I'm going to look the other way. Tell me everything. I've already talked to your partner. I want to know what you saw."

"Okay." Meredith leaned her elbows on her knees, propping her chin up on her hands. "Here's the deal: She was there with Judge Stephen Giroud. I think he asked her because he wanted to make me jealous. You see, I think he's been…" She paused. "…personal and professional boundaries."

Kingston started to speak, but Meredith cut him off. "I know it sounds crazy, but he's been showing up places where I am, sending flowers. That kind of thing."

"No, it doesn't sound crazy." Kingston smiled. "There is no reason he shouldn't ask you out, is there?"

Her heart felt like someone grabbed it and squeezed. She twisted her wedding ring. "Well, yes. I lost my husband four months ago. He knows because he was at the funeral. I'm not ready to see anyone. He doesn't get that."

"I'm sorry for your loss." The detective's eyes searched hers for a moment. "Did you know Judge Giroud before your husband was killed?"

"No."

"Not even in a trial?"

"No."

Kingston dropped his pen on his pad in frustration. "Your husband knew him then?"

Meredith saw the suspicion in his eyes. "He told me he met my husband at a golf tournament."

"Meredith, what aren't you telling me?"

She took a breath. "Here's the thing. Richard didn't play golf. And he never told me about meeting the judge. I would've expected him to."

"So you don't believe him?"

Meredith shook her head.

A heartbeat later, Kingston said, "Okay, let's move on. Did you talk to Astrid that night?"

"Yes, in the ladies' room. She recognized me and introduced herself. Then, she made sure I knew she was with Giroud. She called him, 'my man.' She said he was totally taken with her."

"What do you mean she recognized you?"

"From the Quad shooting. I guess she was in the crowd or something. It happened just outside her office."

Kingston's eyes narrowed. "I thought your name sounded familiar. Now I remember."

"Great." A sad smile crossed her lips.

"Being a hero ain't all it's cracked up to be, is it?" Kingston's comment encouraged her to truthfulness. "It's tough to do something against your nature while everyone slaps you on the back."

"I wish it never happened. I never wanted this." No matter how many times she said it, she didn't think anyone really got it. She dreamt about the burst of blood across Rusty's chest almost every night.

Kingston smiled like he understood. "Let's get back to Astrid. Did she say anything else?"

She sighed. "She said I needed a makeover."

Kingston laughed. "What? Out of the blue?"

"She said she always liked to look her best for her man and that I needed to spice my love life up a little." Meredith couldn't help a wry smile. "She was fishing, I think. Not sure what for. But she asked me if I was enjoying the dinner with my boyfriend."

"She was wrong, by the way. You're attractive just the way you are." He flashed a grin. "You think it was more than casual chatter?"

She shrugged. "It felt like it, yes. I thought she was after something, but I couldn't tell. I didn't want to find out what."

"You were there with two men, right?" His eyes swept over his notes. He put a finger on the page. "Your partner, Nick Reyes, and your brother, David Ryan."

"That's right."

"Do you think she could've been asking about Reyes and your brother for a reason?"

"Like what?"

"I'm asking you. Take a wild guess." Kingston waited, his pen resting on his pad.

She thought it over. What was Astrid's motivation for fishing around about Nick and David? Meredith came up with nothing. She scrolled through the inventory of bullshit excuses she'd heard on the street. Then, a thought flashed through her mind.

"You think the Judge put her up to find out who my brother was? He knows Nick, but he's never met David."

"Your brother wasn't at your husband's funeral?"

She'd hoped he wouldn't pick up on that. Her face grew warm with the embarrassment of her brother missing Richard's funeral. She sank into the sofa. She didn't want to get any deeper into this. "He was on the road. He's a musician. He didn't know until two days ago."

Kingston nodded, paging through his notes.

Meredith filled the silence with a question. "So, am I a suspect because she told me to get a makeover?"

Kingston straightened. "I have no idea what went on in that bathroom. But look at the facts: You've got a dead husband from a felony hit and run, a Superior Court judge sniffing around after you, a brother who throws himself over your balcony. I have to consider you're spinning out of control. Five months ago, you shot a man dead at the courthouse and got a promotion, and you had an on-duty car accident last week. Let's say I know nothing about you. Based on the last six months, who's to say you're not outside that restaurant naked in the back seat of a car with this judge? Maybe hard to prove, maybe not."

Then, he went for the jugular: "Plus, you know every police procedure, every method we use. You'd cover your tracks like a pro."

Meredith squirmed as she looked at the situation from his point of view.

Kingston tapped her knee with his notepad. "It's probably not you, but I got to cover the possibility."

When she could breathe again, she asked the question that had been churning around her brain. "Are you looking at the Judge for this?"

"You know how it works." Kingston's expression was guarded. "We're looking at everyone who knew her."

Meredith winced. "Yeah, yeah, yeah. I know you've gotta say that." That was the only answer a good detective would give to that question. The Judge was a powerful man on a major career trajectory. He'd been front and center in local politics since he arrived. She'd heard vague rumors of a senate campaign in two years. You didn't put a person like him on the hot seat until you had solid evidence. She didn't know what Kingston had, but it wasn't enough to point to Giroud. Yet.

Kingston flipped his notebook closed. He made a production of putting it into his jacket. "Let me ask you a question: you're an investigator, who would you look at first?"

"Giroud." She studied the detective's eyes. Deep brown dilated to the low light in the room framed with crow's feet. She knew what his eyes had seen. The same as hers. He wasn't a fool. "He's the last person she was seen with."

Kingston gave nothing up. "What about motive?"

"I can speculate." She remembered the encounter in the bathroom. "Vachon had a mouth on her, for sure. She could've pushed him, challenged him, seen something...I don't know." She ran a hand through her hair. "I don't know. But the more he's around, the more I'm sure there's something wrong with him."

"Meaning?"

It was hard to put into words. "He doesn't take no for an answer. I've been as diplomatic as I can be because of his position, but he puts himself in my path all the time. You know that I wrecked a car in a pursuit a few days ago?"

"Yeah, I heard."

"Well, Giroud got to someone in my department and got the IA dropped. And, he admitted to doing it." She flung her arms up in irritation.

"Sounds like he's infatuated with you."

"No." She couldn't keep the skepticism out of her reply. Nick said the same thing, but Meredith didn't see it like that. He didn't even know her. "There's more to it than that."

Kingston's mouth set into a thin line below his neatly groomed mustache.

She had to ask. "Have you spoken to him yet?"

"Yes, but it was brief, and I didn't get what I wanted. I have an appointment with him in the morning before court."

She nodded, not sure if Kingston was dodging the question. "What was your take on him?"

He considered his words. "I'll need to talk to him again to form a full picture."

Dodging, Meredith thought. "Really?"

Kingston rose. "I'll leave it at that, for now. Thanks for your time, Meredith." She took his extended hand and followed him to the door, stomach churning. Had she conveyed the almost obsessive pressure Giroud put on her? She sighed. Maybe it didn't pertain to Kingston's investigation. This was his case.

At the front door, his hand paused on the handle. His eyes probed hers. "Watch your six, detective."

Then he left.

Chapter Sixty-Four

"I TOLD YOU IT WASN'T A PROBLEM. TAKE WHAT TIME YOU NEED," Nick repeated. "You can look up the doctor for a progress report, and I'll grab something at the cafeteria here before we go back to the office. You getting any sleep?" At the risk of nagging, he had to ask. He was concerned about her fatigue and stress level.

Meredith rubbed her bloodshot eyes. "Off and on. I'm sure I get more than it feels like." Once again, it ran through her head. "I just can't believe he tried to kill himself." Her brown eyes latched onto Nick's. "This feels all wrong. David's a flake, but he's never been depressed or suicidal." She seemed to plead for him to agree.

"Maybe you didn't know him as well as you thought. He's been hitting the sauce since he came back."

"No, he wouldn't do this." Nick, obviously, was taking the wider view. She changed the subject. "How's your mother? What'd the doctor say?"

"More tests." He sighed. "My sister, Sofia, has taken over her care. She and her husband are moving Mom to Modesto the day after tomorrow. There's an MRI at Sofia's clinic next week. The doctor up here didn't seem too worried."

Meredith's mouth twisted with distaste. "Of course not. She's not *his* mother."

Nick pulled up to the hospital portico. "Hop out. I'll go park and catch up with you inside."

The door slammed behind her. Nick glanced over his shoulder, pulling into the main parking lot. He prowled around, searching for an empty space. He found one in the back, against the back fence, under a tree. It was about as far from the front entrance as he could get. He didn't like parking under trees, especially in the winter when there was little foliage to keep the bird crap off his truck.

He pushed the key fob to lock the Chevy. Leaning into his windshield, he picked at a damp sycamore leaf plastered to the glass.

In his row, a black Mercedes SLS550 sedan sat parked two cars down. He wouldn't have seen it had it not been for the leaf.

Interest piqued, he strolled over to the car. A casual glance revealed it was empty. He checked the bumpers for any stickers, tabs, or anything that might reveal something about the owner. Some cops get good at remembering license numbers. But this one didn't pop out for Nick. He'd notice next time.

Next time.

Nick yanked out his cell phone and flipped it open to call dispatch. After the dispatcher read him the registration, she asked, "Hey, isn't that a judge?"

Not wanting to spend any more time on the phone, he grunted a thank you and disconnected. He hurried to meet up with Meredith, thinking that Giroud was just about everywhere she was, wasn't he?

Made him kind of wonder about David's fall.

Chapter Sixty-Five

MEREDITH POURED A HALF GLASS OF PINOT NOIR AND SANK INTO THE plush leather sofa. Gus hopped up and kneaded her lap, purring shamelessly. She needed to eat but decided to sit with the cat. She was tired and feeling low. This day had gone from bad to worse. Nothing was happening with their homicide investigation. The partners spent the day driving by Sutton's old haunts and talking up former associates but had turned up nothing new. It was like he'd dropped off the face of the earth.

Leahy was rattling his saber: threatening to send in the DA's investigators to review the case. Maybe they could find another angle to work. While she and Nick were all for a fresh pair of eyes, they still had one slim chance to pursue. Meredith had left four voicemail messages for Faye Zelman, who hadn't called back. Meredith was tempted to push Leahy for another trip to San Luis Obispo.

On the way home from the office, Meredith stopped at the hospital. David's condition hadn't changed. She'd missed seeing his doctor, too. She left a message, but experience told her not to expect any callback.

A soft knocking at her front door jarred her out of her self-pity. She didn't feel like seeing anyone now. She wanted to be alone.

Gus squeaked a protest, trotting off to the laundry room when she rose.

She peeked through the peephole and almost dropped her glass. *Giroud*.

He would have seen the lights on so she couldn't pretend she wasn't here. She debated whether to ignore him. The man was too pushy. Maybe she could make him understand that she didn't have the energy to start up a new friendship, much less a romance. She took a deep breath as she pulled the door open.

"Hello." His smile was genuine, his eyes bright.

"Stephen, what are you doing here?" The words were out before she could stop them. She sounded so rude, but now that it was out there, she knew it would set the tone for the rest of his visit.

"I thought I'd see if you had eaten yet. I know you are busy these days, so I thought I'd—"

"That's very kind, but you've driven out for nothing. I'm in for the evening." She shifted position so she could close the door.

A gust of wind blew brown leaves over the threshold. Standing in a tee-shirt and jeans, she shivered. It was going to be cold tonight, down in the 40s.

He took a step toward her, and the toe of his shoe slipped inside. "Well, how about I find something for us here?" He looked relaxed in a cable knit sweater and khakis, yet she felt his determination.

She straightened. She was feeling pressured and didn't like it.

With his forearm and hand, Giroud pushed the door open.

Meredith took a step closer to him. They were almost nose-to-nose. "No." She let the single syllable dangle between them.

His smile faded as he hesitated. He didn't advance. "Stop playing at this."

"No. I'm not playing. I'm dead serious. I am not interested in a relationship." Her chest was tight. She didn't like scenes, and this had the makings of an ugly one. She hated saying these things to anyone.

Giroud studied her. "Stop it." His voice was as soft as velvet. His brows drew together. He was staring at her like his attention would make her change her mind.

"Stop what? I've told you I can't do this. I've been clear, but you don't seem to get it." She squared herself to him, ready for another protest.

He grabbed her wrist, putting his face so close to her that she couldn't focus on him. The words tumbled out, as if he'd been waiting to say this. "Quit pretending. There's no one around to see you play the grieving widow."

Meredith twisted out of his grip. The wine spilled. The glass slipped from her fingers and shattered on the floor. The violence galvanized her energy. Certain now that limits had to be set, she pushed his chest with both hands. "You don't know what you're talking about. I'm not playing at anything. You have to leave. Now."

Over her shoulder, Giroud glanced around the room, then his gaze settled on Meredith's face. "Okay, maybe it is a little too soon. I'll go now, but I will be back. Then, we will have some important things to discuss, like our future together and creating our legacy."

Legacy?

He would have kept talking, pressuring, but Meredith pushed him out and slammed the door. She turned the deadbolt and leaned against the coolness of the door. She slid down to the tile floor awash with wine and broken glass, listening to her wild heartbeat thumping in her ears.

Chapter Sixty-Six

"You think I can take this seriously with no proof?" Sergeant Leahy pushed himself back from his desk. He slapped his arms across his chest, his lips puckered in a smug smile.

"Really? I thought you might be interested in protecting me." Meredith's imagination saw this issue taking flight, wings flapping in the breeze, soaring in thermals, and being everywhere but where it should be—on her boss' mind.

He leaned toward her. "From who? A Superior Court Judge? You're crazy. He's got no reason to pester you. Ryan, get over yourself." He settled back into his chair, his focus on scrolling through his cell phone. "Besides, you have a homicide to work. Not making too much progress, are you?" Without waiting for her answer, he continued. "I'd spend more time on that if I were you, instead of flaunting yourself all over the county trying to catch a new husband."

Struggling to contain her fury, she rose. "You're saying you aren't going to help me?"

He continued tapping his phone. "Go on. You've got work to do."

She squared her shoulders and cleared her throat. "Sergeant

Leahy, I'm going to run this up the chain of command. I'm going to Lieutenant Ferrua."

He sneered at her, then resumed tapping. "Go for it."

TWENTY MINUTES LATER, she was in her lieutenant's office.

"As much as I hate to agree with Leahy, he's right this time." Ferrua tossed a pen across his desk. "I believe you, but Giroud's not a member of this department, so he doesn't have to operate by our rules. He's an appointed official, but he's treated the same as Joe Citizen when it comes to crimes. In this case, he hasn't committed any crime. You need something more than circumstantial evidence. You need physical proof."

Meredith slumped deeper into the chair across from Ferrua's desk. "Oh man," she moaned. She understood Leahy not helping, but Ferrua?

The lieutenant's lips drew into an apologetic look. "I wish I could help. This guy is powerful and has a lot of friends. He won't give a second thought to withdrawing his endorsement of the Sheriff in the election this fall. There has to be a solid case before we take action as a department."

She sat up. She couldn't give up. Giroud's behavior was escalating. He scared her last night. He'd been so aggressive.

"What kind of evidence do I need?"

Ferrua blew a snort of exasperation. "Short of a full confession? How about a video or audio tape of him peeking in your window or admitting his actions? Have you thought about a restraining order?"

Twisting her wedding ring, Meredith grimaced at the idea. "If I could get another judge to sign one, it wouldn't necessarily prevent him from contacting me. If he did, it would mean a citation, then a court appearance later. He is too smooth. Another judge would believe him over me any day."

"It could work." Ferrua's answer packed less conviction than she'd hoped for. He wasn't convinced, either. Why wouldn't he support her?

She stood, catching and holding his attention. With a challenge growing in her mind, she said, "I'll get proof. He is stalking me. He needs to be stopped."

Chapter Sixty-Seven

STILL SMARTING FROM THE BRASS' REFUSAL TO HELP, MEREDITH left a note on Nick's desk, grabbed her raincoat, and left the office. She needed some fresh air.

Slipping the keys into the door lock of her Subaru, she considered her options. Her head wasn't on the Sutton case now. It would have to wait. She wasn't sure how far she would take the stalking issue. Right now, what she wanted the most was to see her brother's blue eyes.

She made her way through the morning traffic and found a parking space near the front entrance of Community Hospital. Getting out of the driver's seat, she marveled that she'd gotten this far without paying attention to the road. She'd been thinking through the evidence suggesting David tried to kill himself.

She dismissed the suicide note early on. David didn't know where her printer was, much less where her laptop was stashed. She'd checked with Peters. Neither piece of equipment was out when deputies arrived. A scuff on the handrail suggested a struggle, that David fought for his life. Although Peters seemed to dismiss the scuff, yes, it was a new mark. But nothing directly tied it to her brother's unwillingness to go over the railing. These clues told *her* that someone orchestrated David's accident, intending it to be his death. There was no way he would take his own life.

Meredith popped her trunk, intending to leave her Beretta inside. She hesitated. Considering she was in the middle of a homicide investigation, however cold the trail, she decided to keep her weapon. She clipped the holster to her waistband.

Pushing open the hospital doors, she was greeted with the cacophony she had grown used to. The smell, not so much. Antiseptics, cleaning products, and alcohol assaulted her nostrils. She was sure she'd never get used to that odor.

She'd called the nurses' station on the way to get an update on David's condition. The good news was that he hadn't worsened; the bad: no improvement. He'd had a CT scan today, and the doctor would be in touch with her with the results. Meredith had no grand expectations for this visit, but felt she needed to be with her brother. She planned to sit down, hold his hand, and talk to him. Lost in the bustle of normal hospital activity, there was the promise of anonymity.

She settled in with no distractions. The bedside chair was not designed with comfort in mind, but she didn't care. She was with her brother.

David was, indeed, the same with his breathing assisted by a ventilator, long tubes disappearing down his throat. He lay in a quiet position that did not appear restful, his arms still restrained. Aside from the lacerations on his cheeks and forehead, one would think he was playing at sleeping. She took his hand, squeezing his long musician's fingers, and spoke as if he could hear her. "How did you get here, David? How did this happen? I don't believe you jumped."

She didn't expect an answer. She hoped articulating her concerns would start her in a direction that might find answers. There'd been no obvious bruising...

"Meredith."

Her head shot up, irritated at the intrusion. The last person she needed to see.

"Stephen."

He swept into the room, sophisticated in an elegant charcoal suit.

His smile was tentative. "I came to visit a neighbor and saw your car in the lot...and here you are." He stood before her, within arm's reach.

"What are you doing?" She couldn't keep her skepticism out of her voice.

His smile faded. "I told you. I saw your car."

Frustrated, she waved his words aside. "Never mind. I..."

Geoffrey Fine, David's doctor, a skinny, pinched-faced young man in a white lab coat rounded the corner into the room. "Hi, Meredith. Sorry for interrupting, but I just have a minute. I got your message, and I wanted to talk to you about moving your brother."

Stephen towered over the physician. The judge's eyebrows raised, and Meredith almost missed the expression. It dawned on her that he just now realized she and David were related. She wondered who he thought David was.

"Why does he need to be moved?" Her attention pulled back to Doctor Fine. She dreaded the answer. As much as she hoped it wouldn't be, long-term care was always a possibility. She needed to plan for his well-being if there was no improvement in his condition.

Fine squatted on his haunches to meet Meredith's eyes. "This is what you need to decide. There is little likelihood of recovery. I see no brain activity with the scan. I'm not sure about his medical coverage, but within the next few days, you're going to have to make a decision on how to proceed with his health care. I assume you are his nearest living relative?"

"Actually, he's still married. His wife filed for divorce, but she's out of state indefinitely." *What was he saying?*

Fine leaned back on his heels. "This complicates things. The wife is the closest relative. Can you get in touch with her?"

"You're telling me we have to decide whether to pull the plug?" She sighed deeply. "He can't breathe on his own, so he'll die?"

Fine stood. "He's not going to recover. I'm sorry."

Meredith rose. "I'll call his wife and give you a decision soon. How long do we have?"

Fine rubbed his pointed chin with his thumb and index finger.

"Let's say the beginning of next week, Monday or Tuesday. That way, you can check on his medical coverage, too."

She nodded, glancing around the room. Giroud was gone. Good.

Meredith followed the doctor out the door. Her brain filled with the details of her brother's imminent death, calling Christy, moving David. She was in motion but not paying attention to what she was doing. She didn't recall patting her waistband where her gun was or searching for her car keys. She didn't know that she had almost knocked over a nurse with a full cart. She didn't remember anything but Dr. Fine's words.

The Subaru door swung open, and she slipped into the driver's seat. Blinking back the horror growing in her chest, she twisted on the ignition. A growl, then another.

If she hadn't been already shell-shocked, she would have been furious. At the moment, she couldn't dredge up the energy. Her brother was going to die. Like everyone else, she was close to. Her father wasn't dead, but he might as well have been. She hadn't seen Terence Ryan since the night he walked out on his family fifteen years ago.

She wished she could cry. Dropping her head against the blossoming headache, she rubbed her eyes and considered what she would tell Christy. The words wouldn't come. Deciding they were stymied by other crises in her life, she gave up for the moment. She had to get back to the office. Pulling the key from the ignition, she dug into her pocket for her phone and punched a phone number. Nick wasn't at his desk, nor did he answer his cell. Oh, yeah. He was with his mother.

She waited through the announcement to leave a message. "Nick, I'm stuck at Community with a broken-down car. I'll call for AAA, but I've got to find a ride back to the office. Just letting you know I'll be late. Hope everything went well with your Mom. Call me when you get this."

Next, she called dispatch. "Maria? It's Meredith. Hey, I'm stuck at Community Hospital, and my car won't start. Can you call AAA for me and expedite them?" She listened for a moment, then gave her vehicle description. "It's a tan over maroon 2006 Subaru Outback, parked in the front lot. It'll be going to the dealership, Paulson Subaru." She listened again. "Next, I need a ride. Can you send me a patrol unit?"

She listened to the dispatcher.

"How long? An hour?" Meredith's heart sank. She hated being late. "Oh, man. Leahy will have kittens. I'll wait." She thumbed the connection closed and slumped against the door. Her head felt like it would explode.

"Excuse me, aren't you Meredith Ryan?" A wiry, Hispanic man leaned on a black Cadillac Escalade parked opposite her Subaru. He was in his early 30's, dressed in a sport coat and slacks. His shoulders had the set of a confident man, one who knew what he could do. *He looks like a cop.* His eyes were busy studying her reactions as he waited for an answer.

Well, let him wait. Cops don't usually admit to their identity without a reason, as a matter of self-preservation. Having a citizen still angry over that ticket you gave them last Christmas was one of the least pleasant perks of the job.

"Who wants to know?" She squinted against the glare of the gray sky.

His brown face broke into the smile of a comrade. "You must be." He advanced toward her with one hand flipping open a flat badge, the other extended for a handshake. "I heard about you. I'm Raul Esparza, Paso Robles PD."

Meredith's gaze glanced over the badge, then she relaxed and shook his hand, mentally doing the geography. Paso Robles was south—a four-hour drive away. She flashed a vague smile. "Nice to meet you. How did you hear about me all the way down there?"

"I'm up here on a special detail. You were big news for a while with that shooting business." He shoved both hands in his pockets, looking at the pavement. "Tough break about the old guy, though."

Meredith took a deep breath, appreciating his response. "Yeah." She couldn't think of anything else to say.

"Say, I couldn't help but overhear your conversation with your dispatcher. I was waiting for my boss, and he's gonna be an hour or two longer. You need a ride somewhere?" Esparza flipped a thumb over his shoulder to the Escalade. "I've got some really nice wheels and an hour to kill. Can I give you a lift?"

Her instinct was to say no, but when she considered waiting an hour for a ride, she changed her mind. She didn't need Leahy on her butt for being late. "Okay, that would be great. Do you know where the Hall of Justice is?" She pulled her briefcase out of the Subaru, stuck the extra key in the sun visor, and closed the door.

"Yeah, the 101 south to Bicentennial, right?" He opened the passenger door. People from the southern part of the state called their highways with an intimacy that Northern Californians lacked.

The Cadillac purred to life. "As long as we're going south, I have a quick errand to run. Do you mind?"

In spite of his earnest expression, she felt the tiniest flicker of concern. "As long as it doesn't take too long. I've got a sergeant who'd love to write me up for being late from lunch."

The Escalade pulled out of the hospital lot at the signal. It eased onto Highway 101 and cruised southbound. A fog of anxiety settled over her. It wasn't just David's prognosis. Talking to Christy, losing David. Grieving for yet another loved one. It tumbled through her mind like a cactus rolling downhill, its spikes picking up additional problems like roadside litter.

Keeping Esparza's profile in her gaze, her concern about his truthfulness began to blossom. The last exit for Santa Rosa came and went as they barreled down 101.

Where was he taking her? What the hell had she done, getting in the car with him?

Chapter Sixty-Eight

"YA GOTTA HAVE A PLAN." FREDO SHOVED THE LAST HALF OF A stale maple donut into his mouth. "Otherwise, all you got is a bunch of crap. Your life is like a jigsaw puzzle that someone dropped on the floor. All the parts are there, but they're not together. Get it?" Impressed with his own philosophy, he snatched a pack of smokes from the table. "Take me, for example. Janette gets out of beauty college in December. When she goes to work full-time, that will help me pay off the boat. Then it'll be mine free and clear."

Sutton nodded, trying to soak up his buddy's wisdom. Fredo was right. A plan—one that included Faye. He wanted to be with her, to make a family. A real one, not like his mother or Theda. Listening to his buddy confirmed he was on the right track. A plan.

Step one, he needed to take her away from Sonoma County. He had too much history here, too many screw-ups, and friends who made him fuck up. Maybe Arizona or Nevada. Not Oregon. Too much rain got on his nerves.

Yeah, that's what he'd do. When the boat docked in two days, he'd get hold of Faye. They'd get the hell outta here and go to Nevada.

Chapter Sixty-Nine

ESPARZA PULLED INTO THE PARKING LOT AT THE HAVEN
Convalescent Home on the southern outskirts of Santa Rosa. The
Cadillac stopped at the green curb in front. He cut the engine and
hopped out, circling the car to the passenger side.

Meredith pressed the button to roll down the window. What now?

Esparza flashed an inviting smile, his teeth white against his dark
skin. "Come on in. You might find this interesting."

"What do you mean?" Her fingers ran over the Beretta at her
waistband.

"Come on and see." He crooked a finger, then tipped his head
toward the building.

Despite her internal warnings, she followed Esparza.

The glass doors of the convalescent hospital slid open to a highly
polished linoleum lobby that branched off to either side. The smell of
disinfectant mingled with cafeteria meatloaf. Meredith wrinkled her
nose.

Before she could read the wall signs, Esparza took her elbow and
steered her to the left.

"Hello, Meredith." Giroud. Oh, my God.

She turned away immediately, bumping into Esparza's chest.

Time to leave. "Come on, Meredith. This will be interesting to you, Esparza said." He pushed her forward.

With a face sharply lined with pride, Giroud said, "Meredith, there's someone here who wants to see you. Give him a minute, then you can go."

"No," she whispered. Esparza held her arm, firmly guiding her down a long hallway, pushing as Giroud led.

In spite of their heavy-handed manner, her curiosity got the better of her. She wondered who wanted to see her. Her father maybe? No. It had been years since she'd seen him. Humiliation warmed her face. She had allowed herself to be detoured like this. Embarrassing.

The drive had been short as the home was just south of Santa Rosa. But she had to get back to work. She also had arrangements to make. She needed to call Christy, deal with the medical coverage, and find a place to care for David until...

She wondered if Giroud was thinking this might be a good place for her brother and found someone to give her a testimonial. He'd heard Doctor Fine's report, hadn't he? No, he couldn't have known about David's prognosis. She doubted that he was that thoughtful. The Judge was a lot of things. She felt silly thinking the best of him.

"Let's get this done so I can get back to work." Meredith snapped. She didn't have time for this.

She glanced at Giroud's striking profile as they walked down the hallway. Handsome or not, she couldn't trust him. No way. Nor Esparza.

The sound of daytime television blasted from many of the rooms. She heard a vacuum in the distance, and metal trays clattering. They were the only visitors. Two doors from the end of the hall, Giroud stopped. Esparza took a post at the door.

Giroud guided her into a room. As they rounded the corner, she glanced at the patient nameplate on the wall. It said, "Ryan."

Damn him. How had he managed this?

A rush of adrenaline staggered her. She leaned against the door-frame. It was him. There was a moment where she thought she would black out.

Giroud stood tall like a boy who'd won the spelling bee. He

made like he was introducing two strangers. In a way, he was. "Terence Ryan, your daughter, Meredith." He smiled at her, saying, "Meredith, your father."

She would've recognized the old man anywhere. He'd aged over fifteen years, and not gracefully. His tall thin frame laid immobile. Skin draped from his face; his hair scraggly and unwashed. Sunken eyes still had the sharp vigilance she recalled from childhood. Red and purple veins covered a bulbous nose, while his chapped lips twisted in a grim smile.

Terence fixed a malevolent squint on Stephen. "This who you wanted me to see? If I'd a known, I wouldn't have agreed."

She straightened, folding her arms across her chest. "We agree on that."

Giroud bent in a gracious bow. "You two are together for the first time in many years. Make the best of it." He spoke with authority, as if he was making a ruling from the bench. Then, he flashed a dazzling smile. "I'll wait outside." He turned and left, but Meredith felt he was acting like a bodyguard.

Father and daughter stared at one another for almost a minute. Meredith broke the silence. "You look pretty sick."

"You have a gift for stating the obvious," Terence snorted. "They don't bring you here to get better."

"Always the charmer, weren't you?" She couldn't say the things she wanted to. No heartfelt reunion of father and daughter? No hugs and kisses of family love lost, then found?

"What did you expect, a party?" His thin lips pressed into a sneer. It was hard to believe her mother ever loved this bitter, angry man. It was also hard to think that she ever felt the need for his approval.

Enough. She turned to leave.

Terence said, "I hear you're a cop."

She nodded. "Sonoma Sheriff's Office. The last seven years."

"Och, those rubes." The faintest lilt of an Irish accent drifted between them. She remembered how much she wanted to please him as a child. How much she had loved him then. "I cleared more cases on mounted patrol in one day than that whole department does in a week." He waved a bony arm, dismissing her livelihood and, with it, the dregs of any hope for respect that she might have harbored.

The invisible armor she used to protect herself slipped into place by long practice, warding off her father's cruelty. Time to go, get out of here.

His chin shifted sideways as he studied her. "You in dicks?"

She nodded. "Violent Crimes."

"Yeah?" He paused. Meredith didn't believe he'd be impressed. "How many brass balls did you have to sleep with to get there?" His head slammed back against the pillow as a laugh seized him, then sunk into a lung-searing cough.

Her anger spiked. She reconsidered the words she'd held back. He didn't deserve kindness. "So, Father, I have to ask. Do you ever regret abandoning your family?" She was curious but didn't think he'd be honest.

The coughing subsided, and his watery eyes snapped. "You have no right to judge me. You don't know what happened."

"So you're not interested in reconnecting with us, making amends?" He wasn't going to admit he did anything wrong. Fine, it'll be between him and God.

His chin set as if in granite. "Amends? Amends for what? You stay out of my life. I was fine before you strolled through that door. I'll be even better when you waltz back out the door." He struggled to raise himself on a scrawny elbow, wheezing. "Don't bother to memorize visiting hours."

Chapter Seventy

Rigid with fury, Meredith marched down the hall and shoved the front doors open. Both men had to trot to catch up with her. Outside the door, she squared off with them both, glaring at Giroud. "It didn't quite work out the way you planned, did it?"

He sucked in a breath, then released it. "No."

"You stay out of my business," she snapped. Her jaw set in granite. "I'll find my own way back. Any objection and I'll file a kidnapping complaint against you both."

Giroud's head dipped in assent, like a child who had been scolded. Esparza turned away to avoid her gaze.

The doors slid closed after her. Flipping her cell open, she called to get a beat unit to pick her up.

Thirty minutes later, Meredith dumped her briefcase on her desk as Nick glanced at his watch. Shrugging out of her damp raincoat, she dropped into the chair, staring at a report on her desk. "Tough morning," she said.

"Yeah? Have you eaten?"

"No."

Nick rose. "Let's get some lunch."

She blinked. "I'm not hungry. Anyway, it's after two."

"Humor me." He made for the door. She followed.

The cafeteria was nearly empty. Nick pulled a chair out for her and scanned the food bar. The lunch menu had been put away, so Nick scrounged an over-ripe banana, a bag of Fritos, and a paper cup of water.

She didn't touch the Fritos but snapped up the banana. Nick was quiet, watching her eat, waiting.

She told him about David. She was almost surprised that she could tell him what Doctor Fine had said. The words carried such a burden, as if saying them made them twice as heavy.

"I'm so sorry, Mere. I'm sorry you have to do this." He reached out to her hand, covering it with the touch of consolation.

Her brown eyes met his across the table. "That's not the half of it."

Nick chewed on a toothpick as he listened. His jaw flexed and relaxed for a while. Then, his jaw locked, and his eyes widened as she recounted her trip to the convalescent hospital. His face flushed as her story ended.

"First, you should've never gotten in the car with that guy..."

"I know." Her shoulders slumped. "He buzzed me. He said he was a cop."

"You should know better." Angry red patches appeared on his neck.

Meredith's hands flew up in frustration, as if she could toss her troubles in the air. She slumped against the chair. No more words came. She couldn't make excuses for her lack of vigilance. She'd been a fool, dropping her defenses. Anything could've happened with this guy Giroud and his man. Was he crazy?

Nick rubbed his face with both hands. From behind his fingers, he said, "You want to go home? I'll take you over to the car dealership, if you want." He dropped his hands and eyed her. "You'll need to talk to Christy and..." his lips twisted while he selected the words. "...make arrangements for your brother."

Meredith straightened. "No, I'll stay. Work will be my therapy." She ran her fingers through her hair. "I'll call Christy tonight. If I call late enough, we can talk without her aunt interrupting."

They were silent for a few moments. "While you were being kidnapped, I was on the phone with Faye Zelman."

Gears shifted in Meredith's head as she focused on what Nick said. "Really?"

"Seems she's had a change of heart. It could have something to do with the warrant she was arrested on in San Luis Obispo County."

Meredith digested this new information. "So she wants to come up here and act as bait for Sutton. Will she testify in court against him?"

"She says she will." Nick nodded. "She wants to get up here as soon as possible. She's scared in jail. She figures the only way to stop being afraid is to put him away."

"But that doesn't make sense. Sutton's nothing to those guys in prison. He doesn't have the power or money to reach out and have her killed."

Nick smiled at Meredith. "She doesn't know that."

She returned his smile. "Do we have an okay to go to SLO County?"

He nodded. "Tomorrow early. I called Leahy at home, and he said to hit the road. We're taking my truck again."

Chapter Seventy-One

THE MARCH MORNING BLEW IN BRISKLY UNDER SOMBER SKIES. JUST a brief shower early last evening made almost three days without substantial rain. A breeze shook the bare branches of the trees along the highway. Meredith was relieved the roadways were dry. Nick was a good driver, although she often thought he drove too slowly. At least wet asphalt wouldn't give him an excuse to plod.

She wanted to get this day over. She wanted to see David, to figure out what to do about Giroud, to catch Sutton. She twisted the gold band on her left ring finger.

She was so engrossed in her thoughts that Nick startled her when he spoke. "You had a full morning yesterday, didn't you?"

"Don't make fun of me." Her voice was flat. "I have no sense of humor right now."

He nodded at the warning, like he had expected it. "What're you going to do?"

"About which problem?"

"David first, then Giroud."

"Christy gave me all the health insurance info. Now, I have to find a decent place for him to stay until…" She took a deep breath. Talking helped, although it only led to one bad conclusion.

"As for Giroud, I haven't figured that out yet. Neither Leahy nor Ferrua are willing to help. I don't think they even believe me. Giroud's got too much clout for either of them to go out on a limb without any physical proof."

Nick straightened behind the wheel. He squinted at the highway. "Is that what they said? You need proof?"

She nodded. "Leahy didn't even give me that. It was Ferrua who said he'd help if he had something to work with."

Nick slammed the heel of his hand onto the steering wheel. "Damn those fuckers. Gutless, just gutless." When Meredith didn't say anything, he smiled. "I've got an idea. What if we get that proof?"

"What are you thinking? Giroud is too smart to leave evidence." He was so slick. Too slick. Even talking about it made her anxious. "He doesn't even think what he's doing is wrong. He's that whacked out. No grip on reality. No grip at all."

"Maybe we can make that work for us." His eyes rounded with excitement.

"Us?"

"Yeah, 'us'." He calmed down, gazing at the road. "We're partners, Mere. You don't have anyone else. Besides, I want to help."

Meredith's cell interrupted.

"Meredith?" The voice on the other end said, "This is Brad Kingston from Santa Rosa PD. Do you have a minute? I need to run some info by you since you're aware of our situation."

She shifted in the seat. "Okay, shoot."

"When you saw Astrid with the Judge at Cabanas, did you speak to him?"

"No, I didn't even make eye contact with him."

"Are you sure he saw you?"

"Yes, he looked at us when we were seated. Nick saw him first." Tension spread through her chest. Feeling like he was pressing her, she was surprised with Kingston's scrutiny, yet gratified. She guessed all cops had that effect when they interviewed people. She made a mental note to be more considerate to people in the future.

"Interesting. He says he never saw you."

What the hell was that about? "Well, that's not true. Nick can verify my statement; he's here with me."

"I'll confirm it with your partner and include it in my report." Kingston sounded distracted. "I'll talk to him in a minute, if I can. There's something you need to know."

"Okay." She drew out the syllables. This conversation was taking a direction she hadn't anticipated.

Kingston cleared his throat. "During the Vachon investigation, we interviewed Judge Giroud twice. Because of his position, we had to tread lightly around the courthouse. But we found out some interesting stuff. Do you know he has a ranch hand named Esparza?"

"Mexican-looking guy? Mid-thirties, cop-type? Yeah, I met him."

"Esparza is more than a ranch hand or groom. He's kind of a jack-of-all-trades. He lives in a trailer on the property there with Giroud. He takes care of the judge's horses, but he also drives and maintains the grounds, the house, and all the vehicles. And, he acts as security." Kingston paused to take a breath.

"I'm not surprised." She didn't like where this was leading. Still stinging with embarrassment over yesterday's debacle, she didn't tell Kingston how she'd met Esparza.

"This character is an ex-cop from Paso Robles PD. He was fired for excessive force."

Ex-cop? He'd flashed a badge. She guessed it was easy enough to scare up a flat badge. She was such a fool.

"How does this fit into your investigation?" She could see Esparza's smug smile.

"Hmm," Kingston said. "I'm tending to believe that he's a hood more than a hand. I'm looking into him as well as the Judge."

The silence stretched between them. For a second, her mind whirled with the dangers of getting into the car with Esparza. It could have gone south fast. She must stay alert. She didn't want to be alone again around Giroud and Esparza. When she could, she drew a breath. "How about motive?"

"We have some possibilities, but nothing concrete. Yet. Anyway, I wanted to pass this info on to you. One more thing.

Giroud is definitely interested in you. We've talked to several people close to the judge who feel that he's fixated. I'm no shrink, but it sounds to me like he is obsessive. Your concerns are well-founded."

She spoke softly. "He's escalated a bit since I last talked to you."

"Anything I need to know about?"

She forced her tone to lighten up. "No, I handled it."

"Be careful. Either he or his man did Astrid Vachon. I just can't prove it yet. Keep it quiet, though. I don't want him blowing town or anything."

"I'll watch out." There's no way Giroud would run. He's too sure of himself.

Kingston asked to speak to Nick, who verified Meredith's statement. After listening a little longer, he thanked Kingston and handed back the phone.

"Sounds like you two are on the road." Kingston was winding up the conversation.

"We're headed to San Luis Obispo to pick up a witness in the McMurray homicide."

"Hm, San Luis? Isn't that close to Paso Robles? That's where Giroud's ex-wife lives. I've been trying to get hold of her, but she won't return my calls."

Meredith exhaled. "Paso Robles is on the way. It's a short detour. Can we help?" What was she doing?

"Yeah, let me talk to my sergeant and I'll call you right back."

Meredith used the time to fill Nick in on the conversation.

Five minutes later, Kingston was on her phone again. "If you could talk to both the mother and the ex, I'd appreciate it. I need background info that would speak to his tendency to violence. If you find anything significant, I'll drive down there myself. Will you have time?"

"We should. What are you looking for, specifically?"

"I'm looking for character here. The ex in particular. I want whatever dirt she can toss our way on Giroud or Esparza. She lives in town. I think she works at an attorney's office near the courthouse, but I don't have an exact address for her. Local law enforcement might have something current. Maybe stepmom has it. Here's her address."

Meredith scratched it on a napkin left over from breakfast. "Got it. I'll write it up in a supplement to your case and send it over tomorrow. What's the case number?" She scribbled it down next to Sally Giroud's home address.

"Hey, Meredith, thanks for this. It'll help me out."

"Sure. It may help me out, too." A sliver of hope took up residence. Maybe she could figure out a way to fix this problem. She shut off the phone, then eyed Nick.

"I get nervous when you smile like that," Nick said.

Chapter Seventy-Two

STEPHEN GIROUD COULDN'T HELP HIMSELF. HE COULDN'T KEEP away. Meredith would be gone most of the day, if not tomorrow, too, leaving him the freedom he wanted. His secretary told him the detectives would be out of the county for the day, according to the duty roster. Having a secretary who has her ear to the ground was beneficial.

Throughout his life, he'd found those women who fell susceptible to his charisma. It was easier than he could imagine persuading them to do what he wanted. His secretary saw his political potential early in her employment. There wasn't anything she wouldn't do to ensure a position in his future career. The records clerk at Paso Robles PD was much simpler: a discreet word put her brother into drug rehab instead of jail. In turn, she would feed him any hint of interest in Lindsay Giroud's death.

All his life, women had wanted him. Even his mother. Then one day, she didn't. And he showed her the price of neglect. His father had been devastated when he found his wife on the floor, dead. But realizing his son's role in the accident, he shifted the blame to his wife. Stephen could not be at fault. His father emphasized the need for a strong woman instead of a weakling like his mother.

Stephen was glad his father had seen through Elizabeth's charade and rose to his son's defense. Stephen was proud of himself for recognizing it, too. He hadn't understood it at the time, but now he realized she sucked the pride out of his father. From that moment on, he vowed his wife would be a pillar of strength standing beside him. He needed a woman who could take care of herself but wanted him to take care of her. She had to be beautiful, a prerequisite for the political path he hoped to tread. But she had to be smart enough to wrangle his opponents, to show them her husband was something so special that she picked him to marry. She would be courageous in the face of difficulty and steadfast at controversy. In all things, she would defer to him. He would be her God, even over the children they would surely have. He would have the power, and she would adore him for it.

Marriage to Lindsay had been a mistake. He'd let lust govern his love life. He sighed, purging the memory of her rebellion. She hadn't been good enough. She wouldn't have been the wife he needed in the future. He forced thoughts of his dead wife from his mind.

Last evening's showers had not relieved leaden skies. His mood had lightened, by contrast, as he parked his Mercedes on a gravel turnout on Mirabel Road south of Meredith's driveway. He followed a damp path that led to his destination. Moments later, he smiled when the latch on the garage door clicked open under his deft fingers. With a silent thanks to Esparza, Giroud pocketed the stolen house key. He stepped inside, pausing to inhale her lingering scent. Right now, it smelled like clean laundry. Last time he was here, she had just left, and her fragrance lasted long enough for him to savor it.

Giroud strode from the garage into the living room. He didn't waste any time in the kitchen. There was little of Meredith's spirit there. He felt her presence most strongly in the living room and bedroom. Standing in the center of the main room, he closed his eyes and pictured her coming home after a long day at work to a nice pinot noir. He saw her drop onto the couch, kick her boots off, and prop her heels on the coffee table. She balanced the pinot while listening attentively to his conversation. A broad, toothy smile flashed across her face as she laughed at some witty story he told.

Something rubbed against his ankle. With reluctance, his eyes popped open to see Meredith's white cat purring while rubbing its face and shoulders against the cuff of his pants.

Giroud could feel the dander rising to his nose. He stifled a sneeze. Then with a grunt, he kicked at the cat. His toe just made contact, but it achieved its purpose. Hunched with indignation, the ball of fur circled around and sauntered toward Giroud's other leg. Giroud scooped up the cat, opened the balcony door, and tossed it. The animal landed on the deck with a dull thump, hissing and scratching the wood to right itself. Giroud hurried to close and lock the glass door.

With that done, he brushed the cat hair from his slacks, trying to regain the mood. Returning to the middle of the living room, he centered his focus on the furniture, books, paintings, and *objets d'art*. Much of it was modern lithographs of Joan Miró and the like. Clearly, her husband, Richard Taylor, had done much of the collecting. The room was too modern for Giroud's classic tastes, surely Meredith's, too. Several expensive pieces of art were displayed, yet there was only one that reflected Meredith's presence, a Chinese warhorse sculpture. Richard had influenced, no, infected the whole house. He had been, after all, an architect. But Giroud was surprised at the lack of personal memorabilia. No family pictures, no photo albums, no silly figurine collections. Only the one wedding photo in the bedroom.

His finger traced the strong lines of the bronze horse sculpture. So delicate, yet strong and enduring, like Meredith. He could see why she was attracted to horses. She shared their elegant way of moving, their down-to-earth sensibilities, and their gentle demeanor, until rubbed the wrong way.

Silently, Giroud moved across the tile floor and into the master bedroom. Heavy wood beams supported oak cathedral ceilings. The walls were painted an edgy shade of russet to accentuate the modern artwork. The simple lines of contemporary furniture added to an angular and austere room.

It didn't suit her, and he hated it. Giroud pictured a warm, inviting space when he thought of Meredith. She wasn't all chintz and cabbage roses, but this was sterile and without warmth. Well, it would all change.

He spent more time at the bed where she slept. It was always made, no matter what time she left for work. He remembered what she looked like asleep, then daydreamed himself next to her.

Kneeling, he buried his head in her pillow, inhaling her smell. Someday soon, he would be able to touch her throat. Right at her pulse point. He wanted to feel her hair, her skin, her essence. Soon, he thought. He stood and made his way to Richard's cherry wood dresser. An 8" x 10" framed wedding photo of Richard and Meredith sat next to a black leather jewel box. Giroud knew the contents by heart. He didn't need to open it. Instead, he wrapped his fingers around a bottle of Richard's cologne. Before he realized it, the cap was unscrewed, and the open bottle was under his nose. The sandal-wood fragrance revolted him. It wasn't cheap, but the cloying aroma stayed in his nose longer than he wished. Seeing the wedding photo with Richard's cologne in his hand brought an unwelcome picture of Meredith's husband, alive. A vaporous image of the dead man materialized before him.

Giroud slammed the cologne on the dresser, scattering tiny droplets on the surface. The impact jolted the photo frame. He grabbed it before it fell, then focused on Richard's face.

"She's mine now," he told the image.

The brushed nickel frame in his hands felt weightless. Same as his substance. Giroud smiled at his secret joke.

He addressed Richard's image as if the man was alive in front of him. Fury rose at the injustice of this man as Meredith's husband. "You weren't worthy of her in life. You are even less worthy in death." His fingers grasped the frame and smashed the picture against the edge of the dresser. Glass shattered, flying in all directions. The frame dropped to the carpet, and the photograph fell last, settling on the debris. He stepped on the photo, the sole of his shoe twisting until the paper shredded.

She is better off without him. She will realize that faster without any of these foolish reminders.

Giroud rubbed his fingerprints off the frame with his sleeve cuff.

He made a mental note to toss the shirt when he got home. It felt contaminated. He didn't want it in his house.

He forced himself away from the mess, irritated that he'd lost his temper. Then, as fast as it had taken hold, the anger was gone. Eager to surround himself with Meredith's things, he moved to her walk-in closet. His breathing calmed as her clothes encircled him. He ran his hand over a row of blouses, feeling the different textures and fabrics. Suits, jackets, and a few dresses crushed under his fingertips. His attention drifted to the built-in mahogany drawers in the center of the room. He reached inside the top and ran his fingers over lacy bras and camisoles. He felt a languorous contentment well up inside him as he touched things that had been next to her skin.

The next drawer held underpants, silk, cotton, knits, and blends, all neatly folded in divided spaces. He handled them carefully, so as not to disturb them. He liked her orderliness. He didn't want her to know he'd been there.

Or maybe knowing could work to his advantage. The damaged wedding picture and frame had made a mess on the bedroom floor. No. He wanted her to feel the power he had over her. When she feels it, she'll be compelled to come to him. She won't be able to resist him. Everyone is attracted to power.

Thinking, he kept his hand on her underwear. When his index finger felt the lace at the bottom of a stack, he couldn't help himself. He gathered it up, studied it for a while, then mashed it to his face.

His breathing became ragged as he felt himself getting excited. A fleeting moment of panic evaporated when he realized he was alone, indeed.

Alone.

As if in a dream, he drifted to the bed. His eyes saw only what he wanted to see, what was in his imagination: Meredith naked, willing, wanting, no, demanding him.

He slumped against the bed, panties in hand, rubbing himself with a frenzied motion. The pumping continued until the tension exploded in his pants. He slid to the floor in exhaustion, his mind reeling with the possibilities.

He didn't bother to straighten the bed. She'd know he'd been there. She'd experience his power over her. He wished he had the energy to observe her tonight. He wanted to gauge her reaction.

Exhausted and unsatisfied, he left the way he came in, tucking the lace panties in his pocket.

Chapter Seventy-Three

NICK AND MEREDITH SETTLED INTO STRAIGHT-BACKED CHAIRS facing the Watch Commander, Lieutenant Lester Franklin of the Paso Robles Police Department. Franklin, in his early forties, had the worn face of a seasoned street cop. Nick hoped he was as down-to-earth as he looked.

With a cautious smile, Lieutenant Franklin listened as Nick summarized their task.

"It's strange that you guys are here to find Lindsay Giroud. I can tell you exactly where she is." In an unconscious movement, he shifted his hip to clear his sidearm of the armrest.

"Where?" Nick was tired and hungry. He wished they'd stopped to eat before finding PRPD. His watch read nine-thirty. He wanted to get this over with so they could talk to these women and get back on the road.

"She's at Paso Robles District Cemetery. She was killed about four months ago. Hit-and-run. Never caught the suspect."

Nick glanced at Meredith's shocked face and then back to Franklin. "This happened in your city?"

Franklin nodded. "We don't take kindly to open homicides in our city limits, Detective Reyes. We've worked it non-stop for months."

"I understand. Did you get a vehicle or suspect description?"

He leaned back. "We found the responsible vehicle three miles away from the scene. Stolen. All surfaces wiped clean. We got some hair that we ran through CODIS but didn't come up with a match."

Meredith had to ask. "Was she a pedestrian, or was she killed in a car?"

"She was in a Lexus sedan. It was totaled."

The detectives let the information sink in and join up with their suspicions. Meredith asked, "She was divorced?"

"Yeah. The senior detective talked to him. I didn't. He was out of the area. Lives up your way. According to my man, his alibi was airtight. He's a judge or something, I heard."

"Yes." The words erupted from her chest. "But that shouldn't exclude him from the investigation." Nick thought she sounded pushy. She'd gone too far, telling him how to do his job.

The lieutenant's lips turned down with the effort to monitor his response. "It didn't, detective. There was no prejudice afforded to him because he's a judge."

Nick knew she'd ask another question, even at the risk of alienating Franklin further. "Did you have any info about the relationship between Lindsay and her ex? I mean, did they get along? Were there kids to fight over? Anything like that?"

Franklin's eyes held hers. "No, no kids. I don't recall word of any hostility between them. No DV priors."

Nick had a thought. "Can we get a copy of your report? We won't need all the lab stuff, just the narrative and scene sketches."

"Sure." Franklin's puzzled gaze drifted from Nick to Meredith. "You have something that might help us with this?"

"Maybe something soon." Nick pulled out his sunglasses. "We're here on another matter but stopped by at the request of Santa Rosa PD detective Brad Kingston. You'll be hearing from him. He's the one who asked us to stop by and talk to Lindsay."

The partners stood, shook hands with Franklin, and expressed their appreciation for the information. At the door, Nick stopped and looked at the lieutenant. "Do you know a guy named Esparza?"

The lieutenant's jawline hardened. "Raul Esparza?"

"That's the one," Meredith said.

"If he's involved in any way, you can be sure it's trouble." Franklin leaned against the door jamb.

"Ah, then you know him." Meredith waited. She'd want to hear this.

Franklin's shoulders straightened, a study of professional discipline. He stepped back and closed the door. "Off the record?" Self-control disappeared, and his face registered something between anger and disgust. He crossed his arms over his chest. "Esparza worked here for over eight years. He was a tough guy to work with, moody and unpredictable. Without getting into his jacket, I can tell you he had anger management problems which sometimes led to complaints. We kept him on because he was good at clearing cases. He closed more open investigations than the detectives. But the last complaint was the straw that broke the camel's back. He beat the crap out of one of our sergeants. Right in the sally port, on camera. We fired him shortly afterward." He paused, looking up, counting, then back at Meredith, "That's been about six/seven years ago."

"Any other problems with him? Alcohol, maybe?" Nick was fishing, looking for information that fleshed out the personality of this bad cop. He and Meredith had to know who she was up against.

"He liked to gamble. The horses, football, the casino down in Santa Ynez. He was always working overtime to pay someone off."

"Do you know what happened to him after he got fired?" Nick studied the lieutenant's face.

Franklin sighed. "I heard he went north with Giroud, working for him. Did something for his horses or something like that. I didn't keep track. You understand."

Meredith understood clearly. The brotherhood didn't extend to fired cops. Even those who didn't make probation and were given a chance to resign before they were terminated didn't count. Cops like Esparza were lepers that most others diligently avoided, afraid some of their bad mojo would rub off.

Nick nodded. "Tell him, Mere."

"I ran into him recently and he ID'ed himself as a Paso Robles

PD officer. He flashed a flat badge, but I didn't actually see where it was from."

It wasn't a crime that would topple the scales of justice, but Franklin would want to know. If Esparza misrepresented himself as a cop from this agency, he could be prosecuted, even though the crime was a misdemeanor.

Franklin didn't let the opportunity pass. He questioned Meredith on the pertinent facts and said he'd talk to the DA about filing charges.

Ten minutes later, Nick balanced the bulky copy of the homicide report in his hand as he got into the truck. Neither of them had spoken since leaving Franklin's office. When the truck doors slammed shut, Nick swore under his breath. "Dang, are you thinking what I'm thinking?"

"Yeah." Meredith's shock hadn't faded. "Wait. What are you thinking?"

Nick looked away, grabbed the steering wheel with both hands, and carefully considered his words. "I'm thinking there are a lot of hit-and-run homicides lately."

"Yeah, both with connections to Giroud." She sunk back into the leather upholstery, staring at the file in her lap. "Circumstantial, of course."

"Two hit-and-run fatalities in the same time frame? Both the same M.O., both indirectly tied to Giroud." He shook his head in disbelief. How hard was it to set up a murder like this? "You just gotta wonder, why would he need Lindsay dead? Wasn't divorce enough?"

Meredith picked up this thread. "Eliminating Richard made me available." She grimaced.

"Yeah, if that was his motive," Nick said. "Taking someone out with a car isn't easy. It's got to be planned to the second. And no forensics left behind? How much prep does it take?"

Meredith sank into the seat. "What if Giroud or Esparza killed Richard? CHP had little evidence found at the scene. I've been calling the investigating officer every week, but they've hit a brick wall."

"And Vachon?" Nick turned toward her. "That was a break from the pattern, but she wound up dead, just the same."

They were silent as each followed their thoughts.

Nick straightened and started the truck. "Get hold of Kingston. Tell him what we found. Tell him we'll meet with him when we get back. He's going to want this report." He checked the clock on his dash. "We still have to interview the stepmother." Nick stopped, hearing their theories again. He looked at her. "Are you okay?"

She nodded. A deliberate murder. Because of her? Nick saw the profound sadness in her eyes. There was only one thing for it. He slammed the transmission into drive.

Suddenly, the urgency to get Faye Zelman back to Sonoma County was secondary to figuring out what Giroud was up to.

Chapter Seventy-Four

"Thirty-seven-oh-two. There it is, over on the left, the gray and white house." Meredith wasn't sure what to expect, but she was surprised at the modest appearance of Stephen's stepmother's home. She had the impression Giroud had money. He didn't seem to be spreading any her way. A small post-WW II ranch-style, the place had seen better days. Overgrown juniper bushes lined the perimeter of the yard, enclosing a faded green patch of invading Bermuda grass. Peeling paint, rusted nail-heads, and brilliant green moss threatened the one-story house. Parked in the driveway was a dinged-up, ten-year-old BMW.

Nick pulled the truck to the curb and turned off the engine. He peered at Meredith over his sunglasses. "Sure you're up to this?"

While she appreciated his concern, he was perilously close to patronizing. Her irritation tempered the worry in his eyes. "I'm fine. Let's get this done."

The sun-bleached door swung open. A pale woman in her late fifties stood with a hand on an ample hip. She might have been pretty at some point, but an extra fifty pounds and a lifetime of alcohol had created a wrinkled relic. A chestnut tangle of hair snugged into a ponytail. Dark eyes, high cheekbones, and full lips were all made-up despite bloodshot eyes. Black yoga pants and a salmon-colored tank top stretched over her curves, revealing too much of her figure.

Sally Giroud glanced at Nick and Meredith through weary eyes. She mumbled, barely understandable. "If you're selling religion, you've got the wrong house." She pushed the door to close it.

Meredith was already moving. Her foot blocked the closing door. "No, ma'am. We're from Sonoma County Sheriff's Office."

Nick flipped out his ID. "We'd like a few moments of your time."

Sally took a step back, eyes wide. "Sonoma County?"

Nick answered. "Yes, ma'am. We're here to ask you some questions about your stepson, Stephen. Do you have the time?"

Sally glanced from one face to the other, thinking it over. Finally, she snorted, laughing at a joke only she understood. "Sure, sure. C'mon in." She stepped back, an arm waving them inside.

"What do you need to know about Stephen? He's a Superior Court Judge in Sonoma County. You must know that."

There was an obvious pride in her voice, and something else that Meredith couldn't yet identify. It all seemed phony.

Meredith smiled, trying to appear pleasantly professional. "We're doing some background information on him for security reasons." The partners had agreed upon this vague explanation for their inquiry. The Vachon homicide wasn't their case. They had no official reason to check into him. As for stalking, the elements of the crime were absent, according to Meredith's superiors, so they had no business talking to Giroud's stepmother. She hoped Ferrua never found out. Meredith crossed her fingers that they would come up with something. Great, now she was acting like her superstitious partner.

Sally's ponytail bobbed as she offered them something to drink. Nick's stomach growled, but they refused. Sally dashed into the kitchen anyway. It gave Meredith an opportunity to study the room.

No pictures of Stephen were displayed, but a framed portrait hanging over the fireplace mantle showed a distinguished-looking man who looked like Stephen might in another decade. Odd to be so proud of a stepson but not have any photos of him, Meredith thought.

Maybe she wasn't proud of Stephen. Maybe she was using his position to her advantage.

Sally returned in a minute with a diet soda. She placed it carefully on an end table and settled into an armchair, tucking one leg beneath her.

"Is that your husband?" Meredith pointed toward the portrait.

Her face slackened, like someone had pulled her chin. "Yes, George Giroud. He passed seven years ago. The love of my life." She gave a huge sigh as she stared at the ceiling, the look of a martyr.

Nick took the opening. "Did Stephen and George get along?"

"Oh my, yes." Her eyes flitted from one detective to the other. "Sometimes I felt like I was a third wheel, you know?" She grabbed the soda can and took a drink.

"Third wheel?" Meredith asked.

"Yes," Sally scrunched her face. "Yes. It was like they were so close they didn't have room for anyone else in their lives. Two peas."

Nick asked, "How long had you been married when he passed away?"

"Three years, five months, and twenty-seven days." Her eyes were moist as her stare returned to the ceiling.

"How did you meet?"

Her eyes settled on Nick. "We met at my niece's wedding. It was love at first sight." Her watery gaze was off again, in a dreamy place. "He was charming. Educated. He was a judge, too, in those days. He drove a beautiful silver Jaguar and lived in a Queen Anne at the south end of the bay called the Gables." Her hand flew to her cheek with the memories. "Oh, and the views—the Pacific Ocean from every room! The antiques and furnishings were impeccable. You see, I'm from a good family, one of the original pioneer families in this valley. But my father lost all our money in the eighties, so I was without resources. When George and I met, I was twenty-one years younger than he. He was a widower, and his son was in college. But we were in love, so we got married. Then a day shy of the ninth anniversary of our meeting, he was gone. One morning, I woke up, and he didn't." She sighed, directing her look at Nick. "You never appreciate what you have until you lose it."

Meredith spoke softly. "What happened, Sally?"

The watery eyes narrowed at Meredith. Her tone sharpened. "What happened? He died, that's what happened." She took a deep breath, grabbed her soda can, and took a sip. "We were happy except when Stephen came to visit. Then we were like children quarreling. It was jealousy, I guess. I think back on it every day. I said some horrible things." She fidgeted with the memory as she put the can down. "George gave him everything: his education, his apartment, a car. Stephen had just passed the bar and was driving a brand-new Beemer. George made things too easy for him. Stephen didn't appreciate it at all. He expected it. After a while, I began to see that he manipulated George. I'm sure George recognized it, but he didn't care. He gave him everything."

Her eyes challenged Nick like maybe a cop would defend her stepson. Then she knocked her temper down a notch and continued quietly. "My husband all but paid that firm in San Francisco to take him on. The two of them had an eye on a judgeship, but he'd have to move north to Sonoma County. George had an 'in' with the governor, you see. Stephen moved, then was appointed to the bench a few months later." She paused to clear her throat. "When George passed, Stephen took control of the finances. You see, our money is in a trust." Her voice lost its softness; the words came out flat and sharp. Meredith began to see who she truly was. "He was named executor in the will. Stephen sold our lovely house, like he never had any history there. Sold everything out from under me." She reached for a tissue and sniffed at her bad fortune.

"With our prenup, I didn't get much. A little monthly income. Everything else went to Stephen, with the stipulation that he'd keep a roof over my head." Sally glared at the detectives, her face hard. "Well, he met the terms of the will, but just. He bought this place before the Gables closed." Her hand motioned to the rest of the room. "He had his man go to Goodwill and buy the furnishings. Then he dumped them in the driveway. Didn't even have the decency to help me move them in. But Stephen met the terms of the will, technically, so I have to accept it."

Meredith took another glance around, taking in the threadbare sofa and chairs. Something caught her attention. "Mrs. Giroud, you said 'his man.' Who is that?"

"Esparza. Can't remember his first name. Mexican guy. He used to be a cop here in town. Stephen hired him to work with his polo ponies." Her face twisted to a depth of bitterness that surprised Meredith. "If you're here to look into Stephen as a security issue, you're on the right track. Don't forget Esparza. That guy is poison. I heard he beat up another cop. I feel like he's capable of anything."

Chapter Seventy-Five

GIROUD WADED THROUGH THE LAST OF A DA'S BRIEF. WHEN HIS private line buzzed, he answered, "Judge Giroud."

The squeaky voice on the other end belonged to a Paso Robles police clerk Giroud had enlisted to monitor activity around the Lindsay Giroud homicide. He'd arranged for the clerk's assistance by having her brother sentenced to rehab instead of the county jail. In return, the clerk would tell him of any interest in the case. Giroud let her believe he wanted to be informed because he'd cared so much about his ex-wife and be sure she found justice. The truth was quite different.

His heart thudded. "Two detectives? Do you know their names?"

"Yeah, we must have their names to release the report to them. They were Nicholas Reyes and Meredith Ryan."

Giroud swore, slamming down the phone.

Chapter Seventy-Six

STANDING NEXT TO NICK, THE JAIL SERGEANT SMIRKED AT FAYE Zelman as she passed through the gate into lockdown. "Protective custody," he snorted. "You're hitting the big time, Reyes. Now you got two women in here."

Nick acted indifferent to the sergeant's remark. "Just watch them. I'm gonna need Zelman in a day or two in one piece, if you can manage it." After he passed the jailer on their way to the exit door, Meredith heard Nick mutter, "Asshole."

Ten seconds later, the partners stood silently while a custodial officer buzzed them out. They'd both worked in the jail before patrol assignments, so they were familiar with all the halls, pods, and common areas wired with audio. Somewhere upstairs, a deputy sat and listened to everything. Meredith was particularly keen on keeping her conversation with Nick private. Their office wouldn't afford any privacy, and she was dead-tired anyway.

"It's past time to go home. I need a ride. My car's still at the shop."

He slid into the driver's seat. "What's up?"

Meredith slammed the passenger door. "I need to talk this over."

"Talk what over? Sutton or the Judge?"

"Let's start with Giroud." She twisted her body to see him. She got comfortable. "We should outline everything we know about him. We've got to find something to convince Ferrua to take action. I mean, if Ferrua understands this situation, he can take it to the Sheriff. Isn't there some kind of judicial reprimand or something?"

"He hasn't done anything under the color of authority. Reprimands and censure pertain to his actions during a judicial case, like trials."

"So, we have to operate like he's Joe Citizen." She shook her head. "He'll laugh at a restraining order."

"I'll start." He frowned. "First, Giroud's wife was killed within a week of your husband by the same method, a hundred and fifty miles apart. And he was with Vachon the night she was murdered."

"Ferrua could say it was coincidence."

"Yeah, circumstantial." His eyes darkened. "That's all we have so far. Giroud is too smart to leave behind evidence."

"What about following me?" Meredith was irritated by how her voice sounded so small. She sounded like a victim.

Nick hmphed. "He meets you in public places where it appears as chance. The one exception is when he came to your house. But we have no witnesses, nothing to corroborate your statement. And," he eyed her, "he left when you told him to, so you can't accuse him of trespassing."

Her chest puffed with indignation. "I made him leave. I almost had to get physical with him." She waved an impatient hand. "I know, it's my word against his."

"How about the trip to your Dad's convalescent home? There were no elements of kidnapping. You agreed to go with Esparza. So, again, we have nothing we can prove."

She had an idea. "Maybe I can get the Chippie who investigated Richard's accident to look at Lindsay Giroud's report. What do you think?"

"Maybe." Nick considered it. "If there's any physical evidence that links the two accidents, it might not implicate Giroud but could finger Esparza. He's probably the doer. I doubt that Giroud did the dirty work himself."

"We should be looking at Esparza." Something was jingling around in her head. What was it? She ran through conversations she'd had with Giroud. *His man*, that's what he called him. Odd jobs? "We should update Kingston about Esparza, too."

Nick nodded. "I have to add one more to our list." He twisted the key fob in his fingers. "I think we should presume that David didn't try to commit suicide, that he was pushed off the deck. I agree with you, but there is no evidence to support the theory."

Meredith took a deep breath of relief that Nick had come to this conclusion without any pressure from her. Relatives rarely had an accurate picture of their loved ones in critical circumstances. She had attended countless interviews where parents declared, "My son would never have hurt another human being." Most parents are reluctant to believe their loved one is capable of anything bad. When it came to David, it wasn't that he was incapable of doing anything like suicide. It was more that he had too much ego to deprive the world of his magnificent presence. She still thought someone had pitched him over the railing. Was it Giroud? Would she ever find out?

Back to laying out the facts. "Okay, what makes you think Giroud is responsible?"

"Instinct. I haven't figured out the motive yet. But it has to do with you." He looked away. When he spoke, his voice was rock bottom serious. "Stalking you."

She studied her nails and considered the possibility that Nick was right. Giroud was stalking her. "Too many accidents happening around here." She sighed. "I'm going to try Ferrua one more time."

"Why? We still have no hard evidence. Even the circumstantial is weak. And for what crime, Meredith?"

Her temper snapped. "All right. I can't go to the brass. What do you suggest I do? Roll over and play patty-cake with Giroud?"

"Easy. I didn't say that." He reached a hand over and settled it on her forearm. "What about going on the offensive instead of waiting for his next move? How about setting him up, like we're setting up Sutton?"

She exhaled. "You have any ideas?"

Chapter Seventy-Seven

THE CHEVY PICK-UP GROUND UP THE DRIVEWAY AS NICK concluded. "It's not a perfect plan, but right now, it's all we have. Let's deal with Sutton. That's the priority."

Meredith fished her house key out of her pants pocket. "Let me think it over. I still may be able to convince Ferrua."

Nick pulled the truck to her front door, threw the transmission in Park, and cut the engine. "Watch your back, girl. You don't know what Giroud is capable of." His warning was quiet, but rock-hard.

Meredith couldn't think of the right thing to say. Her mind was a jumble, no answers came. Hell, even the questions were murky. She wanted Giroud to stay away from her. And she wanted to stay within the law. What Nick proposed was not entrapment, but it skirted the law.

Movement at the front door caught Meredith's eye. The motion detector flipped on the light. There was Gus, in a furry white huff, sitting on the front step.

"Nick, come in the house with me. Gus is out. I'm sure I left him inside this morning."

"Fuck," Nick whispered, pulling his Glock from its holster. They left the truck doors ajar as they sidled up to either side of Meredith's front door. She slipped the key in as quietly as she could. The door was locked. She pushed on the knob and waited as the door swung open.

Nick took point. Meredith came in low, mirroring him in her stance. The house was silent, cold, and dark.

They cleared the living room, kitchen, and dining room. Then on to the guest bedrooms on the south side of the house. Nothing.

She took a breath and held it as the pair swiveled into her bedroom. Dark except for a night light in her bathroom, they searched methodically for anything unusual. When she finished checking her closet, Nick was in the bedroom. "There's no one here." She sighed, holstering her Beretta.

"Got it. Flip on the light."

She did. "How did the damn cat get out? All the doors and windows are secured." She dropped to her bed, holding her head. "This is making me crazy." She stared Nick in the eye. "I know I left him in this morning." Her gaze swept the room, stopping at her rumpled bed comforter. "Jesus, someone's been on my bed. *It was him.*"

He reached out and touched her shoulder. "I believe you." Something on the rug caught his attention.

She followed his look to the glint of splintered glass. "Our wedding picture." Her eyes filled with tears as she bent over the photo. Scraping away the shards of glass, she used two fingers to pull out the shredded portrait. "How could this happen?" She dropped to her knees, letting the photo drift to the carpet. Her chest caught with fury and loss.

For the first time in her life, she felt like a victim. Someone had broken (no forced entry, so a key was used?) into her home, laid on her bed, gone through her things, and let her cat out. She'd felt vulnerable after Richard's death, but this was something different. This new emotion felt physical. He put his hands on her things. This wasn't an errant punch in a bar brawl. This was personal.

"He was here," she whispered.

Nick nodded.

She turned her head toward Nick, tears falling freely now. "Screw the system. We've got to catch this bastard."

Chapter Seventy-Eight

THE NEXT MORNING, THE KEY CLICKED IN THE LOCK, AND MEREDITH elbowed her way into the gym. She hadn't worked out in over a week and needed to blow off steam. Her life was dangerously out of balance. She needed some perspective to make the right choices. Gym time was always that time for her.

As always, the faint aroma of mold, moisture, and mildew greeted her. There was no heat in the old shack, but she didn't need it once she got her heart rate up. She shrugged the gym bag off her shoulder, retied a shoelace, and glanced around at the empty room. Built shortly after World War II, the shack's initial purpose was as a community room. Its most recent incarnation was as the neighborhood exercise room. Nothing of this vintage being insulated, miniature rivulets dripped down the unfinished interior redwood walls. The floor was chipped yellow linoleum from another generation. Free weights, a pair of benches, and a universal gym cage lined one wall opposite a bulky treadmill, aging elliptical, and a large floor fan.

She was used to being alone this early in the morning. Often, she went weeks without seeing another neighbor. It suited her.

Shoving in her ear buds, she jabbed at her iPod, settling on a lively Beyoncé tune. Ten minutes on the treadmill, then to the bench.

It was the upper body routine today—lats, pecs, shoulders, biceps, and triceps. Halfway through a lat pull, it occurred to her that Giroud was a sick man. In spite of his apparent charm, he didn't have a clue how to have a relationship. He pushed and pushed and pushed her some more, beyond what was normal. That might have worked with others but not this time. Not with her. She'd been weak, for sure. She'd let him insinuate himself into her life, and she had let him take control. Her face burned at the recollection of "the rescue" in the hospital parking lot. It had been a set-up. The tow mechanic told her that her distributor cap had been loosened. It made perverse sense, in retrospect. He arranged things so he could be the knight in shining armor. An exploitation.

She wanted no part of him or his ridiculous games.

Meredith lay on a bench with a barbell across her chest. The weights were moderate, 10 pounds in addition to the 20-pound bar. A 30-pound under-handed lift, up, over her head, and down a few inches to work her triceps.

Two, three, four, straining a little, her sweat pooling at her lower back.

The door blew open behind her, blasting the room with a frigid wind. Leaves skittered across the floor as she swung the barbell over her forehead, deciding whether to greet the new arrival, most likely a neighbor.

The barbell stopped at an awkward bend in her elbows. What was going on? The bar felt weightless, as if someone was holding it. She struggled, trying to twist her head to see behind her, but the bar jammed down against her neck.

"Do not bother trying to move. In fact, do not move at all. Just listen."

It was *him*. She couldn't see, but she was sure it was his voice.

"Keep your mouth shut. Do not go to your administration, the DA, or anyone else. Stop digging where you have no business, or your family will suffer even more than they do now. What you have seen is nothing. I am capable of much more than you can take."

As he spoke, Meredith tried to shift her grip on the bar, but he held it close enough to her throat that it immobilized her. His whisper was a caress in her ear. "We could have it all, you and I. More power and influence than you could ever dream, if you just do what I tell you."

He finished speaking, but he pressed the bar closer, tighter against her neck. She twisted, struggling to breathe, but was still pinned against the bench. The etched crosshatching pressed into her skin.

Then she was free. The weight of the barbell fell to her clenched hands, tipping to one side. With a mighty shrug, she pushed the bar and remaining plate up and over. As it clanged to the floor, rolling away, she took huge gulps of air, cold and shocking drafts from outside. Her elbows hurt from being bent at an awkward angle. She rolled off the bench.

Her head whipped around as she moved into a standing position. The room was empty. She dropped to the bench, her chest heaving in great gulps of air.

Thirty seconds passed as she recovered. Finally able to breathe normally, she stood, trying to think what her next move should be. Gravel scraped on the pathway outside. Someone was coming. He's coming back.

Nick's face was a welcome sight. "Hey, how come the door's open?" Without waiting for the answer, he scooped an arm around her gym bag. "C'mon. We gotta go." He tossed it to Meredith's chest. "Theda got shanked last night."

Chapter Seventy-Nine

"WHAT THE HELL HAPPENED?" MEREDITH FIRED AT NICK AS THE gym door slammed behind them. Adrenaline still raced through her body, but now it fired off in a different direction. She pushed the panic and lack of control into a box and tucked it away in her mind until she could address the problem of Giroud's obsession. Trying to re-focus, she shook her head. "I thought they were watching her."

Nick kept his temper under control. She could see, though, that he was steaming mad. The hike from the gym to her house was a narrow dirt track. A cool morning breeze rustled the trees loud enough that they couldn't hear each other on the trail.

At the house, he waited in the hallway while Meredith changed into jeans and a sweater. To save time, he briefed her while she checked on Gus. The cat was safely in his bed in the laundry room. She shoved her phone into her pocket and locked the front door behind her. Outside, she got in the county pool car and slammed the door with unnecessary force. "I need to call a locksmith. Okay. Now, what about Zelman?"

"She's okay, but we've gotta move her ASAP. The staff has locked down the jail but hasn't found anything so far. I'm betting it was a hit from Sutton."

Nick pulled the car out of Meredith's driveway and onto Mirabel Road.

She studied his profile. He'd settled down a bit and pulled at his lower lip with his index finger and thumb. Meredith knew what he was thinking. Theda's death was a shock.

Meredith considered the loss of this woman. She'd led a life on the fringe of society and the law. She hadn't appeared to put herself out for anyone, and Meredith wondered if anyone would mourn her. Sutton surely wouldn't. Theda wasn't crucial for the homicide investigation, but the murder suggested she knew something that Sutton didn't want them to find out. Either that or payback for helping them catch him. There were still questions they'd hoped she'd answer while keeping her safe. The fact that she wasn't safe at all made it imperative that they removed Zelman and stashed her where no one could get at her.

Where to put Zelman? Meredith wondered. "Do we have access to a safe house or anything like that?"

"No," Nick answered immediately. "We'd have to go through the DA, and we don't have the time. We're better off trying a motel."

"Motel? Sounds risky. It would have to be the right one. We'd have to scout all the access points, windows, glass doors…all of that. We don't have a half-dozen cops to help us pick one." Her mind cataloged and rejected motels in the immediate area. Too much hassle. "Besides, it's supposed to flood tonight. The river is predicted to crest at two feet over flood stage. You know how that goes. Everyone will be busy with evacuations and roadblocks. We'll be on our own through the night and plan for the same tomorrow."

"You're right." Nick flashed a grim smile. "If we're going to be on our own, I'd rather be on our turf." His gaze drilled hers. "Mama, Sofia, and her husband are still at my house. They're leaving tomorrow, but tonight…"

"Well, that's the stupidest thing I've ever heard, evict your aging, infirmed mother over a third-rate criminal. No," she raised her hand at his protest. "No, listen. Think about it."

"By tomorrow…"

"Nick, it's my house. Think about this: no one there, no neighbors, and visibility is good all around the house. It's the most sensible choice."

She watched him struggle with the idea. Finally, he nodded. "I'll call Leahy and Traber. Let dispatch know in case we need help."

"That will be after you call your mama and tell her you won't be home tonight." Damn him. He always puts work before his family.

Nick nodded again, his lips curling in an impatient smirk acknowledging her comment was unnecessary. He stopped, staring at her neck, and reached out. When Meredith flinched, he pulled back. "Why's your neck all red?"

He's a detective. Even without seeing a mark, he should've figured there was trouble. Gathering her thoughts, she sighed. "Sutton isn't the only case we have coming to a head." She laid it all out, every frustrating second of what took place in the gym. "His timing stinks," she concluded. "But after we get Sutton in custody, I'd like your help dealing with the judge."

Nick was thoughtful. "You said he was behind you. How did you know it was him?"

"What? Are you on crack?" Her chest filled with indignation. It was his voice...

"No, listen. The DA's going to ask you that when you take this to him. He's going to ask how you knew it was Judge Giroud."

"I know his voice." She could still feel the man's breath on her, his hands pressing.

"You didn't see his face?"

"He was behind me, the bench was elevated enough that he ducked behind it. I know it was him."

"That's not good enough for an ID." He considered it for a moment. "Any defense attorney worth a damn can bust that to pieces. And as for the threat? It's iffy, too. He said that you and your family would suffer if you continue nosing around. He didn't say that he'd kill them or hurt them. This won't be enough for a terrorist threats charge."

"God, he's smart. He knows just what to say, how to say it, and when." She slouched into the worn vinyl seat.

Chapter Eighty

L<small>EAHY LEANED INTO</small> N<small>ICK</small>. "I'<small>M TELLING YOU</small>, R<small>EYES, IF YOU DO</small> this, you are on your own."

"If that's the way it has to be…" Nick spoke through clenched teeth. He was getting a headache, and Leahy wasn't helping things.

"You can't call for back up because there won't be any. Everyone is re-assigned to the flood area until further notice." Leahy's face reddened. A dead giveaway that he was pissed. "You've been through this before. You know it's all hands on deck. Your timing sucks."

"You know that we have to protect Zelman. When Sutton gets wind she's up here, she's at risk."

"Isn't that what you wanted?" Leahy slipped a toothpick between his lips. The logistics seemed to have escaped him.

Nick took a breath to calm himself. Leahy knew all this. "Yes, we have something set up through the local rock radio station, the one he listens to. But we haven't initiated that yet, and we won't—"

"You can't trust the media. Don't be so naive."

"That's right. I can't." Nick let his temper show. He shouted over Leahy. "But if he finds out she's in the jail, he'll get to her. He got to Theda Simms. There's no reason to think he can't find Zelman."

"You don't know that. She's safer in the jail." Leahy put a hand up to stop Nick's comeback. "Besides, they're all dirt bags. She'd go right back to him, given the chance." His gray head shook with annoyance.

Nick was prepared to counter Leahy's argument. "Bullshit on all counts: She's not secure in the jail. Sutton can find her, and she's scared to death of him—she won't go with him. He killed the baby she was carrying and almost did her in, too."

Leahy's thin, pointed nose was inches from Nick's. "Fine, but if anything happens out there, it's on you and your partner. I can't spare anyone to rescue you because you have a broad for a partner. You have been warned. There is no help." He began to raise a fist, then whirled around.

"Warned about what?" Meredith marched Faye Zelman to her desk and motioned for her to take a seat. Meredith watched Leahy's back as he stomped into his office.

"Asshole," Nick hissed. He gestured to Meredith. They stepped out of Zelman's hearing range. "We're on our own. The department is going into emergency mode because of the flooding. There won't be anyone to respond if we call for back up."

"We knew that was a possibility when we started this mess." Meredith waved Leahy and the department aside like they didn't matter. "Besides, it's not like we have a choice, given Theda's murder." She watched the redhead sitting at her desk. The woman's thin frame was shaking, and the room wasn't cold.

"She has to be protected. We pushed her into coming up here and becoming a target. She's scared already, and she doesn't even know what happened to Theda."

The redhead called to the two detectives. "Is there something wrong?"

Nick smiled. "No, office politics. We've got to pick up some equipment, then we're on our way." No need to pile on the drama. There's no telling what she'd do if she knew about Theda.

Zelman's head bobbed with relief.

On his way out the door, Nick asked, "Meredith, can you call the radio station and have their reporter hold the 'media leak'? I'm going to get some stuff from the electronics room."

Chapter Eighty-One

SUTTON LEANED SO CLOSE THAT HE COULD TASTE FREDO'S BREATH. A potato chip crumb stuck to Fredo's quivering lip. He twisted sideways to evade Sutton's intense glare.

"Sorry, dude. I thought you knew." Fredo's beer can crackled under his grip.

Sutton dropped to the bench seat at the galley-table, defeated. "What the fuck..." His eyes latched onto Fredo's again, regaining some hope. Maybe his info was wrong. "How did you hear this? Who told you?" It couldn't be, could it? That bitch found some stupid bastard to take care of her.

"I dunno." Fredo finished the last of the beer. "Some bitch from the cosmetology college told Sarah about it. It was a big secret, huh?"

"A secret?" Sutton slammed a fist on the table. "More like a setup. Who the fuck does she think she is? Like I'd fall for a stupid trick like that." He squashed the fact that he almost had. "Don't even want the hoe."

Fredo burped long and low, a foghorn. He stuffed a handful of chips into his mouth. "My man, you need to teach that bitch a lesson."

"Yeah, yeah." Sutton sank into the greasy pillows behind him. "Whose idea was this, anyway? Faye ain't smart enough to come up with this plan. The cops, you think?"

Fredo nodded. "That's who's got her now. Like I told you, they're gonna use her as bait to catch you."

Sutton studied his palm. "Find out where she is."

Fredo nodded with approval. "I'll check around, dude." An ugly smile spread across his weathered face.

Chapter Eighty-Two

To get into the bookshelf, Nick had to twist like a pretzel. Wires and cables hung over his shoulder at the ready. Books were stacked along the open shelving that separated the entry hall from the main living area. A video camera hiding among them was unnoticeable. From the living room, Meredith could hear her partner's grunts, punctuated by sporadic cuss words. She closed her eyes when she heard a hard thump. Either Nick hit his head, or one of the objects on the shelves fell, she couldn't tell which.

Opening her eyes, she surveyed the house exterior from inside, as if she'd never seen it before, looking for something she'd missed.

"Nick, help me walk the house for vulnerable points."

Another grunt and he was beside her, straightening a kink out of his back.

Huge picture windows stood for walls on two sides of the living room, bisected by a pair of French doors in the middle of each "wall." They stood at the portal that led to a shallow deck running the length of the back of the house. It connected to the north side and another exterior door from the master bedroom. Here, floor-to-ceiling windows looked over a small jungle-like sanctuary bordered by hip-high ferns. Although she couldn't see it, the garden path led to the driveway and eventually meandered to Mirabel Road. "I'm going to keep all outside lights on, even in the garden, with low light on inside." The canopy of trees sheltered the home from the summer sun, but in winter, any passing cloud darkened the house. The absence of light could provide concealment for Sutton.

The home's only solid door was in the front. Meredith thought, with irony, that she should've consulted a crime prevention officer when she and Richard were planning the house. It was one of the easiest structures to get into that she'd ever seen. The glass door off the master bedroom would offer no resistance to a forced entry. Funny, she'd never thought of it that way. In her naiveté or arrogance, she believed that no one would ever find the house to break into.

She still smarted from an epic dose of humility.

Although the rest of the house had windows, none was accessible from the ground. Earlier, with Zelman safely locked in the guest bathroom, Nick and Meredith walked the outside perimeter, looking for weak points.

Nick surveyed the deck while standing at the open door, rain splattering his sweatshirt. "With all this glass, we should be able to see Sutton coming. Then again, Sutton could see us, too." Finding nothing other than glass doors, they returned to the living room, shedding their rain jackets. Nick returned to his cables and twist ties.

Zelman joined Meredith as she looked over the living room. Meredith could watch the French doors easily from her post in the living room. With minimal lights on during the night, she was confident they could see anyone approaching. Inside, a sectional sofa formed an "L" to face the French doors and the view. A pair of club chairs sat kitty-corner to the sofa with a cocktail table in between. From the sofa, one could see into the kitchen and dining room. Guest bedrooms sat behind the kitchen while the master was off the living room.

Nick slapped imaginary dust off his hands. "All done wiring. Where's your laptop?"

Meredith pointed. With an eager smile, Zelman jumped up from her chair, grabbed the laptop, and handed it to Nick. She twisted a carrot-colored tendril around her finger. "Whatcha doing?" she asked.

Meredith smiled at Zelman's growing infatuation with Nick. They hadn't gotten off to a good start at the Circle K. Zelman must have re-considered.

Nick plopped down in a dining room chair, flipped the computer open, and hunched over the keys. "Taking out an insurance policy, Faye."

"Huh?"

Meredith answered for Nick, who continued to download a file. "Installing video cams so we can see what's going on outside and inside." He put the last one in the house by the front door.

Her eyes brightened. "Cool."

Meredith pointed to the framed picture Nick had arranged on the bookshelf. "See that? It's recording whatever happens in the living room."

"Like a nanny cam?"

"Yep."

"You guys expecting problems?"

Meredith shrugged, hoping to appear casual. "No. But if we plan, we'll be prepared. I doubt that anyone will find us here. If they do, we'll be able to see trouble long before it gets close." She leaned toward Zelman, whispering. "Really, I think Nick just likes to play with his tech toys." She hesitated, debating whether to say it or not. "Just the same, if there's any problem, hide in the guest bathroom. It's secure if the door is locked." She didn't say it was a hollow-core door. Easy to break through. "Or go outside."

With a solemn nod, the redhead pointed to the laptop screen. "Are these recorded?"

"Yes, and those are wireless feeds."

"So, is anyone watching it?"

Meredith grimaced. She didn't want to explain all of it. There were plenty of holes in the plan to worry about. She didn't want Faye any more freaked out than she already was.

Zelman's head tipped with impatience. "Is it a live feed? I mean, is anyone watching it?"

"No. This happens to be the worst weekend of the year. Flooding and evacuations are taking up most of the department's personnel." The monitor for the video feed was in the VCI lieutenant's office. No way Ferrua would have it on over the weekend. Nor would he be in his office. Even so, Nick had already emailed the IP address to him.

"Well, what good will it do to record it?" Her face lost its color.

Meredith glanced at her partner.

Nick's fingers paused over the keyboard as he sighed. "Like I said, insurance. If Sutton shows up, we'll be able to see him before he gets to the house." He looked over to the other woman. "But he can't know where you are, Faye."

Meredith nodded. "I called the radio station and postponed our 'media leak'." She waved toward the laptop. "This is all overkill. We're keeping you safe."

"I didn't think I'd be so scared being the bait." Zelman's curls bobbed as she scanned the house. "Is this safer than the jail?"

Meredith cut off this train of thought. "It is for now. Sutton wouldn't know where to look for you." She didn't want to bring up Theda's name, so she said, "We thought he'd be searching down south. We heard he wanted to get back together with you." Meredith threw in the last comment to see Zelman's reaction.

Faye's lips curled into a sneer. "That fucker." She shook her head. "Not a chance. He hurt me so bad that..." The memory softened her face. Her eyes glassed over just before she looked away. "No way."

Meredith was satisfied with Faye's conviction. On patrol, she'd seen too many women drop charges against their batterers out of fear, remorse, obligation for their children, or by falling victim to manipulation. It was far too common to see the victim arranging for bail before deputies cleared the threshold of the jail. Meredith was encouraged by Zelman's resolve.

Meredith went on to the next item for the day. "So, anyone hungry?"

Nick groaned.

"Reyes, don't you bitch about my cooking. I'm just making sandwiches."

He turned toward her with a different concern. "No, no. Ferrua just sent me a text. The media leak just leaked. The word is out about Zelman."

Meredith tensed. It was going to be a long night.

Chapter Eighty-Three

Sutton hissed at the acne-scarred man staring down at him.
"Hey, dude. This better be important."

"Your buddy Fredo sent me." Chapped lips curled in an involuntary grin. It reminded Sutton of a hyena. "Give me the cash." A hundred bucks was all Sutton could scare up in trade for the diamond earrings. This was costing him, big time.

Bony fingers closed around the money. The skinny man stuffed the cash in his jeans. He crossed his arms, trying to appear casual.

Sutton's eyes were slits as he waited. This better be worth it. He took a step towards him, too close. He expected the pressure would force him to talk.

It did. "You know your granny got shanked last night?"

Sutton answered the question with a scowl.

The skinny man shifted from one foot to the other, struggling to keep eye contact. "The cops, they took your girl. My buddy heard them talking about stashing her at one of the cop's houses, the one out at the River, Mirabel Road. That big glass house."

Chapter Eighty-Four

Nick turned on the recorder, making sure the mic pointed to the center of the room. The lens was set at wide angle. The rain had let up for an hour, but clouds kept the sky ashen as night fell. The house sat steeped in shadows carved out from the hillside. Now, persistent rain dampened everything outside and oppressed the inside. Nick felt the weight of their mission squarely on his shoulders.

Meredith and Faye chewed on sandwiches without much enthusiasm. The partners had agreed Meredith would stay with Zelman for the first twelve hours, so Nick could move freely inside the house and outside. Nick made his own sandwich, eating it while standing at the kitchen counter. He preferred making his own meal to eating anything Meredith put together. She was a disaster in the kitchen, even making sandwiches.

When he was done, he grabbed his pocket flashlight, rain gear, not the bright yellow department issue, but his own olive-green jacket and pants, and headed out the side door.

The narrow footpath from the master bedroom door meandered from the garden through the underbrush to the driveway. Even in

March, the vegetation was thick enough to conceal a person. Nick squatted to examine the muddy path and concluded there was no disturbance. He moved on.

On the driveway, he checked to his left, surveying a rugged terrain that sloped toward the abandoned pasture. In dry weather, with solid footing, this could be traversed from Meredith's property. Now it was too slippery to use. To his right was the driveway. Straight ahead to the west, a large promontory hid the view of the house from River Road. Nick studied the outcropping for signs of erosion or slides. This attention to detail was a natural byproduct of ten years in Sonoma County Sheriffs' Office patrol. After working three winter floods, he had developed an eye for problems. Meredith's house was safe from flooding, but the last thing they needed was a mudslide. Most of the area had enough plant growth to slow soil erosion that might undermine the hillside. The cliff to the north where David fell was too steep to climb. On the west, the driveway led to Mirabel Road. That left south and east, heavy brush skirted the south boundary under the deck, and there were no doors or windows low enough to get in.

Nick circled back along the east side. Instead of taking the stairs to the deck, he dropped down, following a muddy game trail under the deck. He trudged as far as he could, making it to the center of the house before a thicket of brambles blocked the path. This part of the structure stood on stilts. Surveying the underside, he appreciated a moment out of the rain. From his pocket, he pulled out a heavy ten-inch Maglite flashlight. Would Sutton come alone? He spotlighted the exterior wall under the deck. There were no hatches, doors, or other access points into the house. He flicked off the light but kept it in his hand. He'd checked. All Sutton's known associates were accounted for. He'd be alone.

The evening grew darker.

He started up the game trail, scrutinizing the path. In the mud, he saw the tread of his own boot. Next to it, facing the same direction, was an impression from another shoe. It looked as fresh as his own print. Nick's fingers tightened around the anodized barrel of the flashlight as he glanced around the slope. He switched the light to his left hand as he dug through his slicker for his Glock.

From behind him came a breath, not his. As Nick turned, a powerful fist slammed into his cheek. Pain shattered his vision, but he reacted even before his brain engaged. He hadn't been quick enough to get to his Glock, but he spun, swinging hard. With his left hand, a quick jab with the Maglite and he made contact with the nose of his attacker.

Earl Sutton's eyes bulged as the aluminum crushed the cartilage in his nose. Blood spurted to the ground between them. With a howl, Sutton's hand flew to his nose, the other to Nick's cheekbone.

Nick ducked. His skin was slippery from the rain, the other man's blow made glancing contact. Nick reached upward and knocked the arc out of Sutton's next swing.

Sutton skidded down the trail, cursing, scrambling. A heel found purchase. He wheeled around to face Nick, his hand making for the gun that bulged out of his pocket.

Nick swung the Maglite at Sutton's fist. He knocked the pistol out of Sutton's hand but lost grip on the Maglite. Hands free now, Nick seized Sutton's left arm, then drew both behind him. Sutton grunted, pulling away toward where the gun landed at the wall of brambles.

Nick gripped a handful of flannel. He steered Sutton to the underside of the house a few feet away. He found a sheltered, level spot in front of the brambles and shoved the man face down in the damp soil.

Nick yelled. "Hands out, where I can see them."

With an ex-convict's automatic obedience, Sutton stretched both arms out.

Nick grasped one, then the other. Securing Sutton's hands with a knee in the man's back, Nick grabbed his handcuffs and clicked them open with his middle finger. Sutton came to life at the noise. He howled, squirming and cussing as Nick snapped the cuffs on securely. Patting him down, he asked if there was anything in his pockets. Sutton ignored him. Nick felt the pockets. The right one had something in it.

Cautiously, Nick reached in. He pulled out a gold filigree bracelet studded with small diamonds and a necklace chain. The pendant was a religious figure set in a silver oval. The Virgin Mary. The chain was a ringer for the casting Ross Proust had taken from Violet McMurray's neck.

"Earl Sutton, you're under arrest for the murder of Violet McMurray. You have the right to remain silent. Anything you say—"

"I ain't saying shit." Sutton spat. Nick finished his admonishment of rights and received a glare for a reply. Nick would have to re-Mirandize him during an interview. With one hand on Sutton, Nick reached for Sutton's revolver in the brambles. A few scrapes later, he tucked it into a pocket and pointed Sutton uphill.

The muddy path complicated Sutton's uneasy balance. It took almost ten minutes to crawl up the hill. Finally, Nick had Sutton stashed in his truck, cuffed to an overhead door handle. "Are you alone?"

Sutton coughed up spit, but mud, blood, and saliva merely dribbled down his chin. His upper lip was too swollen to spit. Nick slammed the door. He smiled at the man, saying, "I'll be right back. You stay here."

IN THE HOUSE, Faye's breathing caught as she struggled to keep her tears in check. "You really got him?"

Nick nodded. "Want to see?"

At her emphatic nod, Nick led her to the front door. He opened it, and the porch light illuminated a drenched and muddy Sutton, handcuffed to the door handle. Zelman gulped, squinting. "He's all bloody."

"It's just his nose. It'll stop soon." He took a good look at Meredith to see how she was holding up. She seemed relieved. "You have a towel I could use? I'll take him down to the sub and lock him up. I'm betting the road is closed. We won't make the main jail tonight."

With a broad smile, Meredith handed Nick a dish towel. "Yep, the radio said River Road is closed at the Highway. The sub's as good a place as any for him. Come back up here when you're done. It'll be smarter for you to stay rather than try to make it home. Your mother is taken care of anyway, right?"

At his nod, she said, "Okay, see you in a while."

Chapter Eighty-Five

MEREDITH'S RELIEF WAS PALPABLE. IT SPREAD THROUGH HER CHEST to her fingertips and down to her toes. Finally, this dirtbag was off the street. He would be held to answer at his arraignment. No way would he get out. She sighed, content as she'd been in a long time.

Silent tears lined Zelman's face. In jeans, a sweatshirt, and tennis shoes, she slouched into the couch pillows. "Oh, God. I get my life back. I don't even have to testify against him."

Gus wandered into the room, leaning against sofa corners, purring. It was clear he thought he was responsible for the elevated mood in the room. He meandered to Zelman, hopping on her lap. She gave a snort of delight.

"Move him off if he's a bother." Meredith stood, gathering dishes.

"No, he's fine." Zelman stroked his long white fur. "He's beautiful."

Over her shoulder, Meredith said, "Yep, and he knows it too. He loves everyone and figures everyone ought to love him." Meredith figured the dirty dishes could wait. She should take her gun off and put it away. After all, she was safe at home.

"Is this it, then, for me? With Earl, I mean."

She studied Faye's expression from across the room. "What do you mean?" Her hand dropped from the gun. Putting the Beretta away dropped lower on her list of priorities. She felt like she needed to support Faye. After all, she'd allowed herself to be bait to catch Sutton.

Faye caressed the cat in long strokes. Gus purred. "No court, nothing?" Faye's gaze met Meredith's.

"Nothing. We're charging him with a murder that had nothing to do with you. You're free to go back to your life without worry that he'll find you. He's going away for a long, long time."

Zelman sighed, burying her head in Gus' fur. She was so quiet, Meredith wasn't sure if she was crying.

Suddenly Meredith heard the snick of the front door lock. Nick didn't have a key to her house. Who? Something moved in the hall.

In the darkness, she saw the figure of a man. His voice broke the silence. "That's excellent police work. Good job, Detective Ryan."

Gus yowled off Faye's lap and ran down the hall. The woman melted into the couch, eyes wide. Meredith stood, stunned.

Giroud.

He walked slowly to the center of the room, staring at Meredith, rainwater dripping on the hardwood floor.

"What are you doing here? How did you get in?" Anger swept through her body like a flash flood as she noticed the front door open. This was crazy. The judge had gone off the deep end.

Holding up a housekey in his fingers, Giroud slipped it into his pocket. He waved off the question. "You are very good at your occupation, Meredith. You deserved the promotion on your own merit."

"On my own merit?" Meredith paused as his words sunk in. "I wondered if you were behind it." Zelman slumped into the couch, her brow drawn up with confusion. He hadn't shown any notice of the girl. She turned to keep Giroud's attention on herself. "You're saying that you meddled in my career. What did you do?" She kept him talking so Zelman could get out.

"Nothing you wouldn't have done for me." He shrugged, the picture of humility. "Flannery is very tractable."

"Flannery? You mean my promotion was engineered? You did

this?" So, she hadn't been promoted on her own abilities. Achieving her dream had been an illusion. Everything she had worked for, sacrificed for, all of it, was erased. It was all a sham.

"I wanted you near me." A breathless chuckle escaped as he studied her. The curve of his mouth made her feel like she was a fool for not knowing the depth of his feelings.

Shocked by his candor, Meredith couldn't think of anything to say.

Taking a step toward her, he reached out a hand. A benevolent, indulgent smile spread across his lips. "Come with me. Let us make the life we were meant to share. I know you want me, Meredith. God knows, I want you." His eyes darkened. "You don't have much time to decide. Your partner will be back soon. He will try to talk you out of coming with me."

"I'm not coming with you." She shook at the unfairness of the situation. He kept moving closer, arm's length now, almost at the corner of the couch between them.

His eyes riveted on her, giving Meredith hope that Zelman could get away without being seen. Keep him engaged. "In fact, Stephen Giroud, if you don't leave right now, I'll arrest you for trespassing. Consider this your warning."

Giroud's lips drew into a smile. "Always the Amazon. What a woman you are, Meredith Ryan. We can have a life most people can't even dream of." He took a step closer to her, then another. "This is no place for you, arresting drunks and chasing burglars. You deserve better. You deserve what I can give you." His hand motioned around the room, but his eyes stayed on her. "I have the means, you know, to give you the best. I can take away all the financial strain you are under, as well."

Indignation drove her response. "Like you did with your step-mother? We saw how she lives, thanks to your generosity. Is that really what your father intended?"

The judge stopped, his eyes glazing over. His hands clenched and opened. "My stepmother got more than she deserved. She's worth-less. The only reason she's not dead is that the police would be suspicious."

Meredith's stomach flipped like she was on an out-of-control roller coaster. 'The only reason she's not dead is that the police would be suspicious?' Did he just say that he could have killed her? She wasn't the only one he considered killing. "Would you have killed her?"

Meredith moved to her left, keeping Giroud's gaze on her and away from the wide-eyed Zelman. Hoping the woman still had a shred of survivor instincts, Meredith inclined her head in a tiny nod. Zelman eased herself from the couch, tiptoeing to the master bedroom. She was gone without so much as a squeak of the door. Gone through the outside door to safety.

"I do what I have to." His eyes challenged her.

Meredith strode from the kitchen to the edge of the living room. Giroud would go to jail. She had Zelman now as a witness for a stalking case. She'd wait for Nick if she could hold out. An extra pair of hands would be helpful to arrest the judge.

Time to up the ante. Keep Giroud talking until Nick got back. Zelman was safe. Nick would be back soon. She challenged him. "You do what you have to? Like with David?"

A burst of laughter exploded in the stillness of the room. "David. Yes, that was interesting, to say the least. Imagine my surprise when I found out he was your brother. Not your lover."

She recalled the surprised look on his face in the hospital room. "You pushed him over the railing." It was a simple statement, a test. See if he'll take the bait. She heard her heartbeat pounding in her ears.

Still smiling, he looked away with false modesty. "He was going anyway, I just helped him."

He's either going to kill her or believe she will stay quiet and go with him. Which was it?

"David would never try to commit suicide." She stepped into the room. It brought her closer to him, but she needed to see the front and side doors. She didn't dare check the clock on the wall.

Giroud eyed her with a critical glare. "I didn't say that he was suicidal. You need to listen better, Meredith."

"You threw David over the railing?"

His eyebrows rose in a 'so what' expression. "Yes."

"Why?" A quick glance to the front windows. Still no Nick. But the camera. The camera was still on. Recording. She wished she could count on Ferrua watching at the other end and sending help. She couldn't hope for that. She was on her own.

Giroud smiled. "Because I thought he was your lover."

Meredith looked away but kept him in her peripheral view. "What about Astrid Vachon?"

"That fool." Giroud's face flushed. "She tried to blackmail me. Can you believe that?" His eyes widened in disbelief.

Giroud was unraveling, she saw it in his rising impatience. Stall for time. Keep him engaged. Nick will be back any moment. "Blackmail you for what?"

"Oh no." He smiled grandly. "That's for me to know and you not to find out. Ever the investigator, Meredith. You truly were made for your job. It is a shame you will not be a detective any longer."

"Who else did you kill?" Had he decided which path to take with her? She still couldn't tell. "Your father? Your ex-wife?"

"My father?" He cocked his head sideways, his eyes narrowing. Maybe she'd gone too far. "No, I loved my father. I would never have hurt him."

Meredith kept her silence, hoping he'd volunteer information about the death of Lindsay Giroud. Meredith stared at him. The judge looked and acted like a charming, sophisticated gentleman. No, he was a remorseless killer.

"As for Lindsay, she simply became too big a liability. She knew too much, started spreading rumors about me all over town. Besides, I didn't actually kill her, like I didn't actually kill your husband." The hair sample Franklin told her about. Maybe it belonged to Esparza. Then Giroud's words penetrated.

"Richard? You killed Richard?" Meredith's voice came out in a raspy scream. He admitted being responsible for Richard's death. She knew it.

"I merely hurried things along. I told you. I had help. Besides, he was adulterous and destined to leave you anyway. I had to level the playing field." His eyes widened as if to show her how logical his decision was.

She fought back the tears of rage. She'd known he'd been involved somehow. She should've trusted her instincts. And done what? Right now, her focus had to be on surviving.

"You had help?" She tried to sound strong.

His lips pressed together as he nodded. A tiny white line of saliva rimmed the corners of his mouth. "All great men need help sometimes."

Outside, the rain had escalated into a full-fledged storm. Redwood boughs slashed against the roof. Propelled by gusting winds, raindrops slapped on the back window like darts. Bursts of rain blew in through the front door.

Even if Ferrua monitored this video feed, he'd have no one to send for help. Evacuations must have already started, tying up all Sheriff's personnel, along with the rest of the county's emergency services. What if Nick had been hijacked at the substation to help? She hadn't thought of that. She was on her own. With luck, Zelman would be safe outside, but she couldn't provide any help, either.

She was alone with this madman.

Chapter Eighty-Six

GIROUD HELD OUT HIS HAND, HIS LONG FINGERS WRIGGLING. "COME with me."

Meredith's body was like a wire, taut and flexible, but strong. She slipped into a warrior mindset and became a weapon. Her right hand eased behind her for the Beretta. She yanked it out and, with a two-handed grip, aimed it at Giroud's chest.

"No. You're under arrest for murder." Damn, she wished her hands would stop shaking. "Put your hands on your head." She was trained to take control in dangerous situations, but even with a gun in her hand, Giroud seemed in control. She stepped toward him, but the judge stood still, ignoring her command.

"Don't do this, Meredith. You don't know what you're starting." His eyes were flat, a lifeless reptilian look. Something was incredibly wrong.

He'd decided. Meredith knew he was going to kill her.

She summoned strength from a reservoir deep within her. "Put your hands on your head. Do it now." She bypassed all the tyrannies of her childhood and the sham of her husband's love. She'd lost a lot in her life, but she'd never allowed herself to be the victim. She was a fighter. A survivor. She'd chosen to deal with Giroud. The second she pulled her gun, she was committed. Proof or not, whether she lost her job or her life, she had to do the right thing—arrest his ass and take him to jail.

Chapter Eighty-Seven

A CLOUD SETTLED OVER GIROUD'S MIND. HE WATCHED HER POINTING the gun at him. She made her choice, and she would have to live or die with the consequences.

A wisp of sadness circled his building rage. Meredith would never know his generosity and never see his greatness. She refused to be a part of his path to power, real power. They could have been a new Camelot, the two of them. Attractive, influential, and much more.

With all that to gain, she chose the other way. She will have to go. She could not be allowed to remain behind to spread rumors, try to ruin his reputation like Lindsay did.

Giroud would not allow it.

His eyes clouded with blood-red fury. Anger swept him forward. Then, out of the corner of his eye, a white mass skittered along behind the furniture toward Meredith.

The damned cat.

He had one last idea that might show her how serious he was. He would give her one more chance.

Chapter Eighty-Eight

MEREDITH SHIFTED HER WEIGHT TO THE BALLS OF HER FEET, TRYING to stay flexible and balanced. The tension of the moment made her body rigid. She was ready. Giroud wouldn't quit without a fight.

She expected an assault, maybe even a retreat. She did not expect him to dive sideways behind a chair. Sliding on the hardwood floor, she lost sight of him.

A hysterical shriek shattered her—Gus!

Giroud got to his feet, the yowling, scratching cat held away from his body by the slack skin of his neck. Gus' claws left threads of blood oozing down the man's arm. Giroud moved across the room to the French doors. He yanked one open and hurled the howling cat over the railing.

A scream erupted from Meredith's throat.

"You see, Meredith." Giroud's chest heaved from the battle he'd just won. "I can make your life a heaven on earth or a hell. Your choice."

Giroud's throw had been inhibited by the fighting cat. So his toss wasn't as far as he intended.

The cat clung to the railing by all four paws. Meredith dove past Giroud through the door, shifting the Beretta to her off-hand. She grabbed the nape of his neck and pulled Gus onto the deck. The cat landed, an indignant cloud of white hair. When Meredith was certain the cat had all feet on the deck, she turned back to Giroud. Gripping both hands on the gun, she said, "I've made my choice. Put your hands on your head."

With a dismissive twist of his mouth, Giroud raised his hands slowly. Meredith darted across the space between them, stuffing the Beretta back in its holster. She gripped Giroud's wrist, wrestling with her cuffs as they tangled in her fingers. She struggled one-handed to open them.

Giroud lunged a shoulder into her, sending the cuffs clattering to the floor. He landed on top of her. His hands pinned her wrists over to the floor as he lowered his head to within inches of hers. Her holstered gun jammed into her back. She could smell his sour breath coming in shallow puffs.

Fighting panic, Meredith brought a knee up, aiming for his crotch. He'd anticipated the move and shifted to a kneeling position on top of her legs. "Don't fight me, Meredith. You've made your decision. Now you have to pay for it."

Giroud clamped her wrists together. He held her with an incredible strength. The other hand slipped around her neck. He squeezed, hard. Meredith fought to free her hands, but she was having trouble taking in a breath.

Had Astrid Vachon felt like this?

Chapter Eighty-Nine

"SORRY, NICK. MIRABEL'S CLOSED UNTIL THE COUNTY ROAD GUYS get the mudslide cleared." Standing in front of a wall map in the substation, Marco Donato's hand traced the path of the slide across the road on the map's surface. "There's no way up there."

There was no immediate need for him to get back. With Sutton cooling his heels in the substation holding cell, Faye was safe. Nick studied the surrounding terrain on the map. Although the aerial photo had been taken during dry season with optimal conditions, he saw clearly that there was no way to walk overland. Sheer canyon walls, sharp ridges, and unstable soil canceled that option. He was stuck with no way to get back.

Donato lumbered back to his office without commandeering him for rescues or evacuations. An opportunity crept into Nick's mind.

He sat down at a grimy keyboard and tapped in his query. Seconds later, the information flashed on the monitor. He considered it for a moment. Knowing that Judge Giroud lived somewhere in west Santa Rosa, Nick had searched for the judge's address. And there it was, not three miles from Mirabel Road. Nick was familiar with the neighborhood, upscale homes, and acreage that catered to the gentleman farmer. In Giroud's case, it would be horses.

Nick moved to the aerial map and found the address. Studying the layout, he figured out a way to get close to the house with minimal hassle.

It's good to know one's enemies.

He didn't know what he'd find, but he felt an itch he couldn't scratch. Seeing where this jackass lived would tell Nick about him. Looking past his veneer of civility, Nick could get a glimpse of what hid in Giroud's shadows, what could be seen when Giroud didn't know someone was watching. Nick also wanted to be sure the judge was at home.

Twenty minutes later, Nick parked his truck on the private driveway off Fulton Road. The rain had let up a bit, but he tugged on his hoodie to cover his head anyway. He snapped on the nitrile gloves he'd put in his pocket. Recalling the images from the headlights, he set off down the side of a pasture fence. Making it to the barn, he kept under the eaves and around to a long, open breezeway that connected to the house.

Lights on. No movement from inside.

He edged closer to one side of a window. A kitchen, unoccupied.

What was he doing here? Time to think this through once more. Just here to look around. He had no plans to confront Giroud or Esparza. Just wanted to see…what? Anything he found that led to an arrest would be disallowed in court as "fruit of the poisonous tree." Evidence found that was illegally obtained.

On the other side of the barn stood a garage. A roof extended from the garage, sheltering a Dodge Ram Pickup and horse trailer. Nick moved to the garage window. The judge's Mercedes was gone. The parking space where Esparza would park his Escalade was empty, too. Nick pulled the hoodie back so he could see peripherally. He heard something, pounding. He made his way through the breezeway, heading toward the sound.

The moment he stepped on Giroud's property, he knew he was going in. Maybe something here could explain the judge's obsession with Meredith. If he had to justify his entry without a warrant, he would say that he heard sounds of a person in distress. But then, a lawful entry was required only if he was going to court. That wasn't going to happen. The "person in distress" excuse was a cliché any DA would see through.

Ten feet away, a screen door banged open in the wind. The door was cheap plywood with glass in the top half, locked. Back in the barn, he found a metal rake. A quick jab with the handle broke the glass. He tossed the rake away and reached through, unlocking the door.

Coming in through the back door brought him through a large, tiled laundry room. Empty. Nick saw organized shelving units, a folding table, and appliances. Very orderly.

From there to a spacious kitchen floored in a mocha-colored marble. Coffee-colored cabinets towered over shiny granite counters. Nick pulled open a cupboard door and found canned food in neat alphabetical rows. Too organized and alphabetical. *Really?* This looked more obsessive than he'd figured. A foreboding settled over him. This was going to hell, fast. A quick look inside to see if he could determine Giroud's next move, then back to Meredith's. He'd figure a way to get there.

The living room was a study in masculinity. Scarlet and brown upholstery. White plantation shutters complimented classic furniture to create the look of an expensive showroom. Nick searched for something out of place, a magazine, glasses, anything, but found no clutter.

A lengthy hallway with windows facing the riding arena and barn took him to the door of an office. Inside, the same décor, with the addition of a desk and a library of law books against two walls. A laptop. Nick pulled open desk drawers.

After a few minutes, he turned up nothing of interest. The laptop could have been important, but he didn't have time to search files or history. Nor did he have a password. He didn't even know what he was looking for.

He moved on. Three guest bedrooms lined the hall, with the master at the end. Disappointed he hadn't found anything, he entered Stephen Giroud's bedroom. The same colors and style followed. Glancing around, his impression was of a gentleman's man-cave. An enormous armoire stood on the wall opposite a mahogany four-poster bed. Nick looked under the bed, into the scrupulously tidy closet, the cabinets in the master bath. He found nothing.

Nick stood at the doorway, thinking about his next move.

The armoire was the last piece of furniture he hadn't checked. In the interest of thoroughness, he padded over and opened the right side. Then the left. He sucked in a breath. He'd expected to see a compulsively neat wardrobe.

Nothing could have prepared him for this.

On a corkboard that extended the entire length of the armoire were newspaper clippings, photos, and maps, all of one subject: Meredith. Printed photos...of Nick's partner at work, shopping, on the phone in her car, jogging, working out. Chills crept down Nick's spine. He spotted some small notebook pages. Dates, times, and locations, a chronology of Meredith's movements, from the day she shot Rusty Webber, until now. The printing was small, angular, and painstakingly clear. Like an old-school cop would print on a hand-written report.

Now. What was the most recent entry? His fingers shook as he paged through the notes.

Saturday. Sunday. Monday.

Here. "Drove witness to her house at 2100 hours with partner. Because of flooding, it's doubtful the operation will go today. They'll want to have backup in place before setting their trap. Probably hole up for a day until the flooding is over. Depending on proximity of partner, this would be a good time to make contact with Ryan."

Nick dropped the book. Small pieces of a torn photo fell out. It took three seconds to figure out they were pieces of a department photo of Meredith in her uniform.

Fuck.

Meredith was a sitting duck. He'd find a way to get to her, even if he had to swim.

Chapter Ninety

"GIROUD, STOP." A MAN SHOUTED, HIS VOICE CARRYING FAINTLY Hispanic inflections.

But it wasn't Nick. Meredith heard footsteps run across the room. Then, Giroud's weight was off her. She rolled to her side, her lungs sucking great gulps of air. *My God, my head is going to explode.*

She heard the man again, stronger. Insisting. "Stop. This has to end. I won't be part of killing a cop." Giroud stood. Esparza faced him, fists tight with anger, ready for a fight. Meredith rolled to her side, pulled her Beretta, and took aim. "Stop, Giroud, or I'll shoot."

Giroud started at Meredith's warning, then ignored it. "You don't have a choice." He answered Esparza.

"I won't do this."

"Later. We can talk about this later." Giroud began to turn toward Meredith.

As her finger pressed the trigger, the judge yanked Esparza in front of him.

The deafening blast filled the house. Gunpowder burned the air as Meredith watched scarlet blossom on the smaller man's shoulder. Just like Rusty. Esparza crumpled to the floor, groaning.

Giroud rushed her, tackling Meredith to the floor. He stepped on her wrists, hard. Her grip loosened. The gun thumped to the floor. He kicked it away, grabbed her bicep, and jerked her back to her feet.

Giroud purpled. "You have fouled this all up. You have ruined everything." He picked her up like a suitcase and threw her through the window.

She thumped hard against the glass. It shattered onto the deck as she broke through, ragged spikes showered over her as she landed. Rain pounded her. She tried to roll to her feet but stumbled. Her right knee gave out. Giroud charged through the broken window. She was up on the other knee when he grabbed her hair, pulling her off balance.

She was simply reacting, her mind overloaded with sensations, the rain, the glass, the gunshot. Blood, adrenaline, and oxygen flowing back through her body. Her own terror threatened her as much as Giroud. If she gave into panic, then Giroud would win.

She snapped out of it. Giroud dragged her toward the railing. She had four feet to make a stand.

She twisted, slamming an elbow across the bridge of his nose. Dazed, he dropped her to the deck. He yowled in anguish on the same place Gus had landed. Then, he bent over and yanked her up, one hand on her jeans waistband and the other grasping a handful of her hair. A wild kick to his knee made him grunt and merely slowed him. She kept at it.

Still holding on to Meredith, he headed for the railing. Meredith screamed at him, swung her feet and fists at any part of his body that could connect until he slowed.

With a scream of rage, Giroud slammed her against the deck railing. He rolled her over and kicked her side. He dropped his full body weight on her torso.

The impact sucked her breath away, suddenly starving her of oxygen. Before she could recover, Giroud grasped her hair, pulled it, and slammed her head on the deck.

Meredith fought for consciousness now. She hurt everywhere and was so exhausted she was tempted to close her eyes. But she couldn't. She wouldn't. She forced her mind to clear. Giroud was propping her body onto the railing.

Then came a sharp crack of a gunshot. Giroud paused, then stumbled against her. He grunted. His grip relaxed as his shoulder nudged her over the balustrade.

She grabbed the wood railing with both hands and hung on for her life. Dangling off the deck fifty feet over the canyon below, Meredith glimpsed and saw Esparza standing frozen in the living room. A tendril of smoke rose from the barrel of the Beretta in his hands, lying on the floor next to her was Giroud.

Giroud lay awkwardly on the deck, rain pounding him, plastering his hair to his face.

She held on, wondering if she was next. She adjusted her grip for a better purchase on the wood. Then, she swung her body to a rail post and caught her toe on a crosspiece. Did the deck sway under her weight? She looked for a sturdier brace. She angled her foot on another timber, hoping it would relieve her weight. Her hands ached.

Giroud's flat, lifeless eyes stared at her from the deck. She caught her breath. Even dead, the man scared her. His reptilian cunning was gone. Even so, her life would never be the same. She'd never forget his eyes.

She glanced at the yawning canyon below. She weighed her chances of surviving a fall into the swaying tangles of vegetation on the steep slope. No better than David's, for sure. Where was Esparza?

She needed help.

A hand reached past her face. Over the howling wind, she heard Nick's voice. "Grab my hand." He reached toward her, grabbing both wrists. Swinging her feet as she released the rail, her fingers caught Nick's and held.

She looked up into his face as he and Esparza dragged her over the wobbling deck banister. Injured, shaking with cold, and wet through and through, but she was safe.

Chapter Ninety-One

GUS LOUNGED ON A CHAIR, LICKING HIS COAT IN A FURIOUS BATH. Across the room, Meredith propped a cushion behind Esparza—the man who killed her husband yet inexplicably had just saved her life. Fighting off revulsion, she turned away. She sat down at the kitchen counter, still shivering under two sweatshirts and a ski parka.

Esparza slumped on the sofa, pressing a cotton towel to his shoulder. Although the crimson ooze had slowed, pain scored his face. A spasm passed through somewhere on his left side.

Nick said an ambulance was on the way, but its arrival time was anybody's guess.

Esparza's watery eyes opened. He studied the body outside on the deck, then looked away, slouched in defeat and humiliation. To Nick, he asked, "What was that question again?"

"Are you sure you want to do this now? Are you physically up to answering my questions? You will be asked the same questions by whoever takes over this investigation."

He nodded. "I want to tell you what happened before it's too late. You're recording this, right?" He glanced at the video camera on the kitchen counter.

"Yes, but you do realize that your injury is not life-threatening. You should recover."

"I'm never getting out of this mess." Esparza's head fell to the pillow. "I don't care. I want to get this down, ASAP."

"Do you want me to Mirandize you again?"

Esparza waved the idea away. Then, he remembered to say it, remembered how to be a cop. "No, I clearly understand my rights." He flashed a weak smile at Nick. "I was a cop for eight years."

Thank God for Nick's initiative. She didn't think she could have questioned him.

"What was your association with Judge Stephen Giroud, and when did it begin?"

"I got fired from Paso Robles PD seven years ago. I knew the Giroud family. Paso's a small town. He was an attorney in Sacramento then, and he said he'd give me work. He needed help with his polo ponies, driving, and "security". I'd never work as a cop again. I needed the money, so I signed on. Things were fine for a year or two. Then he moved to Sonoma County. Not too long afterward, he was appointed to the bench. One day, after Christmas last year, he came home all excited. He said he'd found the woman he'd been looking for." Esparza nodded to Meredith. "That was the day you shot the old guy from the River."

Sadness washed through Meredith. That day had more consequences than she could have imagined. Giroud was so morally corrupt that his malice spread without check. In the end, she didn't need to get proof that Giroud had been stalking her. Nick had told her about the shrine he'd found in Giroud's bedroom. Whoever investigated the judge's death would find it.

Under Nick's precise questioning, Esparza's story unfolded: how Giroud decided Meredith was the one to help him fulfill his political aspirations. Esparza said Giroud talked incessantly about Meredith. Eventually, Giroud focused on the people standing in the way of his goal. The first was Lindsay Giroud. Better to remove her so no one could dig up the secrets she held. When Nick asked about the secrets, Esparza shrugged. "Giroud wouldn't have told me. I wasn't shit to him, a servant. But I'm not stupid. I figured it out."

A simple hit-and-run accident, and the ex-wife was gone. At first, it was hard to kill someone, but it got easier. He claimed he didn't enjoy it like Giroud did. The judge enjoyed every detail of each murder. Esparza said he stayed because Giroud had him trapped, like a junkie, there was no other place for him to support his gambling habit. "I kept back some bargaining chips-evidence like Lindsay's threats to expose him. You'll find it in the horse tack room under my saddle. It's in a box." He sighed. "Then Giroud began to kill. First Astrid Vachon, then David Ryan."

"He started to like killing and the power it gave him. And it was all about power. Life was like a giant chess game to him. If he moved one piece here, this would happen, and so on. He'd spend hours ranting about some little thing that happened that could change his plans." He eyed Meredith. "Then he finally got it. You weren't going along with his plan. He said he'd give you one more chance tonight, but if you didn't go with him, he'd have to kill you. That you knew too much about him already."

Hugging herself, Meredith shook her head in amazement.

Esparza shifted in the chair, then continued. "I told him I couldn't be a party to killing a cop. He didn't care. He figured on doing it himself. Maybe he wanted to set me up to take the fall for all of these homicides. I didn't know what he had in mind, but I had to stop him."

He closed his eyes, tears forming. "I couldn't let him kill a cop." His chin dropped to his chest, and he gulped a huge breath, trying not to cry. "I couldn't let him kill a cop."

Chapter Ninety-Two

FOUR DAYS LATER, MEREDITH AND CHRISTY SAT NEXT TO DAVID'S bed. Meredith was determined to be strong for her friend. She held Christy's hand as her brother took his last breath. His chest fell. She hoped for another yet dreaded it. After some moments, it became clear there would be no more.

Christy dropped Meredith's hand and grasped her husband's. She buried her head in his shoulder, quiet sobs shaking her body.

"He looks more peaceful now than he ever did alive," Meredith said, standing. "I'll leave you to be with him."

Meredith gathered her things. She'd picked up Christy at the airport, and both women had camped out in the convalescent home with David. Her arms bulged with books and magazines as she stood.

She rounded the corner into the hallway. Finally, away from David and Christy, it began to sink in. David was gone. With her arms full, she slumped against the wall, not even trying to control her tears.

Then, there he was. Nick, reaching around her shoulders. The books slammed to the floor as she slumped against him, tears rolling down her face.

She wasn't alone—she knew that now. Whatever was in her future, her partner Nick would be there.

As she would for him.

Acknowledgments

No book is ever less than the sum of its contributors. It took many experts to fill in the blanks in my story. In some cases, the help wasn't technical, it was pure cheerleading. First, thank you to John Ungersma, MD, for his enthusiastic support of early efforts and technical expertise culled from his years as an ER doc and orthopedic surgeon. My critique group: Ron Pasquariello, Robin Moore, George Wilhite, Susan Littlefield, Billie Payton Settles, Andy Gloege, Fredrick Weisel, and Julie Winrich—you all made this a better book and me a better writer. You gently poked and prodded me into digging deeper for a better-crafted story.

Maria Pilgrim, Terri Mazzanti, Rhonda Fitzgerald, LaRae Archibald, Jan Cotter, and Josh Burns read and critiqued for technical problems and continuity. Julia Graves' patient answers about polo proved invaluable. Ann Watters: talk about a cheerleader! Bishop Police Department provided plenty of resources: Officers (now retired Lieutenant) Fred Gomez (Fred was an early inspiration), Danny Nolan, Glenn McClinton, and Sergeant (now retired Chief) Chris Carter.

Mike Worley's critique of the final fight scene was invaluable for authenticity.

Thanks to all who helped. Special thanks to my family for their unflagging hoorays and to Karen Henley for her stellar care of my horse while I was scribbling instead of riding. But especially, thank you to my husband, Danny. Without you, I couldn't have done this.

And lastly, if you read this book and enjoyed it, please consider leaving a review on Amazon. Authors depend on reviews to gauge readership; publishers use them to rate salability, and readers use them to decide whether or not to buy the book.

A Look At Book Two:
Intent to Hold

When Sonoma County Sheriff's Deputy Nick Reyes answers a call from his estranged wife who's in Mexico and in need of help finding her kidnapped brother, he enlists the help of his partner, Detective Meredith Ryan.

Together, they fly out to Mexico where they are plunged into a morass of intrigue and betrayal that threatens their lives and the lives of their family members.

Battling nature, the Federales, a crime cartel, and even Nick's wife, they are determined to solve the kidnapping. But can these two detectives subdue their feelings for each another in order to get the job done and preserve a working relationship?

Intent to Hold is a police procedural thriller about a brave, young deputy who identifies and faces her enemies—both within herself and the real world.

AVAILABLE APRIL 2023

About the Author

Thonie Hevron is a retired 35-year veteran police Community Service Officer, Records Supervisor and 911 dispatcher who grew up in Mill Valley, California. She now lives in Petaluma, California with her husband, Danny, two rescue dogs and a cat. For ten years, she lived in the High Desert town of Bishop, California, working as a dispatcher and writing monthly columns for the *Inyo Register*. Returning to the Bay Area in 2004, she worked for a local law enforcement agency and wrote a regular column for the *Tri-Valley Times* and the *North Valley Times*.

Thonie's writing includes four award-winning mystery novels and short stories. She is a member of the California Writers Association/Redwood Writers Chapter, SistersinCrime/NorCal Chapter and the Public Safety Writers Association.

Her work has appeared in the *Beyond Borders: 2014 Redwood Writers Anthology* and the *Felons, Flames and Ambulance Rides: Public Safety Writers 2013 Anthology*—along with recently releasing in *Cops Writing Crime Fiction: To Serve, Protect and Write*. She is the author of four award-winning mystery thriller novels, re-edited and published by Rough Edges Press. Her website, www.thoniehevron.com, includes a blog with law enforcement guests as well as a writers' column.

When not writing, Thonie rides horses, actively participates in her parish church community and enjoys traveling.